Kirsten Thorup (b. 1942) ... established herself over the past forty years as one of the most widely-read and wide-ranging of modern Danish authors. She has written poetry, plays and novels, often focusing on the fates of outsiders, those who are marginalized because of social, class or ethnic disparities. Much of her material is rooted in her own experiences. The central character of her four novels about Jonna, *Little Jonna* (1977), *The Long Summer* (1979), *Heaven and Hell* (1982) and *The Outer Limit* (1987), comes as she does from the island of Funen and struggles to adapt to big-city life. In *Bonsai* (2000) she draws on her own unhappiness in the story of a wife watching her husband dying of Aids, and in *No Man's Land* (2003) she depicts the dilemmas faced by a family coping with a fiercely independent but failing elderly parent. *The God of Chance* (2011) is a story about the bad conscience of Europeans in the face of global inequality, and the problematic results of our well-meaning efforts to make a difference. Trying to play God can lead to unforseen tragedy for donor and recipient alike.

Janet Garton is Emeritus Professor of European Literature at the University of East Anglia, Norwich. She has published books and articles about Nordic literature, including *Norwegian Women's Writing* 1850-1990 (1993), *Contemporary Norwegian Women's Writing* (1995), *Elskede Amalie* (2002) and most recently a biography of Amalie Skram, *Amalie. Et forfatterliv* (2011). She has also translated Bjørg Vik, Knut Faldbakken, Cecilie Løveid, Paal-Helge Haugen, and Henrik Ibsen.

Some other books from Norvik Press

Jens Bjørneboe: *Moment of Freedom* (translated by Esther Greenleaf Mürer)

Jens Bjørneboe: *Powderhouse* (translated by Esther Greenleaf Mürer)

Jens Bjørneboe: *The Silence* (translated by Esther Greenleaf Mürer)

Johan Borgen: *The Scapegoat* (translated by Elizabeth Rokkan)

Kerstin Ekman: *Witches' Rings* (translated by Linda Schenck)

Kerstin Ekman: *The Spring* (translated by Linda Schenck)

Kerstin Ekman: *The Angel House* (translated by Sarah Death)

Kerstin Ekman: *City of Light* (translated by Linda Schenck)

Arne Garborg: *The Making of Daniel Braut* (translated by Marie Wells)

Svava Jakobsdóttir: *Gunnlöth's Tale* (translated by Oliver Watts)

P. C. Jersild: *A Living Soul* (translated by Rika Lesser)

Selma Lagerlöf: *Lord Arne's Silver* (translated by Sarah Death)

Selma Lagerlöf: *The Löwensköld Ring* (translated by Linda Schenck)

Selma Lagerlöf: *The Phantom Carriage* (translated by Peter Graves)

Viivi Luik: *The Beauty of History* (translated by Hildi Hawkins)

Henry Parland: *To Pieces* (translated by Dinah Cannell)

Amalie Skram: *Lucie* (translated by Katherine Hanson and Judith Messick)

Amalie and Erik Skram: *Caught in the Enchanter's Net: Selected Letters* (edited and translated by Janet Garton)

August Strindberg: *Tschandala* (translated by Peter Graves)

August Strindberg: *The Red Room* (translated by Peter Graves)

Hjalmar Söderberg: *Martin Birck's Youth* (translated by Tom Ellett)

Hjalmar Söderberg: *Selected Stories* (translated by Carl Lofmark)

Anton Tammsaare: *The Misadventures of the New Satan* (translated by Olga Shartze and Christopher Moseley)

Elin Wägner: *Penwoman* (translated by Sarah Death)

The God of Chance

by

Kirsten Thorup

Translated from the Danish
and with an Afterword by
Janet Garton

Norvik Press
2013

Original title: *Tilfældets gud* © Kirsten Thorup and Gyldendal, Copenhagen 2011. Published in agreement with the Gyldendal Group Agency.

This translation and Translator's Afterword © Janet Garton 2013. The translator's moral right to be identified as the translator of the work has been asserted.

Norvik Press Series B: English Translations of Scandinavian Literature, no. 59

A catalogue record for this book is available from the British Library.

ISBN: 978-1-909408-03-6

Norvik Press gratefully acknowledges the generous support of the Danish Arts Council towards the publication of this translation.

Norvik Press
Department of Scandinavian Studies
University College London
Gower Street
London WC1E 6BT
United Kingdom
Website: www.norvikpress.com
E-mail address: norvik.press@ucl.ac.uk

Managing editors: Sarah Death, Helena Forsås-Scott, Janet Garton, C. Claire Thomson.

Cover design: Marita Fraser
Cover photograph: Ximo Michavila
Layout: Marita Fraser

I

The Darkness Out There

By some irony of fate it turned out to be West Africa and not the Seychelles, which had seemed much more appealing, but was long since fully booked by the time she finally found a gap in her calendar. It was a sudden and unconsidered decision taken in a situation of extreme stress, and which afterwards appeared in an almost mystic light. On the rare occasions when she took a holiday she would choose one of the European countries on the Mediterranean, but she could not be sure of the weather out of season. She had attended meetings and conferences in Johannesburg, but did not have any real knowledge of Africa. It was not a continent where she had ever imagined she would play the tourist.

Golden Bay Hotel was unexceptionable, if she ignored the cries of the peacocks from the park and the stink of monkey droppings on the terrace. With a sure instinct for quality she had booked the only acceptable hotel (to judge from the pictures and the description on its homepage) in that part of the country where tourism was concentrated. Under English ownership and tastefully designed, with low pavilions and an elegant main building containing restaurants, cafés, bars and a nightclub with a casino. Below the hotel gardens and with access from the broad mahogany steps lay the tourist beach, where soldiers patrolled in camouflage uniform with pistols in their belts. Zealously and out of pure solicitude for the hotel guests they hunted down the unauthorized sellers of fruit and souvenirs and shooed them away from the fenced-off areas. It took a while to adjust to the fact that she was not on the Mediterranean, but somewhere out of this world, and that her guardians on the beach were black and not white.

She had looked forward, now that she had at last cast off into the unknown, to being able to experience the country and its nature, to wandering around on her own as she was used to doing whenever she was in a southern country. But she had miscalculated. As soon as she ventured beyond the patrolled area of the hotel and strolled up the tourist street with its restaurants, exchange bureaus and supermarkets, she was accosted by young men who offered their services as guides or boyfriends. She made it clear that she did not need either a guide or a boyfriend, but they would not take no for an answer. They stuck to her and wanted her to give, give, give: her rings, her watch, her money, a piece of her white skin. She managed to shake them off and half-ran back to the hotel and complained to the security guards at the entrance, who took her complaints extremely seriously (it was a matter of the country's reputation as a tourist destination and consequently its GNP). She was given a telephone number for the hotline which tourists could use if they were molested. But she would be unable to identify her molesters once they had disappeared into the shade beneath the trees, where they all looked alike.

She did not leave the hotel area after her unpleasant experience with the three 'bumsters', as the guards called the young men who hung out near the tourist hotels in the hope of striking lucky. She could only relax when she had passed the hotel's security guards and was behind the high walls which surrounded the magnificently laid-out gardens with small fountains, a profusion of bird species, tropical trees and a riot of coloured flowers, soft sprinkled lawns crossed by winding paved paths, which conducted the guests around from one exotic African sculpture to the next.

The hotels with their colour-coded sunbeds on their demarcated beach plots were lined up all along the long stretch of sand facing the Atlantic. The beach gave her space to breathe and escape daily from the enclosed hotel reservation. She sat every day on the same spot on the same sunbed on which she had placed her towel early in the morning. If she did not take measures to prevent it, there were no free sunbeds when she sauntered down after breakfast around ten. The first day she had had to leave again disappointed. There was no-one on the beach, but on every single sunbed there was a towel the size of a sheet.

Around four hours after her skirmish in the towel war (the earlier you got up and came down to the beach and deposited your towel, the better placed your sunbed in terms of view and distance to the sea) she returned to her sunbed, dressed in a mint-green bathing-wrap with beach shoes of soft rubber and an extra towel over her shoulder. She sat for most of the day on the sunbed and observed life on the beach, hidden behind her sunglasses. She dare not shut her eyes for fear that someone should invade her space unnoticed. It might be English hotel guests or a fruit and juice seller who in an unguarded moment had invaded the tourist beach from the local beach on the other side of the park, where there were swarms of small light-grey colobus monkeys, who also scampered about in the hotel gardens.

The vendors from the local beach were school-age girls (and a few older boys), gracefully balancing their trays of fruit and nuts on their heads. They were energetically pursued and chased away by the soldiers, and every now and then they got a couple of well-aimed raps across their backs and shoulders with wooden sticks. They returned indefatigably the moment the soldiers in their tight-fitting uniforms had retreated to other parts of the beach or into the shade to relax with a cigarette and cola. It was obviously a matter of life and death for the girls to sell their wares to the wealthy tourists, those bronze gods who lay lounging on the hotel's blue sunbeds or walked in couples along the edge of the beach collecting seashells and conch shells.

For the first couple of days she sat in splendid isolation under her parasol. She felt herself being permeated by the radiant heat, which penetrated right to her bones and thawed out the winter cold in their marrow. She decided not to read

11

the *Wallpaper* magazine she had brought along, an impulse buy from the airport. She was afraid of losing control in the unfamiliar surroundings. And it was a mystery to her how, despite her high state of alert, she did not notice danger drawing near, did not even pick up the slightest little play of light and shade from the corner of her eye.

Without any warning she became aware of the presence of a human being right beside her. She gave a start, unable to move. Her body felt as if it was nailed to the sunbed. Cold sweat prickled her forehead. The sunglasses wrapped closely round her temples restricted her field of vision. She remained locked in an uncomfortable position, trapped in unwilling close contact. She hit out with a flat hand, as if she was waving flies away. Was there no-one there? Was she the victim of an illusion? She dare not turn her head to see whether there really was someone at her left side. She heard something which could be interpreted as silent breathing. There was a cautious hesitancy in the imperceptible breath, something touching and fragile. It was one of the small vendors who had placed herself right next to her armrest, slightly behind her and out of her eyeline.

'Want something?' A voice as if made of a gentle breath had formed an appeal in tense expectation of her positive reaction. Could any human being resist such an assault? Could she?

That was precisely the question. She wished she had been able to resist. But it was not possible. She softened, melted like a snowman in the spring sunshine. The gentle little voice struck her ear and continued in along the auditory canal. She was filled with an unearthly beauty, the fine tinkling of a silver bell. She could not explain what happened. She did not believe that there was a so-called other or higher world which existed beside the material one. Only what could be measured and weighed, heard and seen with the naked eye or under a microscope, could be said to exist. In her view all talk of spiritual and immaterial manifestations was pure superstition. But here on the beach, 'ten thousand light years from home', where sky and sea merged into one, the inexplicable happened. A quivering child's voice forced its way beneath her skin and moved her. She was completely unprepared.

Finally she summoned up her courage and turned her head. The little figure stood planted in the sand, straight as a candle with the enormous tray on her head.

'You want?' The girl pulled at the sleeve of her bathing wrap.

'You want, you want?' insisted the girl. She surrendered. It flattered her to be chosen and feel her defences broken down by such persistence.

'What have you got?'

'Everything.' The girl's grey-black wispy hair was tightly plaited over the crown of her head from her forehead down to her neck, where it ended in small fluffy tufts. The thin plaits were not nearly as wide as the spaces between them, which exposed the tender light-brown scalp. All those tightly pulled plaits must be terribly painful for that sensitive skin.

'Everything' was rather an overstatement. A couple of bags of nuts and a bunch of bananas was all that was left on the tray.

'Bosslady.' It sounded almost threatening.

'Give me a few nuts, just a handful,' she said. Why that idiotic 'just a handful'? she thought, annoyed with herself. The nuts were measured out into grimy plastic bags, which looked as if they had been reused many times. And right enough, the girl emptied a bag of nuts into her hand. How could she pay for them now?

'Help yourself,' she said and motioned to the girl to fish some notes out of the money belt she was wearing under her swimming wrap. She did not go into the water and felt reasonably secure taking her money belt with her to the beach. She could not imagine going out without cash or credit cards on her.

It was only now that she discovered how thin the girl was, just skin and bone. Wrists like pipe-cleaners. Skin more grey than black. Her blouse was dirty and short and looked as if she'd grown out of it. Her face was broad, with coarse features, and her white teeth were stained as if with tiny rust-coloured flowers. She was taller and looked older than the other sellers on the beach. She stood out like an ugly duckling, moving clumsily and abruptly. It took her an inordinately long time to fish the twenty dalasi out of the money belt; she proudly showed her the worn note lying in her cream-coloured palm. She nodded and said 'Thanks for your help', although twenty dalasi was an exorbitant price for that little pile of dry nuts. The girl put the note in her pocket and stood there shuffling on her bare feet under the long skirt. The delay made her feel uncomfortable. The deal was concluded. They had no more business with each other. She needed to be alone. This unwished-for meeting had already lasted too long. She turned away from the girl, but could feel her intense presence and that light cautious breathing which invaded her ears again. As if the scene was going to begin all over again and a mystic ritual repeat itself.

She had to put a stop to this siege and got up suddenly from the sunbed, standing at her full height beside the girl who reached to the middle of her chest. She looked down at the emaciated figure, which looked more like an undeveloped young woman whose growth had been arrested than a child. She looked back with large, guileless and infinitely gentle eyes. Was she mentally retarded?

'What's your name?' she asked to her own amazement.

'Mariama,' said the girl in a barely audible voice.

'Then we are name-sisters,' she exclaimed. Her heart began to thump in her breast. Had chance sent this wretched creature to cross her path and put her to the test?

'Name-sisters?' The girl shook her head and looked as if she was about to take off and flee far away from this white monster (or why not goddess?) which she must appear to her to be.

'I'm also called Mariana,' she explained.

'Mariana.' The girl doubled up with a little soundless giggle.

'Two Marianas.' The girl pointed excitedly to her and then to herself and to her again and then to herself as if in a grotesque pantomime.

'I'm normally called Ana,' she broke in to make her stop.

'Ana,' repeated the girl and stared at her as if she was the eighth wonder of the world.

'My name is Mariama, Mariama … with an m … not Mariana.'

'All right … Mariama with an m … shall we go for a walk?' asked Ana and felt strangely light.

'But I … am at work, doing business.' Mariama blinked nervously.

'I'll buy the whole trayful, how much do you want?'

'A hundred dalasi,' said Mariama and opened her eyes wide. Ana pulled a hundred-dalasi note out of her money belt and stood there with it in her hand. Mariama looked hungrily at the note and handed over the remainder of the day's wares. She put the bananas and nuts on top of her towel on the sunbed, which was her private territory for as long as she remained on the beach.

'You are all alone on holiday?' asked Mariama with a mixture of wonder and sympathy.

'Take that thing off,' commanded Ana instead of answering and pointed at the tin tray.

'And put it on my sun lounger,' she continued with a tourist's assertiveness.

'It will be stolen at once.' Mariama looked at her, shocked, and clearly did not share her evaluation of security on the tourist beach. Ana bowed to her local knowledge and noticed out of the corner of her eye that their little drama had aroused the attention of the hotel guests, who were sitting as one with their faces turned in their direction. Ana's sunbed was at the end of the row, just before the neighbouring hotel's green-and-white-striped sunbeds took over the next strip of sand. What the eyes behind the sunglasses saw she could of course have no idea. But she had never been able to stand being watched. She did not want to be seen, or judged, evaluated, weighed and measured by strangers' glances.

Her innocent initiative, a walk along the beach with the little beach-vendor, should not become the object of curious prying and suspicions of unsavoury motives. In a flash she saw herself with a machine gun, mowing down the gaping flock of sunbed-tourists. These mental images from action films and computer games were a part of her consciousness, although it was her nature to be as peaceful as a quiet summer's day in a birchwood by the Gulf of Bothnia.

Ana did not let herself be put out by her uneasiness at the many sunglasses with a thousand-euro pricetag which were directed towards her and Mariama, who eventually lifted her tray down with an elegant movement. It was smaller and lighter than it looked when it was resting like a heavy lid on top of the emaciated figure of the girl. Ana offered impatiently to carry the tray in her beachbag. But Mariama refused and insisted on carrying it herself. Her impractical obstinacy irritated Ana. She could easily have put the tray in her tasteful wickerwork bag, bought in the hotel's souvenir shop, which stocked everything the heart could desire, from baskets and bags, handprinted material and woven rugs to scary masks and drums in all sizes. Everything beautifully arranged according to country of origin: Nigeria, Burkina Faso, Uganda, Ghana, Congo, Kenya, Senegal, Tanzania. Every evening before dinner, almost like an obsessive ritual, she visited those large airy premises by the hotel entrance. She felt compelled to check whether there was some treasure or other she had overlooked. She had to inhale the dark continent in the concentrated form of the displayed wares and acquire some trendy African design for practically nothing when converted to euros.

Mariama was ready to go and stood waiting for Ana to gather her things together. She left only the towel behind, in order not to forfeit her right to the sunbed. She hung her beachbag over her shoulder, and together they crossed the beach down towards the water's edge, where there were piles of seashells in delicate pastel colours. When they had walked some distance away from the sunbeds and could feel the fresh salty sea air, Mariama took hold of her hand. It gave Ana a jolt like an electric shock passing right through her body. Her hand froze, she could not move it, not withdraw it. It lay cold and stiff around Mariama's warm little living hand. She could not remember having experienced anything like it. She had grown up without physical contact and involuntarily sought to avoid touching anyone else. Even a neutral handshake was something she feared and only returned dutifully in a work context. The touch of a stranger's skin filled her with antipathy and nauseous dizziness. But she had learned to live with it.

Defending herself instinctively, she asked Mariama how old she was.

'Fifteen.'

'So why aren't you at school instead of selling fruit and snacks on the beach?'

'I go to school in the morning.' Her voice shook.

'Are you sure about that?' asked Ana sceptically. On the plane they had seen a short video about conditions in the country, from which it was clear that many families were too poor to send their children to school. And it was boys who were the priority, even though the president had recently decreed that girls should pay only half the school fees. Perhaps Mariama's announcement was just a dream. She didn't look like a girl who could read and write.

They walked along the beach, a stiff breeze blowing in from the sea. They could hear the roaring of the waves, whipped into foam. Ana found a plausible excuse to let go of Mariama's skeleton-like and strangely dry hand. The clam shells were simply too pretty to resist. She stopped, bent down and collected a suitable selection to take home and decorate the bathroom with. She walked on, the shells rattling in her bag. Mariama had dropped behind.

'Hurry up now,' she said, embarrassed that she must look like a tall white woman with a little coolie shuffling along at a seemly distance behind. She did not want to expose herself to moral condemnation or to laughter, and took hold of Mariama's arm. They carried on until they couldn't go any further because of the rocks and scrubland which cut off the beach and ran out into the water.

Ana suggested that they should sit and rest on the sand before they returned. Mariama sat down with the tin tray on her lap. She clung to it as if it was her most precious possession.

'Have you anything to eat? Sandwich?' she asked boldly, looking at her with the direct gaze of the innocent. Ana had to apologise for her lack of provisions. Reluctantly Mariama ate one of the bananas she had sold her, but she would not take any nuts. It was unthinkable to take her in to the hotel's restaurant or pool bar after their walk. Entry to the hotel area was strictly forbidden. Not, of course, for Gambians as a whole, but for the poor and destitute who crowded around the entrance to the hotel and on the beach. And Mariama was one of them. She could not even take her in as her guest.

'Will you be my sponsor, bosslady?' Again her voice had taken on this aggressive insistence.

'What do you mean?' Ana felt uncomfortable at the announcement of this new demand and regretted that she had embarked on an acquaintance with the girl. She thought she had found a little lady's companion who would cheer her loneliness and be grateful for the chance, but there she had miscalculated. This was cool business.

'Sponsor my school, bosslady?' she repeated. This 'bosslady' irritated Ana. It sounded sarcastic.

'I don't believe you go to school. You're just smart enough to know that Europeans love the idea of Africans going to school and getting educated,' Ana returned with an instinctive feeling that it was important to put her foot down from the start.

'I don't lie, bosslady,' said Mariama, revealing an unexpected anger. She looked at Ana with a grimace of contempt. Ana began to feel panicky. After all, Mariama had the advantage of being on home territory.

'Shall we go back?' said Ana; she got up and brushed the sand off her swimming wrap. Suddenly it felt like a handicap that she was not properly dressed. It made her feel exposed and vulnerable.

'I stay here.' Mariama looked around searchingly.

'Don't be so silly,' said Ana with motherly persuasiveness. 'Come here.' She reached out her hand to Mariama.

'No, I wait for my friends,' she went on. Her rejection felt like a slap in the face, a demonstration of Ana's defencelessness as a stranger in Mariama's territory far away from the hotel beaches.

Ana had forgotten that she was anything other than a pitiful figure in the sand, that she had a life outside the tourist area, a life peopled with relations, neighbours, friends, that she had a family with a long history behind it. That was what scared her, that Mariama's existence, when she was out of the picture, reduced her to a faceless nonentity who was indistinguishable from the anonymous stream of tourists. What was she doing here in this wilderness, on this patch of the planet ravaged by drought? A luxury-class, special-offer holiday, a sudden impulse, an escape from the pressure of a full daily schedule. Why in heaven's name did she allow herself to be knocked sideways by the contrariness of some unimportant girl? She was a weakling flown in directly from the West European incubator. The slightest bump, the slightest resistance to her prepackaged planning triggered depression and panic. She must pull herself together and show this girl who she was and where she came from.

'Is something wrong?' said the cautious voice again, fragile as sweet music.

'Now you're coming with me,' said Ana agitatedly and hauled her up by her matchstick arm in a hard grip. Mariama bit her lip.

'It hurts,' she said, at the same time sad and accusing.

'I call my friends.' Mariama made a whistling sound with her lips. Out of the scrub came a girl who looked to be younger than Mariama, but prettier and less shabby.

'Who are you?' asked Ana, irritated by the beginnings of a headache. But she did not want to admit weakness and dive into her bag for paracetamol and a water bottle.

'I am her sister,' said the girl with a self-assurance that Mariama clearly lacked.

'I have a big family, many sisters and brothers,' explained Mariama, less inhibited in her sister's presence. They stood close together, the sister with a protective arm around Mariama.

'I help her.'

'What do you help her with?'

'The bad boys. They chase Mariama and steal her goods and money and sometimes her tray and all. So I hit them.'

'You don't look very strong.'

'But she is, the strongest girl on the beach,' Mariama assured her.

'Do you sell fruit and snacks too, like Mariama?'

'She is not good at business, she is my bodyguard,' Mariama answered for her. 'She's called Madeleine like our grandmother,' she added proudly.

'How old is Madeleine?' asked Ana.

'You think a lot about age.' Mariama frowned.

'Forget it,' said Ana. The sister was an unforseen complication. Ana was a distinctly one-to-one person, and felt she had lost her grip on the situation. She began to walk back towards the hotel beach. The two sisters trotted after her. The sun hammered its clenched fist into the open beach. The sand was at boiling point and burned through her beach shoes. Ana increased her speed. The girls drew level with her and took hold of an arm each.

'Are you angry, bosslady?' said Mariama in her gentlest voice, the one that had disarmed and stirred her. She stopped and shook them off.

'Let me be, both of you,' she said and bitterly regretted her idea of a walk along the beach. Above all she was angry with herself, for having lost her sense of appropriate behaviour, defied her inner warning lights and waded in over the frontier between the locals and the tourists. Frontiers were necessary for the planet to function, and it was especially important not to step over the natural dividing lines, to keep on the right side of the fence and retain the upper hand.

'But I am your friend,' said Mariama in an attempt to placate her. Her sister, the little fighter, had turned round and stood watching them from a distance.

'I'm just in a bad mood, not quite at my best,' complained Ana. Mariama took her hand cautiously. This time it felt more natural.

'Don't be afraid. Rich people are always afraid,' she said comfortingly, and gave her hand a squeeze. With a simple trick she had reversed the roles and got the upper hand.

'You like my country?'

'I don't know anything about your country,' said Ana sulkily, but to her own surprise she kept the girl's hand in hers. Was it so easy and painless to be cured of a lifelong phobia? The sweat was streaming off her beneath her wrap. Her Gucci rubber shoes were chafing, despite the fact that they were lined with thin chamois leather.

'But you know me, bosslady,' said the irrepressible little voice. She began to realise with horror that Mariama had no intention of letting go of her again. That she had given the devil her little finger and opened herself up to the forces of darkness. Mariama was a manifestation of everything she did not want to know about, which she hid away in the black holes of her consciousness under the heading of The World Order. In a moment of distraction Ana had given way to a chance impulse, and now she was trapped.

They carried on walking back along the sand, hand in hand. Ana took a few deep breaths to calm her nerves and steady herself.

'I shall wait for you every day and give you a good price for a walk on the beach,' Mariama carried on optimistically. Ana was caught in a spider's web, but did not try to break free. She repressed the danger signals and concentrated on the beach, the waves and the clam shells, the bright colours and the tropical heat, the high bank of earth with the steps up to the hotel area, from where the armed soldiers kept watch on the beach. For a split second she saw the beach covered in blood-red sand. She shook off the horrible vision and concentrated on relaxing. She was on holiday, and in a week she would be far away from 'the heart of darkness'. Back home again in the temperate climate of the Nordic countries, at home in her own comfortable flat in Copenhagen, that cosy nest where nothing bad could reach her.

They were back by the hotel's sunbeds. Most of them were empty and abandoned. Ana took her digital camera out of her bag and wanted to take a picture of Mariama, so that she could prove to herself and her friends that the girl actually existed in the real world. She was in a better mood already.

'No, bosslady, I don't like.'

'But I'll pay, Mariama,' said Ana, feeling light-headed. By now she had understood the elementary rules of the game. Buying and selling was the universal law. Nothing in this world was free. Everything had its price. How had she been able to forget such an elementary thing, which she had learned as a child, had even studied at university? The heat and the strong sensory impressions must have gone to her head, to make her common sense desert her like this.

'Your camera steals my soul, and I don't sell my soul for money.'

'Oh Mariama, drop that old bullshit.'

'OK, hundred dalasi.' Mariama sighed and looked appreciatively at her.

'Welcome to the twenty-first century,' said Ana teasingly. Mariama smiled uncertainly.

'We are friends?' she said.

'What does that mean?'

'I'll wait for you tomorrow.'

'What time?'

'In the afternoon.'

'All right, we'll meet there.' Ana picked up her towel and walked towards the hotel steps, where every step was painted with the words Golden Bay Hotel in gold.

'You forgot your picture,' said Mariama and put the empty

tray on her head. She posed for the photos, adopting various positions in a professional manner. Ana took a couple of photos of her with the Atlantic and the towering waves in the background. Mariama held out her hand and Ana paid her. They understood each other. She felt that she had already got the measure of this tourist hell, which advertized itself as a paradise.

Mariama hurried away from the hotel beach, half-running towards the local beach which was at a good distance from the fenced-off areas. Ana could faintly make out small groups of people crouching around some kind of cooking pots standing on glowing embers. She imagined that they were families preparing their evening meal on the beach, and that they would later give thanks to their ancestors with the rhythmical drumming which had kept her awake until early morning. She contemplated another sleepless night with pounding drums which went straight through her earplugs. She stood watching Mariama walk away. In the shimmering heat haze it looked as if she was walking and walking without getting anywhere. Every now and then she stumbled and tripped over her own feet, no doubt overcome by fatigue after her day's work and the many trips up and down the long shore. The little silhouette grew smaller and smaller, until it was swallowed up by the haze and disappeared.

Ana celebrated the day's events with a bottle of champagne with the seafood starter. She toasted herself and lifted her glass in greeting to the English couple at the next table. She was wearing an African design in shiny black cotton with a yellow zigzag pattern, bought at the souvenir shop early that morning, delivered to the hotel reception before breakfast and between morning and sunset made up into a traditional outfit at a local dressmaker's. The only thing she had added was a belt of antelope hide, which she had hastily bought in the shop's leather section. Wide, flowing gowns with yards of material were not her style, but held together by a broad belt at the waist the African cut looked quite sophisticated on her tall, rangy, loose-limbed figure.

The couple responded to Ana's gesture by inviting her over to join them at their table for the main course. She had broken through the sound barrier, and felt she was in contact with the whole world. She was already looking forward to seeing Mariama again the next day, and chatted away energetically to the friendly husband and wife. They discussed the standard of the hotel, the furnishings of the rooms, the service, the day's meals and their respective plusses and minuses. Everything that swirled around in tourists' buzzing heads and disorientated senses. They awarded numbers of chef's hats, hearts and stars, clinked glasses and drank deeply as if they had sorrows to drown. Was it nostalgia for familiar surroundings? Was it doubts about whether they deserved to be right here right now? Was it fear of the darkness which lay in wait outside the windows? Of the whispering noises and the approach of night? This lurking fear and unease resulted in exaggerated jollity and the knocking over of a glass of red wine and a smooth and elegant replacement of the white tablecloth.

'I'll give that five stars,' exclaimed Ben. His sympathetic wife Beatrice refilled their glasses, and they clinked, rocking in their storm-tossed luxury liner in the midst of the heaving African ocean.

They had not yet exchanged any personal information. Ana avoided talking about herself as much as possible. She hid behind a neutral and anonymous façade. She felt herself to be different, and functioned best in a professional work context. Social interaction and small talk were an effort for her, as if she were required to complete a task which was beyond her competence. As soon as a conversation became personal and involved feelings she withdrew. She had no soul to lay bare, no feelings to unburden herself of.

'Ana, are you all right?' Beatrice broke through her distraction.

'Sorry …'

'You were far away. Perhaps you were thinking of the

people back home?' said Beatrice in a friendly tone.

'I don't have anyone … back home.'

'There's always someone.' Beatrice was so unexpectedly considerate that Ana was taken aback. Did she see something in her which others could not see?

'Yes, of course,' she agreed hastily.

'When we're away we long for home, and as soon as we're safely home again we're caught by a longing to be away,' Beatrice carried on, as if to herself.

'What brings you to this part of the world?' Ben interjected.

'Chance, a last-minute … holiday,' Ana stammered. She did not want to reveal that her trip was 'time out' ordered by the firm's coach as a measure to reduce stress.

'So you're not in the business, some kind of Africa expert?' Ben was amiability itself.

'Far from it.' Ana's brief answers did not seem to discourage the friendly couple, whose direct and fearless questioning persuaded her to open up.

'Holidays are fine, too,' Ben assured her. He was a little, round balding man in a short-sleeved shirt, safari trousers and canvas shoes. Beatrice was taller than him, with broad shoulders and a slim, wiry figure enveloped in a thin cotton dress with a pattern of small flowers. Ana could not take her eyes off her. She found women more engaging and attractive than men, though not necessarily smarter.

'I wanted to experience … a different world.' Ana had to invent a good reason for making a choice of holiday which was so untypical of her.

'What do you do, then … when you're not on holiday?' Beatrice took over.

'I'm a manager in Rower International. Headhunted when I finished my MBA.' Ana reeled it off as if she was being interviewed for a job. She was not used to talking about herself.

'Clever you,' exclaimed Beatrice. Ana's cheeks became hot. She found it difficult to accept compliments.

'Are you a genius, Ana?' Ben tilted his head sideways and

squinted at her.

'Why not?' Beatrice added good-humouredly.

'I'm governed by my head, not my heart,' she said matter-of-factly, as if she was referring to a fictitious person.

'Only a person with a lot of heart could express themself like that,' said Beatrice with a smile. Her kindness was so natural that Ana's deep-rooted fear of people she did not know dissolved.

'Are you a psychologist? No, you're not a psychologist,' she said to Beatrice. She had consulted several of those without any great success. She did not have the patience to complete the 'course'.

'Good guess, I'm not a psychologist, I'm an anthropologist.' Beatrice clapped her hands.

'I dreamt about doing that once, but didn't have the courage,' Ana exclaimed impulsively.

'What courage?' asked Beatrice.

'To live amongst strangers with foreign customs, in foreign places.' She refrained from saying 'primitive'.

'If you feel a stranger amongst strangers, that's because you're a stranger to yourself,' said Beatrice. Ben laughed out loud.

'One of Bea's hobby horses.'

'Ben works in the animal kingdom,' Beatrice retorted.

'Veterinary, please,' Ben exclaimed, reaching for her hand.

'We're on a mid-term mission, a biosecurity project for Abuko Livestock Centre, Animal Health and Production Department to be quite precise … not far from this hotel,' he added by way of explanation of them staying at a five-star hotel.

'We're trying to make the project's budget balance,' Beatrice put in.

They took turns in telling her about their experiences the previous day, when they had been out in the bush visiting local chicken farmers in connection with a vaccination programme, 'Keep Birds Free From Flu'. Their counterparts were serious civil servants from the Ministry in uncomfortable suits, who complained that the European cost-cutting bombardment of cheap, battery-farmed, deep-frozen chickens was ruining the home market for the country's smaller chicken farmers.

'Just to give you the relevant facts,' Ben concluded in a tone of self-mockery.

'We won't bother you any further with our reliable agricultural statistics and food hygiene,' Beatrice added. Ana just responded with a vague nod. The aid sector was too far removed from her own world to arouse any real interest.

Ben ordered more cognac, confident that the restaurant would remain open as long as there were guests, and the solitary musician in jacket and tie was playing the familiar old evergreens on the keyboard. The room had begun to empty. Many guests would be off early the next day sightseeing. The cool mornings were used for strenuous jeep trips up country.

'So you're in the investment and shares market?' he asked. Ana nodded.

'Then you work round the clock?' Beatrice said.

'I'm married to my work,' Ana admitted in a low voice. Beatrice waved her hand dismissively.

'It's your inbuilt sense of duty.'

'I wouldn't call it duty. I use myself to the maximum and achieve what is expected of me. Call it a fair repayment of what society has invested in an expensive higher education.'

'Work is the scourge of our time, we've become foot-soldiers of employment,' said Beatrice.

'You mustn't discourage our friend,' Ben objected, slightly irritated.

'I'm just telling it the way it is, Ben, we work and we don't know who we are,' said Beatrice, quietly insistent.

'Work is our one remaining vice. They can't take that from us too,' said Ben cheerfully, quoting graffiti from a wall in London City.

'I am glad I met you,' said Ana spontaneously.

'It's mutual, my dear.' Ben's soft squirrel eyes shone.

'My guess is that you don't just work all hours of the day, you also draw on your subconscious and your dream-sleep,'

Beatrice persevered.

'I exploit my whole creative register.'

'It's lovely that you still use the word "creative". It reminds me of the time when we believed in the future and were a part of the global creative class.' Beatrice could be lovely herself, positively worthy of adoration, thought Ana. For a godless person like her it was tempting to make people into gods.

'I live like a nun, work is my prayer'; the words ran through her head like a line of verse. Beatrice looked at her. Ana was drawn to her calm researcher's gaze.

'Our only hope is that we become poor again. Only poverty can bring us back on track as human beings in a human world.' Beatrice directed her attention towards Ben again.

'Isn't that a little over-romantic?' he objected.

'I don't mean misery and starvation, but moderation and respect for a more frugal and sustainable way of life, the good old virtues in a modern framework.' Beatrice had got some colour in her pale cheeks. Ana wondered whether there were children in their marriage, or whether their work was enough. If she had had the chance to choose her parents, it would be those two. She would gladly be their child.

'Riches corrupt our minds and brutalize our senses, give us an illusion of immortality,' Beatrice continued. It sounded as if they were in the middle of a confidential conversation which had not been derailed by Ana's presence.

'All great civilizations have disintegrated from inside,' Ben admitted.

'The Roman Empire.' Beatrice nodded and put her hand on his arm. Ana noticed that she was tired, unused as she was to social interaction outside a regular work context. She wished she could retreat to her room in the bungalow and throw herself on the bed. Beatrice and Ben, on the other hand, seemed alert and talkative despite the lateness of the hour.

Gradually they had been left alone in the restaurant. A waiter was standing ready by the door to the garden, staring into the room with an empty gaze. Two others yawned discreetly whilst they cleared the tables. No-one would ask them to pay and leave the restaurant. As guests they had complete sovereignty and the right to sit there all night if it suited them.

'A whisky?' Ben suggested. Ana couldn't refuse a last drink, and regretted it instantly. But Ben had waved to the waiter, who immediately brought the drink and the bill in a little wooden chest with a rounded lid. Beatrice looked at Ben and stood up. Ben placed a bundle of dalasi bills in the chest, which contained small chocolate gifts and aniseed sweets to cleanse the palate.

'We must keep in touch,' he said in a friendly tone and offered Ana his hand, then checked himself as if he knew she did not like touching strangers. She remained calmly seated, enjoying her whisky in the knowledge that the bill had been paid.

That night she could not sleep. She had not expected to, after the evening's animated company, the many glasses of wine and the cognac and whisky afterwards. Not to mention the enervating, throbbing drumbeats somewhere out there in the darkness of the night. She took a double dose of sleeping pills, but could not switch off. She lay tossing and turning between the stiff sheets, with her head full of plans for the following day together with Mariama. Should she buy her a present from the hotel souvenir shop, or perhaps she would rather have cash? She must be well prepared and write all her questions down on a piece of paper. Perhaps she could simply do something for the family? She was in a state which felt like happiness. She got out of bed and stumbled in the darkness over to the minibar, and with her arms full of bottles she made her way back to the bed and emptied them one after the other. She could not cope with her exalted mood in any other way than by crushing it mercilessly. Was it emotion overwhelming her? Or was it just her imagination deceiving her, giving her the illusion of being in contact with all living things, trees, plants, animals, people? Or was it African spirits which had forced their way in through the walls and the closed doors and windows and robbed her of her rational sense?

She could not just lie there in bed. She had to move, to do something. She got up and got dressed to go for a walk on the hotel premises. Guests had been advised not to go out alone in the area at night, despite the fact that the security guards made their rounds regularly. She dismissed all the warnings and ignored the hotel's security arrangements. Normally she would never pass a No Entry sign or drive through a red light, but she felt trapped and had to get some air.

Wearing a long-sleeved T-shirt, comfortable loose linen trousers and non-slip running shoes, she went out and locked the double security lock on the door behind her. A warm, spicy scent of flowers and dried plants hit her like a euphoric drug. It was dark in the bungalows all around. The grass was as soft as a carpet of foam rubber, where your feet sink securely down to a solid base. She was lulled by a feeling that all was well with the world. Like a babe in swaddling clothes, wrapped up in that immense darkness. Where did it come from, that illusory feeling of security, which she had never felt on her own continent, either in broad daylight or after dark?

She walked away from the beach between the darkened bungalows, which she could just make out in the glow of the lights from the hotel's main building and the low lighting along the garden paths. Her eyes quickly got used to the darkness, so she could find her way after a fashion. Without any warning, as if he had shot up from the ground, a figure was standing right in front of her. She felt a hard grasp on her arm and screamed. It was one of the hotel's security guards. He shone his torch in her face and saw at once that she was one of the hotel guests.

'Sorry, ma'am, you should not be outside at this time of night,' he said in a reproachful, almost hurt tone. If anything happened to her, he would lose his job, he persisted. Her thoughtless excursion was a threat to the very foundation of his existence.

'I'm sorry,' she said with an uncomfortable feeling of

being deprived of freedom. The guard continued in a more conciliatory fashion.

'If you feel the need for fresh air, you can walk with me on my rounds and then let me accompany you back to your bungalow,' he offered. She thanked the friendly man, who was indistinguishable from the darkness. She could see no more of him than the phosphorescent stripes on his uniform. It was a luxury to have a security guard at her side, so that she could forget all about what was moving out there in the darkness.

'Are there not rather too many soldiers on the tourist beach?' she opened the conversation.

'For your safety, ma'am.'

'Security is all very well, but so many soldiers is … frightening.'

'Our president's decision. He is most concerned for the security of our tourists. When the beach has been cleaned up the soldiers will retire and leave the beach to the ordinary police. They are much better trained to deal with tourists.' The guard waved his arms. The luminous stripes on his jacket arms swung up and down.

'Have you had problems?' he continued.

'No, not at all, but the soldiers persecute the little fruit-sellers.'

'They upset the tourists, they ruin our business.'

'They don't do anything wrong.' Ana could not help defending her new friend.

'The tourists complain, ma'am, they want to be left in peace on the beach.'

'Is it not permitted to sell fruit and nuts on the beach?'

'Only if you are authorized and have a permit.' The guard seemed tired and irritable.

'What happens to them if they are not authorized?' Ana asked cautiously.

'Then they are passed to the police and kept in detention until the family comes and pays the fine.'

'Isn't that a little over the top?' Ana objected.

'It is illegal, against the law, you understand?' he explained pedantically.

'I hope my little girl is OK.'

'If she obeys the rules,' the guard assured her. Ana walked behind and to one side, following the luminous stripes on his uniform. He increased his speed. Ana speculated whether he was a devotee of law and order who hated irregularities. Or was it just her, fearful lest her interest in a chance young girl on the beach should appear improper, who attributed to him a distaste for those who were 'unauthorized'? They passed one of his colleagues on the narrow paved path. A series of warm greetings were exchanged.

'My brother,' said the guard gruffly and continued his rounds with Ana on his heels. Suddenly he stopped as if struck by lightening and pointed up at a tree.

'Can you see that owl, ma'am? It is a witch, an evil spirit,' he said in a trembling voice. Ana could see nothing in the darkness. The guard picked up a stone from the path and threw it with all his strength up towards the owl.

'It should be killed on the spot, but unfortunately hotel guards may not carry weapons.' He turned and rushed in a wide arc around the tree and the owl.

'Do you really believe that owls are witches?' asked Ana, out of breath.

'I don't believe. It is a fact.' The guard went even faster, as if in panic.

Without Ana noticing, they had left the hotel area. It struck her suddenly that she had set off into the night in complete confidence that a man she did not know would escort her safely through the darkness. She cursed her distraction and lack of awareness. What had she been thinking of? Was she in her right mind? she thought, as they moved towards a scene of unearthly beauty. Around an orange fire sat boys and girls of all ages, large and small close together in a circle with their legs together and stretched out so that the soles of their feet were turned towards the fire. Dancing women with heavy jewellery and artistically draped headcloths wove in a long chain in and out of the crowd that was gathered around the children. The atmosphere was sombre, vibrating with repressed passion. This was no tourist attraction she was witnessing. Ana felt ill at ease at the response which the deep drumming rhythms awoke in her. She looked round for the security guard. She wanted him to take her back to the bungalow, but could not see him in the smoke from the fire and the flickering chaos of dancing figures, which blended into the darkness so that only their movements were visible.

She felt a hand on her hip and turned round. Behind her stood a little old woman with a face creased into soft wrinkles. She wore a quantity of bracelets set with shells of mother-of-pearl and a broad milled gold band fastened tightly around one upper arm. On her head she wore a scarf in red and orange.

'Where am I?' asked Ana and grabbed the woman's hand.

'In good hands,' answered the woman shortly. Clearly you were not supposed to speak during the ceremony. Ana had no choice other than to remain where she was. Hand in hand they stood in the outermost circle of the crowd of people and the dancing darkness.

Despite her exposed position as a foreign body in the night's festivities, Ana felt remarkably calm. She was on the hazy border between the human and the spirit world, and the thought of death did not scare her. She had a sensation of having reached the end of the road. The only thing she was sorry about was that she wouldn't get to see Mariama again and demonstrate her good intentions. The old woman gave Ana a long thin light-brown twig to chew on. It produced a bitter sap. She dare not swallow, and the sap grew in her mouth and eventually spilled out, out of the corners of her mouth and down her chin. The old woman passed her a screwed-up piece of cotton cloth which she used to wipe herself. She spat the twig out on the ground and refused a new one. The old woman shook her head sadly, making the heavy earrings swing violently to and fro.

She began to push Ana forward towards the fire, where a kind of master of ceremonies in a long damask robe was making the children drink something. She let herself be driven along like a solitary bewildered ox to the slaughter and the black cauldron. Cannibalism like in the old cartoons, where black native kings devour white missionaries, was hard-wired into her subconscious. The fixed ideas and images, centuries old, functioned like an inner state of alertness, which could be summoned up in threatening situations. Yet she had no thought of resisting or defending herself, but only of acquiescing and surrendering herself. She was so far away from her native hemisphere that she had become completely disorientated.

Together with the old woman she had entered the circle of children. The heat from the fire was unbearable. Ana turned her back on it and held her hands up in front of her face. It felt as if her body had been plunged in boiling water. The assembled children were clearly so thick-skinned that the heat from the fire did not affect them. The old woman at Ana's side held on to her firmly. She was under her protection. No-one seemed to notice Ana's presence. It was as if she was invisible and did not exist, as if the ritual was taking place in an alternative reality to the one she was in.

The circle of children had shuffled nearer to the fire, so that the flames were licking the soles of their feet. Piercing shrieks mingled with the insistent drumming rhythms, which had reached a climax. Some of the children broke out of the circle and twisted and turned like mad things as they hopped around on their burnt feet. Their wailing and moaning could be heard through the throbbing drums. Ana bent down and asked the old woman who they were.

'Witches.' Her thin voice was drowned in the noise. Now all the children had risen from the circle. They ran towards her with arms outstretched and wanted to drag her with them into the savagery. Ana clasped her head with both hands and closed her eyes. It was as if the loud shrieks and wailing were coming from inside her and bursting out through her skull.

Every time she opened her eyes the children were whirling around one another in a rain of tiny white shells, weightless as if in a spaceship on its way out towards the flashing darkness of the universe.

Ana awoke late in the morning with a feeling that she was floating up near the ceiling, looking down at herself lying stretched full-length on her bed. The weightlessness had still not released her. She took a few deep breaths to reestablish contact with the earth and make her pounding headache abate. She had nothing to compare her present state with other than the violent hangovers of her student days. The breathing exercises helped her to remember the conclusion of the previous evening, when she had come to herself standing alone by the embers of the burnt-out fire on a broad plain whose close-cropped lawns reminded her of a golf course. Had she been the victim of an illusion caused by hallucinogenic substances from the brown twig the old woman had given her? The security guard had come strolling over to her.

'I'm afraid you must wait until the morning, ma'am,' he said. Ana explained that she was not a golf player. He looked at her disorientated, as if he had never met a European who didn't play golf.

'What happened? A witchhunt?' she asked, uncertain what it was she had seen.

'Are you interested in folklore? We have good museums in Banjul,' he said eagerly. Ana described the ceremony she had witnessed.

'Your imagination has run away with you, ma'am,' said the guard angrily; he sounded as if he was covering over a taboo.

'No, no, I saw it with my own eyes,' Ana objected. Her senses were whirling, confused images were passing through her mind. The guard had taken hold of her arm and led her with a firm grip across the grass, past the gnarled magnolia trees and over to her bungalow. She had lost all sense of time and could not remember whether it was already morning or still night.

Ana got up and dressed in a hurry. The most important item on the agenda was her appointment with Mariama. She could not count on getting a sunbed so late in the day and would have to make do with a more retired position in the beach bar. Thoughts of Mariama made the night's events pale. She inspired a hope in her that she had not known before; she could not interpret it or discover its source. She wanted to get to know Mariama's daily life, her family, her country and to be able to place that fragile little life in a framework of brutal African reality, which she could put straight with small financial contributions.

The beach attracted her more than the restaurant, and she decided to skip breakfast. She quickly put two oranges and a paperback in her beach bag. She did not intend to read the book (she hadn't bothered to note the title). It was a shield on the beach, in the restaurant and the bar, intended to signal that her loneliness was not merely deliberately chosen, but also a deep personal need. That she was happy in her own company and preferred it to superficial chance encounters. She applied her makeup perfectly and left her room, as usual wearing a bikini, an ankle-long beach robe, panama hat, black sunglasses and her indispensable soft rubber beach shoes.

Halfway between the bungalow and the steps down to the beach she was met by the guard who had conducted her to last night's exotic events. She felt no annoyance that he had doubted her nocturnal experiences, just a cool surprise that he was still at work.

'I had to stay at work, staff problems,' he explained before Ana had managed to ask why they hadn't changed the guards between the night and the day shift. Fully conscious of his significance for the security of the guests and consequently for the country's tourist industry, he continued his set route with a friendly 'Enjoy your day'.

Ana hurried on in the opposite direction towards the beach steps. She was as excited as a child at the thought of sitting in the beach bar and passing the time whilst she waited by imagining what she and Mariama would find to do together. She almost tripped on the steps, which were too narrow for her long European feet, so she had to walk sideways. She was reminded of an episode from a finance summit in Hong Kong.

'They just get taller and taller,' she heard an angry Chinese man say about the European delegation, which towered over the other participants. A member of the British delegation had said: 'Sorry, sir, too many vitamins.' This had caused general amusement amongst those standing nearby. And a Russian delegate had shouted: 'Cut down the rations. No more vitamins for the Europeans.'

A sharp, salty blast of sea air hit Ana in the face. She had to hold on to her panama hat, bought in Mexico on a work trip. The beach was suddenly in turmoil. Upturned deckchairs lay in a tangled heap. The air was thick with grains of sand whipping against her sunglasses. She pulled out her silk scarf and tied it over her nose and mouth. A couple of fishermen were busy pulling their boat up onto the beach. Ana went over to them. There were a few limp silvery fish in the bottom of the long, narrow wooden boat.

'Do you know a girl called Mariama?' she began hesitantly.

'We know hundreds,' they said in chorus.

'But one on this beach who sells fruit and nuts?' Ana insisted.

'She will not come today.' The fishermen looked grimly out to sea, from where the strong gusts were blowing.

Further down the beach a single tourist couple were battling against the stiff headwind.

'Enjoying our country?' said one of the fishermen.

'Oh yes, very much,' said Ana, peering towards the local beach from where she guessed Mariama would appear.

'So you don't know this little girl? Mariama?' Ana persisted. The men were busy holding on to their nets, which were spread out on the sand. 'She looks like a street urchin, greyish skin, greyish hair, dirty dress, dirty feet.'

'It could be any girl on the beach.'

'No, the other girls are so nice and clean,' she shouted to make herself heard above the gusty wind. The two men looked at her and shook their heads.

'Sorry about the storm, it should not be such weather, it is not normal for the time of year,' said one of them with earnest seriousness. Ana suddenly saw herself with their eyes. She must look comical with her green silk scarf covering her face from the edge of her glasses downwards, a terrorist in a beach robe. She did not really know how to continue the conversation, and asked whether the few little fish in the bottom of the boat were the day's catch. The fishermen turned their backs on her demonstratively and began to discuss something among themselves in loud voices. Too late she realized that with her casual remark about their miserable catch she had wounded their pride and been guilty of an irreparable insult.

Left to herself, she walked further along the beach. Despite the brilliant sunshine the wind had turned it into a barren and deserted area. The tourists were huddled together around the hotel pools. The fishermen had gone home and the local population stayed away out of respect for the storm approaching from the Atlantic. She had not given up hope that Mariama would appear, even though they had not agreed on a time or place.

She tramped up and down the beach for an hour or so. In the enormous sky above her the clouds had begun to mass together. Out over the sea they were threateningly dark, but over the land they were still light grey. It was just a question of time as to when the rainstorm would break. The wind had slackened a little, holding its breath menacingly. The beach was as good as empty of people. Even the soldiers had retreated. There was not a soul apart from Ana in her idiotic terrorist costume. She decided to go up and change into a more suitable outfit. Solid linen trousers, knee-length leather boots and her light nylon jacket. She ran up the beach steps as fast as her impractical beach-robe allowed, and halfway up it suddenly hit her that she had forgotten to close the safe in her room when she had taken out a bundle of dalasi notes to treat Mariama with when she met her. She sprinted across the lawn towards the bungalow.

Out of breath, Ana reached her door and let herself in to the clean room, which smelt of chlorine. The door of the safe, which was built into the wall between the writing table and the wardrobe, was open as she suspected. She was prepared for the worst, and hardly dared check the contents. Everything was untouched and in perfect order: credit cards, passport, money, jewellery. What honesty! It almost made her feel ill, this blow to her negative expectations when she thought of how poor they were. She closed the safe and locked it with her security code. The sweat was pouring off her. She would have to take a quick shower, but could not relax. She was worried that Mariama was searching for her on the beach. She could hear the little voice calling for her through the gentle streams of the shower. She quickly put on the clothes she had laid out on the bed. She wound the silk scarf round her hair. Her boots felt tight. Her feet had got used to the freedom of her soft rubber shoes.

Just as she came down to the beach the heavens opened and the rain bucketed down in thick ropes. Ana took shelter with her back to the embankment which protected the hotels from the open, uncontrollable beach. She held her bag over her head to ward off the rain. She peered around for the little figure, even though her common sense told her that it was unlikely she would appear in weather which prevented her from doing business with the tourists. She remained standing there with nothing to do except let the rain fall and sink into the nooks and crannies of her mind, which was said to be a miniature version of the universe. 'Il pleure dans mon coeur comme il pleut sur la ville,' was an apt image of the boundless melancholy she felt as she stood there like a drowned mouse watching the rain whipping up the sand.

Her neck and back had grown stiff from standing still, so she walked further along the embankment, still holding her bag over her head and with her eyes fixed on the low skyline of tin roofs behind the local public beach. She passed one hotel beach after the other, all with the streaming wet deckchairs in serried ranks facing the sea and the absent sun. As Ana approached the local beach, she gradually slowed down. In front of her lay what resembled a tip rather than a bathing beach. A bent figure, defying the rain, was rummaging through the rubbish with systematic thoroughness, turning over and inspecting every single piece of garbage before the decision was reached as to whether the object should go back in the sand or into the plastic sack.

The embankment grew lower and lower and stopped where the public beach started. On the last low section there were tunnels dug into the earth. Some of them only went in a few metres. Others were so deep that they disappeared into the darkness. Ana heard someone calling her name. She looked into a couple of the tunnels, but there was no sign of life. She dismissed the voice as a product of her imagination. She really didn't know what to do with herself. She didn't have the courage to carry on along the local beach and wade through rubbish up to her ankles. The violent storm had subsided and was followed by a moist wind. Ana hung her bag over her shoulder and resigned herself to going back to the hotel area and deciding how to make the rest of the day pass.

On the way back she passed the mysterious tunnels again without thinking any more about them. She was making plans for eating dinner with Ben and Beatrice that evening, and did not see the huddled little bundle of rags in one of the tunnel openings until she felt a tugging at her trouser leg and heard Mariama's accusing voice.

'I waited for you all afternoon.'

Ana reached out her hand and helped her to her feet. She looked if possible even more shabby than the day before. She was soaked through, and her dress was sticking to her body, which was just skin and bone. Her tin tray was crumpled up and tossed along the beach like a piece of junk. The little store of goods was scattered in the sand outside the entrance to the tunnel.

'What's happened?' she asked, and tried to put her arm

round Mariama. She pulled away. Was she unused to hugs, or had too many people tried to get too close?

'They caught me.'

'Who caught you, Mariama?' Ana asked carefully. Mariama shook her head. Ana thought it must be the soldiers who had punished her persistent intrusion onto the hotel beaches, or the big boys who her little sister had explained were her tormentors.

'Do you have anything to eat?' Mariama's round face was pale and pinched.

Ana had nothing other than the two oranges and plenty of dalasi notes. She took an orange from her bag and asked whether she should peel it for her. Mariama nodded and sat down on the sand, exhausted. Ana peeled one orange quickly and efficiently with the fruit knife she had brought with her. Without a word, Mariama accepted the pieces of orange and reached out automatically for the next one. She ate both oranges. When she had finished she sat still, staring dejectedly in front of her.

'Business, bosslady, my business is ruined,' she said.

'I'll buy it all …' Ana fished a few hundred-dalasi notes out of her bag. Mariama looked apathetically at the dirty, foul-smelling notes.

' … compensate you for what you would have sold,' Ana continued humbly.

'But what about my tray?' objected Mariama desperately.

'I'll give you everything money can buy,' Ana reassured her.

'Not the tray, the tray belongs to my aunt, my family. She will be very angry with me and hit me hard.'

'So you work for your aunt?'

'She goes to market to buy fruit and nuts which I sell on the beach,' whispered Mariama, looking round scared.

'I don't really understand, can't you explain a bit more about it?' Ana encouraged her. She had a niggling doubt that Mariama was deliberately dramatizing her situation in order to get her to cough up, and at the same time despised herself for her petty mistrust of a destitute child who survived and perhaps even supported her family by serving the invasion of sun-worshipping tourists.

'I get up before dawn and sweep the floors and clean my aunt's house and make sure the little ones get up and have something to eat, if there is anything for them. Then I go to school. In the afternoon I sell fruit and snacks on the beach. And when I come home from the beach I make food and look after the children. I work hard, I have not much time to learn my lessons.' Mariama looked down dejectedly.

'Do you really go to school, Mariama? Aren't you fifteen, nearly sixteen?' Ana asked inquisitorially.

'I go to school, tenth grade.' She looked at Ana with a direct gaze.

'Who pays your school fees?'

'You, bosslady, I hope,' came the swift reply from Mariama.

'If I decide to help you, I say emphatically "if", you must put me in touch with your school.'

'No, you must pay my aunt, she works in a bank, she has a bank account.' Her voice was shrill and aggressive.

Ana suggested that she should go back with her to the steps up to the Golden Bay. Mariama nodded, resigned, and began to shuffle along after Ana, who didn't like to have her on her heels and stopped to wait for her. Mariama looked tired and wretched. Ana said that they could say goodbye if she was too tired to go along all the way, and offered to arrange a new meeting the following day. Their relationship had been transformed into a sensitive business connection with Ana as the investor. Mariama insisted on accompanying her right to the steps. The beach was still deserted and 'dangerous'.

'Last year a Dutch couple were stabbed,' her little protegée reminded her. 'But now the soldiers are cleaning up the beach,' she said reassuringly, forgetting that she herself was one of the objects of the cleaning.

'Where are your parents?' Ana changed the subject.

'My parents and little brothers and sisters live far away in a village. Very poor, very difficult.'

'Why aren't you together with your family?'

'My mother, second wife, is ill. She cannot look after me. So I live with my aunt. It is good for my upbringing, and I get better instruction in housework. Parents are too soft with their own children. They love them too much and do not punish enough for bad behaviour.'

'But shouldn't you concentrate on your education instead of wasting time doing business on the beach?' Ana asked, forgetting she was in Africa.

'Business is needed for my family. We are poor, you see.'

'You mean your aunt's family? Madeleine is not your sister, but your cousin?'

'It is family. We are sisters,' Mariama insisted.

'Who pays for your school?' As potential sponsor, Ana felt she was within her rights to demand an insight into the financial structure of the school project.

'My uncle, Big Man,' said Mariama off-handedly.

'Your uncle?' Ana continued her interrogation. Mariama nodded.

'Do you pay for your school fees by working on the beach in the afternoon?' she suggested, as a possible explanation for her 'business'.

'Big Man can not pay for my school any longer,' she said abruptly.

'Do you only go to school in the morning?'

'I go to school,' Mariama assured her. It was not an answer, but Ana did not want to press her any more. In any case she could not be certain whether it was just a standard rigmarole which Mariama reeled off to soft-hearted tourists, a category Ana now belonged to. She had the choice of whether to stop worrying about the truth and pay a suitable amount of sponsorship and in that way relieve her conscience. Or she could drop her project of assistance and abandon Mariama to the tourists who came after her and simply return home without a backward glance. Every week she had a new chance to reel in one or more benefactors.

'My aunt will soon stop working in the bank,' she said. She had dropped back again. She could hardly drag herself along.

43

'Why?'

'She will just stop,' she said angrily and stamped on the sand with the plastic sandal which was far too large for her.

'You must understand that I need to know your financial situation if I'm going to sponsor your schooling,' said Ana, like a patient teacher. She felt as if she was a participant in a web of hidden truths and lies. Mariama remained silent. Perhaps she did not understand her reasoning, or else she was taking care not to give anything away, Ana wondered. And where did she herself get this ingrained scepticism? Was it from her genes or from her upbringing?

They said goodbye by the hotel steps and arranged to meet the following afternoon. As on the previous day, Mariama could not or would not give Ana a precise time. On the other hand she did suggest that they walk the same way as the day before and meet down by the water's edge opposite Ana's hotel steps. Ana said that she would be on the beach after two o'clock and reminded her that she only had three days left of her holiday, and that she expected Mariama to arrange for her to visit her school and draw up an agreement to pay her school fees directly to the school administration. That was the most sensible and secure way, Ana explained to her, with a feeling that her words were falling on stony ground. Nevertheless she thrust a few notes into Mariama's hand as payment for making sure she got back 'safe and sound' to Golden Bay Hotel.

The next day the weather was once more perfect and demanded that life should be lived. Ana went down onto the beach early with her towel as a weapon and staked her claim on a sunbed in the row nearest to the sea. She did not make use of her claim until after lunch, shortening the time she needed to wait until she hoped Mariama would appear in the afternoon, when she had finished working for her aunt. She sat at her post from two o'clock onwards as she had promised, and did not move from the spot. She was nervous that they would miss each other. Mariama had become a part of her image of herself. A peculiar thought struck her as she sat there on the lounger with her beachrobe fastened, sipping from the bottle of water she had brought and leafing through the airport novel without reading it, the thought that in Mariama she had found her soul, the 'missing link', not in a Darwinian sense, but the missing piece she had been searching for in her individual development towards becoming 'a whole person', which was one of the mantras of the firm's coaches. She suddenly had a clear intuition that Mariama was everything she was not, her platonic other half which she had been separated from at the dawn of time.

Ana was far away in her philosophical reflections when she was caught unawares by Ben and Beatrice, who came strolling along the beach arm in arm and made a beeline for her sunbed. They had clearly taken the afternoon off. Ana got up and said hello. Their cordial and welcoming manner was the same as at dinner in the restaurant. They suggested meeting later for a drink in the bar, and informed her that they were leaving the next day. They had concluded their mission, and could hand over responsibility to their local counterparts in the Ministry of Agriculture. They would like to say a proper goodbye to Ana before they parted. She accepted their invitation with pleasure. The couple continued along the beach in the opposite direction from the way she and Mariama had planned to walk.

Ana was left behind alone. She hated waiting. The minutes passed at a snail's pace. The afternoon was waning. Most of the hotel guests had already left the beach. Some riders rode past bareback at a sedate tempo on a couple of squat horses. They rode along the water's edge where the sand was firmer, away towards the monkey forest and the sunset. Ana had abandoned hope of seeing Mariama again and had adjusted to the fact that her African adventure was over. She took care always to be prepared for the worst in order not to fall into a black hole of disappointed expectations. At that moment she felt the gentlest touch of a hand on her shoulder and a breath from an aerial spirit on her neck.

Mariama was wearing the same threadbare patterned skirt as on the previous days, but was not carrying a tray on her head. She stood there hopping from one foot to the other, keen to get going. She was afraid that the soldiers would catch her and put her in prison, she whispered to Ana, who showed no reaction to her dramatic admission. She quickly collected her things together and let Mariama carry the picnic basket, which she had learnt from experience to order from the restaurant.

They walked hand in hand towards the little thicket of thorn bushes in front of the low rocky promontory. The lazy splash of the waves on the beach and the high-pitched shrieks of the seabirds provided a simple and decorative backdrop of sound. The further they went from the hotel beaches the more Mariama relaxed.

'My aunt invites you home tomorrow,' she said eagerly.

'But the school, Mariama, I must talk to someone at your school before I leave.'

'Not the school, my aunt … my aunt,' repeated Mariama, annoyed.

'That is very kind of her, you must give her my regards and say thank you.'

'My aunt can explain about school.'

'But when can I visit the school?'

'The next day,' she said evasively.

'Sure, Mariama?'

'Sure,' she said and gave Ana's hand an imperceptible squeeze.

'You must understand that I would like to help you, but it has to be set up properly,' Ana continued in a tone of authority.

She had lain sleepless all night and finally decided to pay a year's school fees for Mariama, if she managed to draw up an agreement with her school. She hoped fervently that Mariama was telling the truth about her schooling. That she wasn't leading her up the garden path and making her into a naïve and foolish tourist.

'You sponsor me, bosslady?' she said radiantly.

'Yes, I would like to be your sponsor, so long as you go to school.'

'Just ask my aunt about school. She will look after the school fees,' Mariama assured her. She had not understood, or did not want to understand, Ana's conditions for a sponsorship. She would have to bank on the aunt's willingness to cooperate.

'What is your aunt's name?'

'Rosie.'

'Lovely name, how old is she?'

'Old.'

'But how old?'

'I don't know … old,' she said irritably.

They sat on Ana's towel at the sea's edge with their backs to the thorny thicket. Mariama unpacked the picnic basket and divided the provisions between the two plates placed on the little square cloth. Two cucumber sandwiches, two salmon sandwiches, two cheese sandwiches, a long-stemmed glass and half a bottle of dry white wine for Ana and a coke for herself. She left the fruit cake and the packets of sweets in the basket. They toasted each other and tucked in to the late lunch. Mariama looked around searchingly, as if she was expecting someone or afraid of someone.

'Are you looking for your cousin?' asked Ana, and bit into a delicious salmon sandwich.

'We meet here after work.'

'Why do you live with your aunt?'

'She needs help in the house and I can go to school. In the village there is only primary school.' Suddenly Mariama sounded grownup and sensible.

'And you have enough time to do your homework?'

'Sure, bosslady, very early in the morning.'

'Don't you miss your parents?' Ana enquired further. Mariama jumped up and hurled her sandwich violently far out into the sea.

'I won't answer all your stupid questions.' She stood just in front of Ana with both hands on her hips and shouted like a raging fury.

'You tourists ask all the time about everything.'

'Sorry, Mariama, forgive me.'

'You bring only questions, questions, questions,' she repeated, on the verge of hysteria.

'But what do you want? Just tell me,' Ana said in alarm.

'You have no right to know anything about me.'

'Come here and sit down, Mariama. I would just like to be your sponsor, that's all.'

'I keep you company and you pay for it, but you get nothing else from me,' she yelled, beside herself.

'No more questions and no more answers,' she finished.

'Calm down, Mariama, let's think practically. How do I find your aunt tomorrow? Time and place? I'll take a taxi from the hotel.'

'I'll meet you at the bus station just by Serrekunda Market.' Mariama had calmed down again.

'Where does your aunt live?'

'My auntie is first wife. She has her own house. You will feel at home,' explained Mariama.

'When shall we meet?'

'About 5 o'clock. We will drive to my aunt's in the taxi, I shall tell the driver the way,' she continued.

'Can't you just give me Rosie's address?' Ana said. Mariama looked at her as if she was a hopeless case.

'Let us go back. I am busy,' she said in a business-like tone. She packed the things together quickly and efficiently and placed the plates and cutlery back in the basket.

'But shouldn't we wait for your cousin?' Ana objected and remained seated. She had no desire to leave that sublime stillness and the view out over the boundless Atlantic.

'Madeleine is not coming today,' said Mariama shortly and hitched up the basket.

'Madeleine?'

'Yes, Madeleine, it is a Parisian name. Our grandma is a Christian,' she explained impatiently, and set off quickly without taking the time to wait for Ana. There was no holding hands this time. It was as if she had grown several years older and left childhood behind in the course of an hour or so.

'Madeleine is your cousin, Aunt Rosie's daughter, is that right?' asked Ana, feeling as if she was illiterate.

'Sure.' Mariama looked at her condescendingly.

'Madeleine has problems,' she continued.

'What sort of problems?'

'My uncle. She is a pretty girl, he wants her to work for him.'

'Business on the beach?'

'Job in town, pretty girls have many more problems than ugly ones,' she said, sounding grown-up and worldly-wise.

'I have to go and look for her, she needs help,' continued Mariama, walking faster. Ana began to regret that she had let herself be sucked into this downward spiral, which seemed to twist further and further down into a bottomless darkness.

She had to run to keep up with Mariama, who seemed to be flying over the firm sand along the water's edge. She didn't even glance towards her.

'What has happened to Madeleine?' asked Ana breathlessly.

'Don't ask about it,' Mariama admonished her sternly, 'I'll find her.'

'I can help you.'

'No help, my uncle will kill you.' Mariama's frail, bell-like voice had taken on a decisive authority.

'What about your aunt?'

'You must say nothing to my aunt. Just give her the school money for the next six months,' said Mariama and strode along the sand with determined steps.

They said a hasty farewell by the hotel's advance army of deserted deckchairs. Ana thrust into Mariama's hand more notes of a larger denomination than the day before. She accepted the notes with a professional expression and impressed on Ana that she must be at the bus station the next day at precisely 5 o'clock; then she ran as fast as she could in the direction of the local beach.

Ana sat in the hotel bar, looking absent-mindedly at the wine list. She had changed into a rather gaudy evening outfit, purchased in an exclusive second-hand shop in London. A bottle-green taffeta skirt with black sequinned tulle over it, and a close-fitting black silk cardigan with short sleeves. Ben and Beatrice did not keep her waiting for long. They greeted one another effusively, moved to one of the round tables and collapsed into the deep red armchairs. They were the only guests. Ben asked the bartender to turn down the ear-splitting Afro music and held out a portfolio with a logo designed like an arabesque made of two B's back to back.

'Our consultancy firm.' Ben passed the file over to Ana. It made her feel good having got to know them. She was keen to maintain contact with them, and develop it over time into a friendship.

'A small firm with large ambitions,' Ben went on. Beatrice sent him an affectionate glance. They were both wearing khaki-coloured linen outfits. Ana leafed through the file.

'We are in need of a professional adviser,' said Beatrice neutrally.

'Would that be something for you?' Ben raised his glass.

'I'm not an idealist,' said Ana quietly.

'So call it a hobby,' he shot back. 'We're not idealists either, we are realists. And we would like to continue our collaboration with "big business" in the field of development aid if we can convince them that our projects are sensible and will make a profit in the long run.'

'But why me?' asked Ana.

'Something tells me that you are the right person, that we are members of the same family, so to speak, am I right, dear?' Beatrice looked almost maternally at Ana. She estimated that Beatrice was at most ten years older, but feeling or behaving maternally was not age-related, children could also be maternal.

'It is a rare feeling.' Ana spoke almost to herself.

'Like a tender plant, which needs care and attention,' Beatrice supplemented.

'Far too much feminine earnestness,' Ben muttered.

'We're not married, we're work comrades.' Beatrice looked at him adoringly.

'That's also a kind of marriage,' Ben maintained. 'Our lives are dedicated to our work.'

'How do you see the collaboration between your consultancy firm and the big aid organizations developing over the next five years?' Ana's professional persona had already begun to function.

'So you are considering helping us out as a friend?' Ben's face lit up.

'Is there anything else I should know, here and now?' she said briskly.

'The papers with all the relevant information are in the file.'

'We look forward to you visiting us in London.' Beatrice mopped the sweat from her brow. She was once more unnaturally pale. Ben sent her an anxious sideways glance.

'Beatrice is not as robust as she looks,' he said.

'I think you two would enjoy talking to each other without me here.' Ben stood up.

'No, stay here, I don't want to be left alone,' said Beatrice. Ana felt a jolt. Did Beatrice feel alone in her company? Was she no-one? Ana leafed distractedly through the papers. She felt empty and light-headed.

'You must take your time before you decide,' said Ben to Ana. Beatrice had got up and was standing beside him. How well they looked together, what an attractive couple they made, married or not, thought Ana, and said that she would read through the documents and let them know when she had decided.

'You are a true friend,' they said in chorus.

'Next year, London,' said Beatrice formally, as if it were a password.

'Next year, London,' Ana repeated involuntarily. She felt intensely sad when they were gone. A disappointment which she could not control swept over her. She stayed in her seat and ordered another drink while she recovered. She noticed that Ben and Beatrice's glasses had been left untouched on the table. It was yet another defeat, which underlined her feeling of being abandoned by God and man.

It came as a shock to her that she had formed such high expectations of them. What kind of expectations was not really clear to her. Ben and Beatrice had not made her any promises of friendship, but they had shown their trust in her with their flattering offer of becoming their financial adviser, a task which was well within her competence and which she would consider taking on. Next year, London, she murmured to herself, and ordered another Bloody Mary to celebrate her new utopia.

Next morning she hung the 'Do not disturb' sign on the door handle and stayed in her room until she was due to take the taxi to Serrekunda. She needed peace and quiet in order to prepare herself mentally for the meeting with Mariama's aunt. Rosie was an attractive name, which smelt of roses and poetry. The morning passed at a snail's pace. She emptied the minibar of snacks and water and ordered a fresh consignment. She lay on the bed and leafed through the boring novel she had brought with her as her only reading apart from *Wallpaper* and *Vogue*, which she had long since digested. Ana hoped that Aunt Rosie would be able to let her into the truth about Mariama's schooling. She spent the afternoon finding the appropriate outfit. She did not want to flaunt her wealth, but on the other hand she did not want to give such a modest impression that it weakened her authority.

Ana left the room and walked down the path which led directly to the entrance to the main hotel building. She had asked the receptionist in advance to order a taxi for four o'clock. It was not far to Serrekunda, but sooner get there too early than too late. If she paid the driver well he would wait until Mariama arrived and then drive them on to Aunt Rosie's. The taxi was waiting for her punctually by the entrance. Ana climbed into the back seat and announced where she wanted to go. Before the driver put the car into gear he demanded in insolent English to know her name, so that he was sure she was the person the hotel had ordered him to drive to Serrekunda.

'Mariana Jaeger,' she said in an equally bitchy voice. The car set off with a violent lurch which threw her forwards. The sweat was already breaking out on her temples. She was shaking with nerves at undertaking an expedition off her own bat without a safety net. Her nervousness made her talkative in a way which was not normally in her nature. She did not care to engage service staff in conversation; she was afraid of seeming patronizing and false. Sooner reward good service with cold cash.

Ana sat tensely right on the edge of her seat behind the driver. She could not restrain herself. Questions tumbled out of her mouth. Was there democracy in the country, or a kind of democratic dictatorship? Were the media free and independent? And how did things stand on corruption?

'Our president is working very hard,' the driver broke in, giving her to understand that it was not a topic which was open for discussion. She passed on quickly to the local chicken producers. Were they not threatened by the import of cheap frozen chickens from the EU? Ana sent Ben and Beatrice a grateful thought. Without waiting for an answer she carried on to the education system, which with Mariama had become a matter of personal concern. Was schooling compulsory? Was there a possibility of higher education? Did boys have priority? How great a percentage of the population was illiterate? The questions hung in the air. The driver either shook his head or mumbled something or other which was drowned in the noise from a scratchy cassette player. Ana noticed that they were passing one construction site after another with half-finished concrete frames. That must provide work places to keep the young men at home who would otherwise be flocking to Europe, she enquired.

'Foreign workers,' said the driver tersely and concentrated on driving.

The construction sites on both sides of the road gave way

to barren, reddish-brown patches of earth with scorched tufts of some kind of tall grass and bare trees which stretched out towards the sky. The fields lay fallow. 'What a waste,' she remarked to thin air with not the slightest understanding of the climate or the soil conditions. She had stopped trying to interrogate the driver and just went on chattering, drew her own conclusions and grumbled about all the misery they had created for themselves.

At regular intervals they passed checkpoints manned by one or more guards in military uniform. They stood at the side of the road or sat in small temporary wooden sheds and waved the taxi through, seemingly without taking any particular notice of them. Ana was surprised that this peaceful holiday destination required such security measures, and she asked the driver whether he was ever stopped. He put a stop to her queries with his standard answer: 'No problem, no problem.'

Her thoughts and incessant talking mingled together to form a barrier against the panic which now also embraced the silent driver. She saw him in her mind's eye unexpectedly turning off and driving her along a narrow potholed side road to a sinister cabin, to deliver her to a band of kidnappers who would demand an enormous ransom from her employers, Rower International. And further off on the horizon lurked the fear of what was waiting for her at the bus station, and not least at Aunt Rosie's, when she tried to negotiate a reasonable agreement with her.

They were approaching a built-up area. Grey blocks of houses fenced around with rusty corrugated tin. Heaps of refuse in the grass alongside the road. A mosque with square white towers which ended in little green balls with golden spires. Sellers with an assortment of wares spread out beneath a faded canopy. Car tyres half buried in the loose sand by the roadside. An abandoned trailer eaten up by rust resembled an installation she had recently seen in an art exhibition in Zurich. Peeling concrete facades with brightly-coloured adverts painted directly onto the bare walls. Discarded old televisions and computers stacked up in long narrow storerooms. Some men were sitting eating in the shade beneath a truck. A little girl, almost small enough to be able to stand upright under the truck, was walking around between the men collecting pieces of plastic. Women walked onwards with a calm measured stride, with enormous plastic bowls on their heads and babies tied securely on their backs. At least she was having new experiences, Ana attempted to reassure herself, even though she did not wish to experience anything at all on this doubtful excursion, which should just be over and done with as quickly as possible.

The traffic had imperceptibly slowed, and a flock of children surrounded the taxi. Small greasy hands were thrust in through the open side window. 'Tubaab, tubaab,' piped the shrill children's voices. When the taxi finally began to move again, one front wheel landed in a hole the size of a bomb crater. The driver leapt out and got some help to push the taxi out. In a moment they were ready to set off again. The driver shook hands with his helpers and was given an encouraging slap on the shoulder in return. Ana asked whether he knew people in the district, since he had been able to find help so easily.

'My family lives here, welcome to my home,' he said proudly. Ana leaned back in her seat and took a deep breath. Against all expectations she had met a friendly person. She had underestimated him, but fortunately she could make it up to him with a generous tip.

'Is it far to the bus station?' she asked placatingly.

'I don't know, it depends,' he answered, rubbing his broad back comfortably against the back of the seat.

They drove slowly in towards an area reminiscent of a town centre. More and more cars appeared. Old, unroadworthy lorries, European and American. Streams of yellow taxis. Shops with material, mobile phones, sweets, soap, sewing machines, tools, spices clustered along both sides of the dusty streets. Sellers with bundles of goods on their backs stood in the road in the red dust between the cars. The way into the market with its welcoming green entrance was swarming with people and packed with stalls screened by brightly-coloured parasols. Ana shuddered at the thought of walking alone into that throng of people and being swallowed up in the enormous labyrinthine organism.

The driver stopped the taxi and turned towards her.

'The bus station,' he informed her. The sight which met her eyes was blanketed in the stench of petrol and exhaust fumes, which quickly penetrated the taxi so that she could not breathe. There were rows of buses of all sizes and makes. Some half empty, some crammed with passengers whose luggage was roped to the roof. Waiting men and women surrounded by bags, plastic carriers and cardboard boxes in the exhaust fumes behind the buses. Rubbish and empty plastic bottles lay spread out over the square. The driver asked for payment. Ana explained that they would be going further. She was waiting for a guest, a teenage girl who would explain where they were going. He looked suspicious and asked for an advance for the drive from the hotel. Ana gave him the amount and doubled it with a tip.

The driver calmly lit a cigarette and changed the cassette tape. It was unbearably hot in the sun, and his droning into the mobile phone suddenly got on her nerves. But she didn't dare get out of the taxi. Despite everything it was safer inside than out. She was also worried that Mariama wouldn't be able to find her in the jumble of buses and taxis. She was so busy looking out for Mariama in the seething chaos around them that she had not noticed that the driver had left the car until her glance fell on the empty front seat. Everything went black before her eyes. The next moment anger surged up in her. What impudence, leaving her in the lurch in the midst of this tumult and anarchy. She leaned back and shut her eyes. Shut out the world and refused to be present in this taxi in this bus station on this continent.

Ana was roused by a cautious tapping on the side mirror and started up with a shiver of cold despite the oppressive tropical heat. Mariama's face appeared in the window frame.

At that moment Ana knew that they belonged together. She opened the door and beckoned her into the back seat next to her. Mariama grasped her hand and clung to it as though she would never let her go again.

'My aunt is waiting for us,' she said.

'But where is the driver?' asked Ana. Mariama shrugged her shoulders.

'But we can't keep your aunt waiting,' Ana said in panic.

'No problem,' said Mariama calmly. Her calm transferred itself to Ana and spread through her whole body.

'How did you find me?' she asked.

'You are white … tubaab,' she giggled. Ana wondered what impression she made in her pleated skirt and simple pale blue blouse of Egyptian cotton.

Mariama was wearing a better dress, cleaner and not so worn. They were visiting fine company, thought Ana, forgetting for a moment that she lived with Aunt Rosie. Mariama's hair was gathered into tufts which stuck out in all directions. Not a hairstyle you would associate with a fifteen-year-old. The poor condition of her greyish hair was no doubt due to bad diet and a lack of vitamins. She would have to have a word with Rosie about that. Mariama seemed more cheerful and self-confident than on the beach.

'Have you been to school today?' asked Ana. She nodded vaguely.

'Are you sure?' she insisted.

'How sure must I be?' she answered crossly.

'Sorry,' Ana excused herself in the knowledge of her dependent position. If Mariama got out of the taxi and disappeared into the crowd she was lost.

'What sort of job does your aunt have at the bank?' Ana went on.

'Why do you ask all these questions? You never tell anything about yourself. I don't know who you are.' Mariama pulled away from her and looked out of the side window.

'Perhaps you have a pistol in your bag,' she muttered, 'perhaps you are a dangerous person.'

'Mariama, what are you thinking of?' Ana exclaimed. Mariama turned round and looked directly at her.

'How can I be sure, bosslady?' Her voice had again taken on that soft, fragile tone which aroused so many feelings in Ana. She opened her bag and let Mariama look down into it.

'See for yourself, but don't touch anything,' she added nervously. Mariama threw a quick look into the bag and turned towards the window again.

At that moment the driver opened the door and slipped in behind the wheel. Mariama leant forward and explained to him at length and in detail where they were going. Ana had to take a grip on herself not to ask how far it was to Aunt Rosie's and how long the trip would take. Mariama's criticism of her desire to ask questions acted as a muzzle. Mariama chatted happily to the driver as if he was an old acquaintance. Ana did not understand their tribal language and suddenly felt uneasy at the situation. Was it a put-up job? Where were they taking her?

'Don't worry. We'll be there soon, my aunt's house is on the outskirts of the town,' said Mariama with a touching understanding of her vulnerable position, and went back to her conversation with the driver. They both talked fast and loudly and peppered their conversation with bursts of laughter. Ana concentrated on the surroundings outside the safe, protected refuge of the taxi.

After some time they had left the thick town traffic behind. Ana had a feeling that they were driving back the same way past the same screened compounds, where pale green treetops towered up over concrete or corrugated tin fencing. But she was not sure; all the residential quarters looked alike.

The drive was much further than she had imagined. Mariama's 'soon' was wide of the mark. The buildings thinned out. Suddenly the driver braked sharply, and she shot forward towards the front seat. To her horror she discovered that they had been stopped at a checkpoint. A man in military uniform put his head in through the side window and asked for the driver's papers. It took him far too long to find them, and he passed them through the window with trembling hands. The young man leafed through them and went into the hut to his colleague. Ana immediately felt guilty and went through all the possible crimes she might have committed during her stay in the country. Inside the taxi, time stood still. Mariama kept her mouth tight shut and refused all contact. The driver sweated and wiped his neck and forehead with a multicoloured cloth. An eternity passed before another, somewhat older military man came back with the papers. He looked questioningly at Ana. The driver muttered something which sounded like 'tourist' and 'Golden Bay'.

They were given permission to drive on. The driver was adamant that it was the first time he had been stopped. Ana wanted most of all to forget the unpleasant episode and had no questions. Mariama resumed her interrupted conversation with the driver as if nothing had happened. They had emerged into a scorched yellow bush landscape with low round-topped trees under which a few skinny goats had found shelter. Further off you could make out scattered earth-coloured houses and modest tin shacks.

The taxi stopped in front of a low house which consisted of four clay walls and a flat corrugated tin roof. Ana felt strangely relaxed, as if nothing bad could happen to her after the episode at the checkpoint. All three got out and walked along a narrow gravel path on to the plot, which was surrounded by a wicker fence. The lady of the house appeared in the doorway. She was solidly built and was wearing a white T-shirt and a long boldly-patterned wraparound skirt. She looked disapprovingly at Mariama, as if the visit was inconvenient. Ana had imagined that she would be visiting a compound in Serrekunda and not a mud hut out in the bush, but she didn't want to plague Mariama with further inquisitorial questions. She seemed cowed and somehow stiffer in her aunt's presence. Rosie said something to the driver and then nodded majestically to Ana, as if she had only now noticed she was there.

The driver sat down on a plastic chair outside the entrance.

Mariama and Ana followed on Rosie's heels into the house and came directly into a living room with walls painted green. There was a dining table with two heavy chairs and a sofa. High up near the ceiling was a shelf with various knick-knacks and unframed photos of children large and small. Two curtained-off door openings led to two further rooms. One was Rosie's bedroom. The other was the children's. A mattress almost filled the room. Rosie's children all slept on the mattress, Mariama explained. Where did she herself sleep, Ana wanted to know. Mariama pointed to the narrow strip of earth between the mattress and the wall and passed on quickly, leading Ana out into the back yard where a hole in the ground behind a woven straw screen served as a toilet, and a hearth with a blackened cooking-pot made a sort of outdoor kitchen. Ana refrained from taking photos. She had in general been much less active with her camera than normal when she was in the south. She simply didn't feel like it. A small group of children crowded around Ana and stared at her in an unsettlingly expectant way. She had nothing to give them and felt awkward. Mariama chased them away with a peremptory wave of her hand. It was clear that they respected her.

Mariama explained animatedly that they had moved from Serrekunda because of the pollution, which would have been the death of them all. Especially the little ones, she sighed, picking up a snotty little girl. Rosie and the other townspeople had been given a piece of land by the president and were to build their own houses with the help of family and friends. But it was far from being finished. Mariama pointed up to the tin roof, which covered only part of the house. Ana was more interested in what the move meant for her schooling. There were bush taxis, Mariama explained patiently. She came back at 6 o'clock in the evening, when she had finished her work on the beach. So when did she have time for homework? Ana wanted to know. Early in the morning before the children woke up, answered Mariama.

'Where is Madeleine?' asked Ana.

'At school,' said Mariama crossly, and looked harassed. Ana

felt sorry for her, and did not press her further.

'How many children does Aunt Rosie have?' she asked on the way back to the living room. Mariama tried to count on her fingers, but had to give up. Rosie could not afford to keep all the children with her. Some of them were being fostered by family or friends. Just as Mariama was being fostered by Rosie, her mother's elder sister.

'Auntie Rosie has many children. I have many brothers and sisters.'

'Cousins,' Ana corrected her. 'Where is her husband?'

'He lives with his third wife. Rosie has never accepted her,' Mariama emphasized with a kind of shocked pride. Ana could not work out the relationship between them. She knew only what Mariama had explained. That Rosie needed her to do the housework, and that she in return had the chance to continue her schooling in Serrekunda.

Aunt Rosie was sitting on the sofa and had got changed. She was hung about with heavy jewellery and had her mobile phone in her lap. Her dress was of a shiny green material and sewn in a simple close-fitting style. On her head she had an elaborately constructed turban of the same material. Ana praised the newly-built house and nodded appreciatively at her. Rosie's whole demeanour was business-like. She addressed the subject directly.

'You want to be Mariama's sponsor, right?' she began formally.

'Yes, if you can assure me that she really does go to school,' Ana answered in the same tone. Aunt Rosie looked at her with raised eyebrows. And then over at Mariama.

'What's the problem?' she asked in a shrill voice. Mariama cowered and shook her head contritely, like someone who has not been able to deliver the goods.

'No problem, no problem,' she muttered, looking down at the floor.

'What is that "no problem"? A problem is a problem. Do you hear, do you hear me?' Rosie yelled into Mariama's ear.

'It's not my fault,' Mariama defended herself. Rosie turned

towards Ana.

'Why have you come here, if you don't want to help my little girl?' Rosie's voice had become falsetto. Ana took a deep breath before she answered. Rosie was a formidable negotiator.

'I would very much like to pay Mariama's school fees, but I must be sure where the money goes. I suggest that I pay them directly to the school administration.' Ana had no objection to a round of negotiations with Rosie. Her 'no-nonsense' attitude was a challenge which made Ana feel she was on the same wavelength.

'Make some tea,' she said brusquely to Mariama, who got up obediently. Ana was touched by her meekness.

The driver was still sitting outside, chain-smoking. The sun hung low over the horizon and cast long shadows between the small plots of earth with newly-built mud houses. Soon it would be dark, and she was far from the hotel. Rosie asked Ana to sit at the table. Suddenly the mood seemed tense.

'So you don't trust us,' she said with an undertone of scorn, 'how can that be?'

'You misunderstand me. It is entirely a practical problem. How I should transfer the school fees and to whom. I am prepared to pay for a year in advance.' Ana had already surrendered her doubts about Mariama's schooling. She was willing to send the money to the school administration in Mariama's name just in order to escape Rosie's accusations.

'I have a bank account,' Rosie said meaningfully and got up from the sofa to see what Mariama was doing with the tea. There were no doors to the house, only doorways. A couple of dusty white hens peered curiously into the room.

'I am sorry, but I prefer to pay directly to the school.' Ana accepted a glass of scalding hot tea. Rosie sat down heavily at the table across from her. The chair creaked ominously.

'You have a comfortable home.' Ana tried flattery again.

'I have worked hard for it,' Rosie conceded.

'Does Mariama live here with you?'

'Sure,' said Rosie offended, 'I need her for the housework.'

'Yes, she told me that, I forgot,' Ana excused herself.

'And you look after her?' she continued.

'I am the only one in the family who has a bank account, you understand.' Rosie sent Ana a tired, resigned glance.

'And Mariama's school is in Serrekunda?'

'Sure.' Rosie looked sternly at her.

'What is the name of the school?' Ana was stepping into a minefield. Rosie was getting out of breath. Her colossal bosom heaved up and down. She stared at Ana with wide-open eyes.

'You really do not trust us,' she said threateningly. Ana walked further into the minefield.

'I would like to visit Mariama's school before I leave.' She was tired of this charade. The only thing which interested her was to give Mariama a helping hand. The easiest thing would be to take her back to Denmark and take care of her and her education there, but that solution was beyond the bounds of possibility.

Rosie got up and stood in the middle of the floor with her hands on her hips. Ana was worried that her stilettoes would snap beneath her. Or that she would overbalance and land with all her weight on the uneven floor of trodden earth. But there was no hint of a wobble.

'Will you please leave my house, you have abused my hospitality.' Rosie gave a jerk of her head in the direction of the low doorway out to the small dry patch of earth in front of the house. Ana noticed that the sun was hanging dangerously on the edge of the horizon. In a moment it would be pitch black. Just then Mariama came in with a lamp and looked from one to the other. Ana had risen from the table and stood with her bag over her shoulder, ready to go. Her head was only a few centimetres from the ceiling. That was intimidating as well. In view of the fact that for the amount her Yves Saint Laurent outfit had cost she would have been able to buy the whole hut several times over.

'You must not go, bosslady, what about my school?' Mariama burst out with a scream, and almost dropped the lamp. As if following orders Ana sat down again. The girl had an inexplicable power over her, even though she could well be in cahoots with Aunt Rosie in order to fleece her. Only a few flickering lights in the nearby houses pierced the massive darkness outside. Rosie took the lamp and hung it on a hook in a chain hanging from the ceiling.

'Are you really so heartless? Are you really so indifferent to other people? Are you not aware that this little girl has no other alternative than to go to school or to marry some old man and become his third wife? And the only thing you can think of is where you should send the money and can I visit her school and blah blah blah. You don't believe we have schools in this country. But I am proud of my country. Our president is working very hard for his people.' Rosie had talked herself up to the heights of rhetoric like an opera singer in a brilliant stage set. Ana felt ridiculous, out of place, empty-headed and unbecomingly tall at 5' 10".

'Who do you think you are? Coming here for a bit of fancy sightseeing in the bu-ush,' sneered Rosie, 'drinking my tea and disappearing again back to your comfortable life. Why do you not take photos? Are there no subjects here? Is my house not pi-icturesque enough for you? Is my house not miserable enough for you?' Rosie crossed her arms. Her whole appearance demanded a concession. But Ana had nothing to say in her defence. Rosie's eloquence and fighting spirit had left her dumb with admiration. She would be happy to pay to be allowed to keep Mariama. The question was simply how much she would have to give.

'How much? Just tell me how much you want,' said Ana, playing for high stakes. She was a gambler and felt at home in the cold neurotic darkness of the casino, which was the same everywhere in the world, frequented by the same spectral characters, with their Armani suits and their flashy imitation Rolex watches.

'No ma'am, that is not how things are done here. We are honest people, and we have our dignity.' Rosie shook her head and looked sad. Mariama sat as still as a mouse on the edge of the sofa.

'You do not trust us, but I trust you. You shall have my bank account, the name of the bank, everything you need.' Rosie took a creased piece of paper out of the folds of her dress and passed it to Ana. There stood right enough a bank account number and the name of a bank, written in large letters in pencil.

'How much does the school cost for a whole year?' mumbled Ana, outmanoeuvred.

'Whatever suits you, ma'am, we have several sponsors, you are not the only one.' Rosie looked tired and dissatisfied. It suddenly occurred to Ana that she had not brought a present with her for Rosie. Why had she not thought of that? Back home she never forgot to take a gift for her hostess.

Ana searched in her handbag and found her pillbox with two small diamonds set in the lid. She tipped the pills out into the bottom of her bag and gave the box to Mariama, who quickly slid it inside her blouse.

'Thank you for the tea,' said Ana, turning to Rosie.

'Why did you give Mariama that box?' said Rosie sharply, ignoring Ana's outstretched hand.

'It's just a little souvenir, to remember me by.'

'Why should she remember you?' said Rosie heatedly.

'You can call it a pledge of our friendship.' Ana felt that she was on the point of collapse.

'So you are friends, are you?' Rosie shouted to Mariama. 'Answer me, Mariama.'

'Stop telling her off all the time,' said Ana, looking across at Mariama, who was sitting oddly motionless on the sofa.

'You should be ashamed of yourself.' Rosie came right up close to Ana so that she could feel the warmth of her body. Ana lost control of herself.

'You've no right to tell me to be ashamed of myself. I've not done anything wrong.' She could not hold back the tears. The unsuccessful visit and her own inadequacy had finished her. She felt a tentative hand on her arm.

'It will all be all right, bosslady.' Mariama's voice sounded like music from a higher sphere.

'I will come with you in the taxi,' she continued.

'But it's late.' Ana pointed out into the darkness.

'I am going to my uncle in Serrekunda. He lives near the school, so I shall not have so far to go tomorrow morning,' she insisted. Ana looked at Aunt Rosie to find some explanation of this unexpected announcement, but her face did not betray what was going on behind the mask. Ana could not imagine that Mariama would be going with her to Serrekunda against Rosie's will, and made no more objections. She had already experienced far too much in the few hours she had spent outside the peace and order of the hotel, and needed to rest and recover in its cool, air-conditioned predictability.

Outside by the taxi Rosie gave Mariama a long whispered scolding. She received it with her head bent and a dispirited humility which cut Ana to the heart. Rosie turned on her heels without deigning to glance at her. Finally they could get into the back seat. The taxi moved through the darkness, illuminated only by the front headlights. Ana's visit had clearly had the one objective of furnishing her with the number of Rosie's bank account. Her wish to visit Mariama's school and verify her status as a pupil had not even been a matter for discussion. Was the foreign world in which Ana found herself really so simple? Mariama placed the pillbox discreetly back in her hand.

'Just money, nothing else but money, please,' she said nervously, 'I am not a thief.'

'I am sorry,' said Ana, 'I don't want to give you more problems than you already have.'

'You are a good person,' whispered Mariama. It was like receiving a knighthood. Ana straightened up and said that she was happy to have met her, and that she hoped they could keep in touch with each other in the future.

'Perhaps I can visit you in your country as you visit mine?' She looked hopefully at Ana.

'We have laws which make it almost impossible to have visitors from Africa.'

'That is a pity for you. Visitors are the salt of the day, poor you,' said Mariama. Ana had to admire her ability to turn matters on their head.

'Perhaps I could become an au-pair in your country?' she suggested.

'Do you really want to come to Europe?'

'Very much. I have had good training in housework from my aunt, and I am good at looking after children. But she gives me no money for school lunch, so I am always hungry.'

'But you must finish your schooling before you can travel to Europe, mustn't you?' said Ana, ignoring her last remark.

'I forgot that,' said Mariama in alarm. Ana unfolded the paper with Rosie's bank account number on it and looked at it.

'Do you think I can use this? Will it work?'

'No problem.'

'How many people have been given this account number?'

'Many, many, but we never hear from them once they have left,' she said with naïve candour.

'So who pays for your school?'

'You pay, you pay,' she said eagerly.

'Mariama, honestly. We won't talk about your school any more. I don't believe you go to school.' Mariama opened her mouth to contradict her. Ana stopped her with a deprecating gesture.

'If you just tell me how old you are, perhaps I can get you an au-pair job somewhere in the EU.'

'Fifteen, nearly sixteen,' she assured her.

'Give me your address, and you can have my card.' Ana fished a business card out of its silver box and handed it over. Mariama turned the card around and studied it thoroughly on both sides.

'I have a post-box address, but I would rather have a mobile phone,' she said in a restrained fashion, like someone who has just won a victory. Ana rummaged through her handbag and found a crumpled serviette. Mariama wrote quickly and untidily. Ana had to go over the letters before she could read her scrawl.

'When you are seventeen you can become an au-pair in

Denmark.'

'Perhaps I am seventeen,' Mariama insisted. Tears ran down her cheeks.

'No, you mustn't cry, please.' Suddenly Ana was afraid that she would not be able to shake her off.

'It's just because I am so sad that you are going away soon,' she said ingenuously. It made Ana wonder again whether she was backward. Or whether the simple-mindedness was part of the pretence.

They were approaching Serrekunda. An aura of civilization at last. Ana asked Mariama where she should drop her. She shook her head.

'Where it suits you.'

'What do you mean?'

'It depends on where I'm going to be.'

'Who decides that?'

'My uncle, Big Man,' she whispered. Ana looked at her faded dress, which made her look like an overgrown child, and feared the worst.

'So what was the address you gave me?' said Ana confused, waving the piece of paper.

'It's my uncle's post box. Can't you see c/o Louis Sarr, that means "care of",' she said irritably. Ana noticed that she had a cast in her right eye, which looked out sideways through the side window, whilst the left eye looked straight at her. Ana put her arm around her shoulder.

'Can't I drop you at your uncle's compound?' she suggested, giving her a hug. She felt so slight and fragile.

'No, I have some things I need to do before I go over to my uncle's.'

'But it's dark and dangerous out there.'

'For you perhaps, but not for me. I live here, you know,' said Mariama.

They passed the deserted bus station, where some empty buses were parked for the night. The driver asked whether they wanted to get out here or drive back to the hotel.

'I don't want to go to the hotel.' Mariama pulled away from

Ana.

'I'm not allowed to take you into the hotel anyway,' Ana said soothingly.

'Just drop me here,' she insisted. Ana asked the driver to stop.

'I'm leaving in three days' time. Shall we meet on the beach again?'

'Your card gives me hope.' Mariama held Ana's business card up in front of her face. Ana found a bundle of dalasi notes in her handbag and gave them to Mariama.

'I miss you,' said Mariama in a brusque impersonal voice.

'Just promise me that you will go straight to your uncle's.'

'I told you, I have business to do.'

'But you can do business with me.' Ana was horror-struck at the thought of Mariama's 'business' at this time of night.

'I have my duties,' she said in a grown-up, worldly-wise tone.

'Duties to whom?' Ana pulled her back hard onto the seat.

'Let go of me,' she said angrily, tearing herself away. 'You have no right to … this.'

Mariama got out and slammed the door hard behind her. Ana saw her running in between the parked buses. The driver turned towards Ana.

'Golden Bay Hotel?' he said. Ana nodded and felt like a wrung-out dishcloth.

For the whole of the next day she lay on her sunbed on the windswept beach and watched for Mariama. She didn't even go in to eat lunch. Every single sunbather who passed by was a defeat. Every single souvenir and juice vendor a disappointment. There was non-stop activity right up until nightfall, when the hotel orchestra's drums summoned the guests to a pool party, but not a glimpse of Mariama. Even though she had her reservations Ana had reckoned that she would appear, if for no other reason than that she knew that she would give her some big dalasi notes. Was her money not good enough? she thought crossly, feeling rejected. She now wanted to trample on the very feelings that Mariama had awoken in her. It took her by surprise that her strong feelings for the girl should be accompanied by such explosive anger. Mariama had got her hooked, and the thought of leaving the country without saying a proper goodbye to her was unbearable.

That evening Ana sat at a table for two in the farthest corner of the restaurant and ate her way through a three-course menu without much appetite. She missed the company of Ben and Beatrice and was filled with a melancholy longing for all the people who like Mariama had disappeared from her life. Some were dead or had travelled far away, relationships and friendships had come to nothing. Close colleagues had been transferred to branches on the other side of the world. Ana quickly emptied a bottle of chablis and was well on her way towards the bottom of a burgundy. Her mobile phone, which on the orders of the firm's coach had been hidden away in the safe in her room, lay on the white cloth in front of her. She was annoyed that she had not asked Mariama for Rosie's mobile number, but at least it spared her from exposing herself to new misunderstandings. She made do with sending a text message to Ben and Beatrice, as a confirmation of the friendship which had moved her so deeply.

After breakfast the next morning Ana ordered a taxi in reception. She had decided to use the last day of her holiday to find Mariama. She could not leave for home without knowing what had happened to her after they had parted at the bus station. Her only chance was to enquire at the post office in Serrekunda and try to find the uncle with the help of Mariama's c/o post-box number.

To her surprise it was the same driver who had driven her to Aunt Rosie's. He must be a brother, cousin, relative or boyfriend of the lively young receptionist, she thought; she asked his name, now that he was an old acquaintance.

'Modou,' the driver informed her, and invited her to sit in the front seat. Ana thanked him for the offer but excused herself that she preferred to sit in the back, without mentioning that she could not cope with being close to strange people and their smell. They drove towards Serrekunda. She had become familiar with the road, the many kebab restaurants and shops and at the end by the main road the well-stocked chemist's, which gave her a good feeling of security. Ana started by hiring Modou for the rest of the day. Together they would find Mariama, the teenage girl from a couple of days ago, she informed him. Modou adopted a neutral attitude to the day's programme, and drove her to the post office without comment. Ana asked him to go in with her to interpret, in case her English should be met by a wall of incomprehension.

Inside the pompous colonial building, which looked more like a fort than a post office, it was stiflingly hot. Three sluggish fans on the ceiling were the only attempt at air-conditioning. There was a long queue at the poste restante window. Ana joined the end of it, together with Modou. She could see that her rash plan would be a waste of precious time. She had no justification for asking to be informed of the identity which was concealed behind Louis Sarr's post-box address. The queue hardly moved. Ana stayed put only because she did not know what else to do. She began to wonder whether it would not be more practical to return to the hotel and wait on the beach like the previous day, hoping that Mariama would appear with her tray of fruit on her head. Ana could not bear to leave without having seen her. Once she was back home and part of the rat race again, Mariama would quickly be crowded out. She could not imagine that a post-box address in an African country was any great shakes, and besides, she did not have the nerves to wait for weeks while her letters arrived, and even longer while the replies came back, if they ever materialized at all.

'It's hopeless.' Ana turned to Modou.

'We are moving,' he said and shrugged his shoulders. He looked tired, like someone who has been partying all night.

'It didn't seem as if her aunt liked me,' said Ana, lost in her own thoughts.

'Why should she not like you?' Modou was at work, and had no personal stake in the matter. Nevertheless, his reaction impressed her.

'Perhaps you're right,' she said thoughtfully. Another window was opened, and suddenly things were moving quickly.

In front of Ana stood a tall, imposing man in a white tunic and an embroidered skull-cap, with a black bag on a strap over his shoulder. He leant forward towards the window.

'Louis Sarr, Box 999,' he said. The woman behind the window got up. Ana could not believe her luck. Was that really him standing in front of her? She touched his arm. He turned round and looked at her in surprise.

'Excuse me, Louis Sarr?' She held her breath.

'What do you want?' he asked reservedly.

'I'm looking for Mariama.' Ana could not control her emotion.

'Mariama, you're looking for Mariama?'

'She gave me this address, c/o Louis Sarr.' Ana showed him the crumpled serviette with her clumsy writing.

'We just share the post-box.'

'So you are Louis Sarr, nice to meet you.' Ana held out her hand.

'I would like to say goodbye to Mariama. I'm leaving tomorrow,' she went on awkwardly, and felt the sweat running down her back under her light linen shirt. The man frowned and looked away. Ana regretted that she had embarked on this idiotic excursion and pushed her way in where she was not wanted.

'Is she at school now?' she continued after a long and awkward pause. Suddenly the man's expression changed, as if something had become clear to him. Instead of answering he suggested that they should drive to his compound. Ana looked at Modou in confusion; he introduced himself and shook hands with the man. They embarked on a lengthy discussion. Ana felt sidelined and started to feel impatient. The aim of the day's expedition, to find Mariama, seemed to get lost in their long palaver about how to reach the compound.

After a long drive along barely passable roads through uniform residential districts which reached as far as the eye could see, the taxi stopped in front of the entrance to a compound behind a high concrete wall. Louis Sarr got out and gallantly opened the door for Ana. He seemed much younger than her first impression of him. It was understood that Modou would stay in the car and wait for them. Ana followed Louis Sarr into the shady courtyard, where a few small children were running around noisily, wearing practically nothing. In a corner were some battered tables and chairs and a bundle of clothes, as if someone was in the process of moving in or out. An elderly man was sitting on a low stool brewing tea. He poured the tea in a long stream from a copper teapot with a beak-shaped spout down into glasses with gold rims.

'Where is Mariama? At school?' Ana could not restrain herself any longer.

'How did she get hold of your business card?' asked Louis Sarr calmly, and walked straight over towards the old man.

'We met on the beach. I would like to help her.'

'What do you want to help her with?'

'With continuing her education.'

'She is a young woman now,' he interrupted impatiently.

'But it is her dearest wish. I would never have interfered if she had not asked me.'

'That is not something she decides for herself,' Louis Sarr declared.

'Auntie Rosie agrees with her,' Ana objected.

'I don't discuss family matters with strangers.'

'But education is important,' muttered Ana.

'Mariama works hard and gets good training in running a house. She will be a splendid wife.' Louis Sarr smiled thoughtfully. Ana's heart began to hammer. Was Louis Sarr the man who had picked out Mariama as his third wife? Was Aunt Rosie's threat about marriage not, as she had supposed, general and abstract, but highly concrete and imminent? She wished that she could apologize to her for the day before yesterday, and feared that the school project was a washout because of her own clumsy behaviour. She took a deep breath and said:

'Could you do me a favour, Uncle Louis? I would like to visit Mariama's school.'

'Are you asking me that?' Louis Sarr broke into loud laughter. Ana couldn't help smiling at herself.

'I don't know anything about Mariama's school,' he said gruffly.

'So she doesn't go to school at all?' said Ana despondently.

'That is nothing to do with me.' Louis shrugged.

'But you pay for her school?'

'No I don't.'

'She told me that her uncle pays her school fees.'

'A young person has many uncles.'

'Can you tell me where I can find this other uncle?'

'You are not someone who gives up easily.' Louis looked up into the enormous crown of the tree above them and offered Ana a seat on a stool beside the old man, who passed her a glass of tea with a serious expression. The strong warm drink revived her.

'I would just like to know whether Mariama goes to school or not,' she continued obstinately.

'She does go to school, but not right at this moment,' said Louis reluctantly.

'I would really like to pay for her schooling and for every-thing which is needed in addition, school lunch, uniform, books.' Ana clung desperately to her economic power.

'You shall not interfere in my family.'

'I am only worried about Mariama,' Ana insisted.

'Mariama belongs to the family ...'

'May I ask you something?' Ana broke off.

'Sure, no problem,' said Louis, appraising her with his eyes.

'Is the idea that Mariama should marry you?'

'Me?' Louis Sarr broke out into another gale of laughter.

'I'm not going to marry Mariama, I'm going to marry you,' he said, and was suddenly deadly serious.

'I like you. You are not afraid of me,' he continued.

'I'm afraid of everything,' said Ana, shaken.

'You don't fear death, but you fear life,' he carried on prophetically, observing her intently. The old man was concentrating on his prayer beads and seemed to be lost to the world. Ana drained her glass of tea and said thank you. She wanted to move on, the question was simply where to. The children had moved cautiously closer to her.

'Tubaab, sweets, sweets,' they whispered, looking sideways at Louis Sarr, who raised his index finger. The children disappeared at once, just as noiselessly as they had appeared.

Ana looked after them and felt bad that she didn't have any sweets for them. At the far end of the yard a woman was sitting on some steps, breast-feeding. Washing was drying on a line stretched between two rickety wooden posts. By the well stood some yellow plastic buckets with long ropes attached to the handles. Ana had a feeling of déjà-vu, as if she had been on this precise spot at some time in a previous existence, although she did not believe in any 'before' or 'after'.

'Are you OK?' asked Louis Sarr attentively.

'I would like to visit Mariama's school and make an arrangement about her school fees,' she said in a daze. Louis Sarr laid a careful hand on the old man's shoulder. He gave a start as if he was waking up from a dream.

'Big Man,' called Louis Sarr and regarded the dessicated little figure with reverence.

Big Man, thought Ana in a whirl, he was the very one she wanted to meet. She knew that Rosie's husband lived with his young wife in a village far up the river. Big Man must be yet another uncle. She gave up trying to sort out the complicated family relationships.

'So you're the one who provides for Mariama?' Ana leaned forward towards Big Man. Louis Sarr had crouched down beside him.

'She comes to me when she is in difficulties. I give her shelter,' he said grumpily.

'What difficulties?' asked Ana in alarm.

'She hides from the police.'

'Why?' asked Ana, exhausted at the thought of yet another obstacle in the way of her seeing Mariama again.

'Stealing on the beach. The tourists can't keep an eye on their things and accuse the children of having stolen them.'

'I really hope nothing happens to Mariama.' Once again everything felt unreal to Ana. She could no longer tell whether it was her or someone completely different sitting under the cashew tree with the two uncles, who were deep in conversation in an incomprehensible language. Big Man stood up and wobbled uncertainly on his legs. The light grey suit hung loosely on his thin old man's body.

'Excuse us, time for prayer.' Louis helped Big Man across the yard to one of the rooms in the compound, where they unrolled their prayer mats.

Ana was left sitting alone, and was immediately surrounded by the group of children. They touched her cropped, high-lighted hair, giggling, whilst she talked to them in English and attempted to keep them at a distance. It was not at all her style to get involved with children, but she was not herself any longer. Ana wanted to go out and find Modou, who was waiting for them in the taxi. She extricated herself from the children, feeling as if she was entangled in an unending story which would never lead her to Mariama.

Modou was lying asleep on the back seat of the taxi. Ana opened the door and woke him up. He sat up and yawned. Even though he had parked the taxi further down the street in the shade under the trees, it was suffocatingly hot.

'Where do you want to go?' he said sleepily, getting in to the front seat.

'We are waiting for those two gentlemen there,' said Ana, pointing to Louis Sarr and Big Man, who were on their way out of the compound in the midst of a noisy altercation. Seen from a distance they looked like father and son. Big Man got in beside Modou and Louis Sarr sat on the back seat beside Ana. Her fear of contact was triggered immediately, and she involuntarily moved right over to the window. It almost felt like an anticlimax when Louis Sarr placed a large white cloth bag on the seat between them. Big Man told Modou to drive.

'Where are we driving to?' asked Ana, leaning forward towards Modou, with whom she felt she was more on the right wavelength.

'You want to visit Mariama's school, don't you?' answered Big Man in his place. Ana had nothing against him taking command, so long as he made sure that she got in touch with Mariama before the last day of her holiday was over.

The taxi stopped in front of two three-storey concrete blocks with an entrance between them into a large school playground. There was a lively bustle of pupils coming and going. It was the time when the morning shift gave way to the afternoon shift.

'School,' said Louis Sarr and opened the door on Ana's side. She had abandoned all hope of realising her intention of visiting Mariama's school and was totally unprepared. Obediently she stepped out of the taxi and walked into the playground. She stood for a moment in the shade under an overhanging roof to get her bearings. There were swarms of schoolchildren in blue and white uniforms, the girls in white blouses and dark blue skirts with tightly plaited hair and the boys similarly in white shirts and dark blue trousers. In the middle of the playground stood a cement mixer. Heaps of gravel and building materials were spread around. Ana chose an entrance at random, where a door was standing open in to a roomy office. At the end of a long table placed across the room there sat a middle-aged woman in an attractive, well-fitting outfit, working. On the floor behind her two men were prostrate on their prayer mats. Their prayers did not seem to disturb the woman, who was absorbed in typing numbers into an adding machine. She waved Ana closer and looked up at her over her glasses.

'Yes ma'am?'

Ana needed to pull herself together and work out why she was standing in this office facing this woman. She moved hesitantly towards the table.

'Could you tell me whether a girl called Mariama is registered at this school?' she began.

'Surname please?' said the woman efficiently. Ana realized that she did not know Mariama's surname. She bit her lip, and the sensation of not being equal to the situation floored her. She felt an attack of dizziness coming on, and had to lean against the side of the table. The harassed administrator leafed through the register and ran her finger down the columns of names.

'Mariama Faal,' she said, 'is not in school right now. You're not sure of her surname? Another Mariama changed schools after seventh grade. A third Mariama has dropped out altogether because of family problems.'

'Is it likely that she is still going to school if she is fifteen or sixteen?' Ana was on automatic pilot; she hardly knew what she was saying.

'Why not? If someone pays, everything is possible,' said the woman impatiently.

Ana had not got a single step closer. She was in precisely the same place as when she started. She just stood there, not knowing what she was waiting for. The woman jiggled one foot impatiently and looked enquiringly at her.

'If you wish, you can make a donation to our school. The smallest sum is more than welcome,' she said, preoccupied, and pushed a metal box across the table. Ana put ten hundred-dalasi bills in the empty box.

'Do you know why Mariama is not at school right now?' Ana asked falteringly.

'The school fees have not been paid, but she is on standby. We look after our pupils and keep an eye on them.' She looked down at her papers, signalling that the audience was over.

'Thank you.' Ana left the administrative office and stumbled out to the taxi on her high-heeled cork sandals.

She collapsed onto the back seat, tired to death of this charade which was leading nowhere.

'Tell me, where is Mariama?' said Ana. Big Man turned

round and nodded at Louis Sarr.

'She is at work,' he said.

'What do you mean, at work?'

'In a warehouse by the river.'

'I don't want to hear about it.' Ana's insides were in uproar.

'You don't want to hear, you don't want to see. So what are you doing here?'

'Why are you lying to me the whole time?' Ana was on the verge of an attack of hysterics at the prospect of yet another confrontation with her own ineptitude.

'You call me … us liars? I want to marry you, remember.' Louis Sarr's voice was strident.

'Sorry, it was not my intention to insult you.'

'So what was your intention?' said Louis Sarr coldly. Ana gave up. She couldn't face any more. It was time to throw in the towel.

'Just drive me back to the hotel, please, Modou.'

'You wanted to see Mariama before you leave, so you will see her.' Louis Sarr's stubbornness frightened her.

'No, drive me back to the hotel.' Ana was on the verge of tears.

'You know where we are going?' said Big Man discreetly to Modou, who turned round and looked enquiringly at his customer from earlier that morning. Ana was incapable of giving a clear signal. Modou banged his hands on the steering wheel in frustration, and nodded in agreement to Big Man.

The whole district seemed remarkably colourless and deserted. The roads were empty of people, with the exception of the single figure of a woman with a heavy bundle on her head. Ana could not turn round. She could not even ask to be dropped off. She would never be able to find her own way out and away from this closed world where there were neither street names nor house numbers, where time and place no longer existed, and a slow-motion silence reigned, as if at the bottom of the sea. These pictures of stagnation and hopelessness in various shades of grey undermined Ana's squeaky-clean tourist identity. She was forced to consider whether she could accommodate Mariama in her dream of the ambitious schoolgirl in a newly-pressed school uniform with shiny plaits and the prospect of a place at an elite university. Or whether she should take the unedited version of her life as part of the package.

They were approaching the river along muddy, pitted roads with low bushy trees and tall dry grass on both sides. Ana's insides were thoroughly shaken up, and she felt as if her stomach was in her throat. There was a stench of stale brackish water and shellfish. Clouds of insects swarmed in front of the windscreen. The sun burned through the roof of the taxi. Louis had put his arm around the white cloth bag, which contained his drum, and seemed to be far away. Modou and Big Man exchanged occasional remarks, of which Ana understood nothing. She was left to herself and began to realise that there was nothing to do but allow Big Man to decide the rest of the day's programme.

The gravel track opened up and came to a dead end in a sandy clearing under a little clump of spindly trees, which cast shadows in flickering patterns. Everywhere there were mountains of something which looked like rubbish, but turned out to be oyster shells. Large and small boys and a couple of pubescent girls were crouching by the piles of shells with large plastic bowls between them, scraping and hammering at the inside of the shells. Modou parked the taxi by a baobab tree, its thick trunk decorated with adverts, names, addresses, phone numbers and declarations of love carved into the bark. He turned round to Ana to get the green light from his paying customer to stop at a destination she had not requested. She nodded abstractedly and reluctantly left the enclosed security of the car to join Louis Sarr and Big Man, whose company was after all the guarantee of her safety. The smell and the damp heat made her gasp for air.

The two men walked purposefully towards a narrow wooden bridge which linked the river bank to some decaying straw-thatched wooden cabins built on posts out in the river. They talked to each other in low concentrated voices. Louis had taken his bag with him, and was carrying it over his shoulder. Ana didn't know where she was, only that she would soon see Mariama again and come face to face with the reality which existed around here. She reassured herself with the thought that there could not be any horror scenarios left in this world with which she was not already familiar from the stream of digital images on TV screens and exclusive books of photographs from the earth's disaster areas and conflict zones.

Out on the dilapidated wooden bridge she caught sight of some women with canvas sacks on their backs, standing up to their waists in water by the river bank where mangrove trees hung over the muddy water. Ana had to take some deep breaths so as not to become faint with the heat and the humid air. Then she hurried on to keep up with her two guides. They suddenly turned away from the river and along a narrow well-worn path, where the sun's rays flashed on flattened tin cans, lying along the path as if to mark the way. They disappeared into an overgrown building without windows.

Ana followed them into the dark space, which was unexpectedly large and roomy and with constant movement along the invisible walls. Ana walked carefully forwards, stumbling, hardly able to make out the two men in front of her, but following the sound of their footsteps on the uneven earthen floor. Finally she emerged at the other end, where there was a narrow exit. The building turned out to be an empty shell, the remains of a burnt-out storehouse. Ana turned around, and with the light behind her she could see some children huddled together in a sooty corner of the enormous hangar-like space.

She went back to get a proper look at the huddle of children, hoping to catch sight of Mariama. Some had blankets around them, others lay in plastic sacks, others again on the bare ground. Some were standing together in groups, puffing on pink and pale green cigarettes which poisoned the air with a sweet smell of candy floss. They were scantily covered in random items of clothing, adult sizes which were too big or children's sizes which were too small. She went over to a couple of young girls who were on the edge of the group and asked after Mariama. They reacted by moving away and turning their backs on her.

Ana found Big Man and Louis Sarr sitting on a rusty steel girder in a smaller dump full of electrical scrap. Old-fashioned TV sets, discarded video players stacked up in high piles, mountains of computers and outdated surveillance equipment. Some bigger boys were busy around a primitive fire. Soon they were enveloped in a thick black smoke, which emitted a dreadful stench of rubber and burnt plastic. When the smoke had subsided the boys rooted around in the embers with a wooden stick and collected together pieces of metal and wiring, which they carefully placed in a rusty enamelled container. Then they threw a new portion of the insides of the electronic apparatus onto the fire.

Ana held a handkerchief over her nose and mouth and sat down beside her two guides. They seemed completely unaffected by the fumes of heavy metal and the child scrap collectors who were working in the poisonous smoke.

'Who takes care of these children?' Ana ventured, not expecting an answer. A little boy came out of the burnt-out building, ran over to Big Man and tugged at his trouser leg. Big Man got up and went with him over to a pile of TV sets, which were displayed as if in sorrowful witness to the decay of the old world. Ana seized the opportunity to question Louis Sarr.

'Where is Mariama?' She wanted to get the day's excursion over with and then as quickly as possible back to the hotel to get packed and return home to her own familiar surroundings, before they vanished from her consciousness altogether.

'She is not here.' Louis Sarr shrugged apologetically.

'Where is she?'

'That's what Big Man is finding out.' Louis Sarr seemed tense.

'What are the children doing here?'

'They're collecting copper and nickel from the electrical scrap. It is a good job. Big Man pays them a good price,' he assured her.

'And what about the smoke?' Ana objected.

'The smoke is no problem.'

'It's poisonous,' Ana insisted.

'Poor children are forced to work,' said Louis Sarr angrily.

'And what about the women and children out there?' Ana jerked her head in the direction of the river.

'The women cut the oysters away from the mangrove roots with machetes. They are smoked and sold to restaurants. The children crush the shells into a powder which is used for paint and cement,' he explained slowly and painstakingly, whilst he equally painstakingly unwrapped his drum from his bag.

'Boys in the electronics business are much better paid,' he continued, testing the drumskin with the very tips of his fingers.

Big Man came towards them, engaged in agitated conversation on his mobile phone. Behind him the little boy was busy with the day's work by the toxic fire.

'Where do all these children come from?' Ana felt wretched in this surreal setting.

'Runaways, come from … different places.' Big Man was standing right in front of her.

'Mariama?'

'She keeps on eye on the little ones for me.'

'What about her schooling?' Ana repeated her mantra.

'She has been detained and handed over to the police.' Big Man's mobile dangled from a chain around his neck.

'We must go to the police station at once,' he said. Ana stood up as if on command. Her legs were shaking under her.

'You come with me.' Big Man was stressed and irritable. Ana stood still, waiting for Louis Sarr, who was sitting with his drum between his knees producing some deep suggestive rhythmic drumming.

'I shall perform tonight … in the tourist show on the river.' He pointed towards the floating wooden cabins, whose tops they could just glimpse.

'My wife, you'll come back to me. I am waiting for you,' he continued in his calm arrogant voice. She answered with a nervous little laugh and put her hand to her neck.

Without waiting for Ana, Big Man stormed off in the direction of the taxi. She dashed after him like a brushed-off TV reporter, trying to keep up.

'You owe me an explanation,' she called. Big Man walked faster. The suit flapped around his thin body.

'What has happened?' Ana caught up with him.

'She was on the beach doing business. And then this policeman comes up to her and takes her along, but there are no thieves in my family.' Big Man got in beside Modou. Ana stopped and looked back. The child workers were still sitting motionless in the same position, crouching between the plastic bowls and stacked sacks of pulverized oyster shells. The air laid a glittering veil over the late afternoon, where the sun still reigned at full strength, until imperceptibly, from one moment to the next, it would sink into the river.

As if in a dream, a stocky little man with a knitted cap on his head popped up behind the baobob tree where the taxi was parked and took a bound notebook out of a hollow in its decorated trunk. He came over to Ana and introduced himself as the guide to the oyster farm; he informed her that visitors normally made a donation to a nearby school which the owners of the business had founded. Ana leafed through the notebook of names of foreign visitors, which country they came from and how much they had donated. Ana wrote her name on the list and doubled the largest recorded donation. She refused the offer of a guided tour as part of the deal and thanked him for his trouble. The man counted the notes and with an air of satisfaction returned the notebook to the hollow trunk.

The police station was just off the busy avenue which led to the tourist area, and consisted of some low, relatively modest buildings surrounded by mango trees. Big Man got out of the taxi and slammed the door hard. Ana followed him, with no inkling of what he wanted her for. They went in through an open door in a side building. As soon as they got inside they were confronted by a narrow barred pen running along the mouldy green wall. Fifteen to twenty young male prisoners were standing like sardines in a tin, pressed up against the bars, which ran from floor to ceiling. Some of them pushed gashed wrists out through the bars, others pointed to large blue and red bruises on their arms and legs. One pulled his T-shirt up with a quick movement and showed the bloody stripes across his back. The whole thing choreographed in demonstrative silence. A small thin figure, practically a large child, said hello in a familiar voice to Big Man, who discreetly pressed a dalasi note into his hand.

The corpulent guard on duty at the counter at the end of the cage was indifferent to the stench and the mute lamentations of the prisoners. He was sitting phlegmatically with a bundle of dusty papers in front of him, picking his teeth. On the wall behind him hung a colour photograph of the president and the president's wife, a beauty from the Middle East. By the end of the counter stood a stool with a woven seat. There was nothing else in the narrow, high room except an empty filing cabinet with the doors standing open, hanging crookedly on their hinges.

The two men exchanged a long and fervent handshake. The policeman asked Ana to take a seat on the stool. She sat down on the extreme edge of it, so as not to get her white linen trousers messy on its greasy seat. The two acquaintances (she assumed) talked in low, almost inaudible voices. As if the walls had ears. The sleepy fan on the ceiling emphasized the oppressive damp heat in the stuffy room.

'… good as gold,' said Big Man. The policeman muttered something or other. Ana could only catch the odd word, and imagined that it was a negotiation about the amount needed to buy Mariama's release from the unfounded arrest. Ana was on the point of saying that she would pay whatever was necessary, but stopped herself. It was of course precisely her solvency which was the reason Big Man had dragged her along. The question was only how much she would have to fork out.

The policeman suddenly directed his gaze at Ana, and Big Man explained to him that she was sponsoring Mariama's schooling. The policeman looked at her for a long time. She could not determine whether his face expressed contempt or goodwill.

'So you ... sponsor ... our children?' He spat out the words between his lips. With his short shirt sleeves and the packet of cigarettes in his breast pocket he could be any sweaty official in any public office anywhere.

'Nice, nice,' he smirked. Was that a signal that he accepted Big Man's offer and was ready to pocket the bribe? Ana clutched her handbag and prepared herself mentally to have to pay a considerable sum.

The two men shook hands on the deal. Big Man nodded, satisfied, and muttered that they could go. Ana stood up and wanted to say goodbye to the policeman, but his thoughts seemed to be elsewhere, and he did not notice that she was going. Big Man was already out of the door. Ana hurried past the bars and the hands which reached out for her. Almost like an exorcism she handed out some dalasi bills as she passed, and ran out of the door followed by low cries from the imprisoned men, who had no access to food or water unless they could pay for their keep themselves, or their families brought them food.

On the square outside a police van had stopped with another load of young men rounded up in the tourist area. Ana had seen more than enough, and ran for the taxi which was waiting for her. She fished a wetwipe from the bottom of her handbag, moistened her temples and wiped the dirt and bacteria off her hands. Big Man explained the rescue plan. If she gave him the amount he had agreed with the policeman, then he (Big Man) would personally make sure that the money was delivered to the right place. If she agreed, Mariama would escape any further charges. Big Man gazed thoughtfully out of the front window towards the peeling walls of the police station. Ana asked Modou to drive to the nearest cash machine, so that she could withdraw the required sum at once. Big Man immediately rang his friend behind the counter with the news.

They stopped outside the Standard Chartered Bank. Ana withdrew a large number of dalasi and gave Big Man what he asked for, without questioning the amount. Whether the substantial round sum was the going rate for bribes or a smart fraud she had no way of judging. She registered the financial transaction as a logical consequence of the impenetrable holiday adventure she had got involved in, and could do nothing other than trust that the bribe would help Mariama.

Without asking, Modou drove directly to Golden Bay Hotel. No word was exchanged between them until they stopped at the entrance to the hotel grounds. Ana paid Modou the agreed daily rate plus tip and thanked him for his patience and his safe driving.

'Where is Mariama?' she asked Big Man in a last attempt to make sure that she really was in safe hands.

'At her auntie's.'

'Has she been locked up together with those young men?'

'Men and women are kept separate,' said Big Man with an expression of disgust, as if Ana had said something blasphemous.

'I would like to be able to see her before I leave, to be sure that she is OK,' said Ana without any expectation that her wish would be fulfilled. She was sweating with fatigue, and longing for a leisurely bath and one of Beethoven's string quartets on her iPod.

She prepared to take her leave by giving Big Man her card and asking for his mobile number in return, so that she would be able to contact him. She had plans for the future, she said, plans he would be able to help her put into action. Not without payment, of course. He had no reason to do her any favours for free. He had his business interests. He was a busy man with many irons in the fire. He could regard her as a business partner. She wanted to make an offer concerning Mariama. Big Man straightened up in his seat and finally turned around.

'Mariama … not for sale,' he said.

'It seems that you are really concerned for your niece.' Ana ignored his resistance and tried to convince him of what an opportunity it was for Mariama to come to Europe as an au-pair. And at the same time as doing the au-pair job, to attend a language course and get access to the education system. An education would in the long run help her family and her many brothers and sisters in the village.

'You have no right.' His voice was trembling with anger. Was it Big Man and not Louis Sarr who had picked out Mariama as his third wife? it suddenly struck Ana.

'I am just as concerned about her as you are,' she said, fired by an inner surge of warmth. Big Man got out and opened the door on her side. She had no choice but to get out of the taxi. A sudden impulse made her hold him back. She rummaged feverishly in her handbag, found her mobile phone and took ou the sim-card.

'Please, give Mariama my mobile phone, it is a farewell gift.' Ana gave him the mobile and enough dalasi so that she could buy a new sim-card and a phone card. Big Man took the notes reluctantly, looking anything but satisfied. Without saying goodbye to Ana he got into the taxi beside Modou. She was left standing there with a feeling of having lost the battle, worrying that the emotional turbulence she was experiencing could precipitate her stress-induced depression again at any time. 'Good evening, bosslady,' came the hotel receptionist's voice behind her. Without responding to his greeting Ana dashed past him, past the souvenir shop and through the gardens towards her bungalow. She wanted to get changed and go to the Golden Bay Casino before dinner to gamble away her last dalasi at roulette. As usual she had changed far too much money and forgotten that she could not change dalasi back into another currency.

II

The Consequences of Mariama

The Consequences of Mortality

The first thing Ana did as she entered her flat, relieved and in a good mood that she was finally home, even before she had put down her flight bag and peeled off her jacket, was to ring her coach.

'Fighting fit?' asked Theis, expecting a positive result from his medicine, the stress-preemptive holiday.

'I've been a long way away.' Ana felt that she had not yet landed.

'That was the whole idea. Distance oils the psychosomatic motor.' Theis' jovial directness was a shock.

'I've just been a long way away,' she repeated defensively, and realized that she should have waited before ringing him up, but she needed to talk to someone.

'It takes more than a week in the sun without your mobile and e-mail,' he declared.

'I can't stay away from work any longer.' Ana heard her own voice from far away, like someone else's.

'The most important thing is that you return to optimal functionality,' said Theis. It was kindly meant, but sounded like a threat to Ana's ears. She chose not to hear, and promised herself that she would get up to speed quickly.

'I just have to get back to earth.' Her voice sounded like a ventriloquist's dummy's.

'We don't want to rush anything.'

'There's piles of stuff waiting for me, and my diary is full of meetings,' she interrupted him.

'We'll have a proper talk tomorrow and make a plan,' said Theis, almost solicitously.

'Just give me a couple of days to sort myself out,' she begged again, in this stranger's voice.

Theis had become a more important person in her life with Rower than she liked to admit. She was scared stiff of human weakness, both her own and others'. Weakness precipitated chaos, and chaos was hell. Even though she was a confirmed atheist and materialist, 'the soul' and 'hell' were acceptable concepts in her way of thinking. Really she would have liked to study philosophy and specialize in Descartes, whose thesis 'I think, therefore I am' was a mantra she identified with. She was a thinking junkie. Ever since she was a child, when something upset her she had healed her wounds and neutralized the pain by reflecting and philosophizing, and observing the upset through complicated thought constructions. She had not regretted abandoning philosophy for the secure foundation of a degree in economics and business studies, but philosophy remained her passion, and popped up in pressured situations as snatches and fragments from the time before she embarked on her career, before she and her career became an indivisible whole.

After a few densely packed working days which demanded Ana's full attention, her travel adventures appeared to her as a chaotic parenthesis, a mystical disorder from which she was distancing herself at full speed. She had returned to the world of reality from a dark and ominous dream. There was a reason for everything, but no meaning, she reassured herself, and she could still feel that joyful moment as the plane's landing wheels kissed the runway at Kastrup with a deep sigh. Unutterable relief had flooded her whole body, which had been in a state of highest alert throughout the holiday.

The reason for her holiday outside the firm's normal holiday periods was the latest months' evaluations from her management team. They graded themselves and each other continually according to the evaluation schedule (competence, communication, activity [work performance], responsibility) on a scale of 1 to 7. And for several sessions in a row she had been right at the bottom. Her colleagues' lack of confidence in her was a stress factor which sent her adrenalin levels threateningly high. She had been referred for five sessions with Theis, one of Rower's permanent coaches, who had their offices on the top floor of the corporation's premises on Amager Boulevard. Ana took the referral for stress coaching as proof of the fact that Rower regarded her as a valuable co-worker who was worth investing in and developing further.

She had not personally noticed any problems or conflicts, and did not understand the group's low assessment of her. She had felt aggrieved, and was very angry with her colleagues who could not or would not appreciate her performance as she deserved. She slaved away for sixteen hours a day, and on the odd occasion that she went home at six o'clock she joked that she was taking half a day off. But it was clear that a gulf had opened between her own estimation of her efforts and her colleagues' assessment.

Ana came home late in the evening feeling out of sorts. She had popped in to the nearest pizzeria, and flopped down on the sofa with two slices of pizza and a glass of red wine. All day she had felt an unsettling resistance to getting down to reading the project reports and minutes of meetings which had piled up in her in-tray. She was running exclusively on autopilot and tranquilizers. Her initial relief at being home again and firing on all cylinders had evaporated. It floored her completely that she wasn't turned on by work and didn't get high on the battles to be fought in the client management team and the team-leader group.

The elation she usually felt after nailing a major investment project, which required a dry martini to come down from, was missing. There was only this deathly tiredness and the boundless melancholy of a robot. If her colleagues knew what had happened to her, that the enforced holiday, contrary to intentions, had drained her batteries and pushed her yet further over the edge, they would give her the thumbs down. For there was no other reality than the life she and they were living in Rower International's prestigious futuristic building of glass and steel, and in their attractive private houses equipped with children and au-pairs. Ana identified one hundred percent with those happy/unhappy families, because society belonged to them.

Instead of immersing herself in the work she had brought home with her to prepare for the next day, she allotted herself two hours in the fitness centre across the canal in Fisketorvet shopping centre. She felt a sudden need to drive her soul out of her body, and completely forgot that her soul had remained down there in the tropical heat, where she had no desire ever to return. She could see over to Fisketorvet from her terrace on the eighth floor of the converted double silo, Gemini Residence, and her training kit was always ready in the hall for a quick sortie. She warmed up for the gym by running over the narrow pedestrian and cycle bridge which curved up like a graphic symbol between Islands Brygge and Kalveboderne. She felt that she was truanting from work, and wanted to get through the stolen free time as quickly as possible. When she was not buried deep in her work she was seized by uncomfortable, diffuse pangs of guilt.

Ana checked in with her card and headed purposefully for the changing room. Moments later she was on the treadmill. The sweat was trickling from the pores of her skin, and all mental activity was reduced to hazy images on her retina, which after 30 minutes at maximum speed had been transformed into a colourless vacuum filled with the selection of music from her iPod. She was so familiar with the machines that she could run through her training programme in her sleep. She became one with the twisted metal structures lined up in rows like fantasy creatures from Star Wars, and had difficulty in tearing herself away. She just sat there, leaning forward in the saddle with her head in her hands like Rodin's 'The Thinker', and felt her body dissolving into an amorphous mass of muscles.

Back in the changing room under the shower she was slowly resolved into a coherent body shape again. She was slim and long-limbed, made to reach up high, with well-sculpted muscles under her skin. In the isolation of the sauna her thoughts began to take form, and she pondered how this feeling of inner weakness had surfaced in her, and how she could overcome it. Was weakness built into all people, to prevent trees reaching the sky? Had things gone too well for her, and had a good fairy given her too many gifts, so that nemesis had caught up with her? But she had actually not been given anything for free. Everything she had achieved in financial and career terms she had fought hard for and paid for with blood, sweat and tears. She had got what she wished for, and had finished up where she really wanted to be, in terms of the philosophy that human beings are governed by their innermost subconscious desires in a self-fulfilling process. She felt she was at home in Rower. Here she could make use of her whole intellectual and creative capacity. She was bound to the corporation with strong bonds. She had developed her technical competence, had been professionally moulded and had invested her whole existence in Rower, which was both her close family and her distant relatives, branching out across the whole globe.

Back home in Gemini Residence she indulged in more displacement activity and logged in to the Donor Sibling Registry, where she was a frequent visitor. She was driven by a strong impulse to share what she had thought and experienced with other half-people like herself, despite the fact that Danish law, which protected the anonymity of donors, prevented her from looking for possible half-siblings. The site was her second home and DSR was her second family. DSR's central tenet was honesty, coupled with the conviction that every human being has a fundamental right to information about his or her biological origin and identity. 'There are only two lasting bequests we can hope to give our children. One is roots; the other wings.'

Ana thought about her childhood and the transformation that had occurred at the school leavers' party, when she had found out by accident that her father could not have children and therefore was not her biological father, but just a stand-in for an anonymous donor. At a stroke her parents had shrunk into an egg and an anonymous sperm cell, which had fused together and split into new cells which had turned into her. She felt as if she had been branded on the forehead, and that everyone could see by looking at her that she was an artificial product. She had been so vulnerable as a student at that time, so uncertain of who she was because of that notorious expression, donor child, which had transformed her into someone other than the person she thought she was.

It had not been the intention that she should be told the truth about her origins, even though the whole family knew, along with their circle of friends and acquaintances. But one of the guests, her parents' close friend Uncle Frank, had put his arm round her shoulder in drunken affection and called her 'my donor child'. She immediately suspected the messenger, who was the head of a fashionable fertility clinic, but that had been dismissed as sheer fantasy. Frank had simply provided professional assistance at her conception.

Her parents' large luxury flat was buzzing with merry guests. The scent of lilacs and newmown grass came in through the open windows, and the barrel of beer on the balcony was in constant use. In the midst of all the bustle Ana had felt betrayed and abandoned, quite alone beneath an empty sky. Her parents' love had rested on a lie, and love and lies were, according to her moral precepts, irreconcilable quantities. In her youthful radicalism she rejected her parents, especially her mother whom she could not forgive, and refused to see her again. The revelation of her biological identity had such a devastating effect that she had to undergo therapy in order to piece herself back together. 'Children conceived by sperm donation must be told the truth very early or not at all. If they are in puberty or grown up, the shock and anger at their parents' concealment is too great.' From her own bitter experience she was in complete agreement about this with her fellow victims in the Donor Sibling site's chatroom.

Ana was ashamed of her test-tube origins, which made her a manufactured product conceived by means of artificial insemination or, to use the more friendly expression, assisted reproduction. She was not created by love, passion or violence, but had come into being as a scientific achievement in cold, clinical surroundings. She could not help wondering how much she had cost, and whether her parents had got a special reduction as friends.

Before she knew the reason for it she had reproached her parents that they did not love her enough to give her brothers or sisters, and had often asked them whether she was adopted, since she was fair-haired and did not resemble either of them. How stupid and ignorant she had been. And when she thought about herself before the revelation, she felt sorry for that little girl who had been kept in unenlightened darkness as a victim of her parents' deceit. Her violent anger and desire for revenge were part of the damage which she had worked on with the psychiatrist. She had become world champion in repression. If repression had been a karate technique, she would have qualified as a black belt.

Ana closed down the site and spun round restlessly on her Kiwi chair. By chance her glance fell on the widescreen TV which she had forgotten to switch off when she went to work that morning. The camera was panning in and out through the trees in a petrified forest. The thick silvery-grey trunks glistened in the sun. She sat down on the armchair footrest and waited for the camera to find something interesting between the trunks. An overlooked animal species, a rare plant, fossils from prehistoric times, volcanic rock from a meteor strike. The weekly science magazine was the only programme which disrupted the monotony of the news and entertainment broadcasts. The magazine reminded Ana of the children's programmes of her childhood and the security and warmth they spread in the large playroom, at the time when she still believed she was a whole and undivided result of her parents' love.

Next morning in the middle of the team-leader meeting Ana felt her mobile vibrating in her jacket pocket. Reluctantly she took it out, and saw from the display that it was a Gambian number; she felt a violent revulsion, like when unpleasant experiences unexpectedly emerge from the subconscious. Who could possibly be ringing her from down there? It was true that she had distributed business cards liberally, but it had never occurred to her that anyone would make use of them. She got up and left the meeting room. The sound of Mariama's voice went through her like a jolt of electricity. She had forgotten that she had made her a present of one of her mobile phones when she left.

'Oh, my love, is it really you? What a surprise.' Ana's heart began to beat wildly as a result of her impulsive outburst, which surprised her. On the other end she could hear the urgent restrained breathing which she knew so well from the tourist beach.

'What's wrong? Why can't you talk now? Mariama?' Ana looked at the mobile display in vexation. It was cut off. She rang back at once, but no-one answered. She felt almost faint with anxiety about what could have happened to her little girl (again she surprised herself with her emotional choice of words) since she left the taxi that evening at the bus station in Serrekunda.

Ana went back unwillingly to the meeting room and resumed her place at the oval table with her head full of Mariama, who had miraculously returned to her. Her skinny figure loomed up in the room's windows like a revelation, and squeezed itself in between her and the other participants in the meeting.

'What does Ana think?' said an over-emphatic loud voice.

'Same as before.' Ana had a frog in her throat and had to clear it.

'The only problem is that we've moved to another item on the agenda,' said Kamma. Four pairs of eyes stared at her without expression. Ana felt her neck go red, and looked down. Lack of attention was by definition inadmissible at team-leader meetings, where they took stock of the preceding quarter in the department's five client management teams and decided on the strategy for the next quarter.

'We're on Item 4,' Hans whispered to her.

'Can you please keep private conversations for later.' Kamma's voice sounded irritated.

'Shall we get on,' interposed Gert, who was chairing the meeting that day. The team leaders nodded and came to attention. Ana was grateful for her colleagues' tolerance, outwardly at least. What they thought to themselves didn't bother her.

Later that day she bumped into Hans out by the coffee machine. She was lost in her own thoughts, which had been circling around Mariama ever since the interrupted conversation. Ana left the paper cup standing in the holder and ran after him to apologize that she had not returned his greeting in her distraction. He said it was perfectly all right. He was preoccupied himself with some cost estimates which were not in accord with the client's expectations. Ana nodded understandingly, and to her own surprise experienced a kind of disappointment at being fobbed off with a neutral collegial remark.

'We could have a latte in the canteen around three,' he suggested, harassed, and was already on his way down the corridor. She accepted, even though she did not really have time.

Ana turned up at the canteen as agreed. It was empty in the middle of the afternoon. She had been involved in meetings with clients since they had parted, and had hardly made any impression on the mounds of papers, e-mails and voice messages which always piled up during meetings. Hans gallantly placed the chair for her and fetched two large lattes. He sat down and looked expectantly at her. As if he was really interested in how she was.

'I'm sorry, I've not really come back to earth yet.' Ana mopped some drops of sweat from her upper lip.

'You've lost your poise.'

'I just need to process my experiences.'

'Do you have any photos from down there?' he asked, interested.

'I'm a dreadful photographer, but I might have some from the beach.' Ana did not want to show him the pictures of Mariama which she had on her laptop.

'No need to worry about me. I'm an amateur myself.' Hans' hand lay a few centimetres from hers. He was so natural and sincere that Ana felt nervous that he was not the person he pretended to be. She dared not look at him.

'Have I said anything wrong?' Hans' pupils were tiny black pinpoints. It occurred to her that he must be on coke, but she pushed the thought away.

'No, no, it's just that I've got too many client contracts up in the air right now, and then there's … you know, my private life.' Ana thought about Mariama. She didn't have a private life.

'We're at our best when we're focusing on our work,' said Hans confidingly. Ana was pleased that he had said 'we'.

'I didn't buy a single souvenir to bring home,' she said awkwardly, and not entirely truthfully.

'No, what's the point of all that tat?' Hans' hand came dangerously close. Perhaps it was just her imagination that she could feel the heat radiating from his skin.

'I shan't go back there again,' she continued, moving her hand away. It was actually pleasant sitting at the edge of that large open space, where they could see up through all the floors. The greyish-white table top and the glazed earthenware mugs seemed positively homely, Ana noted to herself. Her mobile rang. Hans stopped in the middle of a sentence and looked enquiringly at her.

'Let it ring,' she said. She was afraid that it was Mariama again. She could almost feel her through the urgent vibrations of the phone.

'Just take it,' Hans insisted.

'Please, call me back,' came Mariama's voice. Ana rang up quickly.

'When are you coming to Gambia again?'

'It will be some time … a long time.' Ana felt bad.

'Time is running out.'

'How are you, my dear?' Ana interrupted, sounding like her own stress coach.

'I am hungry, always hungry. Every night I dream of bread, heaps of bread, please Ana, don't forget me …'

'Trust me, Mariama, you can count on me,' Ana found herself saying, without really knowing what she meant with that 'trust me', which had sprung to her lips unbidden.

'FORGET-ME-NOT …' Mariama's voice was drowned in a half-stifled gurgling noise, as if someone were holding a hand over her mouth. Ana was left with a bad conscience and an uncomfortable feeling of having promised Mariama something she could not deliver, and leaving her in the lurch simply by carrying on living her life as if nothing had happened. Her mind was in a whirl, and she rang back at once, but could not get through. She dialled the number again, and carried on ringing feverishly, but was blocked each time by an irritating buzz.

'Bad news?' asked Hans sympathetically.

'No, not as such … just minor problems.' Ana had to take a grip on herself in order not to break down.

'I'm sorry to hear that.'

'I don't understand what's happening to me.'

'That sounds serious.' Hans was genuinely concerned. The gentleness in his voice made her uneasy. What was he after?

'You needn't worry, I've always managed without other people's …' Ana stopped herself saying 'help'; she did not want to display her weakness. It was more than enough that she had been referred to a stress coach on the recommendation of the group. Even though coaching was the norm rather than the exception in Rower's workforce, it was always the others who had a problem, not Ana. 'Ana never cries,' her school friends used to tease her. The general perception of her as the thick-skinned, invulnerable one did not match her own self-image as a soft-bellied creature, but she had involuntarily come to live up to her friends' pronouncement.

After the revelation of her biological origins the man she had previously called her father mumbled into her ear: 'I'm not superhuman', as a kind of excuse for his infertility and lack of courage to tell her the truth. From then on she had taken this slightly bizarre expression to herself in its positive form, repeating so often inside herself 'I am superhuman', that she came to believe it. Her lightning career affirmed it, and she started to despise her father, to whom she had been very attached, for that negative Nietzsche quotation. She did not want to be like him for anything in the world, and had to remind herself time and again that there was no danger of that, since he was not her real father. In some place over which she had no control she loved him for being everything she was not.

'Thank you for your backup at the meeting,' Ana finally remembered to say.

'It was nothing,' said Hans awkwardly. Ana wondered what he was after, meeting her in the canteen instead of just standing by the coffee dispenser exchanging a few words as they usually did when they bumped into each other. She felt restless, and didn't really have anything more to say to him. Her focus was once again directed towards the work which was waiting for her.

'Thanks for the coffee,' she said and stood up.

'It's me who should say thank you for your company,' said Hans formally, getting up at the same time. Ana felt suddenly that she recognised herself in him, a half-person with just one parent and the other lost in the gaping black void of anonymity. Had he recognised her too? Ana dared not ask him directly. She did not want to reveal herself as a donor child in case her impression that they shared the same fate was just a projection, but she could not find any other reason for his interest and friendliness towards her. She was never open to flirting at work and rarely talked about herself or what she got up to outside 'the glass cage', as the Rower building was called.

Ana was back at her place at her desk and could not

concentrate. Mariama popped constantly into her mind. Just as she was sitting working out estimates for investments in property and crude oil, the girl materialized on her inner screen with a gesture, a smile, a fleeting touch. Occasionally just with her fragile vibrato voice, like on the beach, with some sentence which had remained in Ana's ears: 'You sponsor my school?' 'Got something to eat, bosslady?' Ana had reckoned that she would get Mariama out of her head at the same rate as her holiday memories faded, but contrary to her calculations the image of Mariama had persisted.

Ana hadn't had a proper holiday for years. She travelled so much for her work, partly to visit clients and partly to meetings at Rower's London branch and other sites in Europe and beyond, that she couldn't face packing a holiday suitcase. And on the rare occasions that she took a holiday trip, her work always went along with her luggage. Perhaps she could simply not cope with taking a holiday without e-mail and mobile contact with Rower. Perhaps this unfamiliar weightlessness had made her particularly receptive to new impressions, and contributed to the way her experiences had affected her.

Ana was in a state of paralysis. She could not make contact with Mariama, her mobile was seemingly dead. She had tried to transfer money to Aunt Rosie's bank account with the notification 'Mariama', but the account no longer existed and the money had been returned. This passive uneasiness reduced her time to waiting time. She was annoyed with herself and with the weakness which had sneaked up on her together with Mariama, and the acute anxiety and nervousness which went along with it. She had still not confronted Theis with the consequences of Mariama. Several times she had been on the point of blurting out her anguish, but she had stopped herself. It felt so embarrassing that a complete stranger, a down-and-out on a beach, had been able to move her so deeply and throw her feelings into such confusion. It was true that do-gooding had become fashionable and the aid organizations had become TV darlings, but she could not save Mariama. The distance between them was too great for that, not just geographically, but also mentally and culturally. She had made up her mind that their points of departure were just too far apart.

Ana was having the last of her stress-counselling sessions with Theis. They were supposed to evaluate progress and decide whether she needed to continue. Theis started off optimistically by stating that Ana had sorted herself out sufficiently to be able to function normally again in a work context. She could fly solo, and just needed to touch base occasionally. They were in a kind of study classroom, with a whiteboard on two trestles. Theis looked calmly and expectantly at her. Then he took a felt-tip pen and went over to the whiteboard. His large stomach was confined by a straining shirt with gaping holes between the buttons.

'Let's just summarize … your project before your holiday was?' said Theis, to help her get started.

'To be able to structure my working day better.'

'How?'

'To divide my time into separate compartments, with full concentration on one area at a time.'

'Why is that so important for you?'

'I want to be able to make an optimal contribution. To give Rower everything I have in me.'

'Is there anything in your life that's as important to you as Rower?' Theis put a sticker on the board and wrote on it 'Rower'.

'No.' Ana thought for a long time. Theis waited patiently by the board.

'No? Then I can only repeat to you that you are not the only one,' he said encouragingly.

'Yes … perhaps.'

'Perhaps?' Theis appeared to have all the time in the world for her. Ana held back. Fear lay gleaming in the darkness deep inside her.

'A strange light,' she said, screwing up her eyes. Theis

looked at her in astonishment.

'This is not a therapeutic situation,' he warned her. He was a workman with his toolbox who broke up machine parts with metal fatigue and forged new and more functional ones.

'I know all about that,' said Ana, annoyed at being lectured to.

'Do you have any other projects?' he continued efficiently.

'Just let me think…'

'Think out loud.'

'No, let's drop it.' Ana felt that Mariama did not belong in this clinical room where burnt-out beasts of burden were gathered back into the fold.

'What should we drop?' Theis insisted.

'No, I can't.' Ana wanted more than anything else to get up from the leather chair and flee from the classroom, flee from her life.

'No-one is forcing you to do anything against your will.' Theis had sat down on the chair just behind her. He smelt faintly of sweat.

'I know that.' Ana was tentative and unsure.

'But we should ideally get the pieces to fall into place within a reasonable time frame,' said Theis. He owed Rower a result.

'That's my aim too,' said Ana, but she knew that every single little cautious answer to Theis' simple questions would have incalculable consequences and could turn her life upside down.

'Not that I'm pushing you,' said Theis pedagogically.

'I'm confused,' Ana admitted.

'Well, that's a start.' Theis crossed his legs, looking supremely well-balanced.

'It's not because I don't want to … move forward.' Ana hesitated. Theis waited in silence.

'It can't be reconciled, there's too much distance,' she continued.

'What can't be reconciled and why?' Theis put in.

'It wasn't a normal holiday.'

'No, it was to combat stress, but what's the problem in

concrete terms?' Theis went on, disorientated.

'Work fills up everything.'

'There's no room for anything else?' he suggested, sensing an emotional attachment behind Ana's enigmatic hints.

'Or it's the other way round … perhaps.' Ana could not think the thought through.

'What is most important?' Theis asked. Ana said nothing in reply.

'Put another way, what means most to you?'

'They both mean the same.'

'You must take control. What do you want?' Theis got up and went over to the board and placed a third sticker on it. The question made Ana feel paralysed.

'You have two possibilities: to choose between the two irreconcilable quantities or try to cope with both of them.'

'I can't do that.'

'What can't you do?'

'Cope with both of them.'

'Then you must choose.'

'I can't do that.' Ana felt as if she was being suffocated.

'Try to articulate the problem,' he said in routine fashion.

'I want both. But it's not possible.'

'Why is it not possible?'

'There's not room in here.' Ana pointed at her temples.

'Is there anything you can adjust in your working life so that you make time and space for a commitment outside Rower?'

'It's either-or.' Ana had lost her voice.

'What conclusion do you draw from your statement?'

'I can't do without Rower.'

'Good, then that's the starting point.' Theis put yet another sticker on the board. So far he had achieved the desired outcome for himself and Rower.

'Starting point?' Ana stared at him.

'You've chosen Rower,' he declared.

'I didn't say anything of the sort,' she said. Theis turned round and glanced at her.

'You've chosen Rower,' he affirmed, putting yet another

sticker on the board.

'You're going a bit too fast for me.' Ana was half out of her chair.

'Let's start again. How would you describe your relationship to Rower?' said Theis with professional patience.

'Rower is my family, where I get love and warmth.'

'What does Rower get from you in return?'

'My soul.'

'That's quite a mouthful.' Theis seemed dissatisfied with her answer. 'Can you be more precise?'

'Business analysts maintain that the top level of management are the modern slave-workers.' Ana seized hold of the first thing that occurred to her, fragments of an article she had read on the plane on the way home from a meeting in London.

'Unternehmensknechte.' Ana's voice broke. Theis poured her a cup of elderflower juice. She put the cup in the holder on the armrest without drinking any and began to cry.

It was not the first time tears had flowed in that classroom. Even seasoned workers with something as antiquated as many years of faithful service behind them could dissolve into uncontrolled sobbing. Theis passed her a packet of Kleenex and let her sit quietly until the attack was over. He moved a couple of the stickers on the board, and waited until she was ready to continue. Then he sat down on the edge of the walnut table.

'Can you explain what happened?' Theis looked discreetly at his wristwatch.

'It was that word, Unternehmensknechte, which got to me.' Ana's face was swollen with crying.

'Keep calm, the solution will come to you.'

'I can't see any way out,' she sniffed.

'From what and to what?' Theis looked challengingly at her.

'Sorry, what did I say?' She could not remember what she had just said. She had no contact with the body which was sitting in the black leather chair.

'I heard you say that you couldn't see any way out. So how

does Rower fit into the picture?'

'There can be nothing beside or above Rower.'

'So we're back where we started. Can you structure your working time better, more efficiently, so that you can create time for other matters which are important in your life?' Theis placed special emphasis on 'other matters'.

'It's stronger than I am,' she said. Theis looked at her with narrowed eyes.

'That's important, what you just said.' Theis put a new sticker on the board.

'I wasn't able to separate Rower from myself. We had become fused together,' she said calmly.

'You're talking in the past tense suddenly, what's that about?' Theis interjected.

'I can see the whole thing more from outside,' she confirmed.

'So what was it that happened?' Theis said enthusiastically.

'I don't know. The fog lifted,' she suggested.

'Good.' Theis sat on the edge of the table again.

'This is the moment when you used to light a fag in the old days.' Ana felt unusually light. Theis was no longer an opponent, but an ally.

'Thanks for the invitation,' he said, pretending to take a drag on a cigarette.

'I've had the wrong focus,' said Ana.

'Can you describe that more fully?' he said.

'I've stared until I'm blinded, just like when you look at the sun and you can't see.'

'Who or what represents the sun?' asked Theis.

'Is that so difficult …'

'You must put it into words.'

'OK, Rower, I suppose I'm not all that bright,' sighed Ana.

'None of us are when it comes to seeing through ourselves,' said Theis.

'I've chained myself to my work.' Ana was shocked that she had been so completely seduced by the illusion of being irreplaceable, being immortal.

'My colleagues must think me a complete idiot,' she

continued.

'Why is it important what they think?'

'It's them I measure myself against.'

'By what yardstick?'

'Always to be at the top of your game, to have a 360 degree horizon the whole time and never lose sight of the big picture.'

'Let's meet again in two weeks for a follow-up session – same time same place.' Theis made a note in his electronic calendar. Ana got up.

The next morning during a meeting with partners from Rower's Zurich office Ana had a call from Aunt Rosie, who spoke very loudly and at a frantic speed.

'Call me back, it's urgent,' was the first thing Ana heard loud and clear, and then the line went dead. She set aside all other considerations and ran out to the corridor to ring back.

'Very bad, very bad,' came Rosie's voice.

'What's bad, Aunt Rosie?'

'Everything.'

'How is Mariama?'

'She is OK.'

'Is she living with you?'

'Of course she is.'

'Can I talk to her?'

'It's very, very bad,' repeated Rosie.

'What's wrong, Rosie?'

'We need ten thousand dalasi.'

'What for?'

'Mariama's school certificate.'

'Is she OK?'

'Her school certificate costs ten thousand dalasi, without that she can't get a job.' Rosie was at fever pitch.

'But is she really … has she finished her schooling?'

'Listen, I've lost my job in the bank. I have a large family to take care of and Mariama's school on top of that. You can send the money through Western Union. We have Western Union in Gambia.'

'How much is that in euros?'

'Western Union can tell you the exchange rate. It is the last call. Life or death.'

'What do you mean?'

'Just ring me when you have arranged it with Western Union and give me the reference number on the receipt, so that Mariama can collect the money.' Aunt Rosie's voice faded out.

Ana's relief at having made contact with Mariama was overshadowed by Rosie's ominous 'life or death'. She felt as though she was standing behind a curtain and having to rely on guesswork. She was afraid that it was something much more serious than an exam certificate (which Ana still could not really believe in) the ten thousand dalasi were to be used for. Ana suddenly felt grateful that money was not a problem for her, that she was free to share it. She had never looked at her finances from that perspective before. Once she had made a large one-off donation to the Cancer Trust. Not because she wanted to be a do-gooder or was frightened of getting cancer herself, but to put an end to the insistent calls on her mobile. She had silenced the aggressive phone campaign of the Society for Nature Conservation in the same way. She hurried back to the meeting room and apologized that it was necessary for her to leave the meeting.

She located Western Union on the web and took a taxi out to Nørrebro. Outside on the pavement stood a tattered sign with the day's exchange rates. On the door an official announcement read: 'This office is under police surveillance.' There were no other customers. She stood still, feeling all too visible in the shabby premises.

'Can I help you?' came in halting Danish from the counter, where two men sat behind plexiglass at separate hatches. Ana went over to the one who had addressed her.

'Can I send money to Gambia?'

'We transfer money throughout the world and exchange it into any currency without charges. The cash can be collected two minutes later from any one of our offices in the country concerned.'

'What do I do?' she interrupted nervously. She was not used to being the underdog. The friendly young man passed her a form.

'You write down the name of the recipient. If the person does not have identity papers, you must write a question in that space which the person concerned must answer correctly to claim the money.'

'Any question at all?' she said, disorientated.

'That is up to you.' The young man resumed his conversation with his colleague, a somewhat older man with a bald domed head and a threadbare suit jacket.

Ana was anxious to get the money off quickly. Rosie's 'life or death' was going round and round in her head like a tape playing on a loop. She found it difficult to concentrate in the unfamiliar surroundings; the seedy atmosphere felt like an accusation against her. Finally she composed the question: How old am I? And the answer: 43. She paid in 300 euros and got a receipt. She was not satisfied with her question. It was too childish, but she couldn't think of anything better.

She went and sat in a nearby café in order to ring Rosie and give her the answer for Mariama so that she could collect the money. It struck Ana that it would soon be her birthday, and she would have to invite her closest colleagues and neighbours to a cocktail party. The same narrow little circle every year. In a private context she could not cope with being with many people at once. Professionally it did not bother her attending a conference of several hundred.

She rang Rosie's number. She could hardly speak. She was so nervous that Rosie might misunderstand her, so that something would go wrong and Mariama would be unable to get hold of the money. She impressed on her what the answer was.

'The right answer is 43, you understand ... forty-three,' she repeated.

'Yes, forty-three, you talk like a child,' said Rosie condescendingly.

'I want to speak to Mariama,' she insisted.

'She's at the beach. Ring me again in a few hours.'

'Tell her she doesn't need an identity card so long as she knows the answer to the question.'

'Yes, yes, I know,' said Rosie impatiently.

'I'll ring back.' She gave up.

'Thank you so much.' Rosie hung up.

Ana needed some exercise after that nerve-racking conversation. She walked the whole way home across Town Hall Square, across Langebro Bridge and along Islands Brygge out to Gemini Residence. She swiped her keycard on the entrance post and was admitted into the hall with the lifts. She felt secure in the silo with its CCTV, and let herself into her apartment with a good feeling in her body. She poured herself a double whisky and took it out onto the balcony with her. It was no more than eight months since she had moved in. Living closer to her workplace was a deciding factor when she chose a property to buy.

From the silo to her work was a mere five minutes by bike or a quarter of an hour on foot. It suited her to leave the Porsche in the underground car park for those short distances, whilst the payback was that she was on top form and helping the environment. An added bonus with her new apartment was that it was close not only to her workplace but also to Casino Copenhagen, where she killed time during the night in the periods when she was plagued by insomnia. The excitement of the roulette table could drown out any work-related problem that had got stuck in her head.

Her glance fell on the rubbish dump with the three round hills of refuse sitting in the middle of her panorama like silent exclamation marks. She was surprised that she had not noticed them earlier. Had the area between the new builds down by the canal been converted into a rubbish dump whilst she was away? Or had she just started to see refuse everywhere? She consoled herself with the fact that it was all neatly and tidily sorted, and that the rubbish dump was far enough away for the smell not to be offensive. The surrounding building sites and the cranes, which at night resembled dinosaurs, were a token of growth and progress. The orderliness of everything around her was in sharp contrast to her inner turmoil.

She poured herself another whisky, and was well on the way to getting drunk. She was not at all sure whether it was Mariama's exam certificate (which she still did not believe in), an emergency situation, payment of debts or something completely different she had contributed to, but she would just have to put up with that. She had gradually become a member of the family (in the modest role of rich uncle from America) and had to obey the rules of the game. She could not make her mind up whether Mariama was a blessing or a curse. Perhaps there was not any great difference.

Her mobile rang, loudly and piercingly. She ran around the apartment with no idea of where she had put it. A deafening silence ensued. She carried on looking, more and more convinced that it was Mariama who had rung. Finally she spotted it under the coffee table. There was no number in the display. She rang Rosie and asked for Mariama, but she had not come back from the beach. So she could not be the one who had rung, Ana realized in relief, and she ended the call quickly. Instantly the mobile rang again. She answered without looking at the number.

'Where did you get to?' Hans' familiar voice sounded indignant.

'I ...' Ana could not think what to say.

'We've scheduled another meeting. We couldn't take any decisions without you.'

'I apologize for wasting your time,' said Ana, strangely unconcerned.

'Tell me, are you under the influence?'

'Can't pull the wool over your eyes,' she flirted, emptying the whisky glass.

'Ana, you're not yourself. Can I do anything to help?'

'I'd rather be alone with my ...'

'Your what?'

' … mental state.'

'There's a new time for the meeting. Can you please check the 14th at 13.30.'

'I'm sorry …'

'Yes?'

'It was important,' she went on.

'More important than a meeting which was arranged months ago with our Swiss partners?'

'Only death is an acceptable reason. Isn't that what we usually say?' Ana was falling apart.

'You need professional help,' said Hans cautiously.

'This is not a professional matter,' she brushed him aside.

'So I'll see you tomorrow?' he said formally.

'Is there anything special tomorrow?'

'You'd better check on it.' Hans hung up.

Ana was nervous that Mariama might have rung whilst she was talking to Hans, and hurriedly rang her. She was not quite sure whether it was Rosie's or Mariama's number she was ringing.

'Thank you, thank you so much … but I am very disappointed in you,' Mariama shouted into the phone.

'Disappointed?'

'You didn't send 10,000 dalasi, only 8,500.'

'I'm sorry about that, it must be the exchange rate.'

'I am very disappointed,' sighed Mariama.

'I don't have time to do anything about it either tomorrow or the next day. You must understand that I have an important job which takes up all my time.'

'Western Union is open 24 hours a day,' Mariama objected.

'I am so sorry, I will send the rest of the money as soon as I can.'

'Then it will be too late.'

'What is it you are really going to use the money for?'

'I have told you that many times.'

'Just tell the school office that they will be sent the rest of the money for your leaving certificate.' Ana played her part in the comedy, where she pretended she did not know that they were talking about something completely different when they talked about money for the school, and as if Mariama did not know that she knew. Why was she so weak in her dealings with her? So incapable of putting her foot down and demanding the sponsor's right to know what she was paying for?

'I can't tell my school about the money.'

'Then you could tell me the truth instead.'

'I don't know anything about the truth,' Mariama complained. The line went dead. Ana rang up again and got the irritating buzz, followed by a formal telephone voice: 'The Africell number you are calling is either switched off or outside the coverage area.'

Ana jerked into a sudden razor-sharp wakefulness as the effect of the sleeping pills wore off. The sun was already high in the sky. It was Saturday. She decided to go over to the Rower building, in order to have some peace and quiet to reduce her backlog from the holiday which had been more like a survival course. On the way out it occurred to her that it was a long time since she had emptied her mailbox. When she opened it a pile of adverts and local newpapers spilled out, and an airmail envelope with its clumsy and all too recognizable handwriting landed just in front of her feet on the concrete floor near the lifts. Ana's alarm bells started ringing at once. She tore open the envelope. The letter was written on a page torn out of a lined pad. Inside there were some plastic bracelets in brash colours and a black bead necklace with an amulet, a small white seashell stuck on a piece of leather. The whole thing looked like something which had been made in kindergarten.

Ana read the brief note. 'My Ana. Miss you. You are my hope. Business as usual. Mariama.' She took the touching gesture as a proof of Mariama's devotion to her. What an effort it must have cost her to get hold of a stamp and an envelope and get the letter posted from the post office in Serrekunda, which in Ana's already faded memories of her trip

115

had assumed the form of a seething witches' cauldron. She put the plastic jewellery back in the envelope and took the lift back up again. She would keep the envelope with its precious jewellery in her jewellery box. Those small gifts from Mariama seemed to her to be worth much more than the rest of the contents put together.

Ana came into the open-plan office area to find Hans already sitting at his place. There was no-one else there, they had the whole place to themselves. Most people worked at home at weekends. Ana did not want to disturb him, so she made do with waving to him. She went out to get a mug of black coffee to banish the last traces of the sleeping pills and clear her head. Hans joined her. The coffee machine had become a collective refuge and an excuse for a break.

'What does your family say to you working at the weekend instead of taking the children to Disneyland?' Ana spoke without thinking. The letter with the little homemade gifts had made her feel light-hearted.

'I've neither children nor family,' he answered huffily, and looked away with a hurt expression on his face, which confirmed her suspicion that they might be the same sort of people. The invisible ring he erected around himself, that mimosa-like touch-me-not had from the first moment they were introduced touched a familiar chord in her.

Hans' accusing glance confused her. She didn't know how to interpret it except by egoistically guessing that he too was a donor child, who like her had been denied the truth for too long. Or was it simply the expression of a rejected man's anger? Had Hans made advances to her without her noticing? Had she not been able to see the wood for the trees? Had she wasted the chance to form a close connection with another human being? She wanted to cheer him up again, talk kindly to him, show her interest in him as a person. All those things which were not natural to her, but which she had to keep reminding herself of and make an effort to practise as compensation for a lack in her upbringing or a genetic defect in her brain.

'It does give one a certain freedom,' she ventured, in a light tone. Hans looked at her uncomprehendingly.

'To be oneself without family duties,' she added.

'Those of us who prize freedom are happy to pay the price.' Hans smiled at her. He had nice teeth. Ana started to worry that he might think she was opening the way for an intimacy she was not ready for. Her situation was too fraught for her to be able to cope with a new relationship right now. In her student days she had experimented with celibacy. Abstention had been fashionable for a while and was used to promote success in exams. But during her time at Rower she had had too many casual affairs and had begun to contemplate something more stable and permanent, if that option was still available to her after she had decided against children at an early point in her career.

'You might well ask yourself why we freedom-loving personalities make ourselves slaves to our work and lock ourselves up in glass cages,' said Hans in an ironic conversational tone, expressing the thoughts which had occurred to her upstairs with Theis, and which were new to her and not a little frightening.

In her nervous confusion Ana managed to knock the paper cup off the coffee machine stand; she stared paralysed at the wet stain on her skirt and the little puddle of coffee by the toes of her boots. Hans bent down and picked up the cup, threw it in the rubbish container, picked up some serviettes and wiped up the coffee.

'No harm done,' he said drily.

'I don't think this is my day.' Ana looked down at herself. Hans offered her a new cup of coffee.

'Thanks, I … you are so …' Ana was on the point of saying 'good', but sent him a grateful glance instead. Was he really interested in her or simply unusually well brought up and with a natural desire to help?

'Don't mention it.' Hans was about to return to his place.

'Hans, wait,' said Ana. He stopped and turned towards her.

'I just wanted to say that I'm glad … that we … can meet

like this.' Ana dried up.

'Is there nothing else you want to say?' he asked teasingly.

'Not now … later.' Ana felt driven into a corner.

'I've got plenty of time,' he said gently, and walked off into the open-plan office. She felt like running after him, but stopped herself.

Ana was distracted in her work by fantasies about the tourist beach where Mariama was working for Rosie, at the mercy of the tourists' capricious desires, with nowhere to sleep and nothing to eat but scraps from Rosie's table. In order to escape from her nightmarish fears she rang Rosie's and Mariama's numbers alternately. She rang ten to fifteen times in a row without getting through. She was aware that Hans was sitting watching her. No doubt he was wondering about her monomanic phoning, to which she was devoting much more time than to her computer. She was worried that he would come over to her and ask whether she needed any help.

Finally she got through. In the background was the sound of car engines, hard braking and screaming wheels, as if the mobile's owner was at a crossroads without traffic lights. Ana was sucked in to the throbbing pulse, the rhythms, the strong colours, warmth, energy, bodies, more than anything else the bodies. She had no wish to return to her battle with terror. The terror which lurked behind things, under the thick grass of the plains, hidden in trees and plants, the terror of the spirit world, the non-material invisible world behind the visible one. The noise continued unabated, but nothing else happened. Ana gave up and rang off. She considered the possibility that mobile coverage in the Rower building had been interrupted, and got up to go outside.

At that moment she heard Beethoven's ninth, her ringtone. She heard Mariama as loud and clear as if she had been standing just beside her desk.

'Please, call me now,' she shouted, followed by a silence which impelled Ana to ring back so that the call was registered to her mobile account.

'When are you coming to fetch me?' Mariama's telephone voice was loud and shrill, as if she was afraid it would not be heard.

'What do you mean?'

'You promised to take me with you to Europe, remember?'

'No, no, Mariama, I told you that was impossible,' said Ana firmly and decisively, although she could not rule out the possibility that down there in the tropical heat she had allowed herself to be carried away by Mariama's fantasies in a moment of weakness.

'I don't want to be illegal. I want to have a proper passport and a proper journey to your country,' she yelled desperately, ignoring Ana's protests.

'Listen to me, I want very much to help you, but in your own country. That was what we agreed.' Ana felt like hurling the phone far away from her.

'Big Man can get very legal official papers ... call me later ...' Mariama's voice suddenly changed to a whisper. The phone went dead. Ana was certain that it was Rosie who was standing breathing down the girl's neck. She took a Diazepam (bought over the net) together with a sip of water. It was no longer just work that pushed her needle over into the red. Mariama's desperation put her under just as much pressure. Everything that girl said made an impression as if it were a prediction or an ominous prophecy. She remembered the smallest nuances in Mariama's abrupt sentences and veiled hints, which constantly opened up new abysses. Ana did not know what to do about her. If she had known the consequences back there on the beach, she would never have got involved with her, never mind scattering half-promises around. Why was she so desperate to get away? Why this 'Time is running out'?

Perhaps the solution was to help Mariama get to Europe before she got a message that she had become wife number three of some Uncle-Big-Man or other. A moment later Ana swung back again and reasoned that it was better for her to finance Mariama's education at home where she belonged and had her family. But the prospect of living in constant uncertainty and doubt as to whether the money was actually being used to help Mariama, and being tormented by fear of what might happen to her, was unbearable. It was as if she would never be free of her again. Just the sound of her voice, and she was incapable of controlling her feelings.

Ana stood in the washroom nearest to the office and looked at herself in the mirror over the basin. She did not recognise herself. Her sharp features had become somehow flattened and smudged, her high cheekbones had sunk into her skull and her full lips had shrivelled. She had no intention of repairing the damage and reconstructing a perfect exterior in order to convey the impression of a rock-solid interior which had long ago split apart. She must pull herself together and rise to the surface and begin to function again, but she could not even make her mind up whether she should stay and carry on with her work or go home and collect her thoughts on the question of Mariama.

Just as she was gathering up her laptop and papers in order to dash out of the office, Beethoven's ninth rang out again. It was Rosie on the line.

'What's all this talk about Mariama coming to Europe? Why haven't you told me about it? Why haven't I been told anything? I need Mariama to do my housework and look after my children. You can't take her away from me. If you need an au-pair girl, take my Madeleine. She is more intelligent, more suitable for Europe. She is the one who must have the chance.' Rosie spoke at breakneck speed, all in one breath. Ana had to ask her to speak more slowly and repeat what she had just said.

'I won't let Mariama go, take my Madeleine, you won't regret it. Mariama is no good for Europe,' she finished her diatribe.

'Are you still there?' shouted Rosie. Ana took a deep breath.

'You must understand that I am Mariama's sponsor and no-one else's.'

'My Madeleine is much more suitable for Europe. You met

her on the beach, you saw the difference between the two girls.'

'But it is Mariama I have decided to help.'

'I don't agree with you at all.' Rosie rang off. Ana's head was spinning. She could not think clearly.

'Clocking-off time already,' said Hans' voice behind her. She had completely forgotten that he was there, sitting at his post somewhere in the open office space.

'Yes … no … I'm not sure where I'm going,' she muttered as she slipped past him.

'You're a free individual.' He smiled ironically. At that moment her mobile rang again. She made herself answer it despite the fact that it made her uncomfortable that Hans was nearby. Mariama was beside herself and could not put two words together. Ana calmed her down and assured her that she would not forget her, that she would help her to get an education 'before it was too late'. They were brutally interrupted by the disconnected tone. Ana glanced over to the office where Hans was sitting, so strangely isolated. She felt a sudden rush of tenderness towards him, and hurried towards the lift, where she scanned her company card.

On Monday morning Ana was lying in the bath with a cup of coffee and her mobile ready on the tiled edge. She had been waiting all evening and all night for a call, and could not relax until she had heard Mariama's voice again and made sure that everything was all right. She had to know how she was and keep up with what was happening around her. Every conversation led to new questions which needed to be resolved, new anxieties which had to be quelled. For the first time since her student days, work was not her top priority. The euphoria of work had been pushed into the background and exchanged for Mariama and the endless worries that came along with her.

Had she been wrapped in cotton wool all her life? First at grammar school, then at university and the LSE and finally in Rower's glass houses, where she commuted happily and safely from one to the other. The Hilton and Marriott hotels in Hong Kong, London, Delhi or Johannesburg had the same cool comfort, the same service, the same culinary refinements, the same security. It gave her a special feeling of security to wake up in the morning and for a moment not know where in the world she was, in which hotel in which city in which country, and at the same time have a calm conviction that wherever in the world she might be, there would be a marvellous breakfast buffet waiting for her in pleasant surroundings with soundless air conditioning.

Ana was already on the point of being late when her mobile rang and Mariama's voice reached her loud and clear, with no noise on the line. She continued where she had left off.

'Will you help me before it is too late?' she repeated monomanically.

'What is it that is too late?' asked Ana.

'My life.'

'I promise you,' said Ana as convincingly as she could, and repressed the thought that it was impossible for her to keep her promise.

'But you have promised to sponsor Madeleine so that she can come to Europe too?' said Mariama in her little frightened voice, which had touched Ana ever since their first meeting.

'That's not true, Mariama, believe me.'

'That's what Aunt Rosie says.'

'I'm sponsoring you and no-one but you.' Ana cursed Rosie inwardly for having frightened the life out of Mariama like that.

'I pray to God every day for one thing only, that I can soon come to Europe and live in your big house.'

'It is very difficult for Africans to get in to Europe.'

'I am so little and thin that no-one will notice me. I can get in through the bars in the barrier.' Mariama began to sniff.

'What is it, Mariama? Tell me.'

'I just pray to God,' she whispered and rang off. Ana rang back, but no answer.

She arrived half an hour late for the meeting which had

been arranged in place of the previous one, which she had left in order to send money to Mariama from Western Union. She had had Mariama on the phone again and could not get rid of her. She had to steel herself and tell her that she was busy, and would ring back later.

Ana stepped out of the lift and hurried down the corridor to the meeting room, where she discovered that the door was not just closed, it was locked. She could see in. Her colleagues had not pulled the curtains to the corridor across. She signalled to them that she was locked out, but no-one reacted to her gestures, and the meeting carried on undisturbed. She knocked cautiously on the window. No-one looked up or turned towards the corridor where she was standing. Was the meeting room soundproofed like a radio studio? Suddenly she felt ill, and had to run to the nearest toilet and throw up. She rinsed her mouth and sat on the lid of the toilet seat, cooling her forehead with a wrung-out hand towel. She was shaking with cold and freezing inside as if she had a temperature. She could hardly stand when she got up.

She half-ran back to the meeting room. Now the door was wide open and the light curtain had been pulled across. She looked in. It was empty. Her colleagues had concluded the meeting without her. She went down to the open-plan office and found a free desk. She looked around, but could not spot any of the team leaders. She opened her laptop. A request to add her signature to the final document from the meeting in the team leader group had arrived in her inbox, with no accompanying message. She rang Hans, but changed her mind before he was able to answer. Instead she rang back the number Mariama had rung from, and got hold of Big Man.

'Where is Mariama?' she shouted at him.

'I don't know,' he answered slowly.

'Did she ring from your phone?'

'Sometimes she does.' Big Man's calmness made her even more nervous.

'I have paid the police clerk … your girl is safe on the beach.'

'My girl?'

'Your responsibility from now on … out of my hands.'

'Would you be able to get Mariama a valid passport with a photograph and biometric fingerprint? Before it's too late,' Ana wanted to know, without registering that she had adopted Mariama's 'too late'.

'Passport very expensive,' said Big Man guardedly.

'It's just a query … just for the information,' she emphasized, ' I promised her …'

'Your promises do not count here,' Big Man said again with unruffled calm.

'I cannot let Mariama down, she has the right to a decent life,' said Ana with unexpected energy.

'So have I, so have all human beings.' Big Man hung up.

At that moment Hans rang to remind her that he needed her signature on the agreement from the meeting so that they could send it on to the Moorgate Group. Ana felt a cold sweat break out. The feeling of being sidelined made her throat constrict.

'Shouldn't I just see the minutes first? Just as a matter of form?' she said feverishly.

'That's not necessary. It's all decided, we're just waiting for your signature.' Hans was not inviting any discussion. Ana made a quick decision.

'I'll come over to you with my signature straight away.' She got up and took the lift to the fifth floor, where she made straight for Hans, who was sitting at his computer. The Tokyo stock exchange had just closed, and he shifted to the Moscow exchange. He was so absorbed in the share listings that he did not register that she was standing just behind him.

'Here,' she said, handing him the papers with her signature on three copies. He turned round and looked disorientatedly at her, as if he had been far away. He waved his arm to indicate that she could put the file on the table, and turned his attention to the screen again. Ana stood there, staring at the endless column of company quotations flickering across the screen. Hans was clearly uncomfortable at having her looking over his shoulder.

'I can't talk now. I have a hysterical client who wants to sell at the worst possible time.' Hans' stressed reaction reminded her that she was not the only one working under pressure.

'Let's ring or talk after six, the worst will be over by then,' he said hectically, with his back to her.

'I hope it goes well.' Ana went back to her place in a lighter frame of mind. Hans would be able to explain to her what had happened at the meeting and why there had been a bad atmosphere around her ever since she had come back from Gambia. Not everyone was equally keen on the recently introduced therapy for stress prevention. Ana expected that her status would be discussed in the team leader group in the near future. She ought to forearm herself and prepare a speech for the defence, but she had nothing to say to defend herself.

Ana looked around. The shared office was half full. She felt as if she was going to burst into tears, and rummaged feverishly in her bag for her Prozac. She put her mobile on mute and was just about to look through her client list when Mariama's mobile number lit up on the display. Big Man had clearly taken over the mobile which she had given Mariama in a sentimental moment as she left. He spoke a broken and garbled English which she had to make a big effort to understand.

'Passport ve-er-ry expensive, ve-er-ry,' he drawled. Ana was not prepared to enter into negotiations with him so soon. He had clearly misunderstood her hypothetical question and believed that she had placed an order.

'No, no, I just asked whether it was possible that you might be able to get Mariama a passport, if we ever get that far. It was purely hypothetical. We haven't decided anything yet.'

'So why did you ask if I could give you a price?' said Big Man, offended.

'Mariama would like to come to Europe,' said Ana, uncertain whether she had understood her properly, and whether that was really what she wanted.

'That is not something she can decide herself. A big family

has many decision makers,' Big Man replied brusquely.

'I know, Rosie wants to keep her as a housemaid,' Ana said sharply.

'You will not interfere in my family.' Big Man sounded angry.

'So just give me your price,' said Ana desperately, feeling that she was sinking deeper and deeper into the quicksand. The line went dead.

She rang up again to be met by the disconnected tone, which sounded like a fierce bulldog and gave her the claustrophobic feeling of being locked up. Big Man's rebuff made her nervous that her access to Mariama had been terminated. Neither she, Rosie nor Big Man answered her calls. The image of Mariama as a part of her life had imperceptibly taken root in Ana. She was prepared to pay Big Man whatever it cost to get a passport and visa for Mariama. In her overheated fantasy Mariama's journey to Europe was already a reality, and it was simply a question of the financing of certain problematic logistical requirements.

After a week without contact with Mariama Ana had to give up. She had violent withdrawal symptoms, and could not keep her mind on her work. She left the Rower offices in the middle of the day, treated herself to a lunch in the Custom House on the harbour front and disregarded all duties and appointments. Back home in Gemini Residence she drew the curtains and sat down in front of the television with a bottle of whisky. After several hours of reality shows, talent competitions and scenes from a private health clinic Ana was finally torn out of her cocoon.

Hans rang and informed her that there was a meeting in the team leader group the next morning at seven, and that the only item on the agenda was Ana and her lack of team spirit since her return from her holiday, which seemed not to have had any positive effect on her unstable mental state. A business was no stronger than its weakest link, he concluded his catechism with the firm's internal collegiate slogan. Precisely because she had anticipated the catastrophe Ana's reaction was violent. She blacked out, ceased to exist.

'Are you there?' she heard Hans calling over the phone. She could not utter a sound.

'Ana, are you OK?' he repeated even louder. Ana was incapable of reacting. Her body had frozen. She felt the icy cold rising from her feet towards her heart and her throat.

'No, no,' she shrieked in a stifled voice.

'I'm coming round now,' said Hans. Ana fell onto the beanbag chair in a kind of coma and did not wake up until there was a ring at the door.

As if in a trance, she went out into the hall and switched on the door monitor. On the surveillance camera she saw Hans standing impatiently by the entrance to the lifts, and pressed the button to admit him.

'What do you look like!' he exclaimed in horror as she opened the door and let him in.

'What do I look like?' she asked, strangely indifferent.

'You don't look like yourself.'

'What can I offer you?' Ana regarded him with a calm inward-looking gaze.

'Ceylon tea with milk,' he said, uneasy at her dishevelled appearance.

'Come out to the kitchen and tell me why you've come,' said Ana, and pulled out a stool for him. She put the kettle on and had to search for some time in the drawers to find some teabags. She opened the fridge and discovered that the small carton of skimmed milk was well past its sell-by-date. She threw the carton in the bin and apologized that he would have to manage without milk.

'Do you mean you don't know why I'm here?' he said. Ana shook her head.

'You screamed over the phone.'

'Did I?' she said stiffly.

'We have a meeting of the team leader group tomorrow morning between seven and eight.'

'Yes … that's right … we do.' Ana sat down at the table opposite Hans. The kitchen was lit up by the bright outside lights around the silo.

'I am on the agenda,' she said quietly.

'You are … unstable.'

'Is it that bad?' Ana picked up a bottle at random from the trolley behind her and was about to pour some spirits into her tea mug. Hans took the bottle from her and poured tea for both of them.

'Rower is my life, my whole existence. Rower gives me warmth and love,' said Ana as if it was a quotation from a manual. Hans looked at her, embarrassed.

'You need professional help,' he said unsentimentally.

'Thank you for your kind thoughts.'

'Will you be able to get up tomorrow morning? Shall I ring and wake you up?'

'You must stay here tonight,' she insisted, and could not sink any deeper. She had already stripped herself naked.

'If I can sleep on the sofa.'

'I'll sleep on the sofa. You can sleep in my bed,' she said determinedly.

'You need the bed most.'

'But you are my guest,' she insisted.

'I'd prefer the sofa.' Hans got his way.

Anxiety about the next morning's meeting kept Ana awake despite sleeping pills and exhaustion. Now and then she got up and went over, put her ear to the door of the sitting room and listened to the sleeping man, who breathed, turned over, snored lightly like a child, talked in his sleep, got up and went to the toilet. She made the utmost effort not to miss the slightest sound. She restrained herself from going in, but the need to be in the same room as a sleeping person, register the peace which sleep brought with it and observe the innocence of his face at a distance, grew too strong. She carefully opened the door and left it ajar. She was frightened of disturbing his sleep and went over to the window farthest from the sofa. Hans turned in his sleep with a complaining sound. Scared, Ana hurried back to her bedroom. As soon as she laid her head on the pillow, the phantoms and the transparent figures with white-painted faces appeared. She had always been frightened of the colour white, which made her think of annihilation and nothingness.

It was agreeable and yet unfamiliar to eat breakfast with a friend and sit there relaxed, talking about things other than work, even her experiences in Gambia. She no longer needed to hide anything from Hans, and could tell him about Mariama and her plans for her. Hans asked teasingly if she had gone in for charity work or joined the Salvation Army. Ana explained that it was a deeply personal matter which had nothing to do with charity. She was not one of those people who followed the trend and played at being 'the secret millionaire'. She was not a part of fashionable do-gooding. That was nothing other than image polishing, which made the gap between rich and poor glaringly obvious.

'Now you're sounding like a good old-fashioned socialist,' Hans teased her.

'I don't expect you to understand me,' Ana said, hurt. Socialist was the most painful thing she could imagine being.

'It just sounded a little … comical,' Hans tried to put it right.

'I've been struck by … ' Ana could not find the right word.

'It's an emotional attachment?' suggested Hans. Ana was surprised at his fine understanding and suddenly felt her spirits rise. She took his hand. He started, but did not pull his hand away. They sat for a long time without saying anything, until it was time to set off.

The meeting was held in the Tokyo room. The group was already assembled when they arrived, one a little after the other so as not to reveal their private relationship and arouse suspicions of collusion. Ana sat down opposite Kamma, prepared for the worst. Her colleagues said hello casually, as if this was a perfectly ordinary morning meeting. They were studying the laptop screens in front of them and hardly looked at her. Ana was wearing Mariama's plastic necklace for the occasion. She did not care what the members of the meeting thought about the odd childish object. She needed the amulet to stiffen her resolve and bring good luck at the meeting which was to decide her fate.

'We might just as well get started. Ana, are you in agreement with the agenda?' asked Erik, who was sitting at the head of the table (they took it in turns to chair meetings). There was a friendly and relaxed atmosphere, and Ana began to feel hopeful despite herself. They went round the table, and each gave an evaluation of her contribution (or lack of it), concentrating on her fatal absence from two group meetings. Ana protested vigorously and pointed out in her defence that at the last meeting the door had been locked (perhaps by mistake) so that she was prevented from joining them when she arrived. There was no reaction, just a shaking of heads. Her colleagues either could not or would not listen to her. She began to doubt whether she really had conveyed her objection, or whether it had just happened in her own head.

The faces blurred into one another, the mouths moved in synchrony. She had no sense of how each one evaluated her, who were the hardliners and who the softliners. Throughout the meeting she was aware of Hans' presence in the room, but she did not once look at him. In his extremely brief introduction (time was precious at Rower and measured out in small doses) Erik had emphasized the results she had achieved and her reliable intuition when it came to interpreting the state of the market and the volatile share prices. On the surface in the leader group there was a sense of being an equal amongst equals. Underneath it was every man for himself and Rower, with hidden agendas, plots and knives hidden in sleeves.

From the round-table presentation, where each of them had 30 seconds to put forward a statement, she could clearly remember the order of the speeches and colleagues' placing around the table. Erik, Kamma, Hans, Gert. But who had said what was unclear to her. Their statements were almost identical: weak team spirit, lack of commitment (love for Rower), negligence, as of now the weakest link in the chain. Only Hans said something that caught her attention: that she lacked the ability to listen. That hit her far harder than her other colleagues' standard terminology, which she also had at her fingertips. The meeting was over in less than fifteen minutes. They parted without hard feelings. There was general agreement that Ana was in need of a radical retraining programme. The recommendation would be sent through the official channels to the management team, who had to give final approval to decisions made by the team leader groups.

Ana hurried out of the meeting room and made sure that she took the lift down on her own. She shut herself in at home for the rest of the day, did not answer the phone and did not read her e-mails. She went over and over what had been said and agreed at the meeting. Like a tape playing on a loop that fifteen minutes of hell went round in her head. It was not a question of demotion, but a generous offer, she assured herself. Such a massive investment could only mean that Rower still counted on her as a valuable resource.

The following day Ana was informed by e-mail that at the follow-up meeting in Rower's management team it had been decided that she should be released from some of her areas of responsibility and undertake an intensive coaching programme specially developed for Rower. Theis was to supervise the task: revitalization of her commitment to Rower and restoration of her full working capacity. She had no choice but to accept the offer, keep her head down and conform. She was in free fall, drifting like a little white feather in and out of nothingness. She had an appointment with Theis the next morning, but how the coaching course would unfold and what final goal was envisaged was for the time being under wraps. Ana was to turn up without any preconceptions and as blank as a piece of white paper.

She had slept on a mixture of tranquillizers and sleeping pills and arrived at Theis' office feeling half-stoned. He bypassed the formalities and started directly, shooting from the hip.

'What is your survival strategy?'

'To focus one hundred percent on my work.'

131

'Are you not doing that at present?' Theis looked at her appraisingly.

'A completely new situation has emerged,' said Ana, distracted by the silent vibrations of her phone in her bag. She could not ignore it.

'What is it that stops you giving Rower your full attention?' Theis had changed from warm to cold since their last meeting.

'This number.' Ana stared euphorically at the display. She was again in contact with Mariama.

'You must keep to the matter in hand.' Theis ignored Ana's tête-à-tête with her phone.

'Another life, another place,' she murmured. The phone vibrated again. She got up with an abrupt movement and went out into the corridor. But she was too late. There was no-one on the other end. She went in again and stopped in the doorway.

'I'm sorry, it was important.' Ana looked past Theis to the white exhibition poster. She needed to explain to him that she had a problem with the colour white, that white provoked fear of empty space.

'This won't do. You can't take phone calls.' Theis walked to and fro in front of the whiteboard.

'Shall we carry on where we left off?' Ana held the phone in her hand.

'You must switch that off first.'

'As I said, I have encountered a problem.' Ana reluctantly switched off the phone.

'So actually you want to leave Rower?' said Theis confrontationally.

'Have you already fired me?' said Ana angrily.

'I'm just helping you to find out where you stand.'

'With one foot in each camp,' said Ana, and immediately regretted it.

'You feel motivated to leave Rower, but you're just not quite ready to do so yet?' Theis continued his provocation.

'No, I want to stay where I am.' Her throat constricted. It was as if she had fallen into a trap.

'Consider my questions as tools to help you understand yourself.' Theis changed tactics.

'I don't know which leg to stand on,' Ana admitted.

'What are we talking about in purely concrete terms?' Theis interrupted.

'It's private.'

'Nothing is private so long as you are under Rower's management.'

'My project is to get my work life sorted out, without work I am nothing,' Ana reminded him.

'If you are not honest with yourself, then we can't get any further.' He turned from the board and looked at her.

'I can't live up to my own standards, I feel ashamed to face my colleagues.'

'You have to give yourself permission to have the feelings you have, otherwise you can't separate them from your work.'

'I just feel chaotic inside,' she complained.

'Be so good as to tell me how this chaos has arisen.'

'It's this inequality,' she began hesitatingly, as if it was something criminal she had to explain.

'Unequal how?'

'Economically … '

'What's wrong with that?'

'It's humiliating.'

'For whom?'

'For me …'

'How do you intend to correct this inequality?'

'The more money I send down there, the more unequal it becomes.'

'Down where, to whom?'

'Gambia … a teenage girl and her family.'

'Can't you formalize your payments so that the situation becomes more manageable?' Theis shook his head.

'It never worked out like that. I couldn't get through to them with my suggestions about a regular payment.'

'You're the one who's paying, so surely you're the one who decides how it's going to be done.'

'The situation is not like that,' said Ana, irritated at not being understood.

'Then you must get the situation under control,' said Theis impatiently.

'It's not just a matter of money transfers,' said Ana aggrieved. Theis looked at her expectantly.

'I'm possessed … overwhelmed by her,' she corrected herself.

'What you're saying there belongs in a psychiatric department,' Theis cut her short.

'I didn't express myself clearly, I just want to be able to help her.' Ana could feel a rising frustration.

'Then help her and stick to that. And consider at the same time whether you're going to let a chance holiday acquaintance destroy your working life and career.'

'I'm not used to … feelings like that,' Ana defended herself.

'What feelings are we talking about?'

'For a person who is not close to me.'

'You said just now you were possessed, you can't get much closer than that,' said Theis baldly.

'I mean when compared to collegial relationships or friendships, love.' Ana felt uncomfortable.

'You have no family?'

'No, not any more.' Ana did not want to start on a discussion of family.

'So we can forget about that,' said Theis, satisfied, and continued: 'You must learn to manage these feelings which have arisen as a practical problem with a practical solution. I can't tell you what to do, only provide you with the tools for autonomous decision-making.'

'But this is not a practical problem,' said Ana agitatedly.

'It is what you make it,' said Theis firmly. 'Think positively, enter into your feelings and accept that you have them.'

'Are you trying to manipulate me out of Rower?' asked Ana in panic.

'Message not understood,' said Theis coldly.

'Sorry, that was a short circuit.' Ana was afraid of losing her lifeline to Theis.

'Have we got to the point where your work is irreconcilable with an emotional attachment?' he asked, ignoring her apology. Ana nodded reluctantly.

'If you cannot make room for both your working life and an emotional life, then you will be a bad worker.' Theis looked at her with concern. Ana got up from the leather chair.

'Time out,' she said. She had to get out and get some air.

'I can't tell you which way you should go. Just create a framework to help you understand yourself. The rest is up to you. Make a plan of action by tomorrow. Get control of your – shall we say – sponsor project and place it in a separate box where you can feel all the things you want to, and then we can carry on with a serious discussion of your work situation.' Theis shook hands with Ana. She left his room with an uncomfortable and diffuse feeling of anger.

On the way home she made another attempt to ring Mariama and got through at once.

'Ana, my Ana, why have you been hiding from me?' yelled Mariama into her ear.

'I've not been able to get through,' Ana protested.

'Big news! Big Man can get hold of the papers I need to get a passport.'

'We haven't agreed on that, Mariama.' Ana was not in the mood for new initiatives.

'A real passport, first class with photo and biometric fingerprints,' said the delectable, fragile little voice.

'I don't understand what you're talking about,' she said discouragingly, and felt at the same time strangely liberated by being out of control.

'Do you want to speak to him?' Mariama passed the phone to Big Man.

'Where has Mariama got this mixed-up nonsense from?' said Ana heatedly. She had still not come down to earth after her session with Theis; there was too much going on in her head at once.

'You asked me to give you a price.' Big Man was imbued with a mystical calm.

'I asked if there was a possibility that Mariama could get a passport, purely hypothetically.' Ana was fighting for her life.

'You gave me a commission, I give you a price.'

'And how much is it then?' she said. What was happening to her? She was no longer in control of herself. It was as if Mariama's will had taken her over.

'Fifteen thousand,' muttered Big Man.

'Dalasi?'

'Euros,' said Big Man, annoyed that Ana underestimated the effort involved.

'She won't be able to go anywhere with a passport.' Ana began to realize how crazy it was to consider his offer, even as a supposition.

'You will arrange a visa.'

'I've told Mariama many times that it is impossible for someone like her to enter the EU.'

'Then make it possible,' interrupted Big Man impatiently.

'Is this … a conspiracy?' Ana said gaily; her spirits rose higher and higher as she sank deeper into the quicksand.

'Do you want me to hire a people smuggler?' said Big Man threateningly.

'No, no,' shouted Mariama in the background, 'I don't want to be illegal.'

'Over my dead body,' Ana shouted back, hoping that Mariama could hear her. Mariama was not going to end up in the clutches of people smugglers and die in the desert and turn into a heap of bones in the sand or end up at the bottom of the Mediterranean off a hostile Italian island.

'You promised me, remember, Ana, you promised me.' Mariama had taken the phone back again.

'I didn't promise you anything,' Ana protested without conviction. She saw herself as if in a dream with Mariama at her side, freed from all worries and unease. What a joy to have that little dishevelled creature under her wings and share everything with her. Her solid future-proof finances, her large comfortable apartment, her Porsche, her holiday trips, her philosophy of life and world view. Everything she possessed should be Mariama's as well. Big Man was on the phone again and jolted her out of her dream visions.

'It's up to you. Give me a call when you've decided what you want,' he said finally. Ana was standing at her front door, and could not face the prospect of taking the lift up to her apartment and being alone between four walls.

In a kind of desperation it occurred to her to go and visit Uncle Frank, despite all the years which had passed. Her parents' close friend was to some extent justified in calling her his donor child, since he was the one who had undertaken her mother's insemination. Until now Ana had repressed the desire to uncover the secret of how she had been created, though she had a suspicion that it was not quite so technical as the impression her parents had conveyed. Frank had shown an interest in her and affection for her ever since she was tiny. It was as if he brought love with him. She cheered up and felt her cheeks grow warm when he came visiting and brightened up her parents' large and luxurious apartment, where she had never felt at home.

Frank's fertility clinic in outer Fredriksberg had expanded in line with scientific advances. Ana was the result of the first phase in fertility research, before it became possible to perform artificial insemination outside the womb and create so-called test-tube babies. Ana felt like a foreign body which would never have come into being if it had not been for biotechnological developments in Frank's field of research.

He was surprised and pleased by her unannounced visit, and invited her in to the director's office in the clinic. He asked with interest about how she was. Ana explained briefly that she was undergoing intensive treatment for stress. Their friendly relationship was really in contravention of the rules, and they maintained a strictly formal tone in their meetings. A biotechnologist and his product were not supposed to know each other personally. So there had been a good reason why Ana had not been told the truth about her origins, until Frank's unfortunate slip of the tongue.

'It is important that you respect the symptoms of stress, otherwise you risk them becoming chronic.' Frank chewed thoughtfully on his yellow plastic cigarette.

'I have been brought into the world to work and to fulfil the demands that are made on me,' Ana said awkwardly.

'That requires that you look after yourself properly.'

'You're not normally so … fatherly.' Ana threw discretion to the winds. She had come in order to ask him a direct question.

'You don't normally go on holiday. Thanks for the postcard,' he said. Ana could not remember sending any postcard; it must have been in the first days before Mariama.

'The package tour was an impulse buy, you have to try new things,' she said brightly, though it was not what she was thinking. It was a strange feeling, talking to Frank so informally after being apart for so many years.

'I think it would help you to tell me what's on your mind,' he said in a friendly tone. Ana felt unmasked, and had a strong desire to run away.

'I don't quite understand,' she said evasively.

'You are my own work, but of course that gives me no right to know about your private life and what you get up to on your holidays.' Frank looked over at the farthest corner of the office with its high ceilings.

'But when one of the people around you exposes themselves to danger, then there's a reason to pay attention,' her creator went on thoughtfully.

'You can't pay attention to all your … products.'

'I don't know any of them apart from you, it's against the rules,' he muttered to himself. Ana had never seen him look so shaken, so exhausted. He had gone grey in the face and was breathing heavily.

'Are you ill?' she asked, alarmed. Frank did not answer, but pressed his hand to the left side of his chest.

'Would you mind seeing me home?' he groaned painfully and got to his feet. He stood there swaying. Ana put her arm round him to stop him falling. He pulled her with him out of the clinic and locked the door meticulously behind them. The secretary had gone home.

In the metro Frank perked up again, colour came back to his cheeks and his eyes brightened. Ana went with him right to the door, into the hall and across to the lift; then she stood and waited. She had never visited him privately and was unsure whether he intended her to go up with him. He waved her in, and she managed to squeeze in before the door slid to. They ascended to the top floor. The apartment was just by the lift. Ana felt tense in the unfamiliar situation. She was annoyed that she was not wearing something more elegant now that she was to visit Frank for the first and possibly the only time. It felt like a solemn moment when he opened the door and let her precede him. He lived in a large studio with windows in the roof. The light came in from both sides and fused into a whitish haze which made the room float. Frank offered her a seat at the end of the long dining table while he made tea and buttered some biscuits and cheese.

Ana looked around. Everywhere there were photos of children. The same three faces at different ages. Ana could not take her eyes off them. He poured the tea. The scent of jasmine spread through the room.

'They're mine,' he said casually. They drank their tea in silence until Ana said:

'You have lovely children.'

'They take after their mother,' he said.

'Yes, of course,' Ana replied hurriedly. She did not go on. She had no right to enquire about his private life.

'More tea?' he asked.

'You recovered quickly,' she noted with satisfaction.

'A sudden indisposition is by its very nature something temporary,' he said, again in an almost paternal tone. Ana could not help wondering how he spoke to his own children, when he spoke so lovingly to her. But perhaps she was one of his own children? Ana looked round searchingly again. Frank reacted at once to her hesitation.

'You can talk freely to me,' he assured her.

'I need to share my holiday experiences with you and hear your assessment of what has happened to me.' Ana spoke in a low voice with her hand in front of her mouth, as if to capture the words before they emerged.

'I must make it clear: my professional expertise is all I can offer you. What goes beyond that you will have to find elsewhere.' Frank looked directly into her eyes.

'I have made a promise, and I intend to keep it.' Ana met his glance without blinking.

'What sort of promise?'

'To bring a young girl from down there to Europe.'

'You have lost your grip on reality.' Frank's voice had a metallic sound. The cheese biscuits stood untouched on the dish, the tea had gone cold, but the scent of jasmine still hung in the air.

'On the contrary, I've entered the world of reality,' she objected. Frank's hostility had made it easy for her to leave him.

'A battle of words,' he said dismissively.

'Reality is where Mariama is,' said Ana.

'Reality is where you are, and where I am.' Frank shook his head. 'You can't take over other people's reality,' he went on.

'I can't let her down,' she whispered.

'You are in the reality where you are physically present. And it is there you must fulfil your potential.'

'But my soul is elsewhere,' Ana insisted.

'I'm drawing a line in the sand here. I can't and won't function as your spiritual guide.' Frank got up and took the teapot out to the kitchen alcove with him. Ana got up too. She longed to go home to her own place. She needed time to digest Frank's reproof. The boundaries had been drawn unequivocally. What had she imagined would happen?

'I have you down as a sensible person. You must think this through carefully.' Frank stood leaning over the dishwasher.

'There's no way back,' said Ana quietly. She was glad that Frank did care about her after all.

'You have promised something that's impossible to carry out.'

'I know,' she said, subdued.

'Let me make a final attempt to persuade you not to do it.' He was suddenly speaking unnaturally loudly.

'It has meant a great deal to me that you are concerned for me and interested in how I'm getting on.' Ana had been young for so long, but now it was over once and for all.

'As far as I can see you are a victim of your feelings.'

'It's my own choice.' Ana felt a growing irritation at the fact that he did not understand her.

'You appear very determined.' Frank raised his bushy eyebrows. 'But you have gone astray,' he continued after a pause for thought.

'I'm sorry that you can't follow me.' Ana took her coat from the hatstand and was about to go, but before she had buttoned it up Frank did something completely unexpected. He hugged her, and held her in his arms as though he was never going to let go.

'Freedom means not having any parents,' he said and finally released her. She was totally floored. Her legs shook under her. Again she did not understand what lay behind his words. Whether they were meant as a consolation or whether there was a deeper philosophical meaning. Perhaps they were an answer to the question she had not asked. She looked over her shoulder at the photos of his children and imagined she saw herself. She guessed that they were about her age. Frank followed her gaze.

'They are pursuing careers in various parts of the world.'

'You have lovely children,' Ana repeated, overcome by the unfamiliar feelings his embrace had aroused in her. She had the sensation that she could fall apart at any moment.

'I talk to them once a month on Skype.' Frank's voice trembled, and he suddenly looked lost.

'There are many of us who have need of you.' Ana immediately regretted her cryptical remark.

'Things which should be kept separate must not be mixed

together.' Frank again spoke with distant authority.

'Biotechnology has come a long way since when I … ' she started. Frank shrugged and went over to the door. He stood there undecided. Ana took a last look around the elegant room with its Persian silk rugs, hand-printed cloths from the East and art on the walls. Frank cleared his throat and opened the door, letting Ana go first. Out in the corridor he cleared his throat again even louder, as if he had something stuck in it. He pressed the button and the lift came gliding silently up behind the wrought iron railings. He stood on the landing looking after her as she dropped down through the lift-shaft. She had not got round to asking the question which was burning on her tongue, but the resemblance to his children, especially his daughter, had given her the answer she was looking for. She was sure Frank was aware that she was now certain she had not been created by artificial insemination. Suddenly she saw her father's infinitely sad face in her mind's eye and had a bad conscience about having been born.

Ana got out of the taxi in front of the City Place House where Rower's London office had its premises on the eighth floor. She knew the area inside out and felt at home in the tall black glass building where you could see out but not in. She had been there so many times that the security guards greeted her as a member of the family and politely complimented her on her appearance, which always took her by surprise. She had never learned to see herself with other people's eyes.

The London meeting with representatives of a Dubai-based company ended with them negotiating a particularly successful agreement, so that they could sign a contract long before the estimated time. Ana took it as a sign that she was getting back on form. She sent Hans an affectionate thought. Without him and their relationship she would have been lost. After the obligatory drink with her London colleagues in their local pub Ana arrived at Ben and Beatrice's address in Kensington and realized that she had forgotten to buy flowers for her hosts. She was warmly welcomed, and was touched and grateful that they had made time to invite her at such short notice. They went up to the solidly furnished living room on the first floor, where Ben poured strong dry martinis for Ana and himself. Beatrice just had mineral water. They sat down in the colossal armchairs around a large square coffee table.

'Cheers.' Ben raised his glass and moistened his thick lips with the strong drink.

'Now, first of all the girl,' he said efficiently. Despite his casual clothes, a cardigan and soft corduroy trousers, he looked different and more exclusive than in his leisure wear in Gambia.

'As I said, Bea and I have agreed that we could use a young person to take over some of the daily work in the house.'

'Thank you, Ben, that means a lot to me.' Ana's voice broke. Beatrice excused herself and went down to the kitchen to prepare dinner.

'We're looking forward to having Mariama in the house. Bea is not so strong as she was. In fact she's not at all well.'

'I'm sorry to hear that.' Ana looked enquiringly at him.

'Bea doesn't like me talking about it, but she's in a critical state.' Ben stared thoughtfully into space. 'I really had to persuade her. She wouldn't admit that she can't manage everything herself, but we do need Mariama to help us with the housework. And not least, Bea needs company when I'm away from home on a mission for various lengths of time.'

Ana was ashamed of the stab of jealousy she felt at the thought that Mariama would be Bea's companion. That the two of them would have a much closer relationship than her and Mariama.

'I hope she'll be able to study and improve her English.' Ana mobilized all her altruism.

'For the time being we need to concentrate on getting her a visa.'

'That's what worries me most,' sighed Ana.

'Anyone who does not believe in miracles is not a realist.' Ben was lost in his own thoughts. His nonchalant optimism gave Ana the courage to be confident that the dream of Mariama would become reality.

'I had not expected dinner. It really is too much.' Ana felt that she was imposing.

'You need a decent meal. It'll be a long time before you're back home in Copenhagen,' said Ben. Ana refused a refill and looked around her. She had never been in a home with so many books and so much beauty. She herself had no more than a couple of shelves of airport novels and classical philosophy. Perhaps because she was a little in love, not with Ben but with his and Beatrice's relationship, she could not stop herself asking a personal question. These two people meant much more to her than purely business.

'How did you and Beatrice meet?' she said. Ben did not look upset at her directness.

'When we were students in our first year. Bea was more talented and got better grades than me. She was the star in our field, anthropology.'

'Aren't you a vet?' Ana remembered that from their first meeting at the hotel in Gambia. She had always had a photographic memory.

'I have many qualifications,' he said shortly and continued: 'I really looked up to Bea. Her health was already fragile even then. We knew from the first moment that we were going to be together. Of course we didn't know each other's backgrounds. But we soon realized that Bea's history began with her own birth, whereas mine went as far back as Adam and Eve, so to speak. On the spiritual level we are the same kind. Plato's two halves which seek and find each other, you know.'

'I don't really understand … Bea's own birth?' Ana found it difficult to conceal her curiosity.

'She is a scientific miracle,' said Ben, in a way that precluded further questions.

'Are you thinking of finding a partner yourself?' he went on.

'I have started thinking along those lines,' Ana admitted, 'if the right man shows up … or … perhaps he already has …

I wouldn't have anything against a committed relationship, though I'm perfectly fine with being on my own. I'm not a family person.'

'And who is the lucky man?'

'A colleague and friend.'

'You have to have a resolve to stay together if it's going to work.'

'Perhaps I don't have it in me,' muttered Ana.

'You just have to try it and see.'

'Mariama couldn't find a better place to live than with you.' Ana changed the subject to avoid having to talk about herself.

'You really are concerned about that girl.' Ben looked at her searchingly.

'She's important to me.' Ana cleared her throat in embarrassment.

'Your helpful gene?'

'No, not like that ... she's a ... soul ...'

'Are you certain that the financial sector allows for "souls" in its calculations?' Ben teased her.

'I can't find any other word.'

'Word for what?' Ben looked at her again with his penetrating glance.

'Word for Mariama.' Ana felt free and unconstrained in his company.

'Well, we'll look after your "soul" for you. That's if we can get permission to do so from the immigration authorities, but let's just attempt the impossible.'

'What you mean is that Mariama doesn't have a chance?' said Ana, disheartened.

'The arbitrariness and confusion surrounding the visa regulations in the UK gives us a slight advantage.' Ben radiated a self-confidence which made Ana's tension dissipate. They sat for a moment in silence. He put his hand on her shoulder.

'We are most grateful that you have agreed to be B&B Consultancy's financial adviser.'

'My pleasure,' Ana assured him. Her self-assurance was restored when she was in contact with dry figures, graphs and calculations.

Beatrice called up from the kitchen that dinner was ready. Ben stood up. He looked as if he was in good shape.

'Let us know how matters develop with Mariama,' he said.

'But what if the visa application is turned down?' Ana followed him down the stairs to the ground floor.

'We'll find a way out. There are always other ways of solving a problem.' Ben had connections and could press a few buttons higher up in the system.

'Thank you, dear Ben, thank you,' thought Ana. She looked upwards towards the beautiful wooden ceiling and suddenly doubted whether she was in the real world. Was her obsession with getting Mariama to Europe a fiction which bore no relation to Mariama's own wishes? Ana had never asked her. Just reacted to the girl's vague hints about coming to Europe as an au-pair. Perhaps 'visa' and 'Europe' were dream words which were suspended in thin air like freely available amulets for anyone who needed a hope to cling to.

The dining table in the large open kitchen was laid. They took their places and Ben opened a bottle of champagne. Ana felt oppressed by her knowledge of Beatrice's illness, and did not know what she should say. Outside it began to rain. Ben closed the door out to the terrace and the back garden. It was as if time stood still. They were so far from that euphoric evening and easy-flowing conversation in the restaurant at the Golden Bay Hotel. Beatrice broke the silence with her dark, melodic voice.

'No doubt Ben has aired his concerns for my health.'

'Yes, I'm worried about you, darling,' Ben put in. Beatrice took no notice, and carried on.

'It'll be difficult for me, you see, to have to take responsibility for a young person and make sure she benefits from her stay here. I'm afraid that she will get bored with me and my frailty when Ben is away.' Beatrice looked anxiously at him, and hardly seemed to register that Ana was present. Ana recognised the atmosphere between them from Gambia. Their ongoing conversation, which excluded her and at the same time initiated her into their spiritual fellowship.

'We'll do it together, darling, you're not alone.' Ben passed the toast round.

'When you are out on a mission I'm alone.'

'I shall only go on short missions, one or two weeks at a time, and you won't be alone, you'll have Mariama with you. That's the whole point.' Ben was so certain that he was doing the right thing for her.

'But that's what I mean, I shan't be particularly entertaining to spend time with.'

'You're not suppose to entertain her, you just welcome her and enjoy being in the company of a young girl, listen to music, go to exhibitions, all those things you haven't had time to do for years,' Ben argued persuasively. It was clearly a discussion they had had many times before. Ana did not want to get involved. Most of all she felt like cancelling the whole thing and just being herself again. As if she had read her thoughts, Beatrice suddenly turned towards her.

'You mustn't misunderstand me, Ana. I would be more than happy to have Mariama in the house. I'm just unsure of my own capacity when it comes to it.'

'The girl will be a relief, not a burden.' Ben's patience seemed to be infinite. He collected the plates and got up to serve the main course, pasta with homemade pesto.

'Bea's masterpiece,' he declared proudly. Beatrice's illness was yet another hurdle which Ana would have to overcome if she was to have any hope of bringing Mariama to London. Ben and Beatrice were her only chance.

'You must have faith, darling. Ana wants to help her young soul on its way.' Ben glanced conspiratorially at Ana. Beatrice looked startled, but made no comment. Her face shone with a dull translucency.

'And I will help you, my dear,' Ben added and pulled a face to make Beatrice smile.

'Two against one,' she said seriously, and drank a toast in mineral water. Ana did not like the turn the conversation had taken. She did not want to cause a quarrel between the two of them.

'You mustn't feel pressured,' she said hurriedly, feeling guilty that she had dragged them into her project with Mariama.

'Don't worry, it was a moment's heart-searching,' said Beatrice with her gentle friendliness, and offered Ana more pasta.

'Ben and I agree that we need some help in the house. So why not Mariama?' she said with a lightness which Ana did not find totally reassuring.

'Ana has said yes to being our financial adviser,' said Ben encouragingly.

'Thank you, Ana.' Beatrice seemed as fragile as if she were made of glass. In her naiveté Ana had overlooked the fact that impressions gained from a holiday acquaintance do not necessarily give a true picture.

'Let's give it a chance, shall we, Bea?' said Ben.

'Yes, of course.' Beatrice smiled a distant smile.

After coffee and Bea's homemade blueberry muffins Ben insisted on showing Ana round the house. Upstairs there were three bedrooms. Ben and Beatrice had one each and the third, at the end of the corridor, was to be Mariama's, he explained. It had been the children's room, and had seemingly not been touched since the child (or children) had left home.

'It needs sprucing up.' Unusually for him, Ben sounded tired. Ana noticed that it was an abandoned teenage room with rock posters and a battered loudspeaker with a heap of cables making the floor look like a serpents' den.

'We need a young person in the house, loud music, secret diaries and unrequited love,' said Ben. The thought of Mariama in that solidly comfortable and cultured London home seemed unreal to Ana. Her optimistic plan to give Mariama a better life had lost its gloss. She could no longer picture it.

'Ana, you'll see, it'll all work out,' said Ben as they were standing in the hall waiting for the taxi. Beatrice gave her a hug and assured her that she was a hundred percent positive about Mariama. Ana asked herself: 'Why are they doing this, why am I doing this?'

On the plane to Copenhagen she was overcome by despondency and wondered again whether it would not be more expedient for her to finance Mariama's education at home, where she belonged. A moment later she had swung over to the opposite view. Only if Mariama came to London could she be certain that she would really get an education. She would not spend the rest of her life reproaching herself and feeling guilty that she had not done everything that was humanly possible to secure her future. The more free business-class champagne she drank, the more convinced she became that there was a higher meaning to Mariama coming to London, living with Ben and Bea and being rescued from destitution by her sponsorship.

Ana leaned back in the wide aircraft seat and saw her new life pass before her eyes like a film with two female central characters, who after many tribulations are finally united. She closed her eyes and imagined how, after her emotional arrival, Mariama would slowly, as the months turned into years, blossom into an attractive, intelligent young woman formed in her image. They would become like sisters who resembled each other and yet were utterly different.

III

Imagination

The first Ana saw of her was when the automatic doors had closed behind her; she was standing still, blocking the way for the next group of passengers released into the arrivals hall. Mariama was looking around, irresolute, almost fearful, clutching to her a half-empty nylon sports bag. Her grey-black tufts of hair had been combed out and were as smooth and stiff as a wig. She was wearing clothes that were far too thin for the English climate. Ana had sent her generous funds to buy warm clothing, but they had obviously been appropriated for more urgent needs in the family.

She had become more grown-up, taller and more upright, but also thinner in the two years which had passed before she finally got her visa for the UK. She had not had the best bargaining chips with her incomplete school record. Even with reasonably good final-year marks from Kanifing Secondary School, a student visa was not easy to come by. And there had been an exhausting and nerve-racking process of disappointed hopes and euphoric optimism before Ana could finally pay two semesters' fees for Southwark College in advance, and provide financial guarantees for Mariama's residence with statements from her bank accounts.

In the intervening time, with Hans's back-up and loyal support, she had got herself more or less sorted out and recovered from the bad patch at Rower. The only flaw in her happiness was that she had had to decide to end the affair when she moved to London. She could not cope with a serious relationship and adjust to a new life with Mariama at the same time. She could still feel his body next to hers, feel how she had become a stranger to herself and like someone else together with him. Fantasy, fantasy, she thought and came back to earth again. She would not let herself be governed by a passing sentimentality. She had made her decision and needed to focus on the miracle which by dint of joint efforts had provided Mariama with a visa to the promised UK.

Mariama's effusive joy in the weeks leading up to her departure had been touching. Ana had been bombarded by mobile phone calls and tearful expressions of thanks, 'Thank you, thank you, thank you.' She was staggered that such a comparatively minor outlay could provoke an almost ecstatic gratitude. She had also had Mariama's mother on the phone. She had come in from her village to say goodbye and had spoken to Ana with a subdued, studied 'thank you' and immediately given the phone back to Mariama.

Mariama remained still as if rooted to the spot in the bustle of the airport. Ana waved to her with exaggerated arm movements, and registered a little flicker of disappointment, like the air going out of a balloon. It was almost an anticlimax after the long and tense wait for her finally to appear in the arrivals hall. Ana started to worry that something had gone wrong, that she had not been on board the plane at all. And at the information desk they could not tell her anything other than that the plane had landed on time, and that it was completely normal that it took a long time for passengers arriving by flights from West Africa to pass through passport control.

Mariama caught sight of the only face she knew, and began slowly and by fits and starts to move towards Ana, stopping short a few yards from her.

'I have missed you. My mother sends you her love. She is so happy for me,' she whispered breathlessly. Ana was close to tears.

'Let me take your bag,' she said. But Mariama would not let go of it.

'You must meet your hosts.' Ana laid her hand gently on her shoulder.

'Who?' Mariama pulled away from Ana.

'Just come with me, my dear,' said Ana calmly. 'I have told you that Ben and Beatrice are your hosts, but you can come to my place as often as you like. I live just nearby,' she assured her.

'I don't want to be nearby, I want to live with you,' said Mariama vehemently and turned away from her. Ana said nothing, and did not react to her opposition.

Ben and Beatrice, who until now had stayed in the background, came over to them. Ben held out his hand to Mariama and wished her welcome to London. Mariama reluctantly took hold of his hand with the tips of her fingers.

'Thank you,' she whispered, bending her head.

'Ben and Bea,' Ana introduced them.

'We've been looking forward to having you in the house,' Bea said, and gave her a hug.

'Come, we're going to go home and have something to eat, you must be dying of hunger.' Ben took hold of her bag. Mariama looked at Ana, confused.

'I am going to live with you, aren't I?' she whispered and held tight to her arm.

'Don't worry about it, Mariama,' she said. Mariama gave up and let Ben carry her bag out to the Land Rover which was waiting in the short-stay car park outside the arrivals hall. Bea took Ana's hand and gave it a reassuring squeeze as if to emphasize their joint responsibility. Did this concern mean that she had already lost Mariama to her and Ben? Ana felt strangely calm, like someone staring into the abyss. The diffuse state of fear she had lived in for these months leading up to Mariama's arrival had finally assumed concrete form.

Mariama was shown round all three floors at Ben and Beatrice's in Portland Road. She registered it all without any change of expression, showing no sign of being impressed by the comfortable furnishings. She just nodded in recognition, as if she had seen it all before in another life or in an American TV series. Ana was left to herself whilst Mariama was settled in her newly refurbished room, from which every trace of its former occupants had been removed.

She thought about how much closer she and Ben and Bea had grown through their joint efforts to get Mariama to the UK, and how much their friendship had meant to her during her first months in London. She had steered B&B Consultancy through the economic crisis without any significant losses, and in addition consolidated the firm's net capital. Slowly and surely she had risen in her friends' esteem, and had felt that her strange sensation of familial closeness to them had been confirmed.

During lunch Ana kept an eye on Mariama's reaction to the food, though she could not swallow a bite herself. But Mariama ate politely what was put in front of her. She behaved altogether like a woman of the world, adapting to the unusual situation with a distinctive, diffident elegance. Ana looked forward to going shopping with her and building up her wardrobe, and not least taking her to a good hairdresser. She had agreed with Ben and Bea that she would take care of Mariama's clothes and pocket-money, whilst they gave her board and lodging and a small wage for light housework. Then she could do what she wanted with her wages, that is send them all home to her family to be shared between her mother and Aunt Rosie. Mariama was, as she said herself, 'a good person', and very keen to take over the role as family provider since Rosie had lost her job at the bank.

There was a pleasant atmosphere around the table. Mariama took part in the conversation in the form of brief answers to the questions of her three benefactors. Suddenly she stopped and put down her knife and fork with a loud sigh.

'I am so tired,' she said, looking down at her plate.

'Aren't you hungry any more?' asked Ana awkwardly. She could not get used to her role as third party. Mariama shook her head.

'Why don't you go up to your room with Ana and unpack and have a rest whilst we clear the table,' suggested Bea, looking across at Ben. Mariama and Ana got up obediently and went upstairs.

Ana took the bedspread off and folded it neatly. Mariama threw herself onto the bed with her face to the wall. Ana sat down on the edge of the bed.

'I don't have anything to unpack,' muttered Mariama. Her long narrow back in the thin long-sleeved blouse emanated a heart-rending desolation.

'I do not agree, Ana,' she said and turned around.

'What don't you agree with, my dear?'

'Those two down there.' She pointed down through the floor.

'They are good friends, and like you they are "good people".'

'I miss you.' Mariama took her hand.

'I am right here,' Ana reassured her.

'Soon you will go, and I shall be all alone.'

'But we shall meet every day,' said Ana, knowing well that it would not be every single day.

'Since Aunt Rosie took me from my village to Serrekunda I have missed my mother all the time. I miss her here too.' Mariama sat up on the bed.

'You can ring your mother as often as you like.'

'She doesn't have a phone.' Mariama's eyes filled with tears, and she was once again the little girl Ana had met on the beach below Golden Bay Hotel. She put an arm around her shoulders and rocked her to and fro. She was surprised that she knew what to do without thinking about it. It was as if it was not her sitting on the bed with the child in her arms, but another maternal woman who had taken over her body.

'We'll see it through,' she whispered. Mariama shook herself free with a sudden movement.

'They searched me at the airport.'

'A body search?' asked Ana in alarm. Mariama nodded.

'Was that why it took such a long time for you to reach the arrivals hall? We had started to get worried about you.'

'Like this.' Mariama ignored her question and ran her hands down her body.

'With their hands?'

'With detectors,' said Mariama bashfully.

'Outside your clothing?'

'Of course,' she said not very convincingly.

'Was that all?' Ana insisted. But Mariama clammed up and withdrew into herself. Ana gave up trying to get anything more concrete out of her.

Mariama got up and began restlessly exploring the room and its contents. The writing desk was examined. The blotting-pad was looked at from all sides and put back in its place with the top downwards. The desk chair with its new beige leather cover was twirled round and round. The three empty desk drawers were pulled out one after the other and slammed shut again. She found the wastepaper basket under the desk and put it on her head, as if she was poking fun at herself.

'Put the wastepaper basket down,' said Ana.

'You are not the same Ana as in Gambia.'

'Of course I'm the same, take that thing off please,' said Ana irritated. Mariama stood there unmoved with the wastepaper basket balanced on her head.

'Put the basket down,' Ana insisted. Mariama did not move. Ana waited in silence. Mariama remained equally silent. In the end Ana gave up and went over and took the basket and replaced it on the floor.

'Come over here and sit down beside me,' she said gently. Where did it come from, this instinctive awareness of how to treat a child who was not a child any more, Ana thought to herself. Mariama sat down beside her. Ana felt a violent desire to confide in her.

'I left my job so that I could move to London,' she began. She found it difficult to say it out loud. She had not explained anything about the change in her circumstances to Ben and Bea, and they had not asked. They took it for granted that she had started work in the city.

'No work, no bread,' Mariama stated. Ana's cheeks burned. Her head was spinning. She had still not got over the shock of being informed that there was not after all, as she had expected, a three-year contract for her at Rower's London office in Basinghall Street.

'How can you have money when you don't work?' Mariama repeated sceptically. She was still not quite real for Ana, sitting there on the bed beside her as a strangely alien presence.

'I have money in the bank,' said Ana, giving a simplified explanation of her complicated paper finances. Mariama looked at her anxiously, as if her life now hung by a thin thread. Ana regretted having confided her changed circumstances, and was afraid that Mariama had misunderstood the situation and thought she had become poor, and would throw her over when she could no longer deliver the goods. Ana put her arm around her shoulders and pulled her close.

'Trust me,' she said, and then was almost scared of her solemn promise. Mariama pulled away from her. Her face was agitated.

'I can feel disturbance in this house, there is something here …'

'What do you mean?'

'My mother took me to an interpreter of dreams before I left. She was not pleased that there was a spirit in my dream.'

'But you don't believe in that sort of thing?' Ana felt an odd disappointment. Mariama looked right past her with a stiff expression. At that moment they heard Bea calling from the kitchen.

'What are you doing up there? Come down and have a cup of tea.' Bea sounded happy and upbeat. Ana stood up and smoothed down her skirt. She swayed a little to find her balance on her high heels. Mariama had taken off her uncomfortable shoes and walked barefoot down the steep stairs to the floor below.

Bea was on the way up to the living room with the tea tray. They had so many practical things to discuss, she said in passing. Ana had never seen her so radiant. She hoped it was a sign that she had got over her illness, which she and Ben had never fully explained to Ana. All four of them sat around the heavy coffee table. Mariama seemed oppressed, and kept glancing at Ana.

'Anything wrong?' asked Ben.

'It's just the journey,' Ana said quickly.

'Shall we go for a walk and show Mariama around the district?' suggested Bea. She lived in her own world and had not picked up that Mariama was out of sorts.

Mariama got up from the sofa and ran upstairs. Soon after she came back with souvenirs in transparent plastic bags and gave each of them a bag. A necklace of seashells for Bea, a pearl bracelet for Ana and an unpainted wooden mask for Ben.

'From my mother,' she said ceremoniously. Ana wondered what had become of Aunt Rosie. Had she resigned as foster mother in her disappointment at not being able to keep Mariama with her? Mariama had confided in her that Rosie's anger and curses were feared by the whole family.

'What a kind thought, my dear,' said Bea and embraced Mariama. Ben gave her a hug as well. Mariama looked enquiringly at Ana, which confirmed her feeling that there was a special and deeper connection between them.

Whilst Ana was lost in her own thoughts, letting the pearl bracelet run through her fingers, Mariama had been installed on the sofa between Ben and Bea, who had put the seashell necklace around her neck. Ana could not help admiring her soft dark beauty.

'Let's see your bracelet, Ana,' Ben's voice broke through. Ana passed him the bracelet and wondered that a few tourist souvenirs could arouse so much attention. The homely cosiness around the coffee table made her suddenly restless and gave her the feeling of having sunk into lethargy. She felt an urgent desire to work, to be on the go twenty-four hours a day.

'Can one of these masks frighten away human witches?' Ben held the mask up to his face. Mariama shook her head and searched for words.

'It is an old story,' she defended her reluctance to be quizzed on the West African belief in witches. But she made an effort to be a good guest as her mother had exhorted her.

She had finally found her again after the long time at Aunt Rosie's with no other contact than an occasional greeting sent with relatives who had visited the village. Europe had given her back her mother, and then immediately taken her away again.

'It would be a good idea to show Mariama the district as Bea suggested, so that she can see where I live, that it's quite close to you,' Ana interrupted Ben's intense study of the wooden mask which Mariama's mother had brought with her from the village. Mariama stood up, visibly relieved.

'Then we can all three walk you home,' said Ben enthusiastically to Ana, who longed to get back home and be alone. She needed to let the reality of Mariama in the flesh sink in after the long waiting time full of frustrating phone conversations, money changing hands and worries that she would not get her visa after all, and that the whole project would run into the sand. She needed to get used to Mariama's presence, which affected her as if she had a fever. They parted hastily and without looking at each other near Ana's entrance in Henry Dickens Court, which was ten minutes' walk from Ben and Bea's.

Mariama walked back to the house in Portland Road feeling squeezed between her two hosts. They were two pale white shadows on either side of her. It confused her that there was both Ana, her sponsor, and Ben and Bea, whom she was to live with. She had noticed at once that the narrow yellow house gleamed with order and harmony, but at the same time the splendour was encased in a grey sadness, the same melancholy she had inside herself, and which she would assume as a cloak of invisibility to protect her against evil spirits.

The moment they came in through the door she asked permission to take a bath and spend some time in her room. Bea assured her that that was fine, and she should just let her know if there was anything she needed. They ate at eight o'clock, but she would call her if she forgot the time. Mariama closed the door to her room carefully in order not to draw attention to herself, pulled out her bag and fished a set of clean underclothes out of it. Mariama's mother – it could only be her mother – had placed a prayer mat at the bottom of her bag without her noticing. It was blue with an embroidered pattern in shades of green like the sea at Bakau.

Her mother was aware of Rosie's nonchalant attitude to religious precepts, and in Mariama's hearing she had reproached her for her shortcomings as an educator in that respect. But her mother's timid manner prompted Rosie to defend herself with a violent counterattack, citing her pressurized situation as a single mother of five small children and a foster daughter who required not only schooling but also school materials and school uniform. Mariama's mother admonished her sister that in that case she and her children and Mariama had even more need of Allah's protection. She spoke in such a low voice that Mariama, who was sitting beside her, could hardly hear what she was saying. It was the day before her departure for Europe, which was also the day her mother would leave for the long journey back to her village.

Mariama had a bath and scrubbed herself in a kind of rage with the hard yellow sponge until her body was burning hot and reddish-purple like an aubergine. Despite her strenuous washing, first in the bath and then under the shower, she still felt unclean. The last remnants only prayer could remove. She towelled herself lengthily and thoroughly dry with the large bath towel. She tiptoed into her room and put her long skirt on, and a light scarf round her head. Then she laid the prayer mat out on the floor beneath the window, which she imagined to herself was facing Mecca. She locked the door whilst she prayed, so that Bea could not come bursting in to remind her that time was up. She was grateful for her hosts' hospitality, but her heart was with Ana who had fulfilled the dream she had carried with her ever since she had begun to work on the beach under Rosie's auspices, when she could hardly carry the weight of the heavy fruit tray.

She could feel the rough pattern of the prayer mat against her knees through the material of her skirt. Her mother's thoughts were woven into the little square mat which had accompanied her on the long journey she had so thoughtlessly wished for. She murmured Allah's names and prayed with an intensity she had not felt since she was a small child and prayed together with her mother at sunrise. She prayed for her purity, that the shame which had entered into her at the airport would be wiped from the great balance sheet and she would be reborn as she was before. She let herself be transported into the highest heaven. She was lighter than the birds, lighter than the air, weightless like the angels. She passed cloud castles of mother-of-pearl and fountains with brightly-coloured shoals of fish. She could see into worlds of unknown beauty. With her forehead resting on the mat she sank into eternity.

She stood up and folded the mat. She felt purified and cleaner than clean. 'Cleanliness is next to godliness' was what she had learnt at her mother's knee, but she knew that it only lasted until the next prayer, and that she must not neglect a single prayer if she wanted to keep her cleanliness. She wished she had her mother by her side and could benefit from her spiritual guidance, which she had not felt the need of in Serrekunda, where Aunt Rosie's word was law and she made do with praying every now and then, when she remembered to. But Rosie had kept her promise and had sent her to school for most of the months in the year. Mariama had been lucky compared to other foster children. The stars in the heavens looked kindly on her. She looked forward to becoming a shining star herself when the time came.

Ana had not yet really settled in to the little north-facing flat in Henry Dickens Court. Her involuntary and unaccustomed leisure filled the rooms with an emptiness which provoked migraines, made worse by strong light and sudden move-ments. She walked quietly around in semi-darkness and wore sunglasses when she watched television or went outside in daylight. Mariama's arrival had placed additional strains on her nervous system. For the next few days she would have to cut herself off completely from the rest of the world.

She had brought only a few personal things to the flat. An album of photos from her student days, which immortalized hostel parties and all the lost relationships from the time when the world was wide open. She was quite moved at the sight of all that youth she had been a part of twenty-five years ago. On the windowsill in the living room she had placed an owl in Royal Copenhagen porcelain, which her father had presented her with in order to remind her to use her head and her reason. She had followed his discreet encouragement and had distanced herself so much from her parents that she had completely lost sight of them. When the shame over their betrayal had dissipated, they had simply disappeared together with it. She never gave them a thought. They did not exist in her consciousness, not even as a New Year's resolution. But in that dark little furnished flat, which was the diametric opposite of her banished childhood home's elegant spaciousness, misty flashes of memories began to crowd in on her like filmic flashbacks. Fragments of forgotten episodes, faces which suddenly swam up to the surface, voices which rose from the ocean depths, carried by the freewheeling memory of someone shipwrecked.

The all-absorbing work at Rower had made her youthful memories and ancient traumas disappear into the darkness of repression, where she was convinced they belonged. But things had not worked out as she and the management team on Amager Boulevard had planned. She had anticipated that she would slip effortlessly into the leader team in London, with whom she had worked regularly during her years at Rower International. But the door had been slammed in her face, and remained shut for the time being. Rower's London branch had to reduce its workforce by ten percent. She had however arranged an interview with their HR manager for whenever it became clearer how the financial crisis was panning out.

Ana sat in the kitchen listening to Wagner on her iPod whilst she waited for four o'clock, when she could ring Jakob. She had sent him an SOS text message and got the appointment for her telephone coaching moved forward. She needed guidance to get through the first period with Mariama. She could not control the strong feelings she had for her. She did not understand where they came from and what they involved. Only that they made her forget Hans and erased her feelings of loss of the mental stability the relationship had given her. Jakob had been recommended by the firm coach, and she paid him out of her own pocket. The two courses of eight sessions which Rower had generously funded for her, and which she took as proof that they valued her contribution to the firm, had long ago been used up. But whether they had been a welcome-back present or a farewell present she was no longer so certain.

Normally Jakob answered immediately, but his phone was switched off. That was disturbing, almost against the laws of nature. She sat ready with the phone in her hand and could not concentrate on the book open in front of her. Quite by chance she had found Seneca's little study of the concept of time and human mortality in a bargain book bin on Holland Park Avenue, and regarded it as a sign that she had reached a new phase in her life. She had to read it slowly, word for word, in order to grasp the meaning. That was how far she had distanced herself from her original subject at university, philosophy. In return she had carved out a dream career which brought her into contact with global finance centres and as a bonus gave her a comfortable existence and a solid economic surplus. That meant more to her than all the philosophy in the world. But her disappointment with Rower's London office had given her a need for intellectual nourishment.

Finally Jakob rang back and freed her from her oppressive thoughts.

'Sorry, sorry, my son had to go to casualty after a bad accident on his bike, but it's all OK now.' He was almost shouting.

'Where have you got to right now?' Jakob's tone changed.

'Mariama has arrived in London.'

'And?'

'I can't cope.'

'Why not?'

'I don't know where I am.'

'Let's go back a bit. You have had a heartfelt wish come true.' Jakob did not sound quite so focused as usual.

'Obviously you should be careful what you wish for,' Ana muttered.

'For whose sake did you want to bring Mariama to London?'

'I couldn't bear the thought that she would be lost, without education and without work,' she replied uncertainly.

'Was that a real possibility, or just something you imagined, that she would not get through without your involvement?'

'It's not my imagination,' said Ana hotly.

'So we're talking about emergency aid?'

'No, it's something different.'

'How different?'

'More personal.'

'How personal?'

'I just know there is some kind of fundamental connection between us.'

'How are things with your friends?'

'Ben and Bea are everything I am not.'

'Can you give me a couple of examples of what they are and you are not?'

'They are one hundred percent straightforward in everything they do.'

'And you are not?'

'Mariama is better off with them.'

'Well then, it was quite right of you to leave her with them,' Jakob remarked drily.

'Yes, perhaps, but it doesn't make it any easier,' she said, irritated at his rapid conclusion.

'Easier for whom?'

'For all of us.'

'What is not easy for Mariama?'

'She would rather be with me.'

'Time will tell. - What is not easy for Ben and Bea?' Jakob continued.

'That they have me as a hanger-on, superfluous dead weight.' Ana got up and went over to the window to look down into the yard, where some boys were playing football with an empty beer can.

'It was your project to start with,' he objected. Ana did not answer.

'What is not easy for you?' Jakob was impatient.

'That I'm wandering around here with nothing to do.' Ana sat down again.

'How long have you been in London?'

'Six weeks.'

'Well, that's no longer than a normal summer holiday. Which to the best of my knowledge you haven't had for many years.'

'I am completely useless.'

'Mariama needs you.'

'She is better off with Ben and Bea,' Ana repeated.

'You must not let yourself be ruled by fear.'

'Fear of what?'

'Fear of your feelings for Mariama, when you have after all chosen to put her top of your agenda.'

'Perhaps that was the wrong decision.'

'You can't go back on the decision to have a child.'

'I'm not avoiding my responsibility,' said Ana angrily.

'OK, that's enough for today,' Jakob finished off.

'Thanks for your time. I don't know what I'd do without you.'

'Bye for now and take care.' Jakob rang off briskly. Off to his son who'd had the accident, Ana thought to herself, and immediately rang Ben and Bea. It was Mariama who picked up the phone.

'Where have you been for so long?' she whispered. Her gentle reproach made Ana feel guilty about her passive self-absorption.

'I'm coming over to see you straight away,' she said hurriedly.

'No, I want to come and see you,' Mariama insisted.

'Can you find the way on your own?'

'I have walked over many times and stood in front of your house.'

'What?'

'I couldn't find your name on the door panel.'

'Can I speak to Ben or Bea?'

'They're working.'

'Give them my regards and say you're coming over here. Then they can come and get you when they've finished work,' Ana suggested. If there was anything she had respect for, it was work.

'I'm coming now,' said Mariama eagerly. Ana had to restrain herself from warning her to be careful to find the right way and look both ways when she crossed the street. She found it difficult to imagine her as a town dweller who was used to negotiating the traffic chaos of Serrekunda.

Ana stood on the landing to receive her as Mariama walked up the stairs at a slow and almost meditative pace, gnawing on an apple.

'How are you?' asked Ana.

'Too much housework like at Auntie Rosie's.' Mariama was wearing a blue padded jacket over a pair of loose woollen trousers which hid her slender figure. Ana guessed that they were some of Bea's cast-offs.

'Did you invite Ben and Bea round to tea?' she asked. Mariama shrugged her shoulders and nodded at the same time.

Whilst Ana made tea Mariama explored the flat in minute detail. Ana was not keen on being subjected to such scrutiny and exposing the mess there was in her drawers and behind cupboard doors. Even under the bed her shoes and clothes lay in a tangled heap and had lost all significance as practical items of clothing. Ana called her into the living room. She was not prepared for a visitor and only had some dry biscuits to go with the tea. Mariama sat down in a ladylike fashion with her legs crossed in a way that reminded her of Bea, and looked around.

'Is this your things?' she said sceptically, turning towards Ana.

'I rented the flat furnished,' said Ana. Mariama was visibly disappointed. Ana poured tea and enjoyed waiting on her.

'Have you rung your mother and told her you've got here safely?' she said, surprised at herself for expecting a thoughtfulness from Mariama which she herself had never lived up to.

'I've told you I can't ring her,' Mariama replied impatiently.

'Well Aunt Rosie then?'

'She has gone. Left.'

'Where to?'

'Back to the village. To her husband.'

'You can ring Aunt Rosie from my mobile,' said Ana, trying to adjust to the news.

'I want to ring my uncle in London first.'

'Why didn't you ring him from Ben and Bea's?'

'I would rather ask you,' whispered Mariama, looking around the living room as if the walls had ears.

'Be sensible now, Mariama. Ben and Bea are your hosts here in London, and only want you to do a little housework.'

'A lot of housework,' she protested.

'What is it you do?' asked Ana cautiously.

'I get up first in the morning so that there is not a queue for the bathroom, as Bea says, and make breakfast for all three of us. Ben has a tray brought up. He is not a morning person.' She was clearly not happy at having to provide a report.

'They begin work in the office at half-past eight. I clean the house in the morning and make lunch for one o'clock. When I've finished in the kitchen I sometimes go shopping. And then I am free until six o'clock, when we all join in making dinner in a sort of family way.' Mariama reeled off her work schedule as if she had learnt it by heart.

'You will be well looked after at Ben and Bea's. You just need to get used to being there.'

'But you are my sponsor,' she said, at one and the same time distressed and cross.

'You can come round here whenever you are free.' Ana had to pinch herself to remember that it was not just a dream that she was sitting here on her sofa with Mariama beside her and talking as if they were already part of the same family.

'Thank you, thank you, Ana,' she said irritably, and pulled away from her.

'Is something wrong?'

'They just took us out … and into a little cold room,' Mariama said angrily.

'That does sound unpleasant.' Ana had forgotten all about Mariama's experiences at Gatwick, but she realized immediately what it was she was referring to.

'I had to stand with my arms out to the side and … my legs too.' Mariama had curled up on the sofa.

'Everywhere … under my arms … and under …' she pointed discreetly to her breasts.

'… and between my legs and after that … with their hands,' she whispered and could not bring herself to speak of what had happened, the violation. Ana was struck by a vague feeling of guilt and did not know what to say.

'I felt faint … everything went black … I was allowed to sit down on a bench.'

'What were they looking for?' Ana tried to keep a clear head.

'Drugs,' she said off-hand as though it was something everyone should know. She had had no idea herself what it was the officials were looking for until one of her fellow passengers resisted and shouted out that not all West Africans were fucking drug mules with bellies full of dope from Bolivia. He was quickly overpowered and led away. And she had been very frightened about what might happen to her.

'Fortunately you were more frightened than hurt,' Ana tried to console her.

'I got my passport back … and was taken over to the luggage belt …'

'I'm sure they were just following rules, they have to stop the drug traffic into Europe,' said Ana mostly to herself, whilst she considered whether she ought to complain.

'Then I don't like the rules,' said Mariama again with offended anger in her voice.

'I'm sorry you had such an unpleasant reception. Can't you try to forget it?'

'That's not for me to … decide.'

'I don't want anything bad to happen to you,' Ana assured her, to make her understand how she felt for her.

'What do you mean, bad?' said Mariama in alarm.

'You are so young and pretty,' she said, in order not to frighten her unduly.

'Don't worry, Ana, I am not pretty at all,' she said, patting Ana on the arm.

'In my eyes you are the most beautiful flower in the garden and the loveliest tree in the forest.' Ana wondered where such children's drawing images came from.

'How nice of you.' Mariama was not sure how to react to Ana's maternal declaration of love, which was so different from Auntie Rosie's no-nonsense manner.

'I'll never let you down.' Ana gave her a hug.

'Thank you, thank you, Ana,' said Mariama and passively let herself be hugged. That eternal thank you, thank you, suddenly felt like an insurmountable barrier between them.

'I wish my mother could see me in Ben and Bea's house. I wish she could see that such riches exist in reality,' she suddenly exclaimed excitedly.

'Ben and Bea aren't rich,' Ana objected.

'But the house, the Land Rover, all that furniture and things?' asked Mariama.

'It's just an ordinary house.' Ana suddenly felt doubtful. She herself was in the higher income bracket, and perhaps Ben and Bea's income was at the same level. She had never thought about it. Money was something which only occupied her professionally.

'I don't like sleeping alone,' Mariama went on.

'But it's a lovely room you've got.'

'But so much space all to myself and such a big house just for three people. As if those who lived there are dead and Ben and Bea are the grieving relatives.' Mariama shuddered.

'You must remember that it is their work space as well,' Ana said in defence of her friends' living arrangements.

'I've never seen anyone back home work as much as those two. They work all the time, at night as well. There are no visitors who come to the house, only people who come to meetings behind the closed door of the office.' Mariama spoke so quickly that her words tumbled over one another, and went on to explain to Ana that Bea and Ben never checked whether she skimped her work or left something undone. They were what Rosie called softliners, just like her mother. Softliners did not have the respect of those around them. Ana on the other hand had Mariama's respect because she was not just a tourist on the beach but her sponsor, who made good things happen.

'Shall we find a time to go into town and buy you some clothes?' said Ana, bucked by Mariama's declaration of confidence.

'I miss you, Ana,' she answered a little too automatically. She never looked directly at her.

'There's a lady who sits and begs outside Tesco's,' she continued off-hand.

'I've not noticed that.'

'I give her coins.'

'You should keep away from that sort,' Ana warned her. Mariama stared ahead defiantly.

'I'll come back to Ben and Bea's with you. I don't think we should wait for them to come here.' Ana got up and looked at her watch.

'They work too much,' repeated Mariama worriedly. Ben and Bea were an exact copy of Mr and Mrs Brown in her first English book. They spoke the same perfect English and belonged to the same stalwart British stock who according to the book loved their houses and their scented rose gardens and said 'My home is my castle.'

Ana was on her way to Tesco's on Holland Park Avenue. She liked to go shopping in her faded track suit with just her Burberry over it. At once she noticed the thin fair-haired woman by the entrance, which shone with a blaze of light in the fading gloom of the afternoon. She was shivering in her thin nylon jacket, and raised her cigarette to her mouth with a gloved hand. The pavement between the tall plane trees and the house fronts with shops and cafés looked like an outdoor living area. The woman was sitting there sunk into herself. Her tousled hair swayed like a bird's nest. Then she suddenly turned her head and said something. As if in a trick photo Ana saw Mariama inserted into the picture behind and to the side of the woman on the narrow concrete steps.

Ana stopped with her back to them, examining a shop window with exotic plants and bonsai trees. She could not help hearing fragments of their conversation.

'You stupid or wha'?' the woman said to Mariama, who had politely asked her to repeat what she had just said.

'It's beneath my dignity to repeat myself,' she went on peevishly. She looked ill. Mariama did not respond but just waited patiently. The woman told her to shove off, she couldn't be bothered to talk to people who didn't understand.

'English rules the world. Without English you're nothing,' she snuffled, sucking coffee through the lid of her beaker. Mariama remained calmly sitting there with her shopping net in her lap, watching the people passing by. The woman offered her a sip of the cold coffee; she had obviously taken her into her favour again.

Mariama refused the offer, got up and disappeared into Tesco's.

'Take it easy, take it easy,' the woman shouted after her. She sat there with her empty coffee cup and the placard with its 'Young and Hungry' sob-story, intended to make the well-dressed Tesco customers feel guilty about their full shopping bags. Ana didn't think she looked so young that she should be advertizing the fact. She stood and waited for Mariama to come out with her shopping. In the meantime the woman had been joined by a large-bellied cowboy type, and looked even smaller in his shadow. The mere sight of them made Ana feel a violent revulsion. She and Ben and Bea had laid great stress on warning Mariama that London could be dangerous for a young girl like her, but she had obviously not realized the seriousness of the warnings since she mixed with that kind of riff-raff.

Mariama came quickly out of Tesco's with a few things in her shopping net. To Ana's relief she hurried past the woman and her partner and gave no more than a discreet wave of the hand as she passed. It was only after she had disappeared down Portland Road that Ana approached the entrance to Tesco's and passed just in front of the wretched couple, who were sitting with a joint begging bowl between them, each swigging from a bottle. She felt a strong desire to kick the split plastic cup with its miserable couple of coins into the gutter.

After Mariama started at Southwark College a noticeable change came over her, which became more and more explicit with each weekend visit. Ana was dissatisfied with herself and her lack of ability to handle her relationship with the more independent and autonomous Mariama. She could not cope with emotional conflicts, and attempted to take first a hard line and then a soft one, but was not herself in either of them. They were just roles she assumed like spare coats, borrowed feathers from the fringes of pedagogy. She had no experience from her own life to draw on. When she was Mariama's age she had already broken all ties with her parents.

Every time Mariama was on the point of going out they had a disagreement. She insisted on travelling alone over to her uncle's family in Upton Park and would not be swayed in her determination. Ana warned her that it was dangerous to wander around the streets of London in the evening, with escalating violence and knife crime with young foreign students as particular targets.

'I've been in London long enough, I don't need to be taken everywhere like a little child,' Mariama retorted; she brandished her passport with her date of birth in it and asked Ana to work out her age.

'A birth certificate produced by Big Man, who can conjure up any kind of official document on request, doesn't prove anything at all,' said Ana heatedly, repressing the fact that it was she herself who had paid for the papers.

'The birth certificate got me a passport at the police station in Kotu so that I could apply for a visa to the UK,' Mariama rejoined triumphantly.

'Then you must take a taxi at least,' Ana insisted.

'London is not at all like you and Ben and Bea say it is. I've only met kind and friendly people,' Mariama objected, irritated at her hosts' constant concerns about whether she could cope in London, when she had much more need of their advice and guidance on far more serious questions.

'You mean people like the ones you hang out with down at Tesco's,' Ana remarked tartly.

'They are my friends, Birdy and her fiancé.'

'I don't want you to associate with characters like that.'

'I like the fact that they're always sitting in the same place when I go down to Tesco's. They tell me many things,' Mariama explained.

'They are not good company for you.'

'Then I'm not good company either.' Mariama stormed out into the hall. Ana ran after her and tried to push some notes into her hand.

'You can at least take a taxi,' she demanded. Mariama turned towards her, furious. She had become less receptive to her generosity.

'It's a waste of money. There are so many buses in London. Taxis are a good thing in Africa, where people are forced to walk for long distances.' She spoke to Ana like a teacher, and had begun to talk about Africa rather than Gambia.

Ana imagined that she was under the influence of her fellow students, fanatical types amongst the more diligent and well-spoken student body. She imagined a great deal in order to compensate for the fact that Mariama was not particularly communicative about her college life. Just like when they separated on the hotel beach and Ana was petrified at the thought of what might happen to Mariama in the closed and impenetrable world she was returning to. She feared that Mariama was in the process of creating her own independent life in London, which would be every bit as closed to her.

Mariama was in a hurry to depart, and hardly had time to receive Ana's greetings to her uncle and a box of chocolates for the family. They had agreed, or at least Ana had agreed, that she should be home by midnight at the latest.

'My cousins will meet me at Liverpool Street Station and bring me back again,' Mariama assured her. She could not understand Ana's fixation on clocks and time.

As soon as she was out of the door Ana became restless and could not settle to anything. She made sure that her mobile was within reach, in case Mariama should ring and ask for help, money, anything at all. Any little thing she could do for her would be a relief. She was sitting on the sofa, aimlessly zapping between American shows, when the well-known fragment of Beethoven's ninth rang out like a hymn of liberation. She hardly dared to believe that it was Mariama. Behind her she could hear laughter and loud voices, an unmistakable party mood.

'I shall stay at my uncle's tonight. He does not want me to travel home so late. He sends his regards and thanks you for the present and scolds me and asks why I did not bring you with me. Forgive me, Ana. Next time you must visit him together with me, he says. They all send greetings. I'll see you tomorrow.'

Ana could have fallen to her knees. Thanks to this family which she had feared would reject her, but which had obviously accepted her sight unseen, Mariama was once more the gentle, trusting girl she had met on the beach below Golden Bay Hotel. Ana got drunk out of pure gratitude.

Mariama's weekend visits became shorter and shorter. Their contact had gradually become restricted to phone conversations and brief café meetings. Ana did not know what to say to her to get her to open up. Which questions she should ask, what kind of enticing offers and suggestions she should make to dissolve the tension. Mariama's reticence made her unsure of herself, and she felt that she wasn't good enough. She went to see Ben and Bea to confide her distress, but they had not had the same experience and could not understand her. Mariama had entered wholeheartedly into her studies and had already made friends, they said, confirming Ana's impression that it was her there was something wrong with. Did a couple inspire more confidence than a singleton? Was a singleton in herself the embodiment of a threat to law and order? Was a single existence still confused with good old-fashioned loneliness, which created monsters?

'She is polite and well brought up and doesn't take anything out of the fridge without asking first,' Bea remarked.

'She's miserable and not especially entertaining.' Ben's patience had its limits. He had grown up with servants.

'She's homesick, that will pass,' Bea defended her.

'Perhaps she just doesn't like us,' said Ben ironically, and disappeared down to his office.

'You can't help getting fond of the girl,' Bea continued the conversation. Her attractive hands were folded in her lap.

'That's true,' said Ana evasively. She couldn't bear being reminded that she didn't have Mariama all to herself.

'It is lovely to have a family again,' Bea went on, as if she had read Ana's ambivalent feelings.

'Yes,' said Ana, not understanding what she meant. Bea moved uneasily on the sofa and suddenly looked harassed.

'Ben is very tied up right now. We need to decide soon whether to reduce the number of projects or give one of our ad hoc consultants a permanent contract.'

177

'Can I not help?' Ana suggested.

'You have already helped us by redistributing the firm's assets. Without you we would have gone bankrupt,' Bea said drily.

'You must just tell me if there's anything I can do.'

'But do you have time while you're working?'

'Work is on stand-by for the present. On the other hand it gives me more time for Mariama. That's important for me right now, perhaps more important,' said Ana, uncertain as to whether she really regarded her situation in that light. If she had known just a couple of years ago what was in store for her, she would have regarded her present existence as the end of the world.

Mariama had arrived on an unannounced visit. She had her own keys and was suddenly standing in the living room without Ana having heard her.

'What a nice surprise.' Ana put the TV off and got up from the sofa. She was not dressed for visitors, and felt as if she had been caught napping.

'I've got work at Sainsbury's in Charing Cross Road.' Mariama was radiant with satisfaction.

'So long as you don't neglect your studies,' Ana admonished her, worried that she was already on the slippery slope. Not least after her experiences outside Tesco's and Mariama's defence of her so-called friends.

'I need the money to send home. It's only twenty hours a week,' she added hastily, eager to get Ana's approval.

'But they must understand that the most important thing is for you to concentrate on your studies.' Ana was heartily sick of the family's interference. And Mariama had to explain to her for the hundred and seventeenth time that it was her duty to pay the family back for the life and the care she had received, which from the moment of her birth had left her with a bottomless debt.

'What do Ben and Bea say about you working?' Ana suddenly felt that Mariama's style of dress reminded her too much of Bea's.

'They don't know about it yet.' Mariama looked disapprovingly at the mess in Ana's kitchen, and asked if she might clear up. Ana ignored her indirect reproach and gave her a free hand.

Whilst she did it, Mariama told her proudly about her work as a cashier. She liked all the faces which passed by her with their Sainsbury's discount cards. The customers were of all ages and all colours. No discrimination as long as they could pay for their shopping, the staff manager had impressed on the new recruits who were starting on a two-week probation. But the East Europeans' bad English did annoy her, she complained, nothing but gibberish came out of their mouths. She preferred the regular customers, whose faces she had by now learnt to recognise.

'So you've already started at Sainsbury's?' Ana asked, feeling sidelined.

'I've almost finished my probation, but I will get the job,' said Mariama self-confidently. She had finished putting the dirty cups and plates into the dishwasher, and had to leave.

Before Ana could get round to asking where she was going, her mobile phone rang. Mariama uttered a deep sigh when she saw the number on the display, and disappeared into the bedroom. She spoke in her high shrill voice, which went through doors and walls.

'No, I have no wages yet. I can't do that, it is not allowed for students to work more than twenty hours a week. New roof? And new TV? Yes, but Momo has lived in England for many years. He has his own firm. A brand new car next year? Yes, he is a good son. Auntie Rosie, listen, I'm doing what I can. I shall send you a present soon. I know that you have done everything for me,' she finished impatiently. She came back into the living room and sank down onto the sofa, wiping the sweat from her forehead with the back of her hand.

'What's going on?' said Ana anxiously.

'I'm always being told about the neighbour's boasting: Momo sends this and sends that. They think I can just bend down and pick up fifty-pound notes from the street. They are so ignorant about what it's like in Europe. And I have believed them and listened to them for as long as I can remember,' she wailed.

'Can I do anything?' asked Ana. Mariama waved her hand dismissively.

'My mother does nothing but demand a souvenir from London which she can show off in the village. She rings every day from the neighbour's phone and tells me off because she is getting into debt in order to ring me up.' Mariama suddenly looked tired and stressed.

'She says she has a right to know how her daughter is getting on, now that she is out of the family's reach and has no-one to guide her. I try to calm her by telling her I have Aunt Amina and Uncle Sulay in Upton Park, but I don't tell her that they are too busy to concern themselves with what I am doing and how I am getting on amongst the English. Aunt Amina has a cleaning job in the morning and is a shop assistant in Accessorize in the afternoon until ten o'clock at night, and Uncle drives a taxi twelve hours a day seven days a week, so that my cousins can study.' Mariama got up and was already on her way out of the door. Ana felt powerless when she could not solve her problems with a sum of money.

'Tell me if I can help you with your written work. Don't you have to hand something in soon?'

'There's plenty of time.' Mariama wanted to be off.

'Take care, my dear.' Ana gave up in the face of her evasiveness and let her go.

'Thank you, Ana, for everything.' Mariama gave her a hug as light as a cobweb.

Ana could not control the panicky feeling of exhaustion and abandonment she was left with every time Mariama left the flat. It was much easier back when she lived a single life and was alone with her work. She was also in poor physical condition and had still not pulled herself together to find a sports centre and get started with her training again. Her whole body began to shake as if she was coming off drugs. She had to speak to her coach immediately, and rang Jakob's emergency number. At once she heard his voice on the other end.

'What's wrong?' he said with professional attentiveness.

'Breakdown.'

'How?'

'There's no contact between Mariama and me.'

'What is it you expect?'

'That she confides in me about her studies. That's the whole basis of my sponsorship. If she doesn't get though the preparatory language course she won't be accepted for further studies, and then the whole thing has been pointless.'

'Why shouldn't she?'

'I just know there's something wrong. She's behaving strangely.'

'You must have confidence that she'll get through.'

'But everything is so new and strange for her.'

'You must learn to keep things separate.'

'How?'

'You have a need to help, but does Mariama have a need for your help?'

'If we're talking financially, yes she does.'

'I'm talking about the present situation, once the finances are in order.'

'I don't know whether she needs anything other than my sponsorship, whether I have anything to give her other than money.'

'Now you're getting things mixed up again. It's not a matter of whether you have anything other and more than financial support to offer, but whether Mariama has any need of something other and more.'

'She is so defenceless. She has been so exposed. No real childhood.'

'You need a certain amount of brute strength to get as far as she has,' Jakob interrrupted her.

'But she is all alone in the world.'

'How alone is she really with all that family?'

'The family makes everything more difficult,' said Ana irritably.

'Well, that's the reality you're faced with.'

'It would be much easier if reality did not exist,' said Ana with self-conscious irony.

'Why did you ring my emergency number?' Jakob put in.

'When I look at myself in a mirror, what I see is a mask.'

'What is it you're so afraid of?' said Jakob matter-of-factly.

'In the long run, my financial situation. Without money I can't help Mariama.'

'Forget Mariama. And concentrate on getting back on track yourself. Do you have a reasonable chance of getting a job in Rower's London office?'

'I have good contact with the HR manager. It's up to him to make the running.'

'How long are you going to give him before you look around elsewhere?'

'I can't do anything else,' said Ana horrified.

'Than what?'

'Rower.'

'Aren't you in the process of seeking out new challenges with the leap you've already taken?'

'So far it's just confusion and chaos.'

'You have to think more constructively and then act accordingly.'

'I can't concentrate on anything other than Mariama right now.'

'Leave her out of it.'

'I can't do that.'

'If you need to do something for someone else, why don't you look at helping a charity? Find some voluntary work in a charity shop or a soup kitchen?'

'Are you serious? Work for nothing? With my CV?'

'Why not? If it gives you a focus and restores order to chaos.'

'It's beneath my level.'

'Forgive me for saying so, but what sort of level are you

actually on right now?'

'I know that,' mumbled Ana.

'Your task before next time is to get started on finding something sensible to do. Paid or unpaid. We'll talk soon.'

'Thanks for the pep talk.' She turned her phone off and felt completely wiped out.

Ana had got into the habit of travelling into the City at around four in the afternoon. She took the underground to Bank and rose up into the anonymous security of marble and glass. She felt at home in the City's ivory-coloured concrete desert, where she had been a frequent visitor over the past ten to twelve years. She knew the streets, the cafés, the bars, the smooth upthrust of the buildings which blocked out the sky. She knew the well-cut suits and jackets, the high heels and the brief cases with the same label as her own. She knew the purposeful steps which echoed back from between the walls like the hollow beat of drumsticks.

She had finally arranged an interview with the HR manager. She circled around City Place House where Rower had its premises, and ended up sitting in the large, high-ceilinged bar just opposite. She placed herself strategically at a table right next to the glass façade, so that she had a view of her former workplace. Sitting in the low armchair, she sipped her Campari soda. She leafed absent-mindedly through the *Financial Times*, and felt she was out of circulation. She recognised some of her former colleagues as they walked past on the pavement and cut across the square in front of the entrance.

When Ana had been sitting long enough in those familiar surroundings, looking down the newspaper columns of stock values which fused together into a well-known pattern, she could almost imagine that she had returned to herself, that everything was as it used to be, and that when she had finished her drink she was going back to the meeting room and her laptop. And later, after work, out to eat sushi with some colleagues before she took the late flight back to Copenhagen. She felt quite intoxicated at recalling her working life hour by hour, right down to the smallest details. It was like looking into a lost paradise.

She finished her drink and walked out of the bar and across towards City Place House and the sterile little marble square. With her smart appearance, the discreet elegance of her suit, the shoes moulded perfectly to her feet, and the stiletto heels which added three inches to her height, she looked like the career woman she had been in her earlier life, and blended in with her surroundings. It struck her that the fountain in the middle of the square looked touching in its stripped-down minimalism with the threadlike jets gathered into vertical bundles.

She went into the lobby and over to reception, where she showed her Rower identity card and announced that she had an appointment with Patrick Glover. She was directed to a group of sofas beneath some potted palms. She sat down and waited to be escorted up to the eighth floor by a secretary. She had met the HR manager briefly when she had been a regular visitor to City Place House. But since her move to London she had only been in touch with him by phone and e-mail. She remembered him vaguely as a charming man in the prime of life. In their last phone conversation there had been an undercurrent of flirtation between them. And she had succeeded in getting an appointment to see him. The secretary kept her waiting. Ana had butterflies in her stomach at the thought of meeting this powerful man face to face, but she reassured herself that she had everything to win and nothing to lose.

Ana had installed herself so that she could keep an eye on the lifts, and suddenly saw an attractive middle-aged man emerge into the lobby and make directly for the group of palms. The HR manager himself had come down to fetch her. She felt as nervous as a schoolgirl, and stood up with an awkward movement. But she quickly regained control of herself. The surroundings had a regenerative effect; even a prolonged involuntary break could not eliminate the traces of her former professional self.

'My secretary has a day off today,' he explained his descent from on high.

'I thought secretaries never had a day off,' said Ana with a little touch of irony. She still had Rower jargon at her fingertips.

'It pays to be generous now and then,' he retorted smoothly. She wondered that she had not really noticed him before.

'A good investment,' she supplemented.

'Not to mention the returns,' he said, clicking his tongue. Ana took a deep breath.

'Well, we can't stand here all day,' he went on, placing a hand lightly on her back and conducting her to the lift.

Patrick Glover allowed her to enter first. Their eyes met with a sudden flash in the mirror. An imperceptible suction conveyed them upwards. He made way again with an elegant movement and allowed her to emerge first on to the landing, where there was a small glass table with freshly-squeezed juice and a bowl of fruit.

'Quite nice, don't you think?' he said in an aristocratic tone, and walked ahead of her down the long corridor and into his office right at the far end. She felt a sweet, smarting sensation in her body like a slow resurrection from the dead. It was a long time since she had felt so alive. It made her think of trees in their spring finery; she imagined that leaves and branches were unfurling from her naked arms. Patrick looked back discreetly as if to reassure himself that she was following. Ana stopped herself returning his smile. She was taking nothing for granted. She did not want to tempt fate. For it could only be luck that would save her, a stroke of chance which made some pieces fall into place so that there was an opening for her against all the odds.

They seated themselves on either side of the writing desk in the oversized corner office. Ana sat nervously on the extreme edge of her chair, overwhelmed by the significance of the meeting. When she was in a tense situation there was a parallel track running in her head at the same time, in which she could see herself from outside and provide an internal running commentary on the situation as she conversed with Patrick. He was younger than he seemed at first glance, she noted, and his disarming manner made her relax. They were still at the stage of small-talk, assessing each other's strengths in a ping-pong duel in which hard-hit balls were flying to and fro over the desk.

'You seem so dewy-fresh and untouched, as if life has made no impression on you,' said Patrick with a hard serve as he poured tea for her. He himself was drinking mineral water. His stomach could not tolerate tannic acid, he explained, and herbal tea was beneath his dignity.

'I have devoted the last sixteen years of my life to Rower,' retorted Ana in a sharp and assertive tone. He had no right to get personal. She had come along in order to save her job and her existence. They had the same educational background and roughly the same length of service with the firm. It was just that he had been lucky and she had been unlucky.

'Don't misunderstand me, it's meant as a compliment,' he said, smoothing it over, smiling with brilliant white teeth.

'Your skin is as smooth as silk, you look ageless. I wouldn't even dare guess. Perhaps it's your boyish hairstyle which makes you timeless.' He took a long-handled teaspoon from the tall tea-glass he had not used, and let the cold stainless steel glide slowly down her cheek. Ana felt a tingle down her spine.

'I have always given my work top priority,' she said in a business-like way, straightening up in her chair.

'Rower is generally known for giving its personnel wrinkles and grey hair,' he said ironically.

'I have tried to live up to the demands of my position in the team leader group,' said Ana, glossing over her unfortunate period of stress in Rower DK.

'No-one doubts your qualifications, Ana.' Patrick allowed his glance to rest in hers. There was a cool warmth under the city uniform and the tightly-knotted tie.

'Are qualifications enough if there are too many of us fighting for positions?'

'Yes, if your appearance is in your favour at the same time.' Patrick swivelled his chair round and sat with his back to her, enjoying the view for a moment before he turned back again. He regarded her with the analytical gaze of an expert. Had she already achieved what she had made up her mind to as she sat waiting in the bar opposite? Had he at once picked up the scent that she was easy prey?

'Do you see yourself as a member of our leader team?' he interrupted her thoughts.

'That was what Rower DK led me to expect.'

'What do you know about our new leadership culture?' Patrick asked in a routine fashion. She could not work out whether his question was simply a way of legitimizing their meeting.

'According to the minutes from meetings in 09 and the first quarter of 10 it is a matter of a change from the previous strategy of unanimous decisions to a simple majority, which allows greater flexibility and adaptability to extreme fluctuations in the financial markets,' she answered a little stiffly, like a bright pupil. Her inferior position of suspense prevented her from responding to him with unforced collegiality.

'The administrative leadership has the final word, so in that way the leader team's authority has been transferred to the top of the pyramid,' Ana continued eagerly. It was a long time since she had risen to a purely professional challenge.

'With the exception of?' Patrick pressed his fingertips together.

'Rower Johannesburg, Rower Nairobi. Africa differs from the other markets. Africa is in growth.' Ana enjoyed the feeling of being on an equal footing professionally, and felt her old self absorbing nourishment like a dehydrated plant.

'You know your Rower UK, tell me about yourself,' Patrick broke off, looking bored.

'I started as an investment adviser, mainly for trade and industry, risk assessment, liquidity assessment, cost analysis …'

'With responsibility for clients, then.' Patrick moved her on with a commanding wave of the hand, which made her presentation stiff and uncertain.

'I was in the department's client team, where we worked with about thirty prospective clients worldwide, until I was appointed a hunter, travelling around 200 days a year to meetings with clients …'

'So a hunter, then,' Patrick interrupted again.

'And a dealer?' he went on, staring ahead at a fixed point in the distance.

'Yes, for a relatively short period before I became a member of the team leader group DK. I liked working round the clock, it suited my temperament …'

'Dealer on commission?' Patrick looked directly at her. Ana nodded affirmatively.

'Which function is your preferred one?' Patrick fired off his questions like cracks of the whip.

'All functions have been building blocks in my experience at Rower, but team leader is my preferred one so far,' she said, feeling colourless.

'Let me make it clear.' Patrick was suddenly focused.

'You are still in the running, but you are of course entirely free to look for pastures new. And we would wish you luck if you decided on a new direction,' he summarized. His 'we' made Ana's courage falter.

'I don't know your situation, but I do know that you are restricted to London for private reasons. So we (again that cold 'we') could not move you to Hong Kong or Singapore at the drop of a hat.'

'I have become less mobile,' Ana admitted tersely. She had no wish to discuss her private circumstances with Patrick.

'It has something to do with a foster child, as I understand it?'

'You could put it like that, though no, not really.'

'Adoption? Like Madonna? An effective media stunt, which has given her masses of free PR,' said Patrick indignantly. He wasn't so streamlined as first impressions had suggested, thought Ana in track two.

'No, not like that.' Ana felt outraged at the thought that he believed she was following in Madonna's footsteps, and that Mariama was not her own personal choice but just a symptom of a popular trend.

'So you are not just yourself, you have obligations as well?' he continued, before Ana had managed to think it through.

'I'm sure you have as well,' she blurted out, whilst on the other track she considered whether adoption was a possibility she should explore.

'These two princesses.' Patrick passed her a leather-framed photo of two serious, fashionably dressed girls of pre-school age. Obviously he had had children late. It wasn't too late for her either, she thought again in track two; if nothing else – the thought had never struck her before – she could seek help from a science which was even more advanced than it had been at the time she herself was created. How could such a thought occur to her? She had always sworn that she would never make use of the fertility technology which had brought her into the world. She must have thought aloud, for Patrick asked her to repeat what she had said.

'Did I say something?' Ana was beside herself.

'You muttered something about "courage to act",' replied Patrick, visibly irritated.

'I'm sorry, I was thinking about Madonna's courage,' she improvised.

'That's nothing other than trading in children, consumerism, *so ein Ding muss ich auch haben*,' he said violently. His strong reaction was completely unexpected. Ana felt stung. She could not deny the fact that her relationship with Mariama was primarily a financial one.

'Africans have to find their own way out of poverty. Let them show what they are capable of.'

'The children can't wait that long,' Ana defended herself. She was not prepared to discuss Africa, which she did not feel fully briefed about and had not managed to read up on before Mariama had arrived in London and absorbed all her attention.

'We lost the thread.' Patrick focused on Ana's objectives again. 'You are on our list. You are definitely one of the people we are considering.'

'On a scale of 1 to 10 how do you rate my chances?' Ana had not touched her tea. She was afraid that her hands would start to shake. She felt an urgent need of something to give her strength, and looked longingly at the bottle of gin which was standing untouched on the tray.

'I can't promise anything, but you are, as I said, on our radar. And no less so now that I have had a chance to assess your qualities.'

'Thank you,' said Ana, uncertain of what he intended to convey. He mixed a gin and tonic for each of them and passed her the glass with ice and a slice of lemon.

'A face-to-face meeting is always important.' Patrick emphasized 'face-to-face', and sipped his drink with enjoyment. He looked at his watch. The picture of his two small princesses was still on the desk between them.

'It was good of you to make room for me in your diary,' said Ana formally. She wanted him to make the next move.

'It has been a pleasure,' he answered in the same tone. Ana was afraid that he had already lost interest.

'It's rare to feel you're on the same wavelength,' she said daringly, reaching out for her drink. He would not throw her out before she'd emptied the glass, or at least drunk half of it.

'When I talk to you, I don't notice that I'm talking to a woman,' he said thoughtfully.

'You have a distinctively masculine intelligence,' he continued. Ana could not decide for herself whether it was a damning indictment or a great compliment. She shrank beneath Patrick's X-ray gaze and felt stripped bare.

'I prefer to take that as a compliment,' she said composedly.

'That would not be entirely inaccurate,' he returned quickly, without removing Ana's doubts, and looked at his watch again.

'Unfortunately I can't invite you out to dinner. I have a

meeting out in the sticks at the other end of London.'

'I didn't expect you to do that,' said Ana, slightly confused. Patrick was not exuding the same calm and attentiveness as earlier, but sending out extremely ambivalent signals.

'I'll come down with you.' He got up decisively.

'I'd like to show you my Bedford Square studio. It might be interesting for you to see how the "natives" live. I need to collect some papers for the meeting anyway,' he went on, as he closed his laptop down and placed it in a leather case with a monogram.

'That sounds interesting.' Ana went along with it, picking up her bag.

'We'll take a taxi,' said Patrick on the way out of the lift. Ana nodded in agreement, and wished the new shift on reception 'a nice evening'. There were Rower employees in the building twenty-four hours a day. Some spent the night on an out-of-the-way sofa, others made do with a short power nap with their foreheads resting on their desks.

Patrick's one-room studio flat was a little padded nest with heavy velvet curtains, a thick wall-to-wall carpet which covered the whole of the floor area including the kitchenette, and an oversized bathroom with a jacuzzi. It felt anonymous and unlived-in. No personal belongings or pictures on the walls, apart from a tourist poster from Rome with a floodlit Colosseum. Patrick threw his jacket onto the bed and showed off the apartment with a sweep of the arm. He was obviously proud of his discreet lair. Ana felt trapped, and was unsure whether she had made a wise move. On the other hand, his remark about her masculine intelligence (you think like a man) had shaken her to such an extent that she was determined to show that she was a woman – at least in bed.

'Make yourself at home,' said Patrick in a soft voice, and with a well-rehearsed move he pulled the counterpane from the enormous double bed. He did not have much time.

'What about the mother of your two children?' Ana suddenly had second thoughts, not so much out of consideration for Patrick's wife as out of concern for her position at Rower.

'Isn't it a bit late to start thinking about my wife?' Patrick frowned. He had good reason to be angry.

'Sorry.' Ana was ready to run away. She had the feeling that she was on the point of jeopardizing her future at Rower.

'No need to be sorry,' he said coldly, 'we live together for the sake of the children, but we each go our own way, you know, a "marriage blanc".'

'Oh, right.' Ana sat down cautiously on the bed. She had never in her wildest fantasies imagined using her femininity for professional advancement. She did not define herself by her sex, but by her MA and her profession, and was too ambitious and self-respecting to have used sex as a lever in her career. But she was not herself, and was not behaving like herself. As soon as she got back into Rower everything would become normal, and she herself would become normal again. Normality was her ideal, to be a number in the ranks, enrolled in the army of workers. She had always wanted to be like everyone else, to fit in with her surroundings, to belong. More than anything else to belong, as she belonged in Rower.

Patrick took her by the chin and pushed her backwards with unexpected force; he began to undress her whilst she tried to convince herself that the situation was easier to handle when there were no feelings involved.

Mariama was sitting at home in the flat with her coat on and her nylon bag at her feet, waiting for her. The music from the cd-player's loudspeakers was thumping against the walls. Ana kicked off her shoes and ran across to switch off the machine.

'The neighbours,' she said in the massive silence which followed.

'Haven't you noticed that they have a white flag with a red cross hanging down from the balcony?' She looked meaningfully at Mariama, who just stared at her.

'White Power flag, they're racists the people next door.' Ana realized she was whispering.

'So many people are.' Mariama shrugged her shoulders.

'Not many, my dear, a few are racists, just a few,' Ana corrected her. She would move heaven and earth to make sure that London was good to Mariama.

It was only now that she realized that Mariama looked like someone who had come on a farewell visit before a long journey, and it occurred to her that Mariama should not be at her place at all in the middle of the week.

'What has happened? Are you OK?' Ana's question was followed by a hug which Mariama did her best to avoid.

'I want to stay here with you,' she said.

'What do you mean?'

'I don't want to live with them.' Mariama looked tired and haggard, as if she had not slept for several nights. She followed Ana into the kitchen, the words tumbling out of her whilst Ana made tea.

'You mustn't be cross with me, Ana. It's not because I'm ungrateful to Ben and Bea, but Bea says I bring an old sorrow back into the house,' Mariama began. It made her so unbearably sad to listen to Bea, whose loose clothes in delicate pastel colours reminded her of shrouds. Like an angel who had stepped straight out of the Koran, but she didn't dare to say that to her. She and Ben did not believe in God, on principle, as Ben said, confirmed atheists. It made them a bit crazy and dangerous in her eyes. She could not imagine people who did not believe in some kind of god.

Her grandmother had come from a Christian family, and had taught her about the body and the blood and the resurrection, which she quickly put out of her mind. It was too gruesome. Even though her grandma explained that Isa was also one of God's prophets. So she should not be afraid of this man's body and blood. But the Koran could not help her, because she could not read the language of the Koran. Once the Imam had given her permission to touch the holy book. The touch burnt her hand for a long time after and only stopped when she started school and the English book became her holy book. It was Auntie Rosie who had taught her to love the soft and flexible English language as she loved it herself, because her highest wish had been to become an English teacher.

'But Ben says that it does Bea good to have a young person in the house. She has got much stronger since you moved into the children's room,' Ana objected.

'Don't you know anything about that child who grew into a girl in the house in Portland Road?' Mariama stopped herself saying 'like me'.

'I don't know anything,' Ana mumbled, waiting for her to continue.

'She went out, slamming the door, and left a sour smell of hash behind her and a wardrobe full of empty beer cans which poured onto the floor with a crash and gave Bea her first heart attack. She doesn't want to see them any more, but she rings every New Year's Eve and on Bea's birthday. She's usually high and they refuse to talk to her. It is demeaning both for them and for her in that state, Ben says.'

'This is all news to me.' Ana felt the ground giving way beneath her.

'The girl, Janet, is their adopted child. She came back with them from a mission in Uganda. They were persuaded to save a little girl from an orphanage in Kampala where she hated it and hadn't said a word for many years.'

Mariama's voice grew more and more faint. It was the girl's spirit she had felt from the very first day. And out of fear of the spirit in the house she had begun to do her homework in cafés with an internet connection. She lugged the laptop Ana had given her as a welcoming present with her everywhere. She was neglecting her studies because of the spirit's disturbances and the havoc it was causing in the house in Portland Road. Ana listened patiently to Mariama's many concerns, and was happy that she had a need of her and not just of her money.

'It's not good enough for you to be burdened with Ben and Bea's problems so you can't concentrate on your studies,' said Ana indignantly and took Mariama's hand. She quickly pulled her hand away and hid both hands in her lap. Ana went bright red and regretted that she had allowed her feelings to run away with her.

'Won't you tell them that I'm coming to stay with you?' Mariama kept a constant eye on her mobile phone on the table in front of her.

'Are you sure you want to leave your lovely room at Ben and Bea's and make do with my little guest room?' asked Ana.

'Yes.' Mariama resumed her dramatic report from Portland Road. She could see the spirit clearly behind her when she looked out of the corner of her eye, and was afraid that it was demanding its room back. That poor spirit could not let go of its house and its parents. At night it hid in the walls, behind the doors and under the carpets. It called and wailed like a hyena. Mariama had heard terrible stories about hyenas which ate windows and doors, so that the four winds could blow through the house and take the sleeping people with them.

Mariama's account of conditions in the house in Portland Road had shaken Ana profoundly. She had not had the slightest idea that there was an underlying conflict which was troubling Bea, and might be the explanation for her weak state of health.

'We need to discuss this with Ben and Bea,' Ana asserted, ignoring for the time being the 'spirit', which she did not know how to deal with.

'Can't you talk to them?' Mariama suggested.

'Shouldn't you wait to move until the term is over?'

'I've packed my things.' Mariama lifted up the nylon bag she had brought with her from Gambia.

'We'll go over and talk to Ben and Bea straight away,' said Ana decisively.

'They're not at home. I'd like to sleep here tonight,' said Mariama in a faint little voice. Ana didn't have the heart to say no.

'Do Ben and Bea know you're at my place?'

'They're at a meeting in Newcastle and not back till tomorrow,' said Mariama.

At that moment her phone rang. She went into the bedroom. Ana could not avoid hearing a few snatches of

195

conversation from a low-voiced Mariama: ' … I can't … all right, I'll ask …'.

'Is everything all right?' asked Ana when she saw Mariama frowning.

'There's a wedding in the village and my mother has no money to give the bridal couple. And Auntie Rosie wants to buy a market stall so that she can sell her vegetables at market and provide for her children,' she sighed heavily.

'You can't solve their problems. You need to attend to your studies and not work so much.' Ana was speaking to Mariama's closed face.

'But you can,' she whispered so quietly that Ana had to strain to hear what she was saying.

'Has Rosie asked you to ask me if I will pay for her to buy a market stall?' Ana melted as she realised what a tight corner Mariama was in.

'Will you tell her that she must ring me herself.'

'She has nothing but her vegetables to live off. It is necessary for her to sell them at market. Her husband is old and sick. If she doesn't have a stall the police chase her away, every day they chase her away from the market,' Mariama defended Aunt Rosie.

'Well, I would like to help, but I don't have unlimited funds,' Ana said. Mariama stared straight ahead as though she refused to believe that there was any end to Ana's riches.

'And my mother,' she said cautiously, trying to explain her mother's humiliating situation.

'Ask how much she needs, and we'll send the money through Western Union,' Ana broke in. A 'we' had already crept into her vocabulary, even before it had been decided whether Mariama should come and live with her in Henry Dickens Court.

Ana spent a sleepless night in a kind of intoxication at the thought of Mariama's irregular presence on a normal weekday. This unexpected gift made her life straightforward and everyday. The morning began merrily with eggs and bacon and toast, but even before they had cleared the table they started to quarrel. Ana insisted that they should go over to Ben and Bea's together and talk through the new situation with them. Mariama was sullen and resistant, and didn't think her presence was necessary. Ana tried to make her understand that it was only reasonable for her to take part in a discussion about herself and her wish to move. But she was impervious to argument. She refused to step over the threshold at Portland Road.

'I can't, I'm ashamed,' she wailed.

'Ben and Bea are sensible people, they will understand.'

'No, not them. I'm ashamed to meet the spirit.' Mariama began to shake. Ana took hold of her shoulder.

'What a lot of rubbish,' she said. Mariama stared straight ahead and didn't seem to find it necessary to explain the intrusion of the invisible world into the visible one, and that there were no clear boundaries between the world of people and that of spirits.

'Anyway, I have classes this morning,' Mariama remembered, finding an excuse for which Ana had greater respect than for a poor homeless spirit.

'That must come first, of course,' she said, choosing to believe her.

'Then you can come along afterwards. Ben and Bea won't have time until this afternoon,' she went on.

'Then I have to go to work at Sainsbury's,' Mariama whispered so quietly and indistinctly that it sounded like a lie. Ana dismissed her suspicions. Why should Mariama lie to her?

'I'll talk to them myself,' she terminated the discussion. Once again she had lost the battle to Mariama.

'Thank you, Ana, you are too good, like my mum,' she said in her most fragile voice, and bent down and gave Ana a butterfly kiss on both cheeks.

For once Ana had arranged to meet Bea before she set off for Portland Road. With very few exceptions it was she who visited them and not the other way round. The pressure of their work prevented active socializing. On the other hand their house was always open to her. She was always welcome to drop in and visit Mariama. On the way there, just as she had emerged from Henry Dickens Court, a wizened old woman with a walking frame in front of her came along the opposite pavement. She was festooned with jewellery, jangling bracelets and bangles, rows of necklaces and golden brooches fastened like medals to her lapels. As if she had emptied her jewellery box for fear that burglars would steal her heirlooms whilst she was out taking an airing with her black nurse, who was watching over every step she took and whispering confidential messages into her ear. The oddly assorted couple complemented each other in a perfect match which frightened her, and she hurried onwards as if it were a bad omen.

Bea opened the door almost before Ana had had time to ring the bell, as if she had been standing on the other side waiting for her. Mild and beautiful as always, she radiated a transparent fragility which Ana admired. Perhaps because she herself was made of more substantial material. Bea suggested that they should go up to the living room, where the tea tray stood ready. She was alone in the house. That made it easier for Ana to speak confidentially.

'Where's Ben?'

'He was called to a meeting, emergency. Matters are coming to a head with our vaccination programme. The budget is not sustainable.' Bea's voice had a faint vibrato.

'I'm worried about Mariama,' she went on in her direct and honest fashion. Ana was frustrated that she had not got in first. On the way over she had been practising what to say to Bea. She had to choose her words carefully so that Bea did not get upset or angry with Mariama or with both of them. Ben and Bea had become her family, and she did not want to fall out with them.

'She is literally never here. Ben thinks the situation is intolerable, and that she ought to move out. I think that is very wrong of him. Even though he does want the best for her.' Bea spoke so quickly that she became short of breath.

'I've been talking to her,' said Ana, relieved that they shared the same problem.

'She's not happy in London. She misses her country, she misses her family.' Bea was seriously concerned. Ana did not know what to say. Clearly Mariama had not wanted to be frank about what was upsetting her. That it was in their house she was not happy.

They sat there each with their own thoughts. Bea seemed unwell. Was it the girl from Uganda who was haunting her? Had a curse been placed on the house? Ana did not dare to ask what was wrong with her. Despite her open and friendly manner, Bea had an aura which made her seem untouchable.

'We are close to falling out over this. For the first time in our long life together,' said Bea unhappily, picking up the thread from earlier.

'It's also possible that Mariama herself is ready to try something different, moving to a student hostel perhaps,' said Ana casually.

'She's not ready for that yet. She needs protection until she has settled in properly,' Bea objected sharply.

'Why is she never at home then?'

'Because we are not capable of nurturing.' Bea bit her lip. Ana was startled at her choice of words.

'You have taken Mariama in, given her board and lodging and let her off her domestic duties so that she has more time for her studies. What more can you do?' she protested.

'We haven't had enough time for her,' said Bea.

'Isn't it more that she hasn't had enough time for you?' Ana put in.

'Ana, you don't know how much I'm suffering,' Bea burst out.

'Bea, my dear.' Ana felt an impulse to hold her hand and stroke her hair, but she tried to keep a cool head.

'I'm sorry,' Bea sniffed. 'I got carried away.'

'There's no need to apologize,' said Ana uncomfortably. She had no experience of dealing with sensitive situations.

'I'm all right now.' Bea straightened up and poured more tea.

'Perhaps it's been too much to have Mariama in the house. I mean, with all the pressure of your work,' Ana said carefully.

'It was our decision, and as I remember, it was even Ben who suggested it. We wanted to give ourselves a challenge, see how far we had got with …' she sighed.

'With what, Bea?' Ana risked asking. Bea looked at her as if she had forgotten her presence.

'The loss that sits in your heart like a lump of ice … children are only lent to you.' She sat up in her chair and continued: 'We thought we had learnt something from our experiment.' Bea was pale, almost white in her yellow dress. Ana did not know what to say.

'Please, can you pass me my bag.' Bea put her hand to her chest and gasped for air. Ana passed her the little black leather bag.

'Is there anything I can do?' she muttered.

'No thank you, just stay here a while. I can't be on my own,' she said, and fished a bottle of pills out of her bag.

'I'm not going anywhere,' Ana assured her.

'Mariama must have a chance here with us. It's too early to give up.' Bea was used to having her own way.

'I think she has made progress, she gets on fine under her own steam. Her English has got much better too, she has a larger vocabulary.' Ana tried to put a positive spin on it.

'She hasn't mastered the fine nuances,' said Bea pedantically.

'How far can you get in five months?' Ana defended Mariama, and felt annoyed that she had not given more thought to her appearance, but had just come out in her old Diesel jeans.

'I'm not reproaching Mariama, we are the ones who have failed.'

'You demand too much of yourselves.'

'I have promised myself not to give up,' said Bea.

'I thought it would be good for Mariama to live with you.

That way she could learn the customs of British life and become properly integrated.'

'That was a generous thought, Ana. But we weren't up to it. How many defeats can a person bear?' Bea suddenly seemed unbalanced again.

'Mariama just wants to stand on her own two feet, no doubt,' Ana comforted her.

'Mariama is living here for the time being, never mind what Ben says. He has too little patience with people.'

'But should you not listen to what Mariama herself thinks about the situation?' Ana asked cautiously, without giving herself away.

'I think she is more interested in having fun,' said Bea with a touch of sarcasm.

'What is it in purely concrete terms that causes problems between you and Mariama, apart from the fact that she doesn't spend much time at home?'

'Lots of little things which become magnified and create stupid conflicts, more often between Ben and me than between us and Mariama. She moves things out of her room the whole time, and leaves them lying about all over the place. The things disturb her sleep and invade her dreams, she says. She uses the bathroom as a prayer room, and locks herself in for hours. She maintains that the bathroom is the only room which faces Mecca.'

'She doesn't pray when she's at my place, as far as I know,' Ana put in.

'We don't feel at home in our own house any longer. It's so banal that I'm ashamed of it. Like a pattern that's repeating itself, as if Mariama was a carbon copy of …'

'Of whom, Bea?' Ana interjected.

'It's something we have to live with. Ben won't let her, that ungrateful miss, destroy his life, he says. But for me it's not that simple. Forgive me, Ana. Another time, it hurts too much to talk about it.' Bea made it clear that she was tired and needed to rest. Her insistent agenda had overshadowed Ana's; she had not explained what she had come to say other than in veiled hints, which Bea had no possibility of comprehending.

'Would it relieve you if Mariama moved in with me for a while?' Ana suggested tentatively. Bea had seemingly not heard her. She repeated her question in a whisper. Bea still did not react, but remained sitting beside her, her profile unmoving.

'Bea, have I said the wrong thing?' said Ana desperately.

'You're exploiting our misfortune. I hadn't expected that.' Bea turned her head slowly.

'I don't understand …'

'You want to take over Mariama.' Bea was clearly outraged.

'I want to help, that's all.' Ana cursed herself for being so governed by her fear of other people that she had not stated at once how matters stood, that Mariama wanted to move in with her.

'Mariama …'

'Yes, what of her?' Bea interrupted angrily.

'I suggest that all four of us meet and work out the problems between you and Mariama.'

'Ben doesn't have time for that,' said Bea dismissively. Ana had to show her hand.

'Bea, Mariama came to me yesterday and told me that she wants to come and live with me.' Her voice shook.

'Why didn't you say that from the start? Then we could have saved a lot of time.' Bea looked at her as if she was some strange kind of animal.

'If that's what she wants, then we can't stop her. She is eighteen, as far as I know,' she continued matter-of-factly.

'Or perhaps she could move into a student hostel,' said Ana in a hopeless attempt to smooth things over and reach a compromise.

'That would be expensive for you,' said Bea practically.

'I'm prepared to give her the shirt off my back.'

'You are a good person, Ana.' Bea had regained her equanimity.

'She can wait to move until after the summer holiday,' said Ana suicidally, knowing well that Mariama wanted to move at once.

'Then we can perhaps have time to patch things up,' said Bea with amazing light-heartedness. Ana made a mental note that she did not understand people, but would have to be satisfied with admiring them from a distance.

Mariama was in Portland Road in order to pack her things. She had reluctantly agreed to stay overnight with Bea, who was not happy about being alone. They had got no further than dinner when Bea reproached her for telling Ana about her desire to move without saying a word about it to her and Ben. It was disloyal and unfair, she said with a distorted expression like a mask, which scared Mariama and revealed that she was as unpredictable as the witch people (she shouldn't think like that in London, but she did anyway). Beneath Bea's light and fair exterior there was a dangerous current. Rosie had often warned her about the tides that were governed by the moon, and their alternation between a withdrawn immobility and the rushing incoming tide which no-one could outrun. Bea could change in seconds from a peaceful ebb to a tidal wave which rose like a steep wall and came crashing down on her. Mariama defended herself that Ana was her tubaab mother, and that was why she had gone to her first. But Ana had misunderstood her if she thought it was already decided where she wanted to live. Such a momentous decision demanded much thinking and weighing up.

Mariama felt hurt by Bea's accusation that she was disloyal, and realised at once that she had made a dreadful mistake with her childish 'tubaab mother'. Bea could not bear to hear the word 'mother' in her house because of the girl from Uganda, who had left her in a cloud of curses. Mariama tried to explain to Bea that she needed to have patience. The girl would come back when she had gathered her courage and got things in perspective. She would not desert them. They were her family. And didn't Bea know that Africans were loyal to the point of masochism towards their families? Mariama instructed her in a sharp tone.

Bea's mind was brought down from the stormy heights and back to earth once again, and she wanted to know whether Mariama was taking enough care of herself. It had become far too dangerous to walk around alone in London's streets after dark. She should always make sure she was together with her friends or with someone from her family when she went out at night. Mariama was grateful for her concern, but didn't Bea have anything to say other than to repeat her own and Ana's worries, right now when she was standing in mid-stream and needed their advice and guidance? She had begun to doubt that they really saw her as the person she was, a young person trying to get a foothold in an alien world.

'Let's talk, Mariama,' said Bea as if she had read her thoughts. They were facing each other in the middle of the living room. It was quiet in the house. Ben was at a two-day seminar in Brighton. Bea took her hand and said in her attractive dark voice that they were sensible grown-up people, and that she had had her doubts from the start as to whether she, with her frail health and fragile mental state, was good company for Mariama.

'Oh yes, you are,' Mariama assured her. She could feel that Bea needed her, and was at once ready to put herself to one side. That was what she had learnt as the first commandment at Auntie Rosie's, that everything and everyone had to take precedence over herself.

'It's impossible not to be fond of you,' smiled Bea.

'But what are we doing standing here, let's sit down on the sofa,' she continued cheerfully. Mariama sat down reluctantly on the extreme edge. She didn't have time for all this discussion. She had a meeting with her friend Binta to revise for the exam. Binta was sponsored by her family back home. Her father was employed at the Gambian embassy in Dakar. She felt lonely at the hostel and was putting pressure on Mariama to move in so that they could support each other. At home the social gulf would have prohibited them associating. But Binta's mother was enthusiastic that she had found a friend who spoke Wolof, so that she would not forget her language. She was not happy that Binta gave up searching for words and switched to English when they spoke on the phone. 'In gaining the world, you'll lose your soul', was her standing remark. She could not know that the two friends mostly spoke English together.

'I'm sorry, but I don't have so much time right now,' said Mariama with her eyes on her phone.

'We can make it short. You would like to move. I think we should hear what Ben has to say. This is not a decision you should make alone. We must all make it together,' said Bea. Mariama interpreted this as: she must not only listen to their advice, but also have their permission to move. But perhaps she misunderstood Bea. They so easily found themselves at cross purposes.

Suddenly she became angry and annoyed at herself for getting into this impossible situation. It would not have happened back home, where there was nothing else to do but bite your tongue and put up with things. It was the great confusion she found herself in which made her break into flakes like the millet seed when the women crushed it in the mortar. Her head pounded. She could not determine which decision would be the right one. They all seemed to her to be equally wrong. Whatever she did she would end up by making other people unhappy. She had walked into a sandstorm she had provoked herself, and now she could not see a hand in front of her face. She missed the solid framework of the family pattern with its set rules which had to be obeyed without discussion, and she suddenly felt homesick.

'Mariama, aren't you happy here with us? Are we doing something wrong?' Bea laid a hand on her arm.

'It's the girl from Uganda.' It burst out of her. She could not resist the pressure from inside. Bea went deathly pale and put her hand on her neck.

'She's in the room at night,' Mariama whispered fearfully.

'Let's talk,' Bea repeated. Mariama was reminded that she was supposed to be meeting Binta when another text message beeped into her phone.

'Janet came to Kampala from the north of Uganda, where children were kidnapped by rebel groups. The boys became soldiers or slave workers and the girls were raped and then became soldiers' wives. Janet is the result of a gang-rape of her fifteen-year-old mother. The poor girl didn't want anything to do with her, and left her at an Oxfam office. Janet was our child for twelve years.'

'But she is still your child. She's just not here right now.' Mariama protested violently.

'It's her own choice,' said Bea resigned.

'I'll help you find her,' said Mariama eagerly, and forgot for a moment about her meeting with Binta.

'She doesn't want anything to do with us.'

'Why not?'

'She says nothing. She won't talk to us. We can only conclude that we have failed.' Bea was beside herself again.

'Let's hope we have learnt something,' she sighed. Mariama listened intently.

'Perhaps all experience is an illusion. People make the same mistakes over and over again.' Bea gave an ironic little laugh. Her mood had switched. Mariama feared that the sea would once more gather into a tidal wave.

'I think she needed to find her own way,' said Mariama, as if the unhappy girl was herself.

'It was not my intention to burden you with our problems,' Bea said stiffly, almost distantly. Mariama could not interpret Bea's signals, and was hurt at being excluded from her sorrow. She regretted that she had let herself be persuaded to stay overnight. And she should not have missed the meeting with Binta. She should not be in this house which was possessed by the girl's spirit.

Bea sat in the corner of the sofa, staring empty-eyed like a zombie. She would not notice if Mariama left the living room and sneaked out of the front door. But she could not get up. She was pinned to her seat. Had the spirit bewitched her? Her throat constricted. Sweat poured off her. Bea had left her and gone off into her own world. She was completely alone with the spirit. She could see it behind her right shoulder. She tore herself free from the chair and quickly switched on all the lamps, so that the room was flooded with light. Bea leapt up with a shriek.

'What are you doing?' She looked as if she had seen a ghost.

'It's the darkness,' Mariama managed to stammer.

'I can't bear strong light.' Bea was gasping for breath. Mariama was shaking all over, and was ashamed that she had revealed her receptiveness to spirits. They didn't belong in London. But she was sure Janet was in the house. As soon as it got dark she came to search for food, but she could not help her. It was only Bea and Ben who could. It was them Janet wanted to contact. She was just the one who saw her and passed on her messages.

Bea had put all the lights off again, except for a single wall light over the sofa. Soft dusk fell over the furniture and the piles of books, over the African fertility figures and warrior masks. It suddenly struck Mariama that she would come to share Janet's fate if she carried on living at that house very much longer, and like her be doomed to roam around and never again be able to find firm ground beneath her feet.

'I have got very fond of you, you know,' said Bea, and could not help giving her a hug. Mariama stiffened in her embrace. But Bea did not register her discomfort. She was preoccupied with distancing herself from her and Ben's failure, which he was much better at repressing.

'You have been very kind to me,' Mariama responded to her outburst of sentiment.

'Let's talk,' said Bea for the third time. Mariama was completely exhausted by the evening's tumult of emotions, but sat down politely next to Bea.

'It's perfectly all right if you decide to move in with Ana, but just promise me that you will think about it carefully.'

'I don't know what I want, I just need a break, time out,' said Mariama nervously. Now that harmony had been reestablished, her doubts resurfaced.

'There's no reason to be in a hurry,' Bea assured her. Yes, there was a reason, which she did not dare to mention out loud. Bea was too vulnerable to hear about the spirits and their peculiar entrances and exits. And it was also too dangerous to talk about them after dark.

'You must excuse my temperament. I should not have reproached you. It's natural for you to confide in Ana. She is your main sponsor,' said Bea, smoothing things over. Mariama was glad that there was peace between her sponsor partners once more.

'That's quite all right, Bea. We can all make mistakes,' she said tolerantly. That's what Big Man used to say to her when she complained that Aunt Rosie was hard and treated her and Madeleine differently. It was a long time since she had given him a thought. He was the only member of the family who did not ring up at all times of the day and night and demand that she send presents of money or persuade her rich sponsor to help them in their destitution. Every one of them weighed on her conscience. How could she permit herself to live in all this luxury without sharing it with her family? All her prayers circled around this question. But she had had no answer.

'It takes time and patience to rub off the rough edges and fit in with one another,' Bea said. Mariama nodded without understanding what she was talking about. It was not easy to work her out.

'Perhaps we should retire in good order.' Bea switched off the single wall light and groped her way towards the door in the darkness, where she switched on the stair light.

'Good night, darling,' she said, and hurried downstairs to the work which was waiting for her.

'Good night,' whispered Mariama with her hand over her mouth in terror of waking the spirit. She tiptoed up to her room and lay down to sleep with the light on and her mobile phone clutched in her hand.

For a long time Ana had been pressing Ben and Bea for a solution to the unresolved question of Mariama's living arrangements. But they were deeply involved in the vaccination programme in the Congo and had no time to devote to 'domestic matters'.

'We're drowning in work and losing ourselves,' Bea had said half-apologetically. Ana was disappointed at her friends' desertion, even though she of all people ought to be able to understand that work came first. But she had put a great distance between herself and the imperative demands of a heavy workload. It was precisely 'domestic matters' which preoccupied her now that she had Mariama with her in Henry Dickens Court.

At their last coaching session Jakob had put it to her that she had made herself too dependent on Ben and Bea. And she had begun to wonder whether he was worth his exorbitant fee. In his place, Hans had begun to materialize in her consciousness. At the oddest moments she could suddenly feel his closeness, which reminded her of what she had given up. She had even begun to make plans. If only she could conquer her damned pride and ring him up and tell him that she regretted breaking it off, and she was ready to try again. In the first instance as friends, and then perhaps later establish the sort of long-distance relationship which so many of their circle of workaholics cultivated.

'Did you follow my advice?' Jakob had started off in an inquisitorial tone.

'What advice?'

'To get involved in something meaningful.'

'I've taken a lover. The HR manager at Rower's London branch. He can welcome me back into the fold as easily as snapping his fingers.' Ana sounded more impressed than she had intended.

'But will he do that?'

'That depends on how much he values me.'

'You're playing for high stakes.'

'I'm a gambler.' Ana's voice shook.

'It looks to me as if you're acting out of desperation.'

'I know what I'm doing. I can't let Mariama down halfway through,' said Ana shrilly. 'She doesn't want to live with Ben

209

and Bea, but move over and live with me.'

'How do you feel about her living with you?'

'There is nothing I like more than to have her here with me. But it's perhaps not the optimal thing for her. She gets more out of being with Ben and Bea.'

'Do you have such low self-esteem that you think it's a pity for her to have to "make do" with you?' said Jakob provocatively.

'That's a very drastic conclusion.'

'Are you prepared to take responsibility for her on an everyday basis? Is it not more convenient for you to have her at a distance and just have visits at weekends?' Jakob spoke in a tone of voice as though it was a dispute between estranged parents.

'You're oversimplifying, Jakob.' Ana did not sound entirely convincing. Jakob waited for her to continue.

'It is chance which has brought Mariama into my life. I have met a person who is more important to me than myself. She was a child when we met on the beach. Now she is a young woman,' said Ana with an odd self-reproach in her voice.

'You must decide for yourself whether you want to take on day-to-day responsibility for her.'

'I need to discuss it with Ben and Bea first.'

'They're not the ones who decide what you want.'

'We're a team,' Ana defended herself.

'But you're the one who is the team leader,' said Jakob. Ana was taken aback. He was not giving her what she had paid for.

'I think I know a little more about teamwork and team leadership than you do,' said Ana sharply.

'You're the one Mariama comes to with her problems, so you can't just leave the decisions to Ben and Bea.'

'Perhaps a compromise could be for her to move into a hostel next semester?' suggested Ana.

'Tell me, are you afraid of her?'

'I don't pay through the nose just to be insulted,' said Ana.

'My task is to guide you,' Jakob reminded her.

'OK,' said Ana, calming down, 'I have never been afraid of

anything. As a child I was like the boy in the fairytale who doesn't know fear. I cycled through the forest late at night. I climbed to the top of the tallest trees. I jumped off the ten-metre board. Later on I did bungee-jumping and won medals.'

'All your sporting achievements don't rule out the possibility that you're afraid of people who say BOO to you,' said Jakob.

'I'm not afraid of you … you're the only one I'm not afraid of,' she added weakly.

'So you are afraid of Mariama?'

'I don't like your conclusions.'

'You have to be honest with yourself.'

'I'm afraid of people,' Ana whispered.

'What have they done to you?'

'Nothing. I'm just not on the same wavelength. I don't know what to do with myself. If they come too close, I collapse like a house of cards.'

'How does that square with your position as a team leader in Rower?'

'I function optimally in a work context.'

'Can't you try to see yourself as a normally functioning human being outside the work sphere as well.' Jakob's tone was sharper.

'I'm not normal out there.'

'So perhaps it's yourself you're afraid of?'

'You're turning everything on its head.'

'I'm just asking questions, you have to find the answers yourself,' said Jakob, offended.

'I'm sorry if I overstepped the mark,' Ana hurriedly placated him.

'What are you going to do about Mariama?' he went on practically.

'I'll give more thought to the hostel idea and come to an agreement with Ben and Bea about where she is to live in the meantime.'

'Fine. Good luck.' Jakob finished the session. The expensive time had run out. She was once more left on her own.

Ana enjoyed doing a big shop and serving up the choicest delicacies. Mariama ate like a bird and pushed most of it to one side. Ana should not make so much food for her and not put so much on her plate, she reproached her. She ought to think of the children instead, said Mariama, without identifying precisely which children. Ana was afraid of her anger, and left it to her to draw up the shopping lists. She avoided looking at the luxury articles in the delicatessen and renounced caviar and foie gras. It already seemed as if Mariama had always lived with her, as if her spirit had filled the air she breathed, and had only now materialized as a living being. When Ana came out of Tesco's with her shopping bags, she dutifully put two pounds in Birdy's plastic beaker. She had reconciled herself to her existence, although she refrained from giving her Mariama's best wishes as she had been requested to do.

Ana suggested that they should invite Binta to dinner. She lived in the Nido hostel at King's Cross, and that made her interesting with regard to Ana's future plans for Mariama. But Mariama was far from keen on the idea, which Ana interpreted as indirect criticism.

'You took your friends home to Ben and Bea's,' she said, upset.

'You mustn't put pressure on me, I have so much homework,' said Mariama, in order to avoid explaining to Ana why Binta did not want to visit either her or Ben and Bea.

'Your studies must come first,' Ana agreed, resigned. She was standing behind Mariama's chair, looking down at her neatly plaited hair, which had recovered after the expensive hair damage treatment. Ana felt an urge to stroke over the multitude of thin plaits. But she stopped herself, not wanting to disturb her.

Her glance fell on the computer screen, which was diplaying the ukgambia net forum 'Sex Before Marriage'. Ana held her breath whilst she quickly scanned the screen contents. 'If you gonna have sex with every boyfriend or girlfriend you have. How many people are you going to have sex with b4 u get married? I highly recommend no sex b4 marriage. It just makes more sense.' 'Well, if I had a choice to choose from a virgin and non-virgin to marry, I'll choose the one that I think loves and respects me the most.' 'Sex before marriage or the other way round, it doesn't matter. What matters is: don't do it before you are 18, and when you do it make sure you do it SAFE. The rest of it is just trash.'

Mariama became aware of Ana's eyes on the back of her head and turned round with a jerk.

'I don't like you standing there spying on me,' she said, and quickly closed down the computer.

'I couldn't help seeing what you had on the screen,' Ana excused herself, standing still with a strangely stiff sensation in her body.

'We should have talked about this,' she continued nervously, and had no idea how to go about it. Mariama did not answer. An imperceptible shiver ran down her long narrow back.

'Have you got a boyfriend?' Ana could hear at once that it sounded all wrong. Mariama barricaded herself behind her silence. Her head completely empty, Ana started stroking the girl's hair.

'Not a boyfriend ... but there is someone I think about,' said Mariama when Ana finally moved her hand away.

'Well, that's nice for you.' Ana felt incompetent and not in command of the situation.

'No, it's not nice, it makes me feel split,' declared Mariama.

'Are you in love with him?'

'Perhaps ... it needs time to develop.'

'You should talk to your aunt in Upton Park,' said Ana, grateful that there was an aunt who could take over. Mariama shook her head.

'How long have you known him?'

'I have met him ... once, no twice ...'

'Then it's early days yet.'

'But what if he pressures me?' said Mariama uncertainly, looking away.

'Don't you think you should talk to your aunt about it?' Ana was worried about doing something wrong and giving her advice which was contrary to the norms she had learnt at home. Ana herself had never regarded sex as something which needed any discussion on a moral plane.

'I would prefer to keep her out of it.'

'She would be better able to guide you and help you to make the right choices.'

'She just follows tradition. She has never really moved to the UK, even though she has lived here for twenty years.'

'But she knows what is best for you.'

'You understand my situation better.'

'Have you talked to Ben and Bea about it?' Ana was afraid that she was not able to give the support that Mariama needed.

'I'm living with you, so it is you I talk to.' Mariama wished that Ana was like Ben and Bea, that she could split in half and become two. A woman without a man was nowhere, neither in this world nor in the next.

'Important decisions must be made on the basis of solid facts.' Ana gave advice from the only world she knew.

'Can I be sure of him?'

'You can't be sure of anything in this world. There are no investments which are future-proofed.'

'God,' said Mariama.

'What?'

'You can be sure of God.'

'Oh yes, him.'

'Binta is afraid of atheists. She says they are crazy and unpredictable,' she blurted out.

'Does she really?' Ana started to laugh, and was suddenly reminded that she was forty-five.

'She's frightened of people who don't believe in God,' Mariama insisted earnestly, trying to make Ana understand the importance of the subject. 'She daren't visit me so long as I'm living with godless Englishmen.'

'But you're not frightened of atheists, are you?' Ana wanted to put her arm around her, but she pulled away.

'Not of you,' she said evasively.

'You don't need to be, either. I'm not at all dangerous,' Ana reassured her. The existence of God was not a question which concerned her greatly.

'But Ben and Bea are atheists, Ben said.' Mariama had a worried frown.

'If he says so, then that must be right. It's not something we talk about.'

'I don't understand that,' said Mariama in confusion.

'You don't need to think any more about it. I'm proud of you,' said Ana in order to steer the conversation in a different direction.

'Why are you proud of me ... I shan't pass,' said Mariama crossly, and tears began to run down her face. It suddenly struck Ana that her skin looked so pale. Had she been using that dangerous bleaching cream which gave you skin cancer?

'But my love,' said Ana, and put her hand on her shoulder. 'Of course you will pass.' Ana herself was a top-grade student and could not imagine anything else.

'I'll help you with your homework,' she suggested eagerly.

'I would rather you came to the doctor with me. I am used to having someone from my family with me.'

'Are you pregnant?' Ana couldn't stop herself.

'I am pure,' replied Mariama, unperturbed by her embarrassing question.

'What's wrong with you?' said Ana, with a feeling that she had been neglecting her.

'I can't get enough air, I feel hot and my head spins. Everything churns round and round. My heart is so agitated. I can't sleep. I need something to calm me down.'

'Is it as bad as that?' Ana broke in, alarmed.

'All my fellow students are taking something or other to cope with the pressure.' Mariama opened her computer demonstratively and waited for Ana to leave her in peace so that she could carry on with her exercise on English synonyms.

'I'll make an appointment for you with my doctor, so you

can get a prescription,' said Ana, standing in the doorway. Mariama concentrated on the screen and let her stand there.

'You need to be on top form when your exams start. And we need to decide soon what subject you want to study.'

'Forgive me, Ana, I would rather not talk about that until after the exams,' said Mariama without turning round.

'It could be that you're dreaming of studying something in particular, medicine, law, politics,' Ana suggested. Mariama did not answer.

'Why do you never look me in the eye when we talk together?' Ana wanted to know.

'It is not polite to look someone in the eye when they are older than you,' said Mariama, still with her back turned. Ana opened her mouth, but words failed to come. She went into the living room, switched on the TV and turned the sound down so as not to disturb Mariama's concentration.

They had begun to run together in Holland Park, which Ana liked because of its Japanese garden, its open-air opera stage with the elegant canopy and its peacocks. Their tall, slim figures looked good together. They could almost be taken for a couple of friends of the same age. They ran the same route every Sunday morning, past the tennis courts and round the cricket pitch, down to the play area and then on along the paths through the wood towards the entrance nearest to Holland Park Avenue. Mariama was much faster and improved Ana's performance.

'Ana, you should train more often, it's good for you,' she said.

'I can't talk at the same time,' Ana groaned, straining to keep up with Mariama's tempo. They were like two birds, flying side by side with synchronized movements. Consciousness moved from their heads down through their bodies to their legs, which carried them as if on wings. Ana dropped behind. Her calf muscles went on strike and she got cramp. She stopped briefly to stretch them against the knotted trunk of an oak tree. She fought the pain and carried on at a slower pace, with no chance of catching up with Mariama. She relished following her at a distance, relished observing her elegant and purposeful running style, and was suddenly flooded by a momentary feeling of happiness.

'Your brain grows when you run. Running generates brain cells,' said Mariama, as they sat in the rain beneath a parasol in one of the avenue's cafés, relaxing after their run.

'Well, I certainly need to get into better condition and become a bit smarter,' said Ana with self-conscious irony.

'I don't know anything about you, Ana,' said Mariama in her gentlest voice.

'There's not very much to know.' Ana was reluctant to have attention directed towards herself.

'What about your love life?' Mariama giggled.

'There hasn't really been time for love in my life. On the other hand, I am lucky at cards.'

'Is that why you're not married?'

'I haven't found Mr Right, but statistically it could happen at any time.' Ana decided not to tell her about Hans. It was too painful.

'Do you believe in statistics?' Mariama was teasing her.

'If I have to believe in anything, I believe that it is chance which governs us.'

'Where is your family?' Mariama went on in her own innocent way.

'That's a brief story. My parents only had me, and they were divorced when I was your age … just after my school leaving exam.'

'And the rest of your family?'

'I have no contact with them.'

'It is not good to be alone.' Mariama frowned.

'I have you, that's the most important thing,' said Ana, feeling as if she had won the jackpot.

'Ana, Ana.' Mariama shook her head.

'Here's to you and your future.' Ana lifted her glass. They clinked glasses and sipped their orange juice.

'I want to be a nurse like Aunt Amina,' said Mariama

impulsively.

'They will always be needed.' Ana repressed a twinge of disappointment. 'But it may be that you'll change your mind when you have the exam certificates in your hand.'

'I want to go home and help sick children.'

'You will earn much more if you stay in the UK.'

'I want to serve my country,' she said firmly. Ana did not know how to react to her idealism.

'If I manage to pass the exams,' she sighed.

'Aren't the pills helping you?'

'They did at first.'

'Then you must take a few more until the exam is out of the way.'

'You want the best for me, Ana.' Mariama concentrated on her plate of brunch.

'That's what I'm here for, my dear,' said Ana cheerfully.

'My mother would like to have a photograph of you, so that she can imagine where I am,' said Mariama without looking up.

'Yes, of course,' said Ana, conscious at the same moment of the fact that she had no wish to have her picture lying around in a hut in some dark village stuffed full of black magic and witchcraft. Why did she think in such primitive terms? Was she feeling guilty because she was not happy enough at having Mariama living with her and could not relax in her company? Her moving in had focused the spotlight on Ana's finances. She had spent several days reviewing her investments and after that had calculated how many years she could afford to live in her present fashion, including the expenses for Mariama, on the capital she had at her disposal. And the sums had frightened her. At the same time her hopes that the affair with Patrick would further her career were diminishing.

'Should we not send your mother a picture of the two of us together instead?' she suggested.

'Yes, but also of you alone,' Mariama insisted. 'It's only Rosie who has seen you.'

'If it will make your mother happy, then I suppose it won't

do any harm if she gets my picture,' said Ana resigned, and let her have her way.

The idyllic scene was shattered by shouts and disturbance from further down the avenue. It was Birdy, who had got into an argument with some of her colleagues. They were pushing her and shouting something which sounded like 'cat among the pigeons'. Mariama wanted to get up and go and help her, but Ana held her back.

'It can be dangerous to get mixed up in it,' she said, and Mariama stayed obediently where she was to please Ana. Birdy managed to extricate herself from the struggle without damage, and was once again sitting in her place on the ramp.

'Just a moment,' Mariama ran over to her and put a few coins in her plastic cup. Birdy raised her hand in thanks and played a tune on her harmonica. Ana had to restrain herself from going over and giving the woman an earful for having ruined the pleasant atmosphere so completely.

One Saturday afternoon Aunt Amina appeared in Henry Dickens Court with an enormous enamel casserole smelling of Mariama's favourite dish, chicken pieces in palm oil sauce, marinated in onion, lime, garlic and chili. She would not be able to find her way to Kensington on her own, so one of the cousins must have driven her, thought Mariama, covering up her astonished dismay with a beaming smile, whilst she felt the ground give way beneath her feet. She didn't have time to entertain Amina. She had to finish two difficult exercises ready for submission on the Monday. For the same reason she had as so often before refused the family's standing weekend invitation. Amina did not believe that she had so much homework every single week and had come to find out what lay behind Mariama's evasive behaviour. And if it was really true about all those exercises, why didn't she just bring her computer with her to Upton Park and do the exercises there in the bosom of her family?

'We're worried about you,' said Amina with her head on one side and her upper lip pulled up to reveal the gold crown on her right front tooth.

Mariama tried to make her understand that she did not have time to visit them every weekend, when she had to attend to her studies, her job and her English hosts (whom the family were too wrapped up in their own affairs to take any real interest in). She didn't say it out loud, but it relieved her bad conscience when she discovered that Amina and her uncle were just as hectically busy as she was, and had no time to keep an eye on her. She explained her refusal of weekend invitations with a cautious reference to the fact that she needed peace and quiet to work in order to pass the Advanced English and Foundation Course in five subjects at the end of term and get a place at university, and in that way get her student visa renewed.

As soon as Amina heard that feared and hated word 'visa' she said no more, but asked where the kitchen was, so that she could put the casserole down on the oven. She did not mention Mariama's hosts, whose name she did not know. The fact that she lived at two different addresses was in itself an incomprehensible muddle. Mariama felt it was her duty to show her around the flat, as it was what her aunt expected. Amina walked around as if she was at home and inspected everything in a matter-of-fact way as if she was familiar with every object and detail. Her way of picking up and turning over the precious Chinese porcelain and the silver candlesticks and teapots gave Mariama gooseflesh. She circled around her, petrified by fear that she might damage the hired furnishings for which Ana was responsible.

Finally she got her settled on a chair by the kitchen table, where she served her afternoon tea with all the trimmings. Amina went through her list of accusations, reproaching her for not spending enough time with her family; that was why she had sought an ally in her sister-in-law Rosie, who scolded her on the phone and could not understand what had happened to Mariama in London. Her little girl whom she had brought up to have consideration for others and obey older members of the family. Could it really be right that she had so much studying to do, repeated Amina in Rosie's high descant. It was beyond her experience to understand the pressure Mariama was under, with all the exercises to hand in. Even though her own sons were studying to become engineers, she could not accept that the time Mariama had to devote herself to her family was so limited.

'I'll come and visit you next weekend,' Mariama promised, dazed by her aunt's unexpected visit. The fact that Amina had come all the way to Kensington placed even more pressure on her. She didn't want to risk having her trotting over every Saturday afternoon with home-cooked delicacies, just because she couldn't be sure that she was being properly fed by the English people.

'The whole weekend?' Amina demanded, enjoying every bite of her scone with jam and clotted cream.

Mariama poured her another cup of tea (the fifth). In order to mollify her she assured her that she would be overjoyed to escape from her studies and just relax in the family's overfilled and noisy flat with the thick draped curtains which were always pulled across in the large lounge with the leather sofa and chandeliers and shut out all daylight. And she loved sitting up half the night with her in front of the enormous flatscreen TV, which continuously broadcast (mostly without sound) Nigerian-produced melodramas, watching the far-fetched family conflicts being resolved with the romantic happy ending, whilst she crunched home-made sweet potato crisps.

Amina enjoyed being waited on, and sat there for longer than she had planned. After yet another cup of tea with milk and sugar she sent her son, who had driven her right across London, a text message to say she was ready to leave. She impressed on Mariama that she must remember to bring the casserole dish when she visited them the following weekend, as it was difficult for her to manage without it in the kitchen. Amina had at least eight dishes exactly the same, but Mariama did not betray the fact that she knew that, and promised to bring the dish with her. There came a loud toot from a car horn out on Sirdar Road, and they made haste to leave the flat.

'Why did Omar not come in with you?' asked Mariama, as she walked with Amina along the paths through the green areas between the blocks of flats.

'He didn't want to disturb us,' she said inscrutably, and waved to her son to get out of the car, partly to say hello to his cousin and partly to open the car door for her. Mariama waited until she could no longer see the car. Amina's departure made her sad. The flat felt unfamiliar and deserted after her visit. At the beginning it had been a support for her to know that the family were there for her with advice and guidance, but their expectations and demands on her had become a burden. They wanted far too much of her precious time.

In London she was constantly aware of the time, the fact that time ran more swiftly than a horse could gallop. Time pursued her like a threatening shadow, which calculated the passing of each second into minutes, hours, days, weeks, months. The only place where time stood still was in her prayers. But things had gone so far that she couldn't concentrate on her prayers even for five minutes. She woke in the middle of the night with her heart beating fast and a flickering in front of her eyes, followed by a severe headache. She was worried that there was something serious wrong with her. That someone had asked a marabout to put a curse on her.

She had taken it for granted that she would feel at home in London, as she had felt at home in her dream of London. But she discovered that she was not the girl she had thought she was back home, where children were the family's property and all she had to do was obey. Then she had been on an even keel and knew who she was. She knew the rules and understood when she transgressed them and deserved her rightful punishment from God or Aunt Rosie. Her greatest capital was her good reputation. She was always ready to help others, her younger cousins, especially Madeleine who always got into trouble, and the children in the children's shelter by the dump. She was proud of the fact that she had Big Man's respect. She noticed that he listened to her, even though she was much younger than him, and that her words moved him when she asked him to provide more cassava and yams for the children, so that they didn't need to fight for food. He paid her a small weekly wage which she handed over to Rosie. Poor Rosie had changed since she lost her job in the bank. She had become bitter and aggressive, and expected Mariama to help compensate for her lost salary.

In London an imperceptible change had crept over her. A different Mariama had been called forth as a result of a freer rein and greater independence. She longed to be able to forget herself and not have to think about who she was and what steps she should take. Whether what she was doing was the right thing. She was so tired of this Mariama-in-London, who was constantly aware that time was passing quicker and quicker, so that the dreaded exam was already hanging over her head. She did not live in time. She was not enfolded by time like a bird or a fish in its element. She was strangely separated from time, which passed her by like an evil speed demon. She wished that time would stand still for a moment, so that she could stop and look around and let her eyes sink into the thick mangroves along the river and find a path and a direction.

Mariama had got into the habit of shutting herself in her room after her hour-long baths. It was as if she could not get clean enough, as if she wanted to scrub away the whole world's dirt. From her closed door a deep stillness spread through the rest of the flat and got on Ana's nerves.

'What are you doing in there? I was getting worried that you had jumped out of the window,' she couldn't help saying when Mariama finally emerged late for the dinner which Ana had kept warm for her.

'I become calm,' said Mariama with lowered eyes.

'Better than the nerve pills?'

'I need time to stand still.' Mariama sat down at the table and looked at the empty plate in front of her.

'You must eat something. You've lost weight,' said Ana, and did not enquire further into the mysteries of prayer. She thought that Mariama had started to look like the anorexic models on the catwalk, but she didn't dare say it aloud for fear of her anger. Mariama got up reluctantly and went over and lifted the casserole lid; she had no desire to eat what she saw. Instead she put the kettle on for tea.

'Don't you like my food?' said Ana with a teasing reference to Amina's casserole, which had still not been returned to Upton Park. She had enjoyed Amina's chicken yassa, laughed at Mariama's description of her visit and for once felt that she was on the inside.

'I'm not hungry,' muttered Mariama. It was only now that she understood her mother's warnings. 'Be afraid of your desires. They become your enemies when they are fulfilled.' Ever since she was little she had prayed to God that there would be food enough for the women and children when the men had had their part. Now she had not just food enough, but everything in abundance, and her hunger had departed.

'I'm worried about you. What is it that's troubling you?'

'Nothing.' Mariama shrugged. She could not tell Ana that she was afraid of not being able to live up to expectations, and felt more than anything like leaving Southwark College.

'How are your studies going?' Ana ventured into the mine-field.

'The pills are working,' she said evasively, and did not want to admit to Ana that to be on the safe side she had asked her mother to visit the imam and ask him to pray for her and get some juju amulettes made, which she was wearing on a leather thong around her waist. Powerful remedies were needed if she was to have a chance to pass her exam, but neither prayers nor jujus had as yet had any positive influence on her grades.

'You never tell me anything.'

'You have studied yourself. You know how it is.'

'Advanced English and Foundation Course is not quite the same thing as taking an MA in Economics.' Ana stopped herself, feeling that she had said the wrong thing. But Mariama just smiled and made a cup of tea for herself and a pot for Ana, and retired to her room to think through her situation. She had discovered that she was not nearly as worried about her family back home as she was about her exam. Her exam took up all the space. Day and night she thought of nothing else. It was as if near and far had changed places. She wondered whether she had been damaged, and had become too British inside through living with English people. Was it not possible to be completely happy without having to pay a price for it?

Mariama had quickly finished off her Diazepam pills, and told Ana off for not having arranged for a larger prescription; she insisted that Ana should get her a new one. For the sake of peace Ana gave her some of her own. In general she allowed Mariama to have her own way and decide about their joint housekeeping. She had not noticed that Mariama had changed, and that her gentle reticence often exploded in rage. She had enough to do to combat the fear which was plaguing her at the thought that two photographs of herself were lying around at Mariama's mother's, open and defenceless against evil powers. It had caught her completely off guard that she could be the victim of such primitive fantasies. That she was so entirely at the mercy of her feelings, and could not stop the galloping paranoia.

Why had she not noticed before now that so many of the cashiers and shop assistants in Holland Park Avenue were black? And that the same sight greeted her when she travelled in to the city, where she sat several times a week by the window in the high-ceilinged brasserie opposite the Rower building in Basinghall Street and watched people coming and going, in the vain hope of seeing Patrick come out of the swing doors and stop and look up at the little square patch of sky which floated over the marble court, which would give her time to leave the bar and cross the street and just happen to sit down by the fountain, where his glance would be bound to fall on her.

Ana's research, as she called her trips to the city, was disturbed by a horde of black people in pinstriped suits with briefcases. The foyer in City Hall Building was full of blacks everywhere, under the palms, by the reception counter, on the way to and from the elevator. Why had she not noticed before now that London was invaded by blacks? They came in floods, swamping the British Isles. Why was she seeing these black figures with gleaming faces and high cheek bones everywhere? Was she ill? Had she previously shut out the black figures from the street scene, not wanted to see them? She remembered that Mariama had been surprised at the beginning that there were so many black people in London, and Ana had dismissed it and said it was wishful thinking.

Was it her fear that the photos with Mariama's mother might get into the wrong hands which had summoned up these flocks of well-dressed black people, and made her see things? Her common sense told her (but common sense carried no weight) that London must at present be hosting a political summit meeting or an international conference where Africa was over-represented. Judging by their appearance and clothes, they must be South Africans, whom she was familiar with from her meetings at Rower's Johannesburg branch. She had enjoyed the company of these South African colleagues and been attracted by their sophisticated style, their self-confident rhetoric and their casual arrogance. When she came to think about it, she had once had a short affair with one of the young, go-getting Johannesburg dealers.

It was not only the black throngs in town which forced themselves on her attention and darkened her mind. Henry Dickens Court was occupied by black families and a smattering of socially challenged white English people, bent-backed pensioners who rummaged in containers to find edible scraps and resellable items. Young men with knives in their sleeves and rasta hair. It was only now she had become aware of their massive presence in the yards between the low blocks of social housing. They stood around all day, kicking manically at empty beer cans, which cannoned into everything with nerve-shattering bangs and ruined her pleasure at having Mariama in the house.

Even her dreams were invaded by black people. There was one dream in particular, or rather a nightmare, which came again and again. They were driving in a hotel jeep into a muddy yard in front of two rectangular concrete buildings. Inside there was an out-patients' clinic filled with women and children far down the narrow corridor. They were standing like sardines in a tin or sitting on the floor if they were too ill to stand. The tourist group was guided into a hospital room where there was just enough space for three beds. Pregnant women and new mothers with infants in their arms were sitting or lying in the beds. They were dressed in their colourful everyday costumes, and stood out like decorative flowers against the grey concrete walls.

It was quiet and peaceful, an almost ceremonial atmosphere. A heavily pregnant girl was in labour, lying with her features drawn in pain, waiting for the midwife to come and help her give birth. Two young mothers had all their attention focused on their newborns, who had only just been separated from their bodies. The impression was so overwhelming that Ana had to sit down on the nearest bed.

The woman in the bed smiled at her and pointed to her baby. Ana praised the pretty child. The woman started on a long speech in her native tongue. It sounded like a eulogy, but stopped suddenly as if an electric current had been switched off. She held out the child to Ana with a solemn expression. She didn't know whether she dared to accept the woman's gesture, whether she was capable of holding a stranger's child. She had never held a small baby in her arms, and was afraid that she might hurt it in her clumsiness, but she overcame her fear and accepted the little bundle.

So tiny, so delicate and fragile. So much smaller, softer and more fragile than her childhood's baby dolls. A vibrantly alive black doll, a budding little girl. The mother chattered enthusiastically in her melodic language, and showed Ana how to support the back and head, which suddenly fell back and sideways. She was not sure that she could cope with having so much life and death in her arms, and passed the child back to her mother, who chattered away to her, nodding and smiling in approval.

As she was hastily taking her leave (she could not keep her fellow tourists waiting any longer) Ana held out a bundle of notes to the baby's mother to say thank you. The young mother refused to accept her appreciation, and shook her head, saying:

'Give to hospital. Give to hospital,' she repeated, 'hospital no money.'

Ana put the notes back in her bag, and promised with gestures and sign language to do as she asked. Her little daughter lay peacefully sleeping at her breast. Ana could feel her maternal pride streaming through herself too. Never had she been so closely linked to another human being. She wondered whether in reality she was the young mother in the bed, and in a kind of madness had imagined that she was the stranger, a white woman like an angel. Ana woke up every night at the same place in her dream and found herself in a diffuse chaos, not knowing who or where she was.

Ana's fear had imperceptibly penetrated into the flat, into the walls, along the wainscoting and up under the ceiling. She was walled up in her fear, and imagined that Mariama had had a hidden agenda right from the start, in order to lure her into a trap. She gradually convinced herself that Mariama was conspiring with her mother, who was pulling the strings from back home. That they were plotting together about the photos, wanted to use them to cast a curse on her so that she sickened and died.

Ana was ashamed of her paranoid panic attacks, and lived a double life, one with her fear and one with Mariama. She began to feel uneasy in her company, and behaved with a forced awkwardness as soon as she appeared. She was so shut up in her paranoia that she didn't notice the seriousness of the change which had come over Mariama. And the more violently she reacted to the pressure of exams and to Ana's self-absorption, the more Ana's suspicions grew: that she had let a demon into her house.

In order to arm herself against the witchcraft of a whole continent collected in Mariama's slender, steely person, she had started on an intensive running regime, and was in full swing building up her physique in the spirit of the ancient Greeks: 'a healthy soul in a healthy body'. At the start it had been to escape from her fear and get control of herself and her body, show her recalcitrant muscles who was boss. She pushed herself to the limit, improved her times day by day. Her legs ran by themselves, independently of her will. It was not she who was running but an unknown being whose strength unfolded within her. She would easily have been able to keep up with Mariama's tempo if her exam preparations had allowed her time to train. Ana had begun to think about running the New York marathon, which she had always dreamed of, but her leadership position in Rower had not left her time to do anything about it. When Mariama's exam was out of the way she would suggest to her that they should train together for next year's marathon and find some longer distances than Holland Park could supply.

Ana was in the middle of tying her running-shoe laces whilst she prepared herself mentally for her day's training. Mariama came charging in through the front door and almost knocked her over. They stared at each other in shock, like two foreign bodies from different planets. Mariama started laughing at the awkward situation. Ana felt an almost physical revulsion at being jolted out of focus, and wished that she had been out of the door before Mariama came home.

As soon as she heard Mariama's characteristic laughter, the ill-fated photographs at Mariama's mother's appeared before her mind's eye, and her questions rained down on the girl. Where did her mother keep the pictures? Were they left lying around, or or were they hidden in a drawer? What did she do with them? Did she take them with her when she went out? she asked obsessively.

'She is so proud of them and shows them to everyone in the village,' Mariama assured her, patiently submitting to her cross-questioning.

'Then someone can put the evil eye on them,' Ana went on. Mariama started laughing at her attempts to think like an African.

'I want them back,' Ana persisted hysterically. Mariama's laughter ceased.

'You can't mean that, Ana,' she said. She had got to grips with things better, could work more concentratedly and manage with less sleep since she had started taking Ritalin, which a friend bought for her on the net.

'Even if you can't understand it, you must accept that this is very, very important to me,' Ana insisted.

'Don't you trust us?'

'I trust you and your mother, but I don't know the whole village.'

'No, you don't trust us,' Mariama decided. She was united with her mother and the village, on the same side as them.

'I would just like to have those photos back.'

'It is an insult to my mother.'

'Otherwise I can't be at peace,' Ana complained.

'I can't do that to my mother.'

'It's not very much I'm asking of you, Mariama.' Ana went out onto the kitchen balcony to get a bit of air. Mariama followed her.

'I'll tell my mother to look after the photos carefully, so that nothing happens to them.' Mariama had calmed down again. Ana felt uneasy that she was standing just behind her, almost pressing her up against the railing. She pushed her to one side and went into the kitchen again.

'I am so alone with my thoughts,' muttered Ana, staring straight in front of her.

'But I am here with you. Have you not noticed that?' Mariama came close to her again, making Ana feel threatened.

'Or do I not exist at all?' she said, hurt.

'I'm on my way over to the park.' Ana could not cope with

230

her importunate physical proximity.

'I'll come with you.' Mariama did not have time for a run, but Ana needed her.

'Leave me alone.' Ana shrank back from Mariama, and thought she could see a shadow behind her shoulder.

'Am I bad company?' Mariama stood in front of the door.

'You're misunderstanding me again.' Ana was panting for breath.

'You don't see me as I see me.' Mariama stepped aside and let her pass.

'Our fates are bound together,' said Ana, picked up her anorak and opened the door. Mariama stood still for a moment, looking at herself in the mirror over the chest of drawers. Then with all her force she threw the little bronze figure which stood on the glove shelf against her reflection. Ana heard the unreal sound of splintering glass, and came hurriedly back inside.

'Sorry, I am so sorry, Ana,' Mariama wailed, starting to pick up the splinters of mirror with feverish movements. She cut her fingers, making the blood flow. Large stains appeared on the carpet. Ana sat her down on a chair in the kitchen where the floor could easily be wiped clean and a bit of blood wouldn't do any damage. She wrapped kitchen roll around her bleeding fingers and said she would deal with the mirror splinters. Just so long as she held her hands still so that they stopped bleeding. She must understand that it was a rented flat which must be left in the same condition as it had been taken over.

Mariama looked at her with a veiled glance which came from far away, and was completely unreachable. Ana let her sit there with her fingers spread, and started vacuuming the carpet in the hall. She would have to get hold of a carpet cleaning firm as soon as possible, and get Ben and Bea to agree that they needed a resolution to where Mariama should live until they found a hostel room for her. It was not healthy for a young person not to know where she belonged. She ought to feel at home with them and be happy and bright, otherwise all their efforts were meaningless.

Ana was standing in the queue at one of the tills in Tesco. In front of her stood a large black woman in a gaily-coloured costume and behind her a tall loose-limbed man in a worn beige suit. She could feel his black breath on the back of her neck. Her mobile phone vibrated in her jacket pocket. She had forgotten her appointment with Jakob.

'Excuse me, Jakob, the connection is not very good in here. I'm surrounded by demons,' she explained as if it was an everyday phenomenon. She dropped out of the queue and pushed her basket in front of her with her foot, moving quickly in the direction of the exit.

'Demons?' Jakob fell in with her light tone.

'I see black people everywhere,' she went on.

'That's not so very strange in London, it's full of immigrants from the old colonies,' Jakob said, as if he were speaking to a patient.

'It wasn't like that to start with, but now they're suddenly everywhere,' Ana complained.

'How are things with Mariama?' Jakob wanted to get back on track.

'She's one of them.' Ana had reached the automatic door, and was standing looking down on Birdy's bird's nest. She was sitting faithfully in her place on the concrete ramp, guarding the entrance to the consumer palace.

'One of whom?'

'The demons.'

'What has happened since last time?' asked Jakob, dissatisfied with his client's progress, or rather lack of it.

'It's an invasion.' Ana began to sweat inside her clothes.

'It's perfectly normal that the thing you are focused on right now is what you see everywhere. It's Mariama you're seeing out there. She has overwhelmed you. It will be different when she's become a straightforward part of your life.'

'She hides herself from me. Conceals herself behind a mask.'

'No doubt she's like all adolescents, jealously guarding her private life.'

'Behind the mask she's spying on me.' Ana didn't stop to hear what he said.

'I can't recognise a well-educated career woman in what you're saying.'

'No, I'm not myself any longer.'

'What's happening to you?'

'Mariama has sent some photos of me down to her mother.'

'What's the problem with that?' he asked, tired.

'I'm afraid that someone will use them to put voodoo on me.'

'Who would want to do that and why?'

'You have no idea how poor they are.'

'You are Mariama's sponsor. No-one would dream of hurting you.'

'She looks right through me. She knows what I'm thinking.'

'How can you believe such nonsense?' Jakob interrupted her.

'But I don't believe it,' said Ana angrily.

'So what are you talking about then?' Jakob felt he was wasting his time.

'Something has happened to me … I can't …' Ana was being pushed and shoved by people who were struggling out of Tesco's with their shopping bags.

'Of course something has happened. You've changed your life radically. But there's no need to call it voodoo.'

'Everything's in a mess.'

'You must be patient. Rome wasn't built in a day.'

'Mariama is so distant from me.'

'But that's no reason to demonize her …'

'Why do I do it?' Ana interrupted him.

'To get an explanation.'

'Of what?'

'Of the fact that you've lost control.'

'There's an infernal noise around me. I'll have to hang up.' Ana's voice was drowned out.

'We'll talk again in two weeks, same time.' Jakob was clearly frustrated.

'I'll think about what you've said and work with it,' said Ana politely, and asked herself whether she really had any need of Jakob any more, whether his coaching had not run its course. She put her mobile in her jacket pocket and rejoined the queue, which in the meantime had grown even longer. She suddenly longed for Hans, for his thoughtfulness and balanced overview, his understanding of her peculiarities and his cautious advice, which never transgressed her boundaries. But he had not been in touch since she moved to London, and she could not come crawling back.

Ana had agreed with Bea that she would come over to them in their lunch break between twelve and two. It was the only time of day when they both stopped work. The firm had exploded in the time Mariama had been living with them. They had calculated that the consultancy work for the EU and national aid organizations would decrease with the economic crisis, but it had had the opposite effect for B&B Consultancy. Bea insisted that they should all three meet and draw up a kind of balance sheet of the situation, 'Project Mariama', as Ben in his own ironic way had labelled the lunch agenda. He was of the opinion that the ladies could quite happily find a solution without him, but he had sacrificed himself, despite the fact that he had neither the time nor the energy for 'domestic matters' in the midst of a complicated evaluation report for DFID, who were B&B Consultancy's most important working partners.

'Item 1: Mariama was to help the household run smoothly and item 2: keep Bea company when I'm away,' began Ben efficiently, as if it was a business meeting.

'We have a lodger who is working on her studies, not an au-pair. We have to make adjustments for that,' Bea interrupted him.

'The latter item as Bea's companion has been partly satisfied,' Ben continued, ignoring Bea's intervention.

'I am so fond of her. She's so intelligent to talk to,' she put in. To be intelligent was the highest grade on Bea's scale.

'We and Mariama need to take a break,' Ben said categorically. It came as a surprise to Ana that things had gone so badly wrong.

'As you know, Ben and I are not in agreement. If Mariama decides that she would prefer to live with us after all, then I think we should give it a chance. She has got used to our rhythm. And it would be good for her to be able to concentrate one hundred percent on her exam without having to move in the midst of it all,' Bea asserted. It was as if they had swapped roles. Ben had from the start been the proposer of the idea that they should take Mariama in, whilst Bea had had more reservations.

'You're looking at it with rose-coloured spectacles. We've had a long series of clashes.' Ben threw up his hands in exasperation.

'You're behaving like the spoilt child you used to be, with a nanny and servants,' said Bea, losing her temper.

'I don't think we need to get personal,' said Ben just as heatedly.

'Mariama is not our housemaid,' Bea shrieked in a hoarse crow's voice.

'Please, we have guests.' Ben tried to calm her down.

'Ana is involved in this, she is entitled to know how things stand in this house,' Bea objected. Ben shook his head. He had lost weight and looked exhausted.

'What does Mariama say?' Ana put in.

'I've talked to her.' Bea hesitated.

'Has she accepted your joint offer to move back in?'

'Keep me out of this.' Ben held up his hand dismissively.

'It's not going to work for Mariama if you two disagree.' Ana was concerned about the situation.

'Ben, darling, when you're finished with the Congo report, things will get easier for us.' Bea appealed to his old stable persona. But it was burnt out. Ana felt guilty at having burdened those two dear people with a responsibility they couldn't cope with on top of the extreme pressures of their work. She had done it with the best of intentions, in order to give Mariama optimal conditions in London. In the light of her own failures Ben and Bea had seemed to her to have limitless reserves of energy.

'Would it not be best for all concerned if Mariama moved over to me permanently?' she suggested. Ana found it difficult to imagine not having Mariama living with her.

'I think Mariama should have peace and quiet to work for her exam without the upset of moving,' Bea insisted.

'But she's already installed at my flat.'

'But the mental readjustment,' Bea put in, determined to get her way.

'Ben, do you agree that Mariama should carry on living with you until she has got through her exam?' Ana both hoped and feared that he would say yes.

'I don't like this discussion.' Ben stood up abruptly, making his chair skid across the kitchen floor. 'We're talking about Mariama as if she's a problematic parcel which needs to be deposited where it's most convenient for us,' he continued on his way out of the kitchen.

'But we're just discussing what's best for her,' Ana objected.

'I'm signing off and leaving the parcel to you.'

'Has she not lived up to your expectations?' Ana tried to hold him back.

'It's more that we have not lived up to our own expectations.' Ben paced up and down.

'What do you mean?' asked Bea. Ben's heart-searching had shaken her composure.

'With all our years of experience in Africa, we ought not to fall into the trap called "the white man's burden".'

'Perhaps we have spent too long down there.' Bea's voice was almost inaudible.

'I don't feel that Mariama is a burden, on the contrary, she is the gift of my life, my soul,' Ana burst out, giving voice to her innermost feelings.

'That sounds almost cannibalistic,' said Ben, trembling with indignation.

'No, Ben, you don't mean that, you're not yourself, that's not like you at all,' said Bea in consternation. Ben left the kitchen before she had finished speaking.

'What on earth was it I said that made him so angry?' Ana asked in alarm.

'You just said exactly what you felt.' Bea attempted for a moment to rise above her own agitation which had been caused by Ben's violent reaction.

'How can feelings be so offensive?' Ana picked up a piece of manchego. She had to have something or other to put in her mouth.

'Feelings aren't always right, they represent the most primitive aspect of us, the most offensive, if you like.' Bea was a person who lived on her emotions and knew what difficulties it could get you into.

'Strong feelings are a force of nature which can bring about death and destruction,' she continued with hard-won objectivity.

'That is something I don't understand,' said Ana, feeling lost.

'You must forgive Ben for overstepping the mark. His temperament is like a volcanic explosion. His outbursts don't happen very often, but when they do they're violent.' Bea tried to smooth things over. 'Ben is an idealist,' she sighed, ' he demands the impossible, all or nothing.'

'I thought I was doing something for Mariama, that I was helping her move forwards,' said Ana in a weak voice, drained of emotion.

'It's Ben who looks at things the wrong way. He measures everything against the ideal, but that's also what I love him for. He is a man who won't compromise.' Bea had tears in her eyes, as if Ben's torments with the evaluation report for DFID caused her physical pain.

'Now we'll have a cup of green tea with ginger,' she carried on cheerfully. Ana found her mood swings unsettling. The day's experiences in Portland Road had helped her to understand that Mariama found it hard to feel at home in a house where the air was vibrating with tension and nerves were shredded.

'You mustn't go until Ben has calmed down again. He's so impatient with people. They have to be perfect and live up to his ideals. I do that, fortunately.' Bea gave a subtle little laugh, like someone who has outwitted fate.

'Ben is very enthusiastic about people when he first meets them. Then his disappointment is the greater if his first impressions aren't correct,' said Bea again in a matter-of-fact way, covering her own vulnerability. Ana put two and two together: she and Mariama had fallen short. She shivered. It was as if a cold draught had blown through the kitchen.

'But Ben is so friendly and considerate,' she said surprised, thinking about the trust he had shown her by using her as a financial adviser and putting the financial control of B&B Consultancy into her hands.

'Cheers, my dear, to our friendship.' Bea lifted her teacup and they clinked the thin china. Bea got up and opened the door to the back garden; it was a flower garden without furniture, something beautiful to look at and philosophize about, not a place where you could rest. Ana took Bea's arm and suggested that they should go outside and warm themselves in the sun.

Mariama had been summoned to a 'family meeting' as soon as she came from Nida Hostel where Binta was to show her round. And after that she was going to make a decision together with Ana. Mariama knew that Ana would do anything for her, carry out her slightest wish. She did not understand why, or what all that giving gave her in return, when she did not believe in God. But it would be impolite to ask her about the reason for her overwhelming generosity.

Mariama came into the kitchen, and felt at once that something had taken hold of her with invisible force; she knew that she was lost and did not have any choice. The spirit had chained her to the house in Portland Road. She should not have given in to Ana's repeated attempts to persuade her, but respected the higher powers. She sat down at the table with the remains of the lunch, but could not eat a mouthful. In London it was she who was dependent on others and had to accept help. In London she had neither her good reputation nor the respect she had had back home, even if she had been only a child on the way to becoming an adult.

She began clearing away the lunch and putting the plates and glasses in the dishwasher. When Ana and Bea came in from the garden, the kitchen was as clean as a whistle.

'How beautifully you have cleared away,' said Bea enthusiastically. Mariama shrugged. She didn't like being praised like a child. And besides she had expected to be able to talk things through with Ana on her own. It made her uneasy to be in the minority. She was fond of them each in their own way, and preferred to deal with them separately. She had never imagined that two white women could be so different.

'I don't want to live in Binta's hostel,' she announced.

'Why not?' Ana's mood plummeted.

'It costs so much.' Mariama gave her the papers.

'You mustn't think about that,' she said. Bea felt superfluous and started watering the pot plants with water from a vase of cut flowers. Her home had all the eccentric deficiencies which confirm the stereotype of unworldly academics. Ana sat down opposite Mariama, whose presence made her tense and nervous, like a woman in love in the presence of the beloved.

'But I do think about it,' said Mariama with a forcefulness which brooked no dissent. She did not want to increase her debt of gratitude or challenge fate by acting arrogantly just before the feared exam.

'I want to live here, if Ben and Bea will allow it,' she said, and felt the spirit's breath on the back of her neck. It would not let her go again now that she had crossed the threshold in Portland Road. She looked across to Bea, who was standing with her back to them, picking dry leaves off a geranium. She had a habit of talking to her house plants.

'Yes, dear?' she said, and turned round with a mild,

distracted expression on her face.

'I would like to live here, if you will have me,' she repeated quietly. It upset Ana to see their intimacy. She had to take a grip on herself in order not to hurl the fruit bowl at their heads. She had taken it for granted that Mariama would move in with her or to a hostel paid for by her, and so at any event come under her wing. She was so ready to take over from Ben and Bea. She had begun to dream about a happy daily life with Mariama, like in magazine features about 'ideal homes'.

'I thought ...' she said, confused. Mariama explained patiently that she wanted to wait to move until the exam was over. For no-one knew what the future would bring, ahead lay a black darkness, she added enigmatically.

'Of course you can stay here, that was the idea from the start,' said Bea, pleased. Ana got up; she wanted to go home and recover from her defeat.

'We have both failed, Bea, according to what you confided in me out there amongst the rhododendron bushes about your adopted daughter from Uganda.' Ana had been flattered by Bea's trust in her, but it was worth nothing now that she had won Mariama over.

'Everything is as it was before, Ana,' Mariama comforted her, as if she knew how she felt.

'I didn't try to conceal that I think it is best for Mariama to stay here and get through her exam,' said Bea.

Ana stood there, irresolute and at a loss, as if she couldn't find the door. Her needle-sharp stilettos bored up through her spine and straight into the back of her head. She had to sit down again, and suddenly felt Mariama stroking her hair. It was an upside-down world. It was the grown-up who should be stroking the child's hair, thought Ana, on the verge of tears.

The next day she made another trip to Basinghall Street. She went in to City Place House and gave her name at reception. She had no expectations of her unannounced visit to Patrick, from whom she had heard nothing since their first and only meeting in his studio flat. She felt uncomfortable, and had a strong suspicion that she had miscalculated by embarking on an affair with one of Rower's big guns. The bigger the guns, the more unpredictable and capricious, experience had taught her. Maybe he would refuse to welcome her into the fold precisely because he was afraid of a cast-off lover causing difficulties. One single little false step, and you were lost.

Ana's head was an ants' nest of forebodings as she went up in the lift. As far as she was concerned, their affair could cease without more ado. She was not interested in catching a man, but exclusively in getting that job contract he had held out the prospect of. It had been an expression of unhappiness and desperation that she had got involved with him, and she was ready to back out if that was what he wanted.

On the eighth floor she walked past the seating area and along the corridor to Patrick's office. He was sitting on the edge of the desk talking on the phone, and his expression did not change as she entered. With a slight gesture he indicated that she should sit down at the meeting table. He talked for a long time, and seemed to have completely forgotten her. She was just about to leave when he hung up and came over, formally shaking hands with her as though they had never touched each other before.

'I'm afraid I'm on my way to a meeting, but we can talk in the lift,' he said non-committally. At once Ana knew that she had made the biggest mistake of her life. And it occurred to her that it was a very long time since she had been herself and had just one thing in her head: the current tasks in the client team, with a clearly defined focus which generated a disciplined work ethic.

'What brings you over this way?' Patrick asked neutrally.

'It's ... I hope you aren't ...'

'I'll get in touch when there's an opening in the field,' Patrick brushed her aside, pressing the button for the ground floor and exit. He positioned himself so that she could see him in the mirror as the successful man he was.

'I don't expect our affair ...'

'Affair?' Patrick raised his eyebrows. The lift arrived at the ground floor with a short sigh. He made straight for reception and ordered a taxi. Ana hurried after him.

'Last time we … you said that I was in a strong position.' Ana had no feelings for him, but his powerful status made her run around like a chicken.

'Things are changing all the time. You never know.' Patrick looked around distractedly for the taxi, which drew up by the main entrance. Ana ran after him out into the street. He slid into the back seat, and gave her a brief nod. She remained standing there, looking forlornly at the threadlike jets from the fountain spurting up in thin bundles.

That same evening she began to gamble on the net. Mariama had been to the flat and packed her things, leaving a short message that she would ring, signed 'I miss you. M.' Ana took the hastily scribbled note and folded it up, putting it in her handbag as a keepsake. Her existence had lost altitude. It was time to begin the flight towards the heavens. She went on to gamblenet.com and logged into Rushmore Casino, which gave the highest bonus. She had been on the site a few times to get her bearings, but had not played before. She ensconced herself in bed with her laptop on her knee and a glass of red wine and a bag of crisps on the bedside table. With plentiful rations from the supermarket she made her way into the cosy burrow of the net and further into the virtual gaming hall.

It did not give the same kick as in the casino, but the advantage was that she became completely engrossed in the screen and ceased to exist in the world of reality. She was gambling to win, and that demanded a different level of concentration to just playing with a random sum of money. She needed to fill some substantial holes in her finances. The loss on the sale of the flat, which had fallen in value by several million kroner, and her monthly salary with the various bonus payments which no longer appeared in her account. The many current expenses were reducing the sum at her disposal day by day, and one fine day they would tip her over into the red.

She no longer reckoned on getting work at Rower's London office. Her lack of mobility, the fact that Mariama tied her to London and cut off the possibility of making her home anywhere on the planet where Rower had an office, was a handicap. It was so peculiarly unfamiliar for her to be bound to something other than Rower, to be overwhelmed by a previously unknown feeling for another human being. What was this mystical closeness she felt for this little girl from a continent she knew hardly anything about? The fact that the feeling was not a fantasy or a delusion, but a reality which demanded action, was convincingly demonstrated by the last year's radical change in the circumstances of her life.

The image on the screen changed, and showed that she had entered the game. She might just as well begin in good time, she told herself. Her finances would sooner or later need to be supplemented if she was going to maintain her standard of living and finance Mariama's education as well. She had no expectations of getting anything back in return for her efforts. She had to accept that Mariama had chosen for the time being to stay with Ben and Bea. It made her feel secure to have nothing to lose. She was most comfortable at the bottom of the well. If there was anything life had taught her, it was renunciation. She ought to enter a nunnery, she thought with a kind of excitement, as she waited for the result of the first round. She had eased herself in gently with two hundred dollars on odds.

The well-known feeling of being on the net without limits descended over Ana, who grew bolder as she won back twice her stake. Her self-confidence was strengthened in communion with virtual sums of money. The abstract was her element. In her time at Rower she had enjoyed surfing the net, buying and selling securities and moving seven-figure amounts from one location to another with a single click. Now it was her own finances she was gambling on, her own and Mariama's future.

They had a crisis meeting after it became clear that Mariama had not spent the weekend at Upton Park as she had informed Ana and Ben and Bea. It was almost mid-week before they discovered that something was wrong and contacted her aunt and uncle, whom they were all now meeting for the first time. Aunt Anima had also called in Binta. She was the last one to see Mariama on the Thursday evening, when they said goodbye in front of Liverpool Street Station. Binta had been worried that Mariama was not answering her mobile, and had rung Aunt Amina and asked after her. There was a great stir when the family and the three hosts realized that Mariama had been with neither the one nor the other at the weekend, nor had she appeared at Southwark at the beginning of the week.

They were all sitting around the coffee table drinking tea, the two cousins (who had been out looking for Mariama from early morning to late evening), Amina and Sulay, Binta (on the white leather sofa between the cousins), Bea and Ben (although he did not have time) and Ana, who was sitting on the edge of a deep armchair. It was deathly quiet in the darkened room whilst Amina poured out the tea. The TV was on with no sound, turned away from the coffee table so that the company could not see the picture, just the light from the screen, which shone on the heavy curtain in front of the windows. Amina sat down on Sulay's armrest with her cup in her hands. Ben cleared his throat and broke the silence.

'Might there not be a natural explanation?' he said, glancing round from one to the other to include everyone in the question.

'I suppose the police have been informed.' Ben looked at Sulay. Amina passed him the form recording that Mariama had been declared missing that day. Amina had spent the whole morning at the police station, where a report had been drawn up about the matter. Ben passed the form on to Ana. The words all ran together before her eyes. She could not take in what it said. It wasn't necessary either. The thought of what had happened to Mariama and of her own failure was more than enough. She didn't need any papers to prove it.

Binta was the central actor in the meeting and was asked to tell first about the evening when she and Mariama had gone together to the Al-Badr mosque to a meeting of the study circle of the Gambia Islamic Youth Association, GIYA. She explained that Mariama had seemed nervous and depressed from the outset. She got into an even worse state as they were standing by the bus-stop and she had seen something or other. Binta did not know exactly what it was, but they had joked that a ghost had walked past. Binta had had an uneasy feeling that Mariama was in contact with the invisible world.

Out at the mosque she had behaved strangely. She had fallen asleep in the middle of studying the Koran, as if she just wanted to escape from the whole thing, but then insisted on going over to the Culture Centre afterwards, where they were serving tea. She said that she missed attaya tea with lots of sugar like back home. The worst thing was that she had started to argue with one of the young bearded Koran experts and had quarrelled with him and shouted: 'Why am I here? What am I doing here? Studying Islam?'

Binta explained that at first Mariama did not want to have anything to do with the study circle, and that it had taken her a long time to persuade her to go along. But that evening she had behaved as if she was bewitched. Binta had asked her what was wrong, but Mariama had brushed the question aside, saying that she was stressed and tired because of preparing for the exam, which was worrying her a great deal. Far too much, almost morbidly, in Binta's opinion.

'You said she was depressed. Do you know why?' asked Bea, turning towards Binta.

'I don't know whether anything has happened, or if it's just because our exam is getting close.'

'Did she ever mention us?' Bea went on. Her face was translucent, with an almost greenish hue. Ana thought that Mariama's disappearance must have made her illness flare up.

'Yes … no. Mariama has her own ideas about everything.' Binta was uncomfortable at the question.

'She doesn't let herself be pushed around,' Ben added,

looking discreetly at his watch.

'And that's a good thing.' Bea looked defiantly at him.

'You must understand, this is a terrible blow for us.' Bea spoke as if in a trance. The cousins and Binta sat uneasily on the sofa, not knowing where to look.

The atmosphere was oppressive because those present did not feel at ease with one another. Amina could not hold back her tears, and constantly had to dab at her swollen eyes with a tissue. She had gold-plated chains round her neck and a quantity of thin bracelets, which jangled at the slightest movement. Ana was ashamed to face the family, and had a strong urge to get up from her chair, go out of the door and disappear just like Mariama.

'Does Mariama's mother know …?' she asked, turning to her aunt and uncle.

'That can wait until we know something for sure. My sister has a weak heart,' said Sulay calmly. The cousins nodded and looked down at their shoes. Amina started to sniff again.

'That sounds sensible.' Ben shifted restlessly in his chair.

'She generally rings at weekends to check on Mariama,' Binta put in, with a nervous twitch by one eye.

'So let me summarize. The police are aware, and unless we have any new information it's best that we let them get on with it,' Ben asserted, assuming the lead role again.

'And you two, will you carry on looking?' Bea looked at the cousins.

'We'll leave that to the police,' Ben cut her short. Bea fell silent, aggrieved. Ana had switched off. It was not her but someone else who was sitting on the edge of a chair in the family's living room. A misfortune like this happened to other people, not to her.

'I have asked my sons to enquire about Mariama everywhere where they have been with her: clubs, discotheques, cafés. We must keep going and not give up, not lose heart,' said Sulay with sorrowful dignity.

At that moment Amina's mobile rang. She took it and went down to the other end of the large double lounge. She spoke in a muffled voice, choked with tears. She stayed sitting at the dining table with the high-backed chairs, her head in her hands. Her stiff black wig gleamed in the light from the lamp on the ceiling. Ana looked at the frozen figure and felt like a bird of ill omen who had forced her way in amongst innocent people and caused them grief. How could she ever make it right again? She had nothing to give but money. And that was poor consolation. She got up and went over to sit together with Amina at the table. Amina seized her hand and squeezed it in hers.

'Our little girl. We should have looked after her better. We have let her down,' she sighed.

'Everything is my fault.'

'No it's not. You are not God. We cannot do anything other than pray. Pray and search every last corner of this accursed town.' She let go of Ana's hand.

'You are a good person,' she went on, looking at her as if she wanted to memorize every feature, every line and every shade of colour in her skin. It was almost like hearing Mariama. The same mildness around the solid core. Like the flesh of a fruit around the stone. With herself it was the exact opposite. Hard on the outside and a soft mollusc on the inside.

Amina got up and went back to the group. Ana followed her, more composed and clear-headed.

'Mariama's mother?' asked Bea, as soon as they were in the circle around the sofa.

'Ethel has been ringing all weekend without being able to reach Mariama.' Amina chivvied one of her sons up from the sofa and sat down next to Binta.

'She wanted to talk to the English people, she said.' Amina addressed herself exclusively to her husband and ignored the rest of the company.

Ana suddenly remembered the photos in Mariama's mother's possession, which she had temporarily forgotten. Now her mother really had good reason to avenge herself, and Ana good reason to be afraid. But her fear was gone. Quite the reverse: she was ready to accept her mother's revenge. It would almost be a relief.

'We are most to blame,' she heard Bea say, 'Mariama is our responsibility as long as she is living under our roof.'

'We will of course do everything in our power to make sure that she is found safe and well,' Ben joined in, with an unctuousness which seemed incongruous in him.

'At weekends she stays with me,' Ana objected.

'But on this fateful weekend we were in charge,' Ben corrected her.

'I would prefer to assume my part of the responsibility,' Ana insisted. She had never felt the opposition between herself and them as strongly as she did now.

'Yes, of course,' Bea assured her. She could not bear dissent, and would gladly divide the guilt equally between them.

'We are all desperate, Ana,' she continued, almost reproachfully. Ana could no longer feel any connection to her good friends. They had become alien beings to her.

'Then we must stick together,' said Ana, with an uncomfortable feeling that no-one was receiving her.

'Each one of us will do what we can to bring about a happy ending,' said Bea coolly.

'Of course,' said Ana meekly.

'I'm going to have to go, don't break off on my account. I'll go over to the police station later today and make sure they're working on the case.' Ben got up and shook hands with the uncle and aunt. Bea made a convulsive movement as he went, but forced herself to remain in her seat. Ana felt sorry for her, and wondered what was going on between those two split personalities. She suggested to Bea that they should take their leave and go together to Holland Park. They said goodbye to the family with mutual assurances that they would keep in touch.

Ana was deep into Online Vegas when Jakob rang as arranged. The net was her fixed point in the diffuse vacuum which Mariama had left behind her. So far she had kept her head above water and finished with a modest profit. But there was a long way to go if she was going to have any hope of offsetting even some of her losses, which was the goal she had set herself. She lived and breathed on the net and no longer had any need of Jakob. But she had not got round to cancelling the call and telling him that she had stopped the fixed monthly payment which was transferred to his account.

'I'm in the middle of an important meeting,' she said.

'You can't fool me.' Jakob was so tired of her excuses that he was becoming rude.

'OK, I'm … busy on the net,' she admitted the truth.

'You'll have to put a stop to that if you want to get anywhere.'

'There's nowhere to get. Mariama has disappeared,' she broke in.

'You can't mean that …'

'Please be so good as to register what I'm saying,' said Ana, claiming the right of the unhappy person to be unreasonable.

'I'm sorry, but it can't be true.' Jakob was genuinely shocked.

'You mustn't ask me about anything. Everything is chaos.'

'So it's difficult to …,' said Jakob cautiously.

'I've never had anything to lose apart from my work before. I had made a friend and I was egoistic enough to bring her to London.'

'And your friends?'

'We thought we had agreed where Mariama was to be at the weekend.'

'Is there anything I can do to help?'

'I can't bear to talk about it.'

'You can't just sit and play on the net,' said Jakob. Ana didn't answer. She felt he was invading her boundaries.

'What are your friends doing about it?' He tried a different approach.

'They've hired a private detective who is investigating at the university. Mariama was last seen on Friday evening in the student café. Since then there has been no sign of life from her.' Ana felt that putting the disaster into words made it greater.

'If I can be of any help, as I said …'

'You have been my loyal support. Without you I wouldn't have been able to get through the relocation.'

'It's just my job.' Jakob stopped himself saying any more.

'A paid friendship is more than a friendship, it's the ideal friendship, safe and unchanging,' Ana cut him short. He let her carry on to the end.

'So you must understand that I can't go on. What has happened is so unfair … so wretched … I can't talk about it.' Ana's voice faded out like a sound track.

'Am I to understand that we … that you're stopping here?' said Jakob neutrally.

'I would like to keep open the opportunity to come back to you if I feel I need it.'

'Well, I'm not sure I'll have room. My client list is full.'

'You're not a fucking friend!' Ana shouted into the phone. Jakob hung up.

Suddenly there was no-one on the other end. She panicked at the unexpected abrupt break and hurriedly sent him a text message to apologize for her overreaction. Then she turned her attention back to the screen, where she had put the game on stand-by. For once she couldn't concentrate, and let the laptop switch itself to sleep mode. She moaned softly in front of the black screen. How could she manage without her friend and helper, the only person who was concerned about her when the chips were down? She sent another text and promised to double his fee if he would give her a second chance. But with some part of her she knew that it was all over. She had gone too far and had hit his firewall.

Ana picked up the mobile phone which was lying next to the laptop with shaking hands; it took her a long time to hit the answer button. Mariama's disappearance had thrown her into a kind of mental state of alert. Every time her phone rang her whole body started to shake, and she found it difficult to concentrate on conversations which were about anything other than Mariama.

'Hello,' she said in a fearful whisper. There was just an empty rushing sound, like an echo of nothingness.

'Hello, hello,' she repeated and could hear some distant agitated voices and a muffled sobbing. Her heart pounded in terror.

'Ana?' came Rosie's voice. 'When are we going to get our Mariama back?' she went on.

'Sorry, Rosie, I am so sorry. We're doing all we can to find her.'

'I'm sure she has hidden herself somewhere or other,' said Rosie.

'Do you know something we don't know?'

'I know Mariama,' said Rosie confidently.

'But where would she hide and why?' asked Ana, as if she was speaking to an oracle.

'When she's got herself into a mess, she always hides away, it's been like that ever since she was a little girl,' said Rosie without the least doubt in her voice.

'What sort of mess?'

'How should I know? You ought to know her problems. You should have looked after her.'

'Has she told you she has problems?' Ana was walking restlessly around the flat with the phone to her ear.

'No, but I'm certain she's hiding,' Rosie replied laconically.

'How is her mother?' asked Ana cautiously, fearing the answer.

'She is suffering and praying for her little girl all day long. Listen, you can hear her suffering and prayers,' said Rosie dramatically and held the phone out into the room, from where there came the sounds of loud wailing and lamentation.

'Can you hear her?' she said, and the sounds faded into the background.

'Tell her that I am suffering as well. And give her my heartfelt apologies for having caused so much grief and pain. Tell her that we will definitely find her.' Ana sincerely believed her promise. Rosie's phone call had given her new courage.

'Do you have any idea where we should look for her?'

'Big Man knows Mariama. He is her mentor,' said Rosie formally.

'So perhaps I should speak to Big Man?'

'Yes, you could do that.'

'It's a long time since I have spoken to him. I don't have his mobile number.' Ana's hopes dwindled.

'He changes his number all the time.' Rosie yawned audibly.

'Tell me, what shall I do?' asked Ana.

'How should I know? You just have to find her. Listen.' Rosie held the phone out again, and the cries of lamentation once more became loud and penetrating, as if they were coming from a loudspeaker.

'Her mother is suffering,' said Rosie, as if she was presenting a piece of music. Ana's throat constricted.

'Can you get hold of Big Man's mobile number for me?' Ana pleaded.

'Just remember that I live a long way from Serrekunda, and must look after my business and my market stall.' Rosie sounded pleased with herself. And Ana was equally pleased that the money had done some good.

'So we must hope for a miracle,' she said despondently.

'Mariama will appear sooner or later. I went to the marabout.'

'Does he know anything?' asked Ana. The misfortune had conquered her reservations about the occult.

'He doesn't know, he sees,' Rosie emphasized.

'So what does he see?'

'Mariama is hiding in the darkness and is alive.' Rosie paused for effect.

'Find her,' she said and hung up. The conversation had left Ana with the impression that a breakthrough in the investigation had occurred. Rosie's awe-inspiring power had given her a kind of childlike confidence that the good forces were winning. And it was all the same to her if they were helped by black magic.

Ana wanted to ring Ben and Bea and tell them about Rosie's call, but changed her mind and went over to them instead. For once she ignored the fact that they were probably working. Nothing could be more important than that Mariama came back to them. It was a long time before anyone opened the door. She hardly recognised Bea. She looked even thinner and paler, if that was possible, dressed in layer upon layer of gauzy silk material with nothing inside it.

'Bea, how are you?' Ana hugged her, and could feel the outline of her skeleton.

'Not bad, not bad at all,' she chirped cheerfully, 'but why have you come here at this hour?'

'May I come in?' Ana was standing on the pavement in the rain.

'Of course, do please come in, sorry, Ana.' Bea stood aside so that Ana could come into the dry.

'You need to look after yourself better,' Ana said worriedly.

'I know that, my dear. I have stopped working until Mariama comes back again,' she said, as lightly as if Mariama was just on a trip.

'Can Ben manage on his own?'

'We've appointed a co-worker.'

'Then you'll have more time for yourself,' said Ana, hoping that she would perhaps also have more time for her, that is time to search for Mariama.

'That's true enough, but I'm bored, and I'm jealous of the charming young man who has replaced me.' Bea's gaze became dreamy.

'How is your detective getting on? Any progress?' Ana didn't want to waste time on anything other than Mariama.

'He didn't get anywhere. We fired him and hired a new one, a woman. Mariama is in good hands with her,' Bea assured her.

'But it's time something happened,' said Ana sharply.

'It's out of our hands. I'm relying on her. What's the alternative, after all: the two of us trawling through London, knocking on people's doors and showing them a photo of

253

Mariama?' Bea gave her a mug of lukewarm herbal tea. The atmosphere in the house was cold and dusty, almost unlived-in.

'Well, I'm going to search for her, at least.'

'You'll just get more depressed,' Bea said dismissively.

'I don't give a damn about that. I just want to get Mariama back.'

'We're amateurs. We can't do better than an experienced detective.'

'It's not either-or, it's both-and,' said Ana. Bea's lethargic attitude made her frustrated.

'Why have you come, Ana?' Bea fixed her hawk's eye on her.

'Rosie rang. She's sure that Mariama will be found safe and sound.' Ana sounded more convinced than she was.

'How?' Bea bent over her teacup and breathed in the aroma.

'She went to the marabout,' said Ana. Bea started to laugh at her childlike eagerness.

'You must excuse me, Ana, but you don't mean to tell me that you believe in all that rubbish. It only works for Africans.'

'Mariama is an African, and so is Rosie.'

'If it works, that's fine with me,' said Bea indulgently, and gave Ana the feeling that she was naïve and backward, and couldn't tell the difference between blacks and whites.

'Perhaps we could go through what each of us knows: who Mariama's friends are, where she usually goes, and then agree a plan with her family,' Ana tried again.

'A private detective is what I can offer, and then there's the police as well,' said Bea, irritated by Ana's monomanic insistence.

'But that hasn't got us anywhere,' she complained.

'Ben will sort it out, you'll see. He has contacts at the top of the pyramid ... family connections,' said Bea. Ana was surprised that she was putting so much distance between them.

'Tell me, how do you really feel about the fact that Mariama has disappeared?' said Ana, deliberately challenging her.

'How I feel?' Bea gave a startled little laugh. 'Bad, of course, very bad, I can't sleep, I have nightmares, you know yourself how it is,' she said, sounding strangely detached. Ana felt abandoned.

'It sounds as if you couldn't care less about Mariama,' she said angrily.

'Ana, that is really hurtful.' Bea's pale cheeks became suffused with pink.

'You and Ben leave everything to a private detective. You don't feel any personal responsibility,' said Ana heatedly. Bea stared straight past her and did not condescend to reply.

'You must know something we can go on.' Ana was on the verge of tears. Bea took pity on her.

'We set off early on Saturday morning, it was completely quiet in the house. We didn't say goodbye to Mariama, we thought she was asleep in her room. She had told us, as you already know, that she was going to spend Saturday and Sunday at her uncle's, whilst we were in Newcastle for the weekend. Just stick to your own guilt feelings, please, and stop reproaching Ben and me.' Bea spoke in a calm and measured tone.

'But I need you, I need your help and support.'

'We are doing everything humanly possible to find her,' Bea cut her off.

'You're washing your hands,' Ana said hysterically.

'Why do you keep on insulting us? What have we done to you?' Bea spoke like an injured mother.

'You have let me and Mariama down.' Ana could feel the tears starting to come.

'You are very welcome to move in and live with us, if that would help you.' Bea's suggestion left Ana absolutely speechless.

'Mariama's room is free. We found that she had taken her clothes and everything with her. Probably she's just found a better address.'

'But she's still missing …'

'Think about it, my dear. It's not good for you to be alone.

You need company,' Bea interrupted her, putting her cool hand on Ana's. She was just as alien to her as when they had first met in the restaurant at Golden Bay.

At that moment Ben appeared in the doorway to the kitchen with a young, dark-skinned man of aristocratic appearance behind him. Ben did not seem pleased to see Ana there.

'Are you plotting with Bea?' he asked suspiciously.

'Ben, please. Ana is beside herself about Mariama's disappearance. You must be nice to her,' said Bea firmly.

'I'm on the way to the police station to check whether there's any news,' he said in a harassed tone.

'Would you look after Alvarez and give him some lunch? Excuse me, I must leave you.' Ben vanished out of the door.

'Of course, darling,' Bea called after him.

'It sounded as if Ben wasn't happy about me being here,' said Ana.

'He's just overworked. Isn't that right, Alvarez?' Bea asked.

'Yes, he works far too much.' Alvarez had a charming accent and long curving eyelashes which looked as if they should belong to someone younger. Bea straightened up energetically.

'Now I'll get you some lunch,' she said kindly to him.

'I assume you've already eaten, Ana,' she continued, opening the fridge.

'Yes, of course,' Ana lied, hurt by Bea's inhospitable manner, which was so unlike her. She was always so polite and correct.

'Wine or beer,' said Bea again to Alvarez, who had started laying the table for two.

'Beer,' he said in a soft sexy voice. Ana got up from her chair.

'Are you going already?'said Bea, sounding more than happy at her decision.

'Yes … no … I think I'll wait for Ben and see if there's any news from the police.' Ana sat down again.

'He won't be home till late. I'll ring you,' said Bea, eager to get rid of her.

'OK,' Ana gave up. Alvarez gave Bea a long stare.

'You can find your own way out, dear?' said Bea, pre-occupied with lunch. Ana found it difficult to get out through the door.

'Think about it. You're more than welcome to live with us. You need someone to take care of you.' Bea put a platter of sliced tongue on the table. Ana finally pulled herself together to go. On the way down the stairs she heard Bea's chatter and Alvarez' dark laughter. She had an ominous feeling that they had already written Mariama off.

Ana came out of Tesco's and put two pounds in Birdy's plastic cup; she mentioned with deliberate casualness that the contribution was from Mariama. Birdy was busy on her mobile phone and did not react. Ana repeated as loudly as she could without shouting that Mariama sent her greetings. Finally Birdy looked up, and immediately complained that she never saw her any more; she asked peevishly whether she was too posh to hang around with common folk now. Ana took a deep breath and explained that Mariama had disappeared, and that she was just about to ask her if she had talked to her in the past week, and if not, when she had last seen her. Birdy had first to light a fag and then think for some time. Then she shook her head.

She hadn't seen her for a long time. How long was a long time? Ana wanted to know. Birdy shook her head; she was sorry that she didn't have a very accurate sense of time. The days all ran into one, she explained, when you didn't have a home to keep tabs on time. Ana asked impatiently whether she could remember the last time she saw Mariama. How had she seemed? And what had they talked about? Birdy had to think deeply again, and invited Ana to take a seat on the ramp. Ana sat down at a respectable distance and discreetly observed her new conversation partner with her greasy jeans and worn trainers and a sweatshirt with a Cambridge University logo under her leather jacket.

Birdy sat sunk into herself as if in deep meditation, not

noticing the curious eyes which stared at her and the fine company she found herself in. Ana on the other hand was uncomfortable about the situation, and felt that she was parading herself and her unhappiness. She was getting tired of waiting, and touched Birdy's arm lightly to see if she was awake.

'We mustn't forget Mariama,' said Birdy, confused as if she had been woken from a sleep. 'What do we know about each other?' she went on.

'Try to think. What sort of mood was she in last time you saw her?' Ana moved cautiously, fearful of being brushed off.

'She is a tormented soul, gets far too stressed.' Birdy looked grave. 'God is good, rely on him, I told her, look at me, I said, I'm like the birds of the field, I want for nothing.'

'What was it that tormented her?' said Ana.

'There's always something which hurts and torments. Like she could be thrown out of the UK. She's not one of us.' Birdy started to pack her things together.

'You must have misunderstood.' Ana was indignant.

'I don't misunderstand people,' snapped Birdy, and took a sip from a coffee cup whose contents were hidden under the lid.

'Mariama's papers are in order, and she has a residence permit,' said Ana carefully, not wanting to provoke her further.

'Then it's worries about some exam or other,' Birdy suggested, as if it might be herself.

'As far as I can understand from her, her studies are going well.' Ana brushed the comment aside, repressing what Binta had told her about Mariama's exam terrors, and the fact that she herself had had to supply her with pills.

'Perhaps she has exam fever like all the rest of us in this cruel springtime when the winners win and the losers lose.' Birdy lit a fag with shaking hands.

'Have you ever seen her with anyone?' Ana asked, trying to move on. Birdy pursed her lips.

'She was saying goodbye once ... I don't remember when ... before she gave me some toiletries she'd bought for me in

Boots. So it must have been before, no, don't pester me about what time it was. Everything gets blurred in here.' Birdy held her head.

'A black man? Young, old?' asked Ana excitedly.

'He was black … tall … no, not tall … you must find her,' Birdy snuffled. Ana wondered what was in the coffee cup.

'That's what you're helping me with.' Without thinking Ana put her hand on her arm. Birdy pulled away violently.

'Your help is important, you understand, Birdy,' Ana tried to calm her. 'Did she say anything about having a boyfriend?'

'I don't know whether he was a boyfriend.' Birdy took another sip.

'Did she say what his name was?' Ana was not entirely sure whether the black man was Birdy's own invention.

'He was in the music business, you could see that from the dubious cufflinks, deceived in the sweet time when everything comes into bloom. Daffodils, Bank Holiday, May Balls. Beware of Shakespeare.' Birdy had slipped into intoxication.

'Can't you give me some lead to follow?' Ana felt like shaking her.

'Don't cry, once I too was lost without trace.'

'Ring if anything occurs to you,' Ana finished, giving Birdy her card.

'You are always welcome at my table.' Birdy opened her arms wide, looking unutterably sad as she sat there with her scattered belongings around her.

The clear blue sky and the heat towards midday intensified Ana's longing and the crippling pain in her chest. The bustle of the market and the purposeful activity accused her. She had come with a different aim to that of buying and selling. She caught small glimpses of Mariama the whole time, in a face, a turning away, a nervous laugh. She was everywhere, behind the skilfully piled fruit and vegetables, in the African pop on the CD and DVD sellers' gabbling loudspeakers. She was in the crowd which slowly moved along the wide centre aisle in Dalston market. With her slim, supple figure in tight jeans and a cut-off top she was ten steps ahead of Ana the whole time. And regardless of whether she walked faster or broke into a run, there was the same distance between them. She renounced the pursuit and gave herself plenty of time at each stall, without registering what she was looking at. She annoyed the sellers by standing there taking up room without buying anything.

Eventually she reached the narrow passage where the SeneGambian Minimarket was to be found. It was here that Mariama shopped when she wanted to please Ana on special occasions by serving benachin or chicken yassa and teaching her to eat with her fingers. Just round the corner of the passage there was a shop with piles of rolls of brightly-patterned material in the window. Further down lay the minimarket, diagonally opposite the SeneGambian Money Transfer with favourable rates of exchange and low fees. Ana walked slowly past the baskets of cassava which were displayed outside. She peeped discreetly into the small, crowded premises. Two younger women were standing by the till, absorbed in a heated discussion. Their voices emerged in waves through the open door. Ana carried on without stopping and turned off into a passageway before she turned round and went back.

In that small restricted space she felt like a large, clumsy elephant. She could hardly turn round without knocking cans of food and sacks of rice off the shelves. She walked round looking at the selection of goods with feigned interest and no idea of what was in front of her. She could not bring herself to address the two women, who were following her every movement with their silent presence. On her way out of the door she suddenly turned back and took a photo of Mariama out of her bag to show them.

'This young woman often shops here. Have you seen her recently?' asked Ana breathlessly. The women looked curiously at the photo and shook their heads.

'She has disappeared.' Ana held up the portrait of Mariama again.

One of them, a sturdily built woman with an attractive face beneath a large stiffened headdress, clutched her breast dramatically. The slightly younger woman studied the photo closely.

'Do you recognise her?' said Ana. They shook their heads. Ana was given the photo back. She remained standing there in the hope that something or other would occur to them.

'She loves your dried fish,' she essayed, pointing at the vacuum-packed fish lying piled up on the counter. Again a shake of the head, and an incipient reluctance, which Ana in her manic state did not register.

'You must have seen her,' she insisted. The two women suddenly seemed hostile.

'Who are you anyway?' asked the woman in the headdress in a loud, strident voice. They stood there motionless as statues, close together in a united front against Ana. Their faces were completely expressionless, like visors which would make them invisible to all authorities and immigration police. As if with one movement they moved a step closer to her in silent confrontation. Ana fled out of the minimarket and rushed through the passage and past the market stalls until she reached the safety of Kingsland High Street.

She took a taxi to the nearest underground station and travelled from there out to East Ham. She had not been there since she took Mariama to the Unisex Hair and Beauty salon, where she had her first hair damage treatment. Ana felt wistful at the memory of that first time with Mariama. The impressions were almost too powerful in her present over-excited state. She saw everything with razor-sharp clarity, as if she was on an acid trip. People of varying nationalities, shops and supermarkets with exotic assortments of wares. The strong colours, the noise and the blaring sounds assaulted her nerves. She was wearing far too many clothes in the close, heavy heat, but clenched her teeth and carried on. Suddenly she twisted her foot. One of her heels had got stuck between two paving stones and broke off. She picked up her shoes and walked on with bare feet.

The salon was on a corner with a wide glass frontage. The hairdressing chairs were set out in rows in front of the mirrors. It was empty, not a trace of a customer. A young hairdresser's assistant with short smooth hair was standing leaning on an armrest, studying her face intently in the mirror. A large imposing woman was sitting at the till, staring blankly into thin air. From her name badge it was clear that she was the manageress, and was called Amy. She straightened up with an inviting gesture and a smile as Ana entered to the accompaniment of a loud tinkling from the bell. She explained her reason for coming, and pulled Mariama's photo out of her bag. The smile was extinguished and a tired expression spread over the woman's face.

'She's one of your customers,' said Ana. The assistant came over to them and joined in looking. She had a piercing on her upper lip, a small shiny ball of metal.

'Really,' said the manageress with raised eyebrows. She was wearing tight black stretch trousers and a white sweater.

'I like her hair,' said the assistant, taking the photo.

'You probably styled it yourself, according to this lady she is one of our customers.' Amy put the glasses which hung on a chain round her neck onto the tip of her nose.

'She has disappeared,' said Ana. The assistant looked sceptically at her. Amy closed her appointments book with a bang.

'We cannot help you. It has nothing to do with us. I have been a British citizen for five years. It makes it so much easier to travel abroad. I always carry my passport with me, close to my heart.' Amy placed her hand on her breast.

'I thought … ' Ana searched for words. She felt dizzy. The mirrors all round the walls gave her the feeling of sitting on a roundabout.

' … that she had perhaps been here recently.'

'Listen, lady. You have no right to come here accusing us … '

'You misunderstand. I'm here to look for my little girl.'

262

'We don't want to hear any more about your little girl.' Amy stood up. The hairdresser's assistant summoned up her courage.

'She has been here.'

'When?' Ana held her breath.

'I don't know,' she back-pedalled.

'She must be in your customer file,' Ana ventured.

'Sorry, we're busy.' Amy puffed up her chest.

'If we hear anything about her …' began the young assistant.

'We can't help you.' Amy shrugged. Ana had begun to bore her.

'Then I won't take up any more of your time.' Ana walked towards the door.

'What has happened? Your feet are bleeding,' Amy exclaimed.

'My heel broke.' Ana held out her ruined shoes.

'You can wash your feet here,' the assistant offered, but Ana wanted to get on.

'Have you any objection to putting a notice and her picture in the window?' Ana knew from Mariama that both the owner and the employees were Gambian.

'We never do that, on principle.' Amy had softened a little. Ana's bleeding feet had made an impression on her. Ana herself had not noticed.

'You're not British?' said the manageress self-importantly, with her approximation of an Oxford accent.

'Danish,' said Ana brusquely. There was no more she could do in the salon, so she gave them her business card in case of 'good news'. Amy looked at the card with interest.

'So you're a manager,' she said, clicking her tongue. 'Finance … are you sure this is your card?' She looked sceptically at Ana.

'I hope you find her,' said the assistant, with a little shiver of her bare shoulders. She was wearing a black top and black jeans under her loose beige tunic. Her name badge said that her name was Aida. Ana felt her eyes filling with tears again.

Aida was very different from Mariama, but they were both so young and innocent. All that tender budding growth. Ana felt like hugging her, taking her home and adopting her. She fought back the tears, and felt the grit digging deeper into the soles of her feet. She shifted her weight from one foot to the other and wanted to thank them for their kindness. Amy pre-empted her.

'We'll keep an eye open …' She looked sympathetically at Ana, as if she didn't really believe her story, but regarded her as a pitiful mental case.

'Thank you, that's very kind.' Ana had a strange feeling of security in the company of the two women. In terms of age they could be mother and daughter. How she would love to be them, to work in a safe corner of London, in a pleasant attractive salon where customers enjoyed coming to gossip and relax.

As Ana stood there lost in her thoughts, the first customer arrived. Amy's attention shifted focus. And from the back of the premises came a tall, long-limbed hair stylist in the salon's café-au-lait coloured tunic, ready to cater for the customer's needs. More customers arrived. And with perfect timing, two more hair stylists emerged. Ana suddenly found herself in a largish gathering, and could steal quietly out of the door without anyone noticing her.

Further down High Street South stood The Black Lion, its dark red brick, towers and spires of black, tongue-shaped tiles and flashing Carlsberg adverts in the windows looking as if they were straight out of Grimm's fairytales. Ana needed something strong to fortify herself, and crossed over the street towards the fairytale building, which could also have been an installation in one of Kafka's novels which she had studied in her early youth. On her way up the steep stone steps to the pub she slipped and fell. She was walking in bare feet and carrying a shoe in each hand, and did not manage to catch hold of the rusty iron railings. She slid on her stomach all the way down the steps and landed on the pavement with the torn soles of her feet uppermost.

She just lay there, feeling no desire to get up. She wanted to slip away from her despair and shame at the fact that she had not been able to take care of Mariama and make sure that nothing happened to her. But she had to believe that the miracle would happen, that she would get her little girl back. She felt someone tapping her on the shoulder. She found it difficult to lift her head in the awkward position she was lying in, face down on the paving slabs. Nevertheless she succeeded in raising herself on one elbow. She looked straight into a blurred and distorted face. Her contact lenses had come adrift, and were swimming about somewhere in her eye sockets. A tall slim man in a pale grey suit with a mandarin collar and shiny polished shoes was leaning over her, trying to help her to her feet, but she sank back into a prone position, wondering in horror what she must look like.

She heard a voice saying 'ambulance', and was frightened that she would be taken away and prevented from carrying on with her search for Mariama, which was the only way she could hang on to her hope and her wits. She got up in several stages, and swayed for a moment until she found her balance in an upright position. She left her shoes lying there, and after checking the contents of her bag she staggered unsteadily away from the man with the mobile phone and down towards the underground. She wiped her face with a tissue, and ran her hand through her short wiry hair. There was emptiness and cold air around her.

Ana came up from Upton Park underground station, battered and aching all over as if she had been beaten up. She wandered restlessly up and down the main street, where the shops were tightly packed together with signs in languages she could not identify. She had no clear idea of what country she was in. She was neither in the UK nor anywhere else on the map. The stream of people on the pavement on both sides of the road thronged with traffic was such a motley mixture that there was no point trying to work out where they came from. She was existing at some point in the future where all nationalities had fused into one multifarious humanity.

She wandered round the covered and rather gloomy market behind the station. A quick glance informed her that most of it was pathetic old junk: watches, umbrellas, spare parts, socks, everything at the same magical price: one pound. Ana had a vague feeling that she ought to take something with her to Amina and Sulay's, and went round to the back of the market where there was a seedy flower shop with a miserable selection. She chose a bunch of carnations in vaguely presentable condition.

It was Omar, Mariama's eldest cousin, who opened the door. He smiled mournfully when he saw her. Behind him stood Amina. She was at home in the interval between her morning and evening jobs. Amina pushed past Omar and stood there with her hands on her hips.

'What has happened to you?' She opened her large, soft eyes wide. Ana shook her head. Not a sound crossed her lips. She had come in order to hear any news of Mariama, and whether they had been in touch with the police since the last meeting. But at the sight of those two sorrowful people the words stuck in her throat. Amina made her come inside.

'Have you been mugged?' she asked in concern, and sat Ana down on a stool in the hall. She told Omar to run a hot bath.

'Please, say something,' Amina said urgently.

'Mariama,' whispered Ana, giving her the bouquet. Amina took the carnations, which were already hanging their heads.

'No news is good news.' Amina looked straight ahead and sighed.

'My sister-in-law rings every other hour,' she went on.

'I am so sorry,' Ana apologized. Amina waved her hand deprecatingly.

'It is her right. Mariama is her baby,' she said. Omar came back and announced that the bath was ready. Ana looked at Amina in confusion.

'You need it,' she said brusquely and helped her to her feet.

She had retained the grasp of a former nurse, firm and gentle at the same time.

'You look dreadful,' she stated succinctly.

'You could borrow some of my clothes, but you are so thin, and I am just a little … heavy, you know.' Amina patted her stomach. They had got into the bathroom, and Ana was seated on a stool again.

'This is very kind of you.' She felt quite dazed at the unexpected solicitude.

'You need to be careful.' Amina opened the medicine cabinet, which was filled to bursting.

'This is to rub on your feet after your bath.' She gave Ana a jar of foot cream and found a pair of flipflops and put them in the shower.

'Perhaps not exactly your size, but at least you can get home,' murmured Amina as if to herself.

'Today it is a week since Mariama …' Ana had moved from reality into a dream which was happening in an unknown place amongst strangers whose customs and habits she did not know.

'What shall I do, what shall I do,' she said, so softly that it sounded like a deep sigh.

'Take all the time you need. I'll probably have gone to work when you're finished. Omar will look after you.' Amina went out and closed the door quietly behind her.

Ana undressed quickly. In the fall down the steps the buttons had been torn off her jacket, and her tight skirt had ripped at the seams. She slid down into the warm water without being able to feel her body. The bathroom was a chaotic cave-like room with no window. Dressing gowns and towels hung in layers, one on top of the other. The row of hooks was on the point of coming loose from the wall. Soap, toothpaste, cotton wool and nail brushes, bath sponges, nail files, scissors, combs lay in baskets. Plastic sandals, buckets and stacks of toilet rolls spread over the floor. She was in the centre of the family's busy daily life and the grooming requirements of four active people. Ana was not busy. Her world was empty.

And the emptiness made her restless. She could not relax, and got out of the bath without taking the time to enjoy it. She grabbed the nearest towel and dried herself quickly. It was unpleasant to have to put her dirty clothes on again. She sat down on the toilet seat and pondered what she should do with herself when she came out of the bathroom.

She did not know how long she had been sitting there when there came a hesitant knock at the door. The knocking became more and more insistent. It was not until she heard Omar saying her name that she came to herself and opened the door a little.

'Sorry, I'm occupying the bathroom,' she said, bewildered.

'No, no, take your time. I just wanted to see if you're OK,' he said. Her frozen expression made him take a step backwards.

'Could we just talk for a moment?' Ana came out of the bathroom like a snail leaving its shell.

'What about?' said Omar unresponsively. He spoke entirely without an accent, in contrast to his parents.

'Do you have any idea about what has happened to Mariama?' Ana sat down in the same armchair as she had sat in just a short week ago. Since then the shock had lodged in her body like a crushing dead weight.

'She was not happy to be here.' Omar poured boiling water into two mugs with teabags in.

'What have we done wrong?'

'Forgive me, I mean, of course …'

'So you have no idea about what has happened?' Ana repeated. Omar did not answer.

'Could she have gone off with a boyfriend?' Ana suggested falteringly.

'I don't know anything about a boyfriend.' Omar spoke reluctantly; he was not serving tea on his own initiative but because his mother had asked him to. Ana had no idea how to carry on with her questions, which seemed to awaken no response in Omar. He was sitting uneasily and staring straight ahead distractedly, not touching his tea.

'She was very nervous about something,' he began,

breaking the awkward silence. Ana leaned forward towards him.

'About what?'

'She didn't say.'

'Had she got into the wrong sort of company somehow?'

'I wasn't her bodyguard.' Omar retreated into himself once more. Ana did not like the fact that he was talking in the past tense again.

'But what is your opinion?'

'I have no opinion.' Omar got up, and suddenly added unhappily: 'We are all worried.'

'So am I … and Ben and Bea.'

'I don't like them,' Omar muttered. Ana gave a start.

'Has Mariama said anything about Ben and Bea?'

'Yeah, something … not very much …'

'What did she say?' asked Ana agitatedly.

'I don't know anything,' said Omar. There was something about his impatient reticence that reminded her of Mariama.

'Did she ever complain about us?'

'Sorry, I have an appointment.' Omar checked the time on his mobile. Ana could not pull herself together to leave. Mariama's family was her only hope.

'I'll see you out.' Omar walked quickly out into the hall without checking whether Ana was following him. He removed the safety chain, unbolted the many locks and opened the door for her before she had come out into the hall.

'Thank you for the bath and the tea,' she said humbly, almost pleadingly, and avoided looking at herself in the full-length mirror.

'I can't help you,' he apologized.

'Has Mariama gone back to Gambia?' Ana knew the moment she said it that it was a stupid question. When she was with Mariama and her family she involuntarily started to act as if she was retarded. She held Omar's hand in hers a moment too long.

'Her mother rings us the whole time,' said Omar dismissively, and pulled his hand away. Ana was left standing on the landing after he had closed the door behind her. She looked down at the shapeless sandals of garish yellow plastic. She did not know where to go. Only that she did not want to go home to the flat in Henry Dickens Court.

Mariama was standing in the queue by the entrance to the School of Oriental and African Studies, SOAS, where shaven-headed Hare Krishna monks in orange gowns distributed free soup every afternoon to needy students. Her appetite had vanished along with the board and lodging at her English hosts. Most of all she felt like lying down in the green grass and listening to the trees, the birds, the lizards, the sea and the sky over the beach and letting her rational self go to sleep; but she forced herself to eat in order to get the strength to carry on without her college and outside the bounds of the law. But as yet her visa had not expired, as yet she still had a little refuge, still a brief respite.

It had been a strangely turbulent and weightless time, a time of rainbows and roses, since she had packed her things and left Portland Road and the spirit, with which she had made a deal that after her exit it would only haunt her in dreams. She hoped she would be able to find Janet before the spirit appeared again. She had searched for her in vain together with her cousins, at discos and bars. And they had agreed that Janet was probably not a fan of Afro-music.

It was on one of these forays looking for Janet that she had met Gehran, a friend of her cousins. That evening in The Passing Clouds her favourite band, Wormfood from the Congo, was playing. (Aunt Amina, who was always waiting for them in her pink bathrobe and cross-examined her the moment they came through the door, could not stand the name of the band, which she maintained was blasphemous and disrespectful of the dead.) Gehran had come over to her and asked why she wasn't dancing, why she wasn't happy. She replied calmly that she was working hard at her studies and her job at Sainsbury's. He offered to buy her a drink, but she preferred cola. They sat down in the lounge. The cousins joined them.

Gehran had lived in the USA and done very well in business over there. So he could pay for his studies at the London School of Law himself. He was from a fishing family, but there were no more fish to be caught in the sea near the coast. His father had taught him to rise early and work hard, and he would teach his children the same. He wanted to work for human rights when he had taken his MA, and help young Gambians who were stranded in London. They came on a visitor visa and stayed in the UK when it had expired. They couldn't get a job and had nothing to do. They opened a beer as soon as they got out of bed in the morning and continued with skunk or pot. The whole day they sat in front of Sky Channel and didn't go out until after dark, and then only to cause trouble. The youngsters ought to learn from the Americans. Gehran himself had become like the Americans, he said, they are entrepreneurs in their own lives, self-made men. Mariama felt an unaccustomed security in Gehran's company. She had not heard anyone talk like that about illegals without being patronizing. Her cousins' presence could not prevent a sympathy emerging between them the very first time they met in The Passing Clouds, which quickly developed into something more.

Mariama had not lost her smart college look. She took great care to keep her clothes neat and clean, so that she could assume the appearance of a student who was standing in the soup queue and making use of the sect's generous offer. A homeless woman who looked like a gypsy sat leaning against the wall of the university library with a pile of *The Big Issue* in her lap. She had her eyes closed, and was dressed in a thick layer of knitted sweaters and waistcoats and a profusion of voluminous skirts; she did not look to be particularly interested in selling her magazines. Mariama made sure to keep her distance from her, so that it should not one fine day be her sitting there from morning till evening in the English rain and wind, offering her fate for sale.

She thought mournfully about her final meeting with her tutor. She had been sorry to disappoint that mild and helpful man who lived and breathed for his students and was happy to advise them if they had problems with their tasks and their studies. He had devoted extra time and effort to Mariama's pronunciation. The social conventions and the slang in Sainsbury's crowded, smoke-filled staffroom (which she found it easier to slip into than Southwark College; she did not have to put on a front and could be more herself) limited her vocabulary and had a negative influence on her pronunciation, Mr Townsend had made clear to her.

He was a living incarnation of Mr Brown in her English book, with his tousled brown hair divided by a white parting and the same buttoned-up tweed jacket and solid walking boots with the laces in neat parallel stripes over the ankle. With his big boots he looked like a giant in the cluttered little office on the third floor with the number 292 on the door; he looked more like a wild man from the woods than a college professor. She had confided in him, and asked if it was possible to take a break from her studies. She needed breathing space, which would help her to see her situation more clearly. A break would give her an overview and renewed energy for her studies, so that she would be better prepared to pass her exams.

Mr Townsend regretted that he could not give students on visas leave of absence or time off from their studies as he could with his British students, and certainly not so early in the course. He tapped the pile of papers on the desk in front of him and advised her to stick with it if she wanted to have any hope of being allowed to remain in the UK. He did not hold out any false hopes, but promised on the other hand to give her all the help she might need. She had not quite reached the standard of proficiency, they would need a miracle, he smiled in an attempt to cheer her up, but he didn't sound as if he believed in miracles. On the way home she had made her decision without discussing it with anyone, not even Binta with whom she otherwise shared her thoughts and dreams.

Gehran had told her beforehand that he was ready to support her, just so long as she herself was convinced that it was the right thing for her to do.

No-one noticed Ana with her disordered clothes and plastic sandals, which had already given her blisters. In the soup queue all were equal in the eyes of the Lord, and if Ana really believed in the god of chance, the moment was approaching when she should fall to her knees. In the row of students in front of her there were a number of black people of whom she didn't take much notice. Her sensory register stood at absolute zero. Her strength was spent. She was floating free in the air like a balloon which a naughty child had let go. She had not eaten anything all day and practically nothing on previous days either, but now hunger announced itself with a sickening gnawing in her stomach as the spicy vegetable aroma reached her nostrils. She was reduced to a cipher in the queue with one single requirement: a paper bowl of steaming vegetables swimming in a pale liquid with pearls of fat.

Right at the front by the monks' black vat of soup, which was transported on a trolley, was a couple, each with a filled bowl. As they left the queue and turned to go towards the steps up to the main faculty building, Ana hardly registered that they were black, only that she had moved forwards two places and was no longer at the back of the queue. She would not have taken any further notice of the couple if she had not heard an embarrassed giggle as a bowl of soup landed upside down right in front of her feet, and a young man with trimmed Afro hair muttered 'sorry' and bent down to try and shovel the vegetables back into the bowl with the plastic spoon that came with the soup. Ana's legs had been splashed with the soup, but she was not perturbed by the accident. The young man walked off again and threw his bowl in the bin, then sat down on the steps beside his girlfriend, who shared her soup with him.

It was only then that Ana registered something familiar about the young woman and thought she had gone mad and was hallucinating. She wanted to run over to the steps, but her body felt like lead and her feet would not obey her. She blinked hard, but the vision would not disappear. Mariama had revealed herself to her as if by magic. It was up to her to believe in the magic and make herself known. She hesitated; something held her back. The certainty and the relief that she had found Mariama safe and well was all she desired for herself. Her first impulse was to let her vanish again and be satisfied with the fact that she was alive and in good spirits (that was how it looked from a distance, at least), pass on the good news to the family in Upton Park and inform them that they could find Mariama in the Hare Krishna soup queue at SOAS the next day, same time, same place.

The couple got up and set off towards Malet Street. Ana stepped out of the queue, which had grown considerably shorter, and followed them at a safe distance. She felt she had not deserved to get Mariama back so quickly, and still did not dare to believe her eyes, that she really was walking in front of her, large as life, and was not simply a mirage. The two youngsters were strolling at a leisurely pace and were too absorbed in each other to notice that they were being shadowed. Up by Euston Square they said goodbye to each other, and the young man disappeared down the steps to the underground station. Mariama stood for a moment looking after him, then waved and turned back in Ana's direction. She could not do anything other than stand still and wait for Mariama to get close and notice her. But she turned off down University Street, and Ana hurried after her so that she should not disappear again before she had proof that it really was Mariama she was seeing, and not a hallucination. As she was catching up with her, Ana called her name. Mariama turned round. Her face dissolved into a smile. How much she looked like her old self! And yet so changed! A black plastic slide held her hair back off her forehead. She had harder lines around her mouth and a different look in her eyes.

'Where have you been all this time?' The words burst out of her.

'I'm sorry, Ana, I got lost, but now I'm finding my way back.' Nervously she fingered the thin gold chain Gehran had given her.

'Why have you done this to me?' Ana was amazed at the violent anger which overshadowed her joy at finding her safe and well.

'I am so sorry. I had to get out of that house before the spirit took me over. Believe me, I did struggle, and I'm still trying to find Janet.'

'You owe me a better explanation than that,' said Ana with an icy coldness she had not known she had in her. She was on the wrong side of the sun.

'She wouldn't let me go as long as I stayed in that house,' Mariama explained. But Ana neither saw nor heard her.

'Binta said you saw a ghost outside Liverpool Street station. Was that her?'

'No, it was Gehran, my boyfriend.' Mariama's face lit up.

'Why didn't you tell me you had a boyfriend?'

'It happened so quickly.' Mariama lowered her eyes.

'So you haven't been taking your exams, just fooling around with some random Afro character.'

'I've dropped out,' said Mariama in a low voice.

'Then you'll be in real trouble.'

'I am already. The checks on foreign students with student visas have been stepped up.'

'What do you mean, stepped up?' Ana could not control her anger.

'If you don't attend college, they throw you out of the UK.'

'Have you become illegal?' Ana could hardly get the words out. All her efforts had been in vain. Her great plans for Mariama as a success story had crashed to the ground.

'When my visa runs out, I shall overstay it and stay in the UK,' Mariama explained serenely.

'But that's against the law.'

'I work full-time in Sainsbury's,' Mariama defended herself.

'Then you might just as well have stayed at home.' Ana spat the words out.

'There's no job there,' said Mariama sharply.

'Do you really not have any higher goals?'

'Working full-time means I can send more money home to the family.'

'Does Sainsbury's employ illegals?'

'I wasn't illegal when I got the job.'

'Where have you been since you took yourself off from Ben and Bea's?' Ana was as if possessed by rage.

'Gehran is helping me to find places to stay,' she said evasively.

'But it's not feasible to live underground. No security. No help to be had if anything happens to you or you become ill.'

'That is my life right now.' Mariama had a distant look in her eyes.

'Who is this Gehran? What does he do?'

'He's studying law. He's working for human rights and doing voluntary work to assist young Gambians who are stranded in London on a visitor visa. There's no human dignity in their lives, he says. They have nothing to do other than cause trouble. It's a waste of resources.'

'Why don't they just go home?' Ana was on the point of losing her patience.

'They are caught in a trap. They don't want to bring shame on their families. They can't go home without having achieved success and expensive habits, and in the UK they get nowhere.'

'What does a future solicitor want with friends like that?'

'He wants to teach them to survive. Like Americans, who are entrepreneurs in their own lives, self-made men.' Mariama had warmed to her theme, her eyes shone.

'You're illegal too, just like his friends.'

'But I work hard,' said Mariama assertively.

'You must come back to Ben and Bea and me, otherwise you'll be ruined,' said Ana, aware that Mariama was already beyond her reach.

'Gehran has a job with a solicitor who might be able to help me.'

'What sort of solicitor?' asked Ana, resentful at being side-lined.

'He has a law firm in Banjul and a London-based branch in Dalston. I have had a conversation with him.'

'How can you afford to go to a solicitor?'

'He gives free legal advice to illegals and tries to normalize their status, but the chances are small, he says.'

'So it is really your intention to become illegal?'

'I am so sorry, Ana, I will always be grateful for everything you have done for me. At first it was just a dream, then it became reality.'

'I think that deep inside you want to go back home again. I will be happy to buy you a single ticket to Banjul.'

'I can't go back. The family depends on me. They have nothing else to live on but the money I send.'

'You must think of yourself. What is going to happen to you?' said Ana. It was beyond her comprehension that Mariama had no use for her. That possibility did not exist in the world of her imagination.

'I shall manage.' Mariama shrugged. Her insistent optimism was offensive to Ana.

'If the police find you, you will be deported.'

'They can't find everyone … it's a matter of statistics,' said Mariama with a teasing reference to Ana's belief in statistics and chance.

'I had no choice,' she concluded.

'I don't recognise you, Mariama.'

'London has transformed me.'

'Yes, in the wrong direction. The idea was that you should get qualifications.'

'I'm sorry, Ana,' said Mariama contritely, 'my body got too much information. Learning, learning, learning, I became too full and did not have the chance to digest it. Time had become my enemy.'

'That's all meaningless.'

'I'm sorry,' repeated Mariama, 'my head shut off, my body rebelled, I needed to breathe and feel the world around me. I had to get out into the light again. I can see more clearly now. I have dropped the pills and I'm waiting until the time is ripe.'

'You just drop out without saying a word to anyone. You have been given board and lodging, pocket money, clothes money, not to mention the fact that it costs a fortune to go to college. You did it all under false pretences, you never took your studies seriously.'

'I could not cope with the pressure from all sides,' said Mariama quietly.

'So what are you doing here?' screamed Ana.

'Working so that I can support my family.'

'But there's no future in that,' Ana continued in a transport of rage.

'You don't understand the situation, Ana.' Mariama, by contrast, was calm and self-possessed.

'I understand enough to see that I've been cheated and deceived.'

'I am so sorry,' said Mariama for the third time.

'If you carry on with your "sorry, sorry" I'll strangle you.' Ana had reached breaking point and no longer knew what she was saying or doing.

'I have learned a great deal and know much more than when I left Banjul. Then I was an ignorant little girl who did not know the world and could not see beyond the tip of her own nose. Everything I am today, I am thanks to you.'

'You are nothing. The project has failed completely,' wailed Ana.

'Believe me, Ana. I shall make it. I have a plan for my life, and I'm not alone.'

'Surrounded by down-at-heel illegals, what help is that?'

'And Gehran,' Mariama corrected her.

'Once he gets started on his career, his illegal friends will be a millstone round his neck.'

'You mustn't talk like that about my boyfriend,' said Mariama heatedly. At last Ana had succeeded in provoking her.

'Is he the one who got you into this mess? So that he can

save you with his "human rights"?'

'It was my own decision. I had got too far behind with my college schedule.'

'So how does your Gehran fit into the picture?' Ana wanted to know; she sounded like an inquisitor.

'He's trying in the first instance to get me a work permit. Perhaps my job at Sainsbury's will help me.'

'That's not realistic. I would like to talk to the solicitor that this young man is working for.'

'He's called Jamil Jawara, you can look him up on the net. He's a well-known solicitor, famous,' said Mariama, proud of her successful compatriot.

'So that's the thanks I get, no good, over and out,' Ana broke in.

'You misunderstand.'

'You're the one who won't understand that our fates are bound together.'

'You don't see me as I see me.' Mariama shook her head indulgently. Ana had moved close to her and could feel her heart beating in rhythm with her own. They stood facing each other, powerless, bound together by good intentions and frustrated expectations.

Suddenly Mariama became aware of Ana's dishevelled appearance and the round-toed yellow plastic sandals which looked completely wrong on her. Her elegance, the well-groomed stylishness which in the beginning she had admired and envied, had disappeared. Before her stood a plucked bird, without the brightly-coloured authority of its feathered plumage. Before her stood a naked human being, neither rich nor poor, just a human being like herself, like her mother and Rosie. She felt relieved and liberated. Ana had come down from the clouds. She didn't need to look up to her, she could just see her like herself.

'Ana, what has happened to you? Are you OK?' she said, putting her arm around her shoulder and pulling her close. Mariama's unexpected gesture caused a short circuit in Ana's head. A sharp boring pain on the left side, which warned her from a remote-controlled microchip that she was in great danger. Thousands of flashing lightbulbs exploded on her retina.

In an overexposed flashback she was standing in a photographer's studio in her matriculation gown. A butch-looking female photographer in a striped suit was ordering her about in front of a black backdrop. First she was placed on a stool, then posed with her arms crossed. Now she had to smile, now to be serious, now show her teeth, now keep her mouth closed and lower her eyelids. After that she was ordered to place her hand on her chin, on her hair, on her cheeks and temples. The photographer became more and more irritable as the photo session went on.

She left the tripod and returned a moment later with a glass of whisky in her hand, which she emptied in one gulp. Ana apologized for the fact that she was not photogenic and thus made the woman's work more difficult. She dismissed Ana's words with a theatrical wave of the hand, saying that it had nothing to do with being photogenic or not. A skilful portrait photographer could get a good result from any face, even the ugliest and most disharmonious one. The thing that was wrong with Ana was that she had no soul, and a person without a soul could not be photographed. There was simply no image appearing on the photographic plate. Nothing was transmitted. The woman poured herself another whisky, remarking that she had never in her long career come across a phenomenon like Ana. Yes, a phenomenon, that was what she was. She had no other word for this peculiar aberration.

Ana's first reaction was that someone must have made a mistake in the lab with the artificial insemination, and that she was a kind of second-rate scientific product. Before she had managed to think the matter through, she felt the photographer putting her arm around her shoulder. The dark figure cocked the coarse mask of its face on one side as if to comfort her. Ana shoved the woman away from her with a violent movement as if she was defending herself from a demon which terrified the life out of her with its clinging embrace. The falling body transformed itself into a diffuse mass and split into a tangle of black shadows, which formed a circle around her.

Mariama felt the back of her head hit the kerbstone with a dull sound which shattered her consciousness. She slipped into the magical kingdom of the spirits. First of all it was pitch-black as if in a thick blanket of smoke. Then she could make out a faint flashing light which revealed the enormous starry sky. The great emptiness of space was filled with cold planets and burning suns, which thawed the permafrost and made the icebergs melt. She caught hold of the thin veil of the Milky Way and lowered herself down towards the blue planet. She landed in the vicinity of the equator at Serrekunda market, far too far away from her beloved. A white woman was wandering confusedly around the market. There was something familiar about her. But she couldn't see her face, which was covered in a mask. Why was she hiding? Why didn't she want to be the one she was, but another, with a breeding place for evil spirits inside her?

Ana had lost herself in the throng of black souls. Were they in reality white ones, who had coloured themselves black with make-up and body paint? Would all that blackness rub off on her tender white skin? Had she already become black amongst blacks? She gave up trying to find herself in the market's noisy tumult of parading devils, and hid away in a secluded gallery where friendly souls served her strong sweet tea. She just sat there resting, until one of the black figures laid a hand on her shoulder and wanted something from her which she could not understand. And without a context she could not function. Her rational mind was disturbed, and she did not want to know anything of a world her brain could not grasp. But the black soul had already infiltrated her thought processes with its simple touch.

Mariama listened to her own voice as she listened to the birds and the wind. It was a different way of talking. 'You only remember the bad things, you don't remember the good things,' she said to Ana, who had disappeared into the market's labyrinthine alleyways, where only someone with local knowledge could find their way. Mariama could feel the pulse of silence, and out of the silence Janet came to meet her, enveloped in a black cloth. 'You are light, I am darkness,' she said. 'I have searched for you, so that together we can lay the spirit to rest,' answered Mariama. 'Don't go out. When the sun is highest in the sky, your shadow will vanish and with it your soul,' said Janet, mild as a sister. 'I was forced to leave the spirit in the English people's house,' Mariama said regretfully. 'I jumped out of the frame. I didn't want to be a picture on the wall,' said Janet. 'You must fetch the spirit so the white people can have peace,' Mariama insisted. 'I can't give them peace.' Janet changed colour, first to red, then to yellow and to white, and finally she was once more the black colour which contains all the colours of the rainbow. She was about to disappear into the silence again, into the pure clear air which abolished time. Mariama tried to hold Janet back before she woke up from her dream. But the spirit had deserted her.

Ana was no longer mistress of herself. It didn't help that she tried to remind herself that it was not the colour black but the colour white she was afraid of, the white clown who had frightened the life out of her the first time her parents had taken her to a circus. Her common sense struggled in vain against the all-powerful fear which created monsters. She had to annihilate those devils. Stamp them out once and for all, so that they could not invade her innocent pure white consciousness. She was riding on waves of superhuman strength. Her cold rage stifled the homeless voice which sounded like a little bell calling inside her. 'Don't be afraid. I am your friend.'

Her mother's distant voice came closer and closer, right inside her ear, and inside her head the voice was drowning in the unusual noises which had awoken her mother before sunrise. The noise of unfamiliar lorries and buses, the noise of hard braking, the noise of boots tramping, the noise of doors being broken in, the noise of hand-to-hand fighting, shouting and screaming, the noise of heavy vehicles driving away again, the noise of the silence which descended heavily on the village, and her mother's fearful whisper: 'Armed with rifles and spades they took women and men with them, also my brother, your uncle. Some have come back and told us that they were forced into buses and driven to the President's home town and herded into military baracks and forced with a pistol to their heads to drink a bitter and foul-smelling herbal drink, which gave them hallucinations and made them behave strangely, some got diarrhoea and vomited, some died from kidney failure, some were raped, they were forced to confess that they were witches. Rumour says that the witchhunters were the president's personal bodyguard, who invaded the villages together with witch doctors from Guinea. The witchhunt is supposed to be revenge for the death of the President's aunt. He says it is the work of human witches, but the victims are ordinary men and women with no knowledge of witchcraft. Your uncle has fled to Senegal out of fear that the President's men will return.' Her mother's voice was muffled and incoherent, as if she had her hand in front of her mouth. Those sorts of happenings you don't talk about out loud, you hide them away quickly like something unheard-of which has never happened.

All at once Ana was back in her own body, which felt like a thin shell around an empty interior. The violence had made her unrecognisable. The mask had fused with her face. She saw Mariama fall backwards and hit the kerb of the pavement and paid no heed to the fact that she had killed her soul. She saw only Mariama's large oval eyes staring at her in mild reproach, and the red-black lips trying to form some words.

The noise of sirens, the noise of doors being flung open, the noise of small squeaking wheels, the noise of starched sheets and soft blankets, the noise of the oxygen mask, the noise of heartbeats. 'We are born in order to die.' 'We meet in order to part.' 'We receive in order to lose.'

Ana did not have the patience to wait for public transport, and took a taxi to Harrods. She kitted herself out from top to toe, from satin underwear to a white mink cape. She paid with her gold Mastercard and asked the elegant assistant, who at first had refused to serve her, to get rid of her old rags. After that she drove directly to the Ritz Casino on Piccadilly. It was getting towards evening, and the gentle dusk helped to soothe her nervous excitement. The doorman in a tight-fitting charcoal-grey uniform held the glass door open for her, and she glided easily in her ivory-coloured silk dress with the mink cape over her shoulders into the blaze of lights in the foyer with its islands of extravagant lilac and red floral displays. She walked purposefully towards the hotel casino, in through the circular anteroom lined with champagne-coloured silk, stepping from there into the main gambling hall. Three bankers were sitting at the exchange counter behind bullet-proof glass. They bore a striking likeness to one another, both in their dress (the obligatory black tie) and in their appearance, all the way to their protruding left ears and a swirl at the hairline, making their hair fall the same way at the front. Ana changed five thousand pounds and asked for a mixture of fifty and hundred-pound chips. She had bought a hand-embroidered Thai silk bag for the chips, so that they would not rattle about in her handbag.

She stood still in order to take in the large high-ceilinged room with carved wood and walls covered with leather hangings in every conceivable shade of red. No windows, no doors. Time stood still in this Mecca of money. The lighting, which came partly from crystal chandeliers on the ceiling, and partly from candelabras which were large enough to grace a baronial banqueting hall, created an intimate, cavern-like atmosphere in spite of the enormous dimensions of the central casino hall. There were five poker tables, seven blackjack tables and five roulette tables. A brocade curtain which stretched from floor to ceiling with twisted ropes of golden silk ending in huge tassels could be drawn aside like a theatre curtain. Behind it there was a side room with extra gaming tables in case the pressure on the tables in the main gambling hall should become too great.

Ana chose the outermost roulette table and took her place in the ring of bodies behind the innermost circle, who were sitting on high-backed chairs. She noted the strategies of the various players, their preferences for high risk or caution. She always started with roulette, and then later went over to blackjack when she needed to take a breather. She could feel her heels sinking deep into the Persian carpet, and found herself filled with a sense of divine calm, together with a superstitious belief that if she won the jackpot in the Ritz she would also win back Mariama. Like the moon, the force of the game would draw the waters together, and a tidal wave would carry Mariama to her.

She seized her chance when there was a space at the table and took her place in the innermost circle, sitting right by the croupier. She began by placing two fifty-pound chips on three, which was her lucky number and the nearest she could come to Christianity. She believed in the magic of numbers. She was not an atheist, rather a heathen who lived magically in the world. Mariama felt so close to her in the gambling hall, where no unauthorized people could enter. Around the roulette wheel stood people in evening dress with greedy staring eyes, following the rotation of the little metal ball up and down. A deathly silence greeted its final standstill on three in red. A hushed sigh went round the circle by the table. No-one moved a muscle, not to mention taking any notice of Ana, as the croupier pushed two tall piles of chips over to her. They were already preoccupied with placing their next bets. After announcing no further bets, the croupier pressed the button concealed beneath the table and set the roulette wheel going.

Ana could feel the adrenalin coursing through her veins, and knew that luck was with her. She had been right down, scraping the bottom, and feared nothing. Not even dying in poverty. She bet on red, and won four times in a row. Then her luck turned. Despite the fact that her losses were greater than her profits, she was convinced she would win. She had an almost childlike belief in roulette. It was her only salvation, and therefore she had to believe in it. But here no prayers would help. The laws of chance and statistics were inexorable. The ball landed seven times in a row on red, then suddenly changed to black. Ana had betted the maximum amount allowed, trusting to her luck on red. She had heard that the ball had been known to fall on the same colour up to 20-25 times in a row. But this evening the curve was broken after only seven. Ana had lost five thousand pounds in less than an hour, and had to change more money with the croupier.

The roulette filled her whole consciousness and crowded out her fears about her finances, which were not so future-proofed as she and her colleagues at Rower had taken for granted. That, too, had been an article of faith, like luck at roulette. She had ordered a drink, which stood ready on one of the round tables placed on the periphery of the hall, like black toadstools on high steel stalks. Ana started with high stakes and bet on black. And carried on betting on black. The piles of chips towered up in front of her. She should have left the gaming hall there and then, quietly drunk her drink on the way out and exchanged her bag, chock full of chips, for cash. But she was in another world, and wanted to challenge fate and statistics.

After her luck turned she placed larger and larger bets. She wanted to win back what she had lost in one fell swoop. And in order to win you had to bet high. Her head spun in time to the ball which danced up and down in the row of numbers, and only stood still when the ball landed in its stall. Ana bet on zero, which pays thirty-five times the stake. A gentleman

beside her, who was keeping tally and jotting down prob-
ability percentages on a discreet little notepad, looked at
her in amazement and remarked on her eccentric choice by
raising his eyebrows. It was forbidden to speak out loud at the
gaming tables. Now things went downhill rapidly. She bet on
zero three times running, making the players standing around
her shake their heads. The croupier pulled her piles of fifty and
hundred pound chips towards him with a horrible whistling
sound. She left the game to lick her wounds over her vodka
cocktail, which tasted flat after standing too long. She drank
it in one swallow and went back to the gaming table. She
did not have time to wait, but pushed her way through into
the inner circle. She registered how the game immediately
stimulated her brain and made her see clearly.

Ana changed tables twice during the evening and night,
but it made no difference. She had not made the god of
gaming swear not to harm her, and was completely cleaned
out. Late in the night she tottered past the exchange counter,
where she had earlier had to empty one of her reserve
accounts to be able to carry on playing. The three bankers
nodded in synchrony, as if according to a carefully calculated
choreography. She went out into the hotel foyer and asked at
reception if they had a room available. She needed rest and
time to think in pleasant surroundings, and complete peace
in order to work out a strategy for the next day. She ordered a
bottle of whisky for her room. It was time to break away from
the modest existence she had so far led in London.

Translator's Afterword

Chance – 'tilfældet' – is the deity which rules Ana's life. 'If I have to believe in anything, I believe that it is chance which governs us', she explains at one point (p. 217). It is by chance that she takes her holiday in Gambia, and it is chance that determines her meeting on the beach with the little Mariama, who is to assume such a dominant role in her life. Time and again she trusts to chance, taking the fact that she stumbles on a book about Seneca's philosophy as a sign of a new departure, hoping for a stroke of luck to give her a job in the London office of the multinational finance company Rower, and finally staking her financial security on the turning of the roulette wheel. But chance is a fickle protector, and Ana's reliance on it leads to risky and ultimately self-destructive behaviour.

As the plot of this novel unfolds, however, the reader becomes aware that Ana's assertions of her own motivation and beliefs are themselves not to be relied on. Most of the early part of the narrative is related from her point of view, but she is subtly undermined by the narrator. This confident, independent career woman, who wishes to use her abundant wealth to transform the life of an African waif, is in fact needy and insecure. Her material success has not compensated for the fact that she feels incomplete and unloved, a half-person who was created with donated sperm – though it was actually she who rejected her parents, as she also later rejects the man who feels genuine affection for her, her colleague and lover Hans. When she meets Mariama, her almost-namesake, she fantasizes that she finally has the opportunity to become a complete person, that she has found 'her platonic other half which she had been separated from at the dawn of time' (p. 45).

Even more than that, Ana feels that Mariama has given her an identity; before meeting her, she literally did not know who she was. She has no soul to lay bare, she reflects in her conversations with the English couple she meets in Gambia, Ben and Bea. With Mariama it occurs to her that she has found her 'soul' – a startling over-reaction and a word she starts to use frequently, to the alarm of her friends. When she tells her mentor Frank that her soul is elsewhere, he refuses any further discussion of the matter; when she claims to her fellow sponsor Ben that the girl is her soul, he accuses her furiously of cannibalism. Her project of helping Mariama to get an education is equally a project of helping herself to become whole.

Money and power and the relation between them are central to this story. At the start Ana is confronted by the contrast between her relatively enormous wealth and the destitution of Mariama and her family; her money, she feels, gives her the power to change lives and to bring hope. She is used to a corporate world of financial dealings, and approaches the project of Mariama with the same negotiating attitude which has made her a high-flier in the past. But she soon realises that the power her money brings is severely restricted in this very differently-structured society. The pendulum begins to swing the other way as her image of herself as a benevolent benefactor is challenged by reactions she finds impenetrable and threatening.

When she finally manages to bring Mariama to Europe, the longed-for sisterhood also turns out to be more problematic than Ana had envisaged. Her reaction to the girl has always been a mixture of attraction and fear; now she wants Mariama under her protection, yet not too close, sending her to live with Ben and Bea rather than taking her in herself. She focuses on her own needs to the extent that she does not see Mariama as a separate person, does not listen to what her protegée feels but rather tells her what to feel. Mariama is to be a kind of shadow, an alter ego rather in the sense that the shadow in H.C. Andersen's story of that name is meant to be a double of the protagonist; but as in Andersen's story, the shadow demands a life of its own.[1] Ana's therapist tries to warn her of what is happening, but she cuts him off when he gets too close to the uncomfortable truth. Her insecurity develops into paranoia, and she suspects a conspiracy to harm her; Mariama is bringing evil spirits into the apartment, and her mother is putting a curse on her based on the photographs she has asked her daughter to send.

The colours black and white also permeate the novel, initially in the obvious sense that it portrays a meeting between white Europeans and black Africans, and the culture clash experienced by Europeans in Africa and Africans in Europe. But black and white have an extended meaning for Ana; she has always been afraid of the colour white, which makes her think of annihilation, of empty space. The white face of a clown terrified her as a child. Increasingly, though, it becomes the colour black which sets her alarm bells ringing – black magic, black masks, black devils, black souls. London is suddenly full of hordes of black people who are flooding the streets, swamping the country, even invading her dreams. It is black which lets her down at the roulette table when she starts to gamble seriously. It is as if she has opened a door which she can never close again.

During the course of the novel Ana slowly disintegrates; what started as work-related stress develops into a paralysis which spreads across all areas of her existence. She loses her work, her home, her friends, her ability to think clearly and plan logically. She becomes incapable of structuring her life, even of tidying the flat in which she is surrounded by random anonymous furniture. Her disintegration finally extends even to her physical appearance, as she loses her shoes and tears and dirties her clothes, wandering around the streets of London like the tramps she had previously so despised. Mariama in the meantime has resolved the conflicts between the demands of her family back home and those of her sponsors in London, and found a context in which she can regain the harmony she lost when she left Gambia; the struggle between black and white has for her been subsumed in 'a time of rainbows and roses' (p. 270).

The last meeting between Ana and Mariama takes place on a London street, where they are finally on the same level; Ana's dishevelled appearance makes Mariama suddenly conscious that she too needs support. It is also the last time in the novel where chance seems to be on Ana's side, as the narrator points out: 'if Ana really believed in the god of chance, the moment was approaching when she should fall to her knees' (p. 273). But Ana's joy at discovering Mariama safe and well soon turns to anger as she realises that the girl has dropped out of school and that she can no longer influence her; in their circular conversation she again asserts her own project repeatedly, rather than listening to Mariama's needs. When Mariama in a role reversal tries to help Ana by putting her arm around her shoulders, she precipitates a flashback-cum-hallucination in which Ana is told by a photographer that it is impossible to take photographs of her, because she has no soul. The attempt to make herself complete by fusing with another person has failed, as it was bound to; as Ana strikes out hysterically and Mariama falls, she feels that she has killed her own soul.

The God of Chance is an acute psychological study of two women and their search for a sense of meaning in their lives; but at the same time, like many of Kirsten Thorup's novels, it has a far wider reference. In this novel Thorup takes up the fraught question of global inequality and our attempts to redress it; what are we doing when we provide so-called aid, and is our help really altruistic or just a sop to our bad consciences? Can our model of what constitutes a good life be applied to other cultures, or are we destroying a functioning social structure and leaving people rootless? The urge to help in the face of extreme deprivation seems laudable, yet it can so easily turn into another form of imperialism. Ana really wants to help Mariama and her family, but she wants to get something out of it herself too, and she reacts angrily when the expected gratitude gives way to importunate demands. At the same time her work for an international capitalist organization based on a profit motive may well be undermining all her individual efforts to improve conditions in the Developing World.

Science and ethics is another contemporary topic of heated debate which is explored in this novel. Ana is a product of anonymous donor insemination; she does not know who her biological father was. She discovered the truth by chance when it was too late and she was already grown up – and she was the only one in the family who did not know. It is to this history that she attributes the fact that she feels rejected and alone in the world; she has no family – she severed relations completely with her parents and projected her feelings of being unloved back to her childhood. She is close to no-one and lets no-one get close, for fear they abandon her again. At the same time this makes her intensely vulnerable, so that the mere sound of Mariama's voice in her ear makes her melt 'like a snowman in the spring sunshine' and fills her with 'an unearthly beauty' (p. 12). A scientific advance has made it possible for her to be conceived, but science is not enough to produce a well-rounded person.

Working on this novel has involved an unusually close collaboration with the author, to whom I am grateful for her perceptive comments on my translation and a fascinating discussion of the background to its composition. The descriptions of luxury hotels in Gambia, modern corporate life in Copenhagen and the multicultural community of London are based on Thorup's first-hand observation, and the complications of entanglement in an individual project to help an African girl get a good education are also derived from her personal experience. We have agreed small adjustments in the text to accommodate an English rather than a Danish reader, but I have otherwise done my best to reproduce the deceptively straightforward everyday language of the original.

Janet Garton

1. I am indebted to Jørgen Veisland's article 'A mysterious closeness. Africa and Europe in Kirsten Thorup's *The God of Chance*' (*Forum for World Literature Studies*, 2013) for this observation.

HANNE MARIE SVENDSEN

Under the Sun

(translated by Marina Allemano)

Written in 1991, *Under the Sun* is the story of Margrethe Thiede, the daughter of a lighthouse keeper in an unnamed small fishing community on the north-western coast of Denmark. We follow Margrethe through her childhood, her years as a student in the capital, her marriage to a mentally unstable man, her involvement in the peace movement, and her old age.

The novel is also about a changing community where fears of violence at sea and rampant commercialism on land are strong undercurrents. The building of a naval base and the ominous presence of foreign submarines intimidate the fishermen and their families, and an accident caused by one of these intruding vessels forms the catastrophic climax of the novel.

ISBN 9781870041621
UK £9.95
(Paperback, 256 pages)

HELENE URI

Honey Tongues

(translated by Kari Dickson)

The honey tongues of the title belong to four friends in their thirties who have known each other since school. They make up a 'sewing circle' where no sewing is done, but much exquisite food is lovingly prepared and consumed and increasingly bitchy gossip exchanged.

The novel follows their three-weekly meetings over six months, as they take turns to entertain each other; we are privy to their thoughts and memories and discover how apparently innocent actions are motivated by emotional hang-ups with their roots in childhood traumas. The tension builds towards a gourmet trip to Copenhagen to celebrate their friendship, where during an eight-course meal the masks drop and undisguised fear and loathing are revealed. Shocking secrets are unearthed as the balance of power subtly shifts from one member of the group to another. Brilliantly observed, this is female bonding at its worst, manipulative and psychotic, exposing the dependency and deceit behind the compassionate and affectionate façade.

ISBN 9781870041720
UK £9.95
(Paperback, 192 pages)

SVAVA JAKOBSDÓTTIR

Gunnlöth's Tale

(translated by Oliver Watts)

This spirited and at times sinister novel ensnares the reader in a tangled encounter between modern-day Scandinavia and the ancient world of myth. In the 1980s, a hardworking Icelandic businesswoman and her teenage daughter Dís, who has been arrested for apparently committing a strange and senseless robbery, are unwittingly drawn into a ritual-bound world of goddesses, sacrificial priests, golden thrones, clashing crags and kings-in-waiting. It is said that Gunnlöth was seduced by Odin so he could win the 'mead' of poetry from her, but is that really true, and why was Dís summoned to their world?

The boundaries dissolve and the parallels between Gunnlöth's circle and the strange company into which Dís's mother is drawn as she fights to clear Dís's name grow ever closer. The earth-cherishing goddess seems set on a collision course with strategic thinker Odin who has discovered that iron can be extracted from the marshes where she resides, and environmental disaster also looms in the modern context, brought into sharp focus by a shocking world event.

ISBN 9781870041799
UK £9.95
(Paperback, 232 pages)

Jørgen-Franz Jacobsen

Barbara

(translated by George Johnston)

Originally written in Danish, *Barbara* was the only novel by the
Faroese author Jørgen-Frantz Jacobsen (1900-38), yet it quickly
achieved international best-seller status and is still one of the best-
loved classics of Danish and Faroese literature. On the face of it,
Barbara is a straightforward historical romance. It contains a story
of passion in an exotic setting with overtones of semi-piracy; there
is a powerful erotic element, an outsider who breaks up a marriage,
and a built-in inevitability resulting from Barbara's own psychological
make-up. She stands as one of the most complex female characters
in modern Scandinavian literature: beautiful, passionate, devoted,
amoral and uncomprehending of her own tragedy. Jørgen-Frantz
Jacobsen portrays her with fascinated devotion.

ISBN 9781870041225
UK £9.95
(Paperback, 304 pages)

Lightning Source UK Ltd.
Milton Keynes UK
UKOW03f0607041213

222329UK00001B/17/P